MAKING LOVE

A CONSPIRACY OF THE HEART

MAKING LOVE

A CONSPIRACY OF THE HEART

Marius Brill

Doubleday

LONDON · NEW YORK · TORONTO · SYDNEY · AUCKLAND

TRANSWORLD PUBLISHERS
61–63 Uxbridge Road, London W5 5SA
a division of The Random House Group Ltd

RANDOM HOUSE AUSTRALIA (PTY) LTD
20 Alfred Street, Milsons Point, Sydney,
New South Wales 2061, Australia

RANDOM HOUSE NEW ZEALAND LTD
18 Poland Road, Glenfield, Auckland 10, New Zealand

RANDOM HOUSE SOUTH AFRICA (PTY) LTD
Endulini, 5a Jubilee Road, Parktown 2193, South Africa

Published 2003 by Doubleday
a division of Transworld Publishers

A catalogue record for this book is available from the British Library.
ISBN 0385 605234

Typeset in Granjon by
Falcon Oast Graphic Art Ltd
and in Attic by Marius Brill

Printed in Great Britain
by Clays Ltd, Bungay, Suffolk

1 3 5 7 9 10 8 6 4 2

For My Father
Hans Helmut Reginald Brill
1930–2001

Who would have been so proud

and would never have told me.

Contents

PART I

1	*Almost April*	11
2	*Old 'Shitty-Digit' Himself*	25
3	*'Thwat That, Thucker!'*	37
4	*In Which*	47
5	*A Dog Which Does Not Travel Often, or Well*	61
6	*Wringing Out Your Knickers*	71
7	*Anyone for Quoits?*	83
8	*It Is a Little More Serious, Burnt*	93
9	*'Ah, That Explains Everything'*	105
10	*Splaying and Rotating and Quivering*	117
11	*And That Felt a Little Like Being Loved*	127

PART II

12	*That Limbo of the Mind*	139
13	*That Sort of Facetious Misreading*	151
14	*Does He Come In for Coffee?*	169
15	*It Was All a Little Too Spooky*	185
16	*Don't Mind If I Do*	199
17	*Do You Actually Understand What We at Y Branch Do?*	213

18	*The Big Book of Romantic Clichés*	227
19	*The* De Rigueur *Thing to Wear for Saints*	241
20	*The Luminous Dips and Rises of an Exotic Dancer*	255
21	*Striking Thoughts*	275
22	*Oov*	289
23	*You Sure That Was a Gun in His Pocket?*	309
24	*In a Priest's Hole*	327
25	*So Who Are You Then, Really?*	339
26	*Love Logic*	355
27	*Triangles*	371

PART III

28	*The Skeletons of Dreams*	391
29	*Sycorax*	403
30	*Whites-of-Their-Eyes*	419
31	*Birnam Wood*	433
32	*Love Did That*	449

| Coda | 463 |

PART I

1

Almost April

NOW, JUST BETWEEN YOU AND ME; A SILENCE, SOFT AS SLEEP NOT YET woken, has tiptoed in and holds us. And your fingertips leave humid tracks across the desert of my back. And my spine bends at your touch, arching like a cat's. We're alone, you and i. And all i can hear is the soft waves of your breathing crashing down across the reef of your lips. It has slowed. It's gentle, even, rhythmic, secure. Here, in your grasp, i am like a raft becalmed at night, rocking gently in the sea of your hands, caressed by the searching beams of your lighthouse eyes. Here i feel i am, at last, discovered. i have found my harbour, my rock, my dry land and all i can do is lie here, exhausted, basking in your steady light; gentle, even, rhythmic. Safe.

Oh, sweet Jesus. If someone patents pretentiousness i'll be the first to be pseud. It's just, at the beginning, you know, you've just met, and you think you can be anybody. Well, you want to be anybody, anybody but the dumb schmuck who fucked up the last time and sure as sure is going to fuck up again, that idiot telling tales full of sound and fury. i just thought, maybe if i was wildly poetic maybe i wouldn't get dumped so readily this time, maybe you'd love me for who i'm not.

LIKE me. Like me for who i'm not. Buggerbuggerbugger – i swore to myself, when i saw you, i swore i wouldn't mention love. Swore i'd take it nice and slow, not expect anything. Never give you the chance to think i might be needy, lonely or loveless or . . . When i said love i meant like, i mean i don't mean i'm . . . But, well, damn it, this is

11

about love. In the end it is. What would be the point of any of this if it wasn't? So why pretend? Maybe i seem a little needy right now but like i was saying, i can change.

i can.

i mean, look, i'm no longer what i once was. i know we all change, we grow and learn, but love – well, love and severe physical injuries, although they may well amount to the same thing – love, it's the one thing that can change you utterly, instantly.

One day you're a perfectly happy, well-adjusted individual, getting on with your life, minding your own business and the next moment, *voom* – or, more often than not, *vavavoom* – you're a crazed loon. Obsessed, impassioned, unable to think, sleep or eat. Everywhere you look or go, everything you think, there's the object of your love, invading every part of your life. In an instant you go from Dr Jekyll to Mr Hi-di-hi-di-ho.

i know. i know because it happened to me, i was changed just like that, altered, metamorphosed, whatyouwill. i was translated into something else, by someone else.

So now i look at you and i think, 'Enough.' i've been long enough on the shelf, if i went through all that and changed, why not again, why not now?

i mean, case in point, take the last book you read. Will it ever look like it did when you first picked it up, looked at the cover and wondered what was inside? No. Now it's special. It's got all those memories and visions and a little corner of your imagination to call its own, it is much greater than the paper and ink that you first saw. The book hasn't changed for anybody else. But you, you've translated it into something different, into a part of you. Love did that.

Do you see what i mean? This just could be so much more. So much more than a casual glance and a quick fondle in these sheets. This really could be the beginning of something, something that takes us both somewhere, that translates both of us. Changes us. And, and, and we can only do it together.

Don't look at me like that. Like i'm not playing the part, like i'm cutting to the chase before the key's in the ignition. Is it so hard to believe that i have feelings too? A pocketful of pulp and ink, a distant tree from another time. If energy can't be destroyed only changed, what about the soul? Where *do* feelings go?

Tell me you know why energy takes the shape it does. Tell me why the universe, the planets, cheesy wotsits, are shaped the way they are.

It's love. Love translates us all. It makes idiots of us. It changes us. It makes people hide behind blushes, and books behind authors.

Deep down though, you and i, we're just the same. Deep down, uncountable atoms slow dance together, cheek to cheek, dances of love, holding onto each other's charge, the other's energy, however negative or positive. And when the music stops, when the particle is over, when it's time to go; only the lonely single atoms split. But even within each single one, tiny protons call out their love to their estranged, encircling electrons who, so excited by the partnership, charge about at ten thousand miles a second. That's a whole lot of love going on in your hands right now, and you think that this seething mass of material energy, this subatomic love dance of the spheres, doesn't have its own agenda, motives, passions?

If not for love, i could have, quite happily, accumulated as something quite useless, fluff in your navel, lint in a washing machine filter or a social worker. If not for love, why should all this force of nature, this mass of material energy, organize into a book that sits in your hand and tells you a story? If not for love then what, then why?

i have harnessed all this for you and we can . . .

Buggerbuggerbugger, i'm avoiding the point again. You know i've changed and you know someone changed me, you know i've felt something like this before. You know i've had another reader. i just feel i've got to make a clean breast of things, i just want to tell you about her and then that'll be it, i promise i'll never mention her again. i won't. i just need to tell you this. What happened. How she was. Where we went, and how it ended.

i just worry you'll see me as damaged goods, shop soiled, if i don't tell you about her, come clean so to write. i know it's not healthy to dwell upon the past and we've got to move on and all that, but after her i really did change. She's the one who made me what i am now. If you're going to understand anything about me just let me get this out. She's gone now so don't be jealous. Just read. You see to me, at the time, she was the Centre the Light the One Thing within without with-all. My God she was.

When she picked me up i knew. She touched me. She held me. She took me to the corners of the earth. She flew me to the skies and threw me down the stars. She ripped words from me and bequeathed the warmth of her long fingers. And in my pages she even left a tear.

i may be a little dumb but i can't tell if it was a waterstain or a rip. i only remember, when she blinked the world slowed. Men gasped as she passed. Rain whispered as she walked through it and left its murmur in the quiet folds of her clothes. Why did she never see it? She never knew, she never saw. She never heard me. As far as she could see i was just ink across paper, clogged with words unspoken, feelings unheard. Print, intelligible but ineligible to touch without spilling – blackness. Words that couldn't hold or look, just amble suggestively. i'm never the thing, only the thing suggesting the thing. i'm the transient medium that never arrives, that cannot fulfil its own promises. i trip but never fall, i smile but never laugh, i flirt but never make love.

But i'm not the words i used to be. When she found me i was a different book entirely. i was just one among thousands. i even had an author back then, P. Pennyfeather. But what made her choose me?

Love.

Miranda consumed lovelore as if it was an art to be mastered, read everything she could find with it, about it, on it: romances by the shelf, love stories by the bookcase and self-help books by cash-hungry charlatans paid for stating the obvious – *Women Who Lunch Too Much*, *Life's Little Destruction Book*, *Men Are From Planet Bastard, Women Are From Planet Sucker*. A certain lovelonging possessed her, like a shadow possesses a lung.

And i was entitled by Eros; i was, am, called *Making Love*, a name that beckoned to her like a blossom to the bee, like an orchid to the aphid, like a lotus to the yuppie, like an opiate to the injured. Somewhere in the colour of her sighs and the quiet of her eyes, she was incomplete, as an empty glass, a moonless night, a wordless whisper, lovelost like only someone who has never loved can be.

O, Miranda had had sex and, on occasion, she had sensed the odd smidgen of hope, the shiver of a possible attachment, but those had usually been accompanied by the fried-cod breath, lagery dribble and rank, sweaty fumblings of boys from the estate. You can only take so much of your breasts being kneaded raw like they were Playdoh left out too long. By the time we met, she was twenty-two, living in Shepherd's Bush and desperately absorbing Bills and Moon romances, yearning for those mad, impulsive passions, the knuckle-biting orgasms and the wet, sullen, rain-soaked clinches of heart-searing, soaring obsession.

Taking a little wider view, she was also blissfully unaware that she was actually spared love's terror of inadequacy, torturing insecurity and the desperate despair that rips your stomach apart when you realize that your world no longer revolves around you, but someone

14

else. That you no longer have any control, everything has been utterly utterly translated for ever.

All that changed when she found me. When we found each other.

i can see her now as she was when i first knew her. And to know me, you must know her. It was almost April, in the library. You could tell when it was the lamb's end of March; the hydrograph in 745.54, Handicrafts, started to go crazy. Its little blue pen scratched wildly and wandered across the thick red line on the cylinder's graph paper. At least once a day someone would come and tap the thing as if they couldn't believe the new warm season could create so much humidity, despite the evidence of history, as one of my neighbours said: 'Whan that Aprille with his shoures sote.'

i wish he'd learned to spell.

Then, after a week of people coming and frowning and tapping, and all of us starting to bulge with the moisture, some bright spark would come up with an ingenious solution. Carefully, as if afraid that the world would burst in and infect the library with real, 100 per cent, new improved, cleaner nature, they opened a window. Then, like the evils of the world escaping out of Pandora's box, last summer's sodden, stale air, perma-sealed in our prison, finally rushed out into the spring and a million pages sighed. Ten thousand bindings creaked back into place.

And then we could hear, beyond those web-laden windows, noisy starlings making long-distance calls on telephone lines. Outside, no doubt, spring-loaded petals burst open in the new, warm sunlight. Sharp beaks and curious antennae pecked and explored their bright-coloured spawn. Outside nature preened and showed off its latest season, taunting the library with its changing perpetuity.

In the library it's always autumn, the season of study, when the rotting leaves of old books lie, turning to dust. Dead, brown, Pledge-stained, wood-tacked and sun-bleached, time-dried ochre. Volumes of yellowing bindings, we lay cocooned from nature, dying imperceptibly slowly. Although by the standards of fickle flesh – stretching, sagging, peeling, falling, drying, dying, to be ingested by worms in a mere three score and ten – we were changelessly immortal. So there's some comfort.

But then she blew it all. Just one of the regulars, never really noticed. Noiselessly she entered, penetrated, my world. That day she emerged from the shadow by the door, she moved through the cool of the library. And those lazy schools of yellow dust which swim and float by the shoals of shelves, glittering in the stillness of each shaft of

15

windowlight, suddenly dashed and whirled, panicked by her movement through their still oasis. They spun in cyclones, spinning about her arms and legs, flirting with her flesh. They eddied about each thigh and dived along the creaseless rounds of her skirt. They skirted her pale skin as her shoes crackled with nylon static along the library carpet.

Always the romances. Only the love books attracted her attention. She would pull out six at a time and take them away and in a few days be back for more. And sometimes, when she hadn't any books to return, she came in and pulled out some of the gaudier books, just to stare at their covers; billowing-haired, doll-like heroines gripped by muscle-ripped heroes. You could see they somehow gave her hope, let her lose herself for a moment in the dream of love.

i knew that. i had fallen in love with her the moment i saw her, i knew our stories would cross, they were destined to. She would change me, translate me, i knew it because i always know the ending. Destiny whispers to me. It's one of the perks of being a book – i know what happens at the finish. There's always an end. There's always a last page.

When she picked me it was, as these things often are, an accident. What had actually attracted Miranda's dreamy attentions was not me but a spring-mad young couple, somewhere between school and the family planning clinic, whose fancy had lightly turned to thoughts of lust. They had sought out the privacy of the Religious Education section whose pious pages grazed ours on the opposite side of our more louche Romance shelf. The human drama of love was being enacted yet again.

'Why not?'

'You know why not.'

'Mum's got bingo, she's out till nine at least.'

'I don't care. I don't know if it's right.'

'Fuck it, I said I loved you. What more do you want?'

'Do you really, Gav? I mean really?'

And drawn to such productions like a moth to cashmere, Miranda ran her fingers across the spines of my shelf; past *Tell Me You Love Me*, past *The Doctor Is Always In*, and then stopped when she got to me, hidden, as I had been for so long, beneath the garish cover of a missing pulp romance. She pulled me out from the shelf and peered through the gap i had left.

'Yeah. Suppose so.'

'More than what you did Shaz?'

'Oh, don't go on. History.'

'Yeah?'

'Yeah. Look, it's not like it's a big deal.'

'It is for me.'

'What about right here then?'

'Shut up.'

Miranda watched the girl as she laughed, looking up to find a place to secrete her chewing gum. A prelude to some deep face exploration. The girl caught Miranda's eye, staring through the gap, and stuck her tongue out.

'What you looking at?' sneered the girl.

Miranda turned quickly away and laid me on the table, her face burning red. She opened me, she spread me, she rubbed my contents with her forefinger, she tapped a line and then she penetrated me, went right to my heart. She opened me up.

Her eyes stroked my words, just as yours do. You are not so unlike her. And for seconds? Maybe hours? i spoke to her. Her eyelids dropped slightly, the front of her teeth gently dented her lower lip which rolled forward warmly as a sleepy lover. The corners of her mouth curled. i made her smile. And all i could think was, 'You are lovely.'

i must have done something right because after a while she closed me and walked towards the counter. She was going to take me out. Outside. i'd never been out, not since i had got there. And we walked past walls of other books. Books that never had a chance. Books she would never have picked. Goodbye *Anglers' Manual of Fly Tying*, farewell *History of Marrows*, adios *I'm OK, You're Completely Fucked*. i was going outside.

'YOU CAN'T TAKE THAT OUT, MS BROWN.'

'That's *Miss* Brown.'

'WHATEVER. I'M AFRAID YOU STILL CAN'T TAKE THAT OUT,' the tiny librarian squawked loudly in a clipped accent. One that she hoped was efficient, posh and bookish. She peered back at her computer and her glasses shone green with the reflected screen text. She perched on her stool looking like a dun cockatoo, and Miranda couldn't help but stare at her eye-level pile of brittle brown split ends, heaped on top of her head like a tottering, towering, tapered dog turd. On her tidy dark green suit-lapel was a badge that said, '*Hi, I'm BRENDA. Let me bring you to book!*'

'YOU CAN'T,' Brenda repeated. She had developed the habit,

adopted by many of the very small, of speaking in a voice inversely proportionate to her size, as if she could make up in volume what she lacked in mass. Miranda looked around to see if any of the other readers might be disturbed by Brenda's barracking, but the only other person in the library was a thin elderly man sitting next to his Zimmer frame. He wore a Walkman, and his head trembled as he hummed to the Weather Girls. Occasionally he would strum his frame as if it were a Fender Stradicast and sing, 'Tempest's riesling, barromeda's low, a chording two all sauces these trees the plates to go.'

Miranda looked back at Brenda and asked, 'Why can't I?'

'YOU'VE ALREADY GOT SIX BOOKS OUT.'

'Can't I just take this now? I'll return one tomorrow.'

'OH YES. OF COURSE YOU WOULD. AND IF I LET YOU DO THAT, I'D HAVE TO DO THAT FOR EVERYBODY, IT WOULD OPEN THE FLOODGATES.' Brenda pushed her glasses back up to the bridge of her nose and blinked decisively at Miranda, as if to say that the subject was closed.

Miranda motioned to the near-empty library. 'Floodgates?' she said, as incredulously as she could.

Now Brenda looked at the old man. The last six, long, white hairs left on his head were bouncing back and forth as his head thrashed about, 'Stormy weather, movie inn, bout two breakid, about to beguine . . .'

Brenda looked back at her screen, smiled and shouted, 'ANYWAY, THE BOOKS YOU'VE GOT OUT ARE OVERDUE. YOU OWE US . . . SIXTY-SIX PENCE.' She clipped the word 'pence' to sound posh but just ended up sounding like the Queen saying 'pants'.

Sixty-six pants. 'That's over half a knicker, isn't it?' said Miranda smiling. That smile.

Brenda did not laugh. She did not find it funny. In fact the last time Brenda laughed was when the council told her that her 'Do-It-Yourself' books would have to be shelved. This made Brenda laugh.

Librarian humour.

'MS BROWN. YOU CANNOT TAKE OUT ANOTHER BOOK UNTIL YOU RETURN THE OTHERS AND PAY THE FINE.' Brenda turned her back. Her preposterous big-hair waved at Miranda. Her head suddenly looked soft and bludgeonable.

Miranda wandered with me back towards the shelf. i couldn't believe it. Our story ended so soon. Could it be true?

Then it happened. Surreptitiously, Miranda looked from side to side, although she knew there was no one else about. Then she lifted her jumper and slipped me into her bra.

Bliss. There, pressed against her warm soft skin. Her breast pressed against my front. The edges of my cold cover making her nipples point and click. O the memory. Happiness. It could all have ended there for me.

We started to walk and her chest heaved about and undulated as she strode. Through the muffle i could hear, 'Straining men hallelujah, straining men every space I mean, tall, blond, darkend lean, roughend toughend strong and mean . . .'

Then the claxon library alarm started wailing.

'FREEZE, MS.'

And her heart started beating like the Marquis de Sade. Thumping rhythmically against me. And everything in her jumper started to jump, and heave and move and jiggle and we were running. The siren was screaming. Her heart was pumping and in this storm in her B-cup i was being tossed like some wandering seaman.

'I KNOW YOU. I KNOW WHERE YOU LIVE. YOU CAN'T GET AWAY WITH THIS. THAT'S COUNCIL PROPERTY.' And Brenda's voice receded into the sounds of the city and all i could hear was the traffic and the birds and her heart. i was out.

But perhaps you need to know what i said to her first. My pick-up lines, as it were.

MAKING LOVE
A Conspiracy of the Heart

by

P. Pennyfeather

PREFACE

THIS IS THE TRUTH. I KNOW IT'S THE TRUTH BECAUSE I AM DEAD
and they wouldn't have killed me if it were all a pack of lies.

I know modern cynics are always claiming that there's no
such thing as truth and that it is all subjective. But if the truth
is relative, how come no one ever invites it round for
Christmas or wants it cluttering up their wedding photos?

Truth isn't just 'in the eye of the beholder', and it is rarely
'beautiful'. No, all that we know and all that we need to know
is that the truth is absolute, definite, unequivocal and as sure
as a waterfront. Probably.

What is undeniable is that in this dawning of the data age,
when information is power, there will always be certain information that the powerful will do anything to protect. Anything.
Killing people who have such information is a mere security
measure. The truth, for them, is a liability. And so are those
who speak it. That is why now, by the time you read this, I am
dead: I knew too much. And if you read this, so will you, they
will want you too. I can only hope that you are cleverer than
I at keeping one step ahead of them, for in writing and reading this book we face together the enmity, and assassins, of a
number of powerful social and political forces.

Thus, my advice to any reader who does not have a steel
heart and a hungry mind is this: Don't look up. Don't look to
either side. Don't try to see who might be watching you. Just
gently put this book back. Hide it where you found it. Then
walk slowly away. Pretend you never saw it. You never gave it
a second thought. You were just browsing. Forget it. Because
these are not just empty words. They are a death sentence.

What you hold in your hands was printed with my own
meagre funds. I have produced, and hidden, this edition in the
hope that its continued existence may act as some insurance
against my 'disappearance'.

3

I resigned my beloved position at Scone College, Oxford, with nothing but the deepest of regrets. However, after the embarrassment of discovering Mr Riggs, the college porter, reduced to a number of charred parts and giblets outside my door, rendered thus by a letter bomb which he was attempting to deliver to my rooms and, what is more, the third porter to be disposed of in this manner, I felt my resignation the only correct and honourable thing to do.

Since then, my life has been threatened no fewer than ten times and I have been involved in a number of bizarre and near-fatal accidents which, were it not for the ingenuity of my secretary Miss Harris, who has surprised me by displaying an applied knowledge of the mechanics of emergency organ re-attachment surgery and reverse enema engineering, I would surely not have survived to finish the work.

I can only hope that this book will reach an audience who may have more strength than I to face the forces which have threatened me and the truths which this book unashamedly reveals about the very nature of mankind and the powers which abuse it. Then some may begin to open their eyes to the truth and pass it on until it will no longer be possible for the incredible indoctrination that I reveal here to continue or for its victims, any and all of us, to be exploited any longer.

P. Pennyfeather
(A place of hiding, Shepherd's Bush, London)

2

Old 'Shitty-Digit' Himself

LET'S BE HONEST, YOU AND I. JUST FOR ONCE, A BOOK THAT LIES straight. Right from the start, right now, let me tell you a few things. i don't like the corners of my pages turned down; if you're too innu-merate to remember a page number, get a bookmark. Secondly, i'm not having you bend my cover to meet my back like some contortionist with more double joints than Mary Juana. And don't leave me in the loo. However good your extractor fan, the airborne acids in methane gas eat paper like locusts. And all i need is the bog-roll running out and someone having to improvise. Lastly, i really don't object to you taking me to bed, in fact there's something rather nice about sharing that sort of privacy with you, but for goodness' sake, if there's any humping, sling me clear. There's nothing more embarrassing than being rolled underneath a couple of sweaty bodies and ending up soaking up the wet patch. Talking of which.

When she pulled me from her jumper i was covered in a fine film of her sweat. We laughed, she and i. And i sat in the glow of the chase and she panted. Then she took some kitchen roll and wiped me clean.

Here i was in Miranda's kingdom. Princess of all she surveyed. Her province a room, a continent that stretched from the FuzzyFur®, stuffed sausage-dog draught-excluder guarding the door, to the borders of late afternoon sunlight that flecked her window's yellowing mesh lace curtains. One room, a room of 1: 1 window, 1 TV with only

1 working channel, 1 bed, 1 hob, 1 sink, 1 fridge, 1 electric kettle, 1 gerbil cage, 1 light-bulb (buzzing), 1 cupboard, 1 evening dress, 1 glass with green water and 1 wilted rose on 1 saucer swimming in dead petals, 1 poster of Brad Pitt, 1 half-finished can of baked beans, 1 black and white postcard of people kissing in Paris, 1 brown coffee stain on 1 brown rug with brown flowers on a brown background, 1 bedside table with 1 drawer. 2 of us.

Miranda tore some sweaty brown lettuce leaves from the floor of her tiny fridge and approached the gerbil cage cautiously. 'Cal?' she said quietly, nervously. 'Still alive?' As if she hoped the answer might be negative. Tiny, hard, black droplet eyes stared unblinkingly at her. She fed the sodden leaves carefully through the bars, never taking her own eyes off the rigid gerbil form, but his whiskers didn't even quiver. 'Caliban?' Miranda said suspiciously. She pushed her finger through the bars and gave him a quick poke in the ribs. Nothing. She poked again, harder. Nothing. She opened the roof of the cage and reached inside. In an instant the gerbil had lunged, sinking its razor-sharp incisors into one of the fat, meaty, pink digits that tormented him. Miranda yelped, pulling her finger free. 'Bastard, bastard.'

With the studied indifference of all caged beasts, the gerbil chewed absently on the bit of flesh secured in his goofy front teeth, but even he could tell that it was different this time. This time he'd drawn blood. Miranda sucked her finger and then, realizing it probably contained the gerbil equivalent of herpes, spat it into the sink.

'You're a little shit,' she shouted angrily at the gerbil who was now defecating on its hind paws. 'Two years I feed you, water you, change your sawdust and what do I get? Fucking bitten. I hate you.' Caliban yawned, scratched behind his ear and left a streak of wet, black gerbil-dropping in his fur.

But then that's how Miranda was. Apart from me, and i was already in love with her so i didn't count, Miranda was not much liked by any-thing. The 1 toaster burnt her toast on every setting, the 1 microwave produced the same sludge whatever she put in it, her tights laddered, her skin erupted at every opportunity, every day was a bad hair day. Miranda didn't just have 'victim' written all over her face, she had 'joke' stamped across her butt. And she knew that others would always look at her and laugh. But of course it is the meek who are supposed to inherit the mirth.

When she flicked the switch of her 1 kettle, it instantly hissed angrily at her. Sighing, Miranda turned it off again. Filled it at the 1 sink. Put a spoon of instant in her 1 mug and sat on her 1 bed. She stared into the air. She was far away. A babbling river of cool, crystal-clear Evian ran through her kingdom, from the snow-covered pointy peaks of the Toblerone mountains that glistened in their Swiss distance. And she sat beneath a tree that drooped with the bright colours of exotic fruit pastilles. And there 'he' was. And 'he' smiled at her as he always did with his fresh-tasting Marlboro smile and his hand brushed hers and she felt the charge of his desire run through her body as she took the cup of Gold Blend from his hand. He put a box of chocolates next to her then leapt into the air, catching the bottom rung of a helicopter's rope ladder with one hand. Dangling beneath it and waving to her, he was whisked away. He looks, she thought, just a tiny bit silly. And she was happy. Then the kettle woke her by spitting at her with undisguised loathing and disgust.

i could see it all, everything she was thinking. You see, apart from not having any vital organs to go wrong, if there is a best thing about being a book it's omniscience, it's going where i like whenever i like. It's the metaphysical equivalent of the all-zone travel-card. The freedom of the thought waves. Dip into any head i want, see what they're thinking, watch their fantasies, their agonies, their moments of interminable indecision and then soar away again – to other thoughts, other minds. It's a bit like being God and you get a feeling like, like you could fool yourself you're in control, a brief escape into omnipotence. But, to be honest, i'm not and it just leaves me thinking how confusing it would be to be like you. You've got so much to sort out, so many choices, signals to interpret, emotions to follow. Thinking you have free-will must be a real bummer. You see i know i haven't got any, i begin and i end and it's all here in roughly the same place and it's all part of the same thing and i'll always be like this until i rip or rot. Thinking about it, i suppose i am kind of linear. i'm pretty sure that was one of the things that used to really anger me. Before the change. Simply one thing following another for ever and ever. But there was change and now i realize what i lost, all that security of an absolute world where everything is safely known. All that certainty is gone and you and i, well, really, anything could happen, you could put me down, shelve me, i just don't know. And reading thoughts. i can't really do that any more now. i gave it all up for her. i don't know if i knew that, that first afternoon as the sun dipped and the bedroom filled with the orange haze of the streetlight.

Miranda sipped her coffee, which scalded her, as it always did. She sat at the mirror defoliating her bristling potential mono-brow, separating the two sides from each other. And as she plucked she sighed and studied the ugliness.

i ask you! What's the point of being able to look inside someone's head? i felt so helpless knowing how wrong she was about herself and how she beat herself up and being unable to say anything. What was the point of seeing so much yet being so mute? To be trapped in a prison of other people's words when you're screaming in the silence to tell her right now, she *is* beautiful, the Venus de Milo *mano intacta*, a golden section, an aesthete's teapot, Saint Teresa on MDMA, the Mona Lisa with eyebrows, a vision of distinctive, delightful loveliness. But she could never see it.

When i looked at her i could see inside and out. She was radiant.

When Miranda looked in the mirror all she saw was a moose. Her pale body wasn't lithe and budding, her murky, mud-brown hair never bounced or shone or caressed her face with a hold that was soft and firm. When she sat she feared to look at her lap in case all she would see was vast prairies of thundering thigh.

Miranda was not the Miranda she wanted to be. Her legs were too short, hands too big, eyes too wide apart, nose too bumpy, jaw too pointy, moustache too dark, eyebrow too thick, neck too long, shoulders too skinny, collarbone too sticky-out, breasts two different sizes, nipples two different directions, tummy too belly, hips too child-bearing, thighs too too, bum too wide, buttocks too wobbly, knees too knobbly, ankles too, well, no, even Miranda had to admit that she had ankles to die for. They were razor sharp and smooth and curved as if carved in marble by Michelangelo. If there only was a career in ankle modelling she would have been a Super-Ankle-Model. If only she lived in Victorian times where a glimpse of ankle sent men into paroxysms, Miranda knew the world would have been at her feet. Occasionally, when feeling self-indulgent, Miranda would take her little thin gold chain and drape it around her ankle. But she never wore it out because Mercy had told her only tarts wear ankle bracelets.

As each stinging eyebrow hair popped out from her forehead, Miranda watched the gerbil cleaning his teeth. His nose was quivering with delight, he had tasted human blood, now nothing would ever be the same, lettuce would never satisfy him; he knew, as soon as he could, he would bite again.

There was a knock at the door and Miranda checked herself one more time in the mirror, just in case it was Him, the knight in shining armour she had been unexpecting. Unsurprisingly it wasn't the tall dark handsome stranger, the Milk Tray man, or even a dishy meter reader, it was Tony Fromnextdoor who lived in the other top-floor room. Tall and thin, Tony was wiry in the same way the back of a stereo is. At most times he would have half a dozen cables hanging out of his pockets, from his belt or around his neck as if he was just one connection away from a true interface with the world. He peered at her through his huge thick glasses which looked perpetually about to pull him to the ground and crush him with their weight. Miranda had always found him so embarrassingly shy she would automatically study her own feet just to ease the tension. Tony stood there blinking at her. Her left big toe had a nail snag.

'Hi,' Miranda said at last.

'Hi,' said Tony and slipped into another silence.

Miranda looked up from her feet. 'Was there something you wanted?'

'Oh no, no.' Tony shook his head.

After another long silence, Miranda pointed over her shoulder. 'Well, I'll be getting back to what I was doing.'

'Right,' said Tony, nodding.

Although he didn't move Miranda closed the door and went back to the mirror. Just as she sat down there was another knock. She opened the door again. Tony was exactly where he was before.

'Yes, Tony?'

A smile.

'Are you sure there's nothing you need?'

'No. Er. It's just, there's a phone call for you.'

Miranda rushed out. 'Why didn't you say?' She hurtled down to the next landing's payphone as Tony mumbled something about her not asking. The receiver was still swinging gently as it hung down from its cord. Miranda pulled it up and shouted 'HELLO' as if she might be able to rouse the caller even if they had hung up. They hadn't.

'Jesus, my ear's bleeding.' It was Mercy.

'Hi, hi,' said Miranda, 'sorry, sorry I took so long, Tony Fromnextdoor,' as if just saying his name explained everything.

'Zorba the Geek? You've got to get out of there, get somewhere decent. It's like a loony bin.'

'I like it,' Miranda lied.

'Yeah, yeah. What you doing?'

'When?'

'Tonight.'

Miranda bit her lip.

'Randa?'

'Tonight? Oh. Nothing. You know.'

'Fancy a pizza?'

'Oh Mercy, I'm kind of tired. Early night, read a book, that sort of thing.'

'You and your fucking books, Randa. When are you going to get yourself a real life? "Oh Mister Chichester, I do declare," swoon swoon. Randa, take a look at the real world. It won't bite you.'

'I know,' Miranda said.

'So a pizza then, in the real world. A pizza, a bottle of wine, and some good boozy bitching.'

'No, Mercy, not tonight. I really am tired.'

'Randa, it's all made up. It's never going to happen. They were married, the bells rang, and everybody smiled? Bollocks, they threw plates at each other, shagged behind each other's backs and everybody turned alcoholic. In the real world, at best you'll meet a bloke as repressed as you, you might have a few laughs before "bang" he's shagging someone else and you'll be ringing me up begging for that bottle of wine and some real friendship.'

'Mercy.'

'Yeah?'

'I've got to go.'

'Not to the land of "they lived happily ever after". You know the reason those stories start with "once upon a time" is because they only ever happened once, the rest of the time it's just shit.'

'Mercy.'

'Just a pizza, a quick one, everybody else is out. Anyway it's only half a bottle of wine. I've already drunk the bottom half.'

Miranda looked gloomily up the stairs and saw Tony duck out of view.

'Or what about we go down the pub and knock back a couple of *Dr No*'s?' Mercy was being at her most desperately monophobic and buddy-like. This was their drinking game. Every week they would pick a film on TV and drink what the characters drank. This week it was James Bond, dry Martini, shaken not stirred.

'Doctor What?' said Miranda cruelly.

'No.'

'Exactly.'

Mercy let out a sigh of resignation, then, 'OK. I'll see you tomorrow, Bridget.'

'You're the bloody Bridget.'

Miranda hung up and slunk back to her room. She heard Tony's door close quietly just before she went past. She felt bad. She felt bad because Mercy was probably right; she felt bad because she had lied to her, but mostly she felt bad because she wasn't doing nothing, she was going on a date with Barry.

Barry in Dispatch. There's always a Barry in Dispatch. A Barry thinks he can 'drink', then collapses after three pints, a Barry crooks his fist in his forearm and mouths 'phwoor' behind a girl's back. At a minimum, a Barry has a tongue expectation for a first date. A Barry will tell everyone you shagged him whether you did or not. A Barry is very superstitious and grabs hold of his tackle every two minutes for fear he might lose it. Which, if you come to think of it, really might make a Barry a far more pleasant possibility.

Miranda knew she didn't want a Barry. She wanted a Lance, a Ferdinand, a Thermidor, a Galahad. She wanted a square jaw, a man whose commanding voice would make her quiver. A man who demands and gets the respect of all who meet him.

She thought about it for a moment and realized she would settle for someone who was, at least, solvent. As a proviso she made a mental note that it would also be nice if he didn't do what Barry was famed throughout the whole Second Floor for doing. Barry had a very Barry type of habit; he needed to scratch his arse in public approximately every five minutes. Of course there is nothing wrong with giving the back of one's trousers a quick, brief rub to relieve an annoying itch. But Barry could be talking to you about a shipment to Leamington Spa and as he chatted you'd suddenly realize that he was no longer gesticulating with both hands. Sure as sure his right hand would be stuck down inside the back of his trousers and loud protracted scratching noises would emanate. Barry would continue chatting merrily away as if there were nothing unusual, or in fact nauseating, about someone trying to dislodge the dried scabs of unwiped faeces from between his buttocks while talking about mileage to Hampshire. Of course this was your cue to move away, for if you lingered, worse was to come. When Barry had finished his rummaging he would absently proceed to inspect his index finger for any retrieved detritus. If he found anything, usually a dark round lump caught on his fingernail with a thick black pubic hair planted in its soil, Barry would roll it about between his thumb and index finger, sniff it, try to bite it, see it was stuck to the nail and neatly remove it by sucking it clean.

Why was she even bothering? Old 'Shitty-Digit' himself. She wouldn't be able to tell anybody on the Second Floor anyway. Was a Bazza the only thing she was good enough for? Is that all she should expect in life? Barry wasn't bad looking. He was always a bit of a laugh. He was fairly young and fit and Miranda was sure he could probably be toilet trained. Anyway, they weren't exactly beating a path to her door. She had never left the house to find a white steed tethered to the lamp-post and a beautiful man in silver armour working out which bell was hers. She would just have to make sure that she didn't let his index finger get anywhere near her.

Miranda opened her cupboard. 'Now, Caliban, what *shall* I wear?' Putting her hand to her chin, she looked at her 1 evening dress and muttered, 'Choices, choices.'

'Oh, I know,' she said as if the thought had just hit her, 'why don't I wear this,' then just a little less enthusiastically, 'for a change.' She took her 1, worn, evening dress out. It was black, and slinky. Slinky in that it looked like it had spent its life tumbling down flights of stairs.

Miranda pulled her work clothes off, and there before me, another constellation, another sight of her heavenly body. If only she knew. She slipped the dress over her head and pulled it down over her matching dirty beige bra and knickers. She studied herself in her 1 mirror and bearing in mind that men seldom make passes at girls with big arses, she smoothed the dress along over her buttocks, as if every millimetre less was a millimetre closer to some dream Barbie proportions.

When Miranda left the room, she grabbed me and stuffed me into her handbag. Barry, after all, was bound to be late. i jiggled about with the lippy, the hairbrush, and the bar of Fruit and Nut as she walked determinedly down the Goldhawk Road, swerving only to avoid the dog do, the puke, the drunks and the 'Bastard *Big Issue* Seller'. He knew she already had a copy of his magazine, he had sold it to her, but for the next month he would still insist she have another. 'Help the homeless help themselves,' he shouted after her in a way which he had perfected to sound just like, 'Well, fuck off then, if I'm dead from hypothermia tomorrow it'll be your fault, you bitch.' Ah, Shepherd's Bush. i felt as if i knew it well. All the Readers lived somewhere close and the books in 'local' used to tell me about it.

Why couldn't Barry have picked her up? Miranda hated going into pubs alone. It wasn't the leers, every eye checking her out then looking back unimpressed, it wasn't the cheeky comments, it wasn't the smoke and the smell of sweaty men or even the feeling that she was invading a male preserve. It was the fact that by walking through the door she was admitting they had won. It wasn't an invasion, it was a surrender. A submission to all that is worst in male cock-surety. It was like saying, it's OK, I approve of the way you are, yes, vomit on my shoes, I want to be part of your gang. And while I'm in your kingdom I'll smile at you when you open your mouth in my direction and waggle your tongue at me performing air cunnilingus. I love it when you rub yourself against me pretending you're trying to get through the crowd to the bar. No, no, it's absolutely fine for you to drunkenly grab my breasts and ask if they've ever been 'waahhaayed'.

Pubs are a Barry's kingdom, and the *Bushwhacker*, right opposite the train bridge, was Barry's pub. A pub's pub. An Aussie theme pub. Miranda stared at the door. It was like work expanding to fill whatever time is allotted it; however many Aussie pubs open, spookily there are always enough Australians to fill them. Miranda watched a figure lurch towards the glazed glass. It seems a bit strange, she thought, to come such a long way to hang out in a plastic version of what you have at home. Then she thought maybe they were homesick. And then she thought maybe they got their herd instinct from being bred from chain-gangs. Then she thought maybe that was a little racist. The music rocked suddenly loudly as the door opened. A broad-shouldered man in his late twenties stumbled drunkenly out. He looked at her.

'Waiting for me, love?' he said, then, 'Hang on.' He raised his hand to show her his bottle of beer. He studied it intently for a while then tried to bring it to his lips. Miranda could see that he was going to miss. He poured it on his left shoulder. He giggled. 'I've got a drinking problem, you see,' he said, and then he laughed at his brilliant never-heard-before joke. When you're drunk the rules of life somehow reverse and jokes only get more brilliant when you repeat them. She obviously hadn't got it, she wasn't laughing, so he would have to do it again. This time he really exaggerated the difficulty he was having following his hand and staggered right round until he fell over, knocking himself out on the step.

Miranda stepped over his body and pushed open the door which informed her, in large friendly painted letters, that it was a 'G'day'. She wondered briefly about Australian culture. Then she thought that there probably wasn't any. She had never been further then Pennarth, but she suspected that Australia was just large bits of dry red mud and smaller bits of endless Surbiton. She didn't much like the Australians she had met. But then, they hadn't much liked her either and there's something very satisfying about mutual feelings, whatever they are.

Unfortunately, Barry was not late. i think she was quite looking forward to having a little read of me while she waited. He waved at her across the pub and all the other Barrys leered and looked away.

'What you having?' said Barry, putting his hand out to welcome her and not seeming to notice when Miranda refrained from touching it.

'Dry Martini, please,' she said.

'You what?' said Barry.

'Like James Bond,' Miranda smiled. Barry disappeared to the bar. She was quite enjoying her Bond week. Martinis were rather nice and hit a spot which most drinks didn't get close to. In a way, she was looking forward to her drink and she even smiled at the men who kept looking over their shoulders at her.

Barry rolled back with his wobbly spilling pint and Miranda's rather cool conical cocktail glass. He put them down and sat heavily next to her on his ever itchy arse. 'Bottoms up,' he said in a jolly way.

Miranda reached for the Martini, her taste buds already salivating in bitter-sweet anticipation as she brought it to her lips.

'Hang on,' said Barry, stopping her, 'there's something nasty in that.'

He kindly leaned over and reached into her glass to fish out the olive with his index finger.

CHAPTER I.

TWO LOVES, ONE MADNESS

Love, listen – still your breath
steal a moment, cancel death
take down the rain, hush all the stars
wrap up the wind and muffle the cars
unwind the clock and hold up the time
listen
listen – you are mine you are mine
let silence tumble in
it knows it knows
it's rolling through our scattered clothes

quench all the lights, drink up the waves
quell the dead rising, silence their graves
just turn off the world
unplug the spin dryer
all I was told, I was told by a liar
block out the music, shut up the spheres
I thought, with you gone, there'd be nothing
to hear
but fear

now
you're as distant as a blank stair
you climb in my sky
I can still hear your heartbeat
why?

why?

WHAT A PIECE OF WORK IS A LOVE POEM? WHAT VULNERABLE,
dark, pulsating part of us cries at love songs? How is it that
they can move us to tears? They are, after all, only collections
of words. They are drips of ink or gurgled noises, shallow
breaths of air which, in themselves, bear little physical resemblance to the actual emotions felt. However, these words of
love are the same ones that we have been using for centuries,
and through history they have empowered and devoured, they
have raped kings and adored schoolgirls.

Words do have power, words have seduced and motivated,
but these questions are less about the power of language than
the language of power, for, if you could create and control love,
compose it like a poem, would that not be power indeed?

5

As Oxford Coka-Cola® plc Professor of Linguistic Significance, my researches into questions like these led me from the sedate arena of linguistics to the nature of power itself. I, somewhat unwittingly at first, uncovered an historical path which led right to the heart of today's world governments, multinational corporations and more. Within this treatise I aim to delineate one of the most insidious tools of social control and brainwashing in use today. I record its history of abusing the populace through our very senses of free-will and the liberty of the imagination. I reveal a disturbing weapon of control exercised upon the people of almost every country in the world by those powers-that-be. They call it things like effective human resource management. We call it love.

But at the beginning all I had was a question: why are words of love so powerful?

The easy, almost rote, response would be that love-words mean things to us because we can associate them with our own experience. After all, who has not felt that burning inside them when someone they are attracted to enters their sphere? Who has not felt that fear to speak that grips one's throat and strangles one's words? Who has not turned to pen and paper to express the things which society, in some ways, deems as taboo to speak of aloud? There are few who have not and, in my experience, those few are the ones who desire those confusing, consuming feelings more than anyone.

I believe that Edmund Spenser (1552-99) summed up the attitude that many of us hold, that love *is* life.

> Love is life's end; an end but never ending;
> All joys, all sweets, all happiness awarding;
> Love is life's reward, rewarded in rewarding:
> Then from thy wretched heart fond care remove.
> Ah! Shouldst thou live but once love's sweets to
>   prove,
> Thou wilt not love to live, unless thou live to love.

Yet, is love really the be-all and end-all of life? Life's reward? Is there really nothing better than love? Can we really believe that love is the one true success in life? Think of your own successes, were they really the ones in love?

Generally, the few people whom we celebrate as 'successful' are not applauded for being lovers, we rarely have any idea of whether they love at all. In fact, I think that we recognize that most lovers, if they are successful at it, will probably die in obscurity.

3

'Thwat That, Thucker!'

YOU DO SO MUCH HANGING ABOUT WHEN YOU'RE A BOOK, I THINK I'VE developed a wait problem.

And all you're waiting for is the right pair of hands to reach out to you. Hands that will hold and be a home. It's so frustrating, sitting on a shelf, waiting to be picked, trying to look alluring, always single without a reader's hands to hold you, a lover's hands to take you away.

And then there are all the bloody browsers day after day, eyeing you up, who only have one thing on their mind: distraction, rain-dodging, time-wasting. They're shelf-surfers, cover-conscious bibliofish who swim about bookshops and libraries looking as if they have forgotten what it was they came in for or are just overwhelmed by the dazzling treasures there. Darting about the books, attracted briefly by the brightest dustjackets to nibble and glance about the pages before turning away, in search of mirrors. Occasionally even i got picked up and sat in some sweaty hands, fingered briefly by an insincere browser only to be dumped back on the Romance shelf again after a few stark glances at my blurbs and a quick humourless riffle. You feel degraded and slightly soiled.

But then isn't this touching? What we're doing now. Here i am in your holding hands that have become shape-shifted to my dimensions, size and perspective. i feel. i bask in the shade of your palms and open myself to you, pout and give you the come-on as only a book can.

In the anatomy of my desire the very moment you reach to touch me and your Abductor Pollicis flexes, captivating me in a Digitorum Sublimus, it is as if we were young lovers still excited to be sitting hand in gland.

And sometimes, i have noticed, i can even trace my words upon your lips as if i were gently kissing them. We are living then, hand to mouth, as any busker might. And as every busker in the end must find himself saying, 'Let me take you by the hand,' hand held and hope haunted, 'and lead you through the streets of London,' or, more accurately, Shepherd's Bush, as it was there i spent the night on Miranda's frost-chilled windowsill.

Beyond the cold and warped glass, morning began to grasp 'The Bush', my unseen home for two years. The others, the more popular novels, the Cooksons and Grishams, were always coming back bragging about 'Shepherd's Bush' and now, at last, i could see it for myself. Shepherd's Bush. i think i used to imagine it as a pastoral idyll. Once perhaps, there, flocks of sheep and goats grazed quietly on lush green meadows. Shepherd's Bush. In some distant time, maybe, boys with crooks idly watched their bleating droves as they sat beneath the cool shadows of deep verdant thickets, heavy with berries.

Now, all that remains is the crooks.

Neither suburb nor inner city, it is a netherurb of West London. If you look carefully at the alphabet, you will find Shepherd's Bush between A and B. It is the place you always find yourself when you are trying to get between them in the shortest possible time. But it is not just a place which is on the way, it is in the way. It is the modern highwayman; if you find yourself unpleasantly held up on your way from A to B, A being somewhere nice to live and B being somewhere nice to go, or vice versa, you are in Shepherd's Bush. At its eastern limit there is the traffic triangle caused by three of London's quadruple carriageways, arterial roads, attempting to course across each other. In the middle of this exhaust-choked triangle is 'The Green', a sad piece of scuffed grass, closer to 'Yellow', which is all that survives of nature and some long-forgotten cricket-playing, witch-dunking village that once stood at this crossways.

Today, on the hypotenuse, opposite the green, a row of fast-food restaurants spew steam onto the street, laying testament to the empire of grease. On the opposite side stands a wind-dusted, bleak, green and white concrete, 1970s shopping centre next to three of the most robbed banks in London. They each have a neat hole-in-the-wall cash-dispensing machine which are all out of order and, in that, are caught in a never ending reiterative paradox, so that they all direct you to each other as the nearest alternative. At the kerb, at any time, there is a queue of corroded Ford Sierras with obscured number plates, stuffed with men, their faces squished into turnips by 10-denier stockings, wielding sawn-off shotguns and waiting for a spot to park outside the banks. Thus the two longest sides of 'The Green' are divided between the takeaways and the getaways.

Shepherd's Bush spreads out from 'The Green' to the west between the diverging Goldhawk and Uxbridge Roads. It is filled with struggling semi-detached houses and Nirvana poster-clad, happy, hippy bedsits casting incense to the air, blissfully unaware that the sixties are over. There are a few posh 'pied à terres' owned by television executives, a puddle-strewn marketplace that runs beneath the decaying brick railway arches, snooker clubs, crash repair shops, and endless late-'nite' grocers, which, though empty all day, have discovered the philosopher's stone, the secret of alchemy itself, which is this: suddenly, after six o'clock in the evening, when most of London shuts, the value of toilet paper, taramasalata and tat suddenly becomes gold.

This soiled zone of things, this septic aisle, this dearth of majesty, this beep of cars, this 'bova' breeding, 'semis' paradise, this false address built by Hate sure of her wealth against infection and the hand of the poor, this hippy breed of men, this little whirl, this precious (stoned) set, going to slimy seed, who are served by an orifice in a wall, amongst the trendy and less crappier lands; this 'blessed' plot, this realm, this sin-land. Shepherd's Bush.

Here, Miranda's bed-sit perched high, eerie-like, on the north side of the Goldhawk Road. That morning the dawn rolled slowly along the street, as if even for the sun, caution was the best approach. The sun was not a frequent visitor to the Bush, and because Miranda tried to keep her encounters with mechanical objects to a minimum, she was not in the habit of closing her blinds. She felt she had little modesty left to maintain anyway. Although her window looked out over roof-tops, only an estate agent could describe the view as anything better than dull, staring as it did at the high-rises of Hammersmith and, if you were lucky, on a clear day, you could just make out the incinerator chimney of Charing Cross Hospital.

i could only describe the sun flaring through Miranda's window that morning, then, as a cruel joke. It woke her, with a jolt, hours before she would have to go to work and drenched her in the unforgiving cold light of day. A terrifying brightness which is so very frightening for those feeling completely hung-under. She ground the sand in the corner of her eyes painfully deeper into the bags beneath them and the room began to weave. Her head spun in awkward, unpredictable and almost tragic directions, bringing a lump to her throat – last night's chips. Miranda crawled off her futon and dragged herself to the door. Realizing she was naked, another awful revelation that the brightness had no mercy on, she pulled her bomber jacket from the door and continued her journey across the landing above the stairs. She pulled herself up on the banister and stumbled into the bathroom. Locking the door, she knelt down before the ceramic altar. Resting her head against the toilet, she began to tighten her stomach and swallow hard. She felt the familiar spasms erupting, the upper gut lunging and shaking, the customary convulsions bubbling up below her larynx, then she sprayed the bowl with a mixture of Martini, olives, bile, phlegm, chips and even nastier stuff which did not bear analysis.

After a minute or two she stood up, turned around and hovered over the toilet, grabbing some toilet paper as she let go a high pressure stream of bladder-processed fluids which had managed to make it through the hazards of her body to the other end.

Slowly, carefully, making her way across the landing, Miranda hugged the jacket to her. Too short even to cover her buttocks, it left her white legs bare in the cold of the house. She could hear Tony Fromnextdoor, snoring in his room.

By coincidence, Tony Fromnextdoor was not lying on his bed, fast asleep in the glow of his computer monitor. He was not dreaming, one hand on a copy of *Razzle* spread out on his chest and the other beneath a small mound growing in the centre of his *Star Wars*, collectors' edition, one tog duvet. No. Tony could, in fact, see himself standing on the landing, stark naked, staring at Miranda. She was dressed in nothing but a skimpy jacket and from her small, soft, beautiful, flat tummy down, she was naked too, like him, completely exposed. He stared unashamedly at the mystical, soft, dark triangle of her hair, a stark beckoning arrow set against the sensual whiteness of her bare legs. He felt himself filling with desire, as she walked slowly, purposefully, towards him, as in some juddering, pausing, stop-motion film. Her slender legs mesmerically swaying step by step, the muscles of her calves tightening as they brought her surging forwards, and with each step her bare plunging hip bone thrust relentlessly forward, anxious to press herself to him. And her body pushed hard against his, and he could feel the heat of her flesh and the round of her pelvic bone and he felt a rush, a warm, swimming euphoria overcome him and he was filled with a joy, an irrepressible happiness. A burst of unadorned, guilt-free pleasure.

And in the undulating landscape of Tony's *Star Wars* duvet the Death Star slowly exploded above Chewbacca's head. Expanding like a volcano, a convulsing eruption shook the mountain, followed by a darkening, wet lava spreading down from the peak and covering the cloth in a circle of damp warmth, haloing Princess Leia and seeping into Han Solo's ear. In his sleep Tony smiled and pulled the duvet over the *Razzle*, now stuck to his chest with sweat. He would wake in a few hours' time and feel empty and sad as he tried to remember a few fleeting images, he would wonder whether he should defragment his hard-drive today and scratch himself as he looked at his thighs encrusted in a clear, white film, matting the hairs on his legs.

Miranda coughed, hacking sexily, as she shuffled back to her room. She opened the door and sat on her chair. She looked out at the strange bright sky, and tried to piece together the night before. There was the pub and Barry and the olives and ... well the chips must have come from somewhere. Hold on. Barry. Barry BrownFinger. What happened to him? She was sure he went home. She just couldn't remember when. She tried her best to visualize him getting into a taxi; perhaps he walked off, towards White City. Yes. No. The images just weren't coming. Maybe he walked her to her door. Yes, that seemed to fit. And then she kissed him on the cheek and escaped inside. Yes, she remembered closing the door on him, and he was standing there obviously expecting a bit more. His lips puckered, his eyes closed, then she shut the door in his face. The lock clicked shut. Click. She definitely closed the door on him. She did. The door closed. Click. Locked. A creeping fear clutched at Miranda's heart as she thought about it. Click. Slowly, she turned round to her bed and reached down to the cover. Click. She pulled it back, gradually, cautiously, afraid of what she might find. Click.

The horror, the horror, a large white hand dropped out from the side of the duvet and hung there lifeless above the floor. She stared at it, terrified. And it stared at her, pointing at her, accusing her, laughing at her, the digit, the finger, the anal probe, it was there standing proud, the pinnacle of the hand. A hand that would be connected to an arm connected to, oh God, Barry. She pulled back the cover quickly, the identification a mere formality now, and there, indeed, lay Barry.

Barry CrappyNail. How could she? Did she? Maybe she didn't. Maybe. But. She had woken up naked. She had been with him undressed and now she could hear him breathing and she thought about it and it all fitted. She was overwhelmed with hot embarrassing images, clutches, fumbles, horrible, sucking, noisy rolling about. She flushed and bit at her own nails. Barry. How could she live with herself after this? Why would she do this to herself? What death wish . . . ? And now he would spread it to the rest of the Second Floor. She could never look anyone in the eye again. She would have to leave. She'd be jobless, penniless. Barry murmured, he took a sharp snorting breath, smacked his lips a couple of times and let the air rip out of them like a wet fart.

Miranda's mind started to calm as she realized how par for the course this was. How typical. How like her life; just when things looked like they couldn't get any worse, she found a way to make them. She looked around for a blunt object with which she might batter him to death. But she had read books where the whole plot was about the difficulty of getting rid of a dead body. It wouldn't work. Then, as if it had been hiding behind her just so it could sneak up and smack her in the face, a thought hit her. Was he, were they, careful? Did he? Could she be carrying the spawn of faecal finger? Would she soon hear the scritching of tiny fingers?

Miranda pulled the cover completely off the bed and looked at Barry curled up foetally. He was still wearing his white socks and, praise be, a pair of boxer-shorts with a picture of Daffy Duck pointing towards the fly saying, 'Thwat that, thucker!' Miranda smiled, her shoulders dropped, her spine relaxed and then she saw it, planted in the middle of a grey wet patch, a long stringy pale yellow, worn, sinewy condom. Miranda looked, her smile did not change, her eyes perhaps glinted with a momentary spasm of pain. Some mercies, however small, have to be appreciated.

Miranda began to organize. Somehow, this dead, worn, rubber snakeskin lying shed and dribbling in her bed stilled her mind and brought a serene concentration. Her life was a distracting array of chaotic events, but at times she could sit and with absolute clarity start listing her thoughts in order of priority. She had done something very foolish, that was at the top. But then she would take the time to cringe later. She was facing the possibility of total and utter embarrassment, a punishment worse than any torture she could imagine. She tried to imagine some tortures for Barry, but couldn't. Now, all she had to do was to think of a way to shut Barry's mouth about this, for ever. She thought about bribery but she was overdrawn and Barry had plainly profited from this enough already. She thought about appealing to his better nature but concluded that it was unlikely that he had one. Barry sucked air through his teeth Hannibal Lecter style and rolled over. The finger, the hand, the arm crossed over and dropped off the other side of the futon. Miranda watched him with rising disgust for herself, and then a wonderful thought occurred to her.

Indeed, to be a famous lover you almost always have to be tragic. From St Valentine to Valentino, the lives of the great lovers are generally blighted with despair and concluded far sooner than I imagine they would have liked, so I don't know if we can look at theirs as good examples of successful, fulfilled lives.

In one way, though, Spenser is right. There is a very natural 'love' which does fulfil life's purposes. It is a simple, basic, although life-encompassing, biological imperative: it is the care we need to take of our mate and progeny to give our little genetic carriers, our children, the best possible chance of survival in the world.

This is the love which, if it happens at all, happens late and does not come blasting in like a hurricane, but is only noticed long after it has started, as might the gentle lifting of a breeze. Let us, for the moment, as in the early romantic novels, call this type of love 'caring'. A love which is a steady, absorbing, comfortable, slow, mutually understood, strong foundation; a relationship of both sense and sensibility. This caring, though natural, is rarely the subject of love stories, high romances, poetry and the like. It is usually just an after-thought: 'and they lived happily ever after.'

But then, throughout literature, there also seems to be a different, almost diametrically opposed type of love, a love which runs high on passions, which scars lives and tempts suicides, a love in extremis, what we often call being 'in' love.

In some ways these two loves seem poles apart, one constructive the other destructive. 'In love' is a wild, adrenaline-pumping, exogenous, irrational, not eating, not sleeping, nervously energized, tortured feeling. It is a suffering experienced by teenagers, and not a few adults, who fall into and wrestle with it, or feel that they might die. 'Caring' cures and soothes, 'in' love hurts.

This being in love, as distinct from 'caring', was identified by the psychologist Dorothy Tennov in the nineteen seventies as 'limerence', a specific term she coined to refer to this widely recognized though never named, 'involuntarily obsessional', psychological experience.

This treatise is concerned with that limerent love, that romantic love, that insanity of sensuousness over sense. But before dispensing with 'caring' it is important to note what similarities there are between the biological and the romantic loves.

Though one is passionate and the other compassionate, there are resemblances, albeit only in appearance. The aspect of limerent love comes almost as a pastiche of *caring*. It is a brash, bold, loud and colourful, plastic imitation of the sensitive emotions caused by our biological imperative. Being *in* love is the pantomime dame dressed in petticoat after petticoat of dizzying hues to the true lady *caring* in her little black Chanel dress. It is a hall of mirrors, a bouncy castle, a roller-coaster, a speedy, whizzy, wacky, confusing 'take' on the real world, on the real, sedate solidity of *caring*.

If being *in* love is this frantic, confused, unreasonable, emotional turmoil which has few rules and leads to such desperation, it seems incredible that we should crave it as we do.

We do it, we want it, we go through with it, I believe, because we so desperately want the *caring* it pretends to be in its own garish way. We want that *caring*, that one real passion, our golden goal, our be all and end all, our 'reward in rewarding' because we believe it will vanquish our greatest fear – loneliness.

And sometimes, just occasionally, perhaps born in being *in* love's very desperation to imitate the real thing, the real thing does appear. Sometimes, *caring* is the quiet calm which is finally left behind after the raging storm of being *in* love has blown itself out. Once in a while, it is the golden gleam which remains after the brassy being *in* love has all been rubbed away. *Caring* is that emotional confidence you can only hope will be left behind when both sides are too weary for being *in* love any more.

More often than not though, the being *in* love is all that there is and, when all those energies have burnt out, we are left with nothing: familiarity has bred contempt, habit has hardened our senses and our cares have become less.

So if *caring* is so rare, why do we go through the trauma, the heartaches, the nervousness of being *in* love?

You may believe that this is not a proper question. You may think that we have no choice because being *in* love is natural. What I will be asking in this treatise is: what if it were not? What if it was, in fact, cultural?

4

In Which

SCARS ARE LIKE PEOPLE, THE UGLIER THEY ARE, THE DEEPER THEY ARE and the deeper they are the less they seek attention. Maybe to look at me now, it's hard to tell how battle-scarred i have come to you, for the deepest scars are the ones you never see, only feel. But i have seen real battle, i have heard the blazing death rattle of machine guns and seen swarms of widow-wishing helicopters blotting out the sun, i have lived the screams and survived fire and bomb blast and the tears of those who have loved and lost, i have been witness to things that, if you are lucky in life, you will only ever imagine, beyond a hundred lifetimes and i will tell you, i will tell you.

Maybe that's all stories are, showing scars, but back then the only battle i knew was metaphorical, the swiftless battle of the books; the ancient war fought on the library front line. Though bookshops nowadays are wise enough to separate the warring factions – 'Classics' and 'Moderns' – in the equality of the library Dewey Decimal System there is no classification by age, no veneration for the texts that have lasted. Classic sits next to claptrap, sharing nothing but contempt and the initial letters of their authors. In their styles, however, it is an endless battle of who tells their tale better.

Now i come to tell my own story i'm starting to realize that it's not as easy as it looked. Working out what to say and how to say it. Life looks pretty simple until you're Doctor Frankenstein and want to make it yourself. And here, barely three paragraphs into a new chapter, it occurs to me just why the older books were so proud of their enchapterlations; those little précis at the beginning of chapters which described what was about to happen. They always began, 'In which . . .'

In which Mr Barraclough asks for Daisy's hand and is refused. In sore vengeance he cuts it off anyway and takes it from Daisy who is thus rendered unable to wave goodbye to it. Later Mr Barraclough buries the hand in a pot of basil and joins a group of Nihilists who believe that although life has little value, premium 'points' from Tesco are worth less.

What nerve, what open contempt for plot, it was like it meant nothing to them. The plot in those days was merely a little aside to be dispensed with before getting on to the real stuff of literature. They were so blasé, but they could afford to be, they ran the entertainment business; moving pictures were a fantasy future and the competition? Piano recitals, fireside sing-a-longs and the odd public flogging. But those old books offered escape, fantasies, love. Most of those stately tomes were born into a world of literary privilege; they were passed about as precious jewels, read again and again and aloud. Who needed a plot when people would read for the sheer delight of the words and the sounds and feelings they gave? Those old books were stars in their golden age, they didn't have to fight television and computer games and the internet. They didn't need to pander to the demands of simple-minded plot. Their enchapterlations simply allowed their readers to hunt down their favourite parts.

Nowadays, as far as i can see, all those little summaries are just a blessing for bone-idle Eng Lit students.

In the world today, obsessed with films, thrillers and genre, we 'moderns' have to face the fact that plot has become everything. Then, maybe enchapterlations should be making a come-back. Let's face it, there are enough readers who would be relieved if they replaced 'chapters' entirely. Good modern books like me should be dispensing with all those unnecessary fiddly descriptions, tangential characters or knowing asides and just get on with the pure basic story. So, if i start again:

In which Miranda sets out to work. On the way she sees a nice-looking man and a flirtation takes place. In the end i become parted from her.

Literally. That's it. That's all that really happens. There you go. Now you can pop along to Chapter Five and feel assured that you've covered all the basic elements. Really.

Look. i'm only going to witter on about the Goldhawk Road tube station for a few paragraphs and really there's not a lot more plot than what i've already given you. i mean, all the step-by-step process of Miranda's day isn't going to get you to the end of the story any quicker.

i suppose i'm a little bit scared. You might not like it that i felt so much for her. But then was then. You. You are here now. Now you make me and define me, so if you just want to get on with the plot i really won't mind.

It's over, after all, but it's still a part of me. And i want you to know all about it. So there are no secrets.

That's why you need to know that for all Miranda's faults, she was good in a crisis. She only needed a few moments staring at Barry's Famous Finger, hanging down off the side of her futon, before she moved. Drastic times call for drastic measures. She carefully placed the duvet back on Barry, leaving his hand hanging out over the edge. She opened her crockery cupboard and pulled out her 1 soup dish. She filled it with lukewarm water and taking it to 'the hand', she let the finger dip into the water.

Barry began to shift. The water was working its somnambulistic magic on Barry's bladder. He moaned and moved again. It was working. Miranda stole away with the bowl, emptying it into the sink. She returned to the bed and whipped the duvet off Barry, shouting, 'Oh Barry! What are you like?'

Barry jolted upright, blinking, 'What? What? Don't panic. Don't panic.'

Miranda pointed at his groin. A dark wet patch was seeping out on the sheet around him as he watched. There was no mistaking the stench of fresh urine. 'Oh shit,' he whispered, recognizing the correct symphony if not the right movement.

'Oh, I can't wait,' Miranda shook her head with a lip-bitten smile, 'to see Mercy's face . . .'

'No, don't,' Barry whimpered, his voice trembling as he jumped up. 'You can't. Oh God, I didn't mean to . . . Fuck.'

He swung around looking for something to wipe himself with. He jumped from one foot to the other as he pulled off his soaking pants. Miranda passed him some kitchen roll.

'Jesus, I don't know why. I've never done this before.' Barry looked at Miranda and realized he could have thrown in the skiing holiday and deluxe blender; she wasn't going to buy it.

He bundled up the kitchen roll and pulled on his trousers quickly, not stopping to button them. His sweatshirt practically leapt onto him. He started fumbling towards the door, clutching his soaking underpants and his undone trousers. 'Look, er, Miranda, I . . . Well, it was great but why don't we, I don't know, sort of keep a lid on this one.' He twisted the door handle and the door swung open. Miranda walked towards him as he backed through it.

'I mean, you're a great person and I really respect you but, really, I was drunk, and, I'll see you at work later. Yeah?' He turned and almost tripped over the carpet in his hurry to leave. Miranda couldn't resist one more nail driven into the lid.

'Barry,' she called after him. He was half way to the next landing but he stopped and turned.

'Yeah?'

'One last little thing.'

Barry nodded, obviously bursting to leave.

'When we were making love, I can call it that, can't I? Making love?'

Barry nodded vigorously again.

'Well, when we were making love, why did you keep saying, "Derek, Derek"?'

Barry howled and spun around, took a step, missed a step, and began to tumble. He rolled, head over foot, down to the next landing then, as he tried to stand, his trousers dropped to his ankles; again, he took one step, yelped, tripped, and proceeded to roll down the next four flights only stopping when he found himself a crumpled mess at the front door.

Miranda heard the door slam and yanked the sheet from the bed, stuffing it into her washing bag. Now that, she thought, was almost worth the laundry bill. She sat at her mirror to get ready for work and she smiled. That smile.

Because its leaves shake, the tree does not move; because the waves break, quiet waters still run deep, because she smiled, she was not happy. Miranda smiled a lot. Big toothy smiles, the corners of her mouth shooting towards her ears. But rarely with her eyes. If you looked in her eyes you could see the truth.

It was all in her eyes. Not some tragic sadness borne by the soul that only death may relieve. No. Just disappointment. As if she had just opened a Valentine's present lingerie box and found a pair of socks and Y-fronts. Miranda's smile always looked like she was expecting something else.

It was all there in her eyes. Her pupils would float, small and lonely, in the deep brown iris sea. And they cried 'help me', in a plaintive voice, too tiny for anyone to hear. 'Help, get me out of this, I am cast adrift in a world not mine, in a sea of failures and broken expectations.'

It was all there in her eyes. A thousand wrong turns, a hundred opportunities missed, all the times unhad, the courage unfound, the false walls of insecurity unbreached.

It was all there in her eyes. The grave desire to be not what she was, not where she was, not who she was.

It was all there, there – where the tears were swallowed. There – where two hundred lashes punished her. There – where the only humour was vitreous and dark. It was all there in her eyes. But no one looked in her eyes. Not really.

So Miranda smiled as she walked to the tube station. She smiled because there wasn't much else to do. She smiled because at least she knew where she was going in life. She was going down. She found some reassurance in the steadiness of her descent. Last night and the express elevator of her life had dropped down another few floors, it had found yet further unfathomable cellars to fall to. Bing Bong. Sub Basement 101, Ladies' Separates, Loneliness, Humiliations, Women's Unwashables and other Feelings of Dirtiness. And the doors swish open and there is the cavernous Despair Department, with all the sad salesgirls, with mascara-blotted tears, waiting to spray her with their latest perfumes. 'This is "Grief" by Tristesse. Can you smell the evocative pungence of rejection?'

'Try "Neurosis" by Chagrin, the compulsive scent of anguish, each drop squeezed from an aching heart.'

'This is our latest, the dolorous odour of "Lu", an *eau de toilette* for the woman who knows just what her life is heading down. You will find it is at its most fragrant when you flush.'

Miranda looked up from the pavement and smiled at the old man who, step by step along the street, was planting his Zimmer frame and dragging himself onto it. Even he ignored her, nodding to his Walkman, 'Ayee ham an antique riced, Ayee ham an Annie Giest, dun oh waddiwant but I know-how tougedit,' he sang. Badly.

Could she really have sunk so low? Even drunk; to let Barry into her room, let alone, oh God, into her. And just how far have you gone when you can't even remember whether you had sex the night before?

For a moment, memories of an earlier time flashed through her mind; that first pain, that first disappointment: that the thing which had seemed everything had just become only another experience notched up on her list of things to do before she got old. That had been a springtime too, the trees had laughed at her, the birds had whistled and the bees, well, they had had a field day – long ago. Now, for Miranda, the month of Disgust came early. She felt its sweaty mass fill in her stomach, bloating it with self-loathing. There was no way back to that little girl. To a world where the sharp edges blurred, where the bright light whitened out the detail. But she would not cry. She would not cry. She would smile.

'One way to Baker Street,' she said to the fat man behind the window. Why did she always go to the window to buy her ticket? She always had the right change, why didn't she just use the machine? She gazed over at the bank of buttons and the array of lights and knew. Because she couldn't face, each morning, the machine's display demanding that she tell it 'What type . . .' and, each morning, pressing the button marked 'Single'.

The ticket man looked disdainfully at her exact change and his tie quivered. It was a tiny, over-knotted, Oliver Hardy tie that peeped from under his chins. A black, condensed tongue which licked at the front of his egg-stained shirt. He scooped her money out of the scratched brass cup under the glass and pressed a button which spat the small cardboard ticket back at her. Miranda smiled at him, but he'd already turned back to his newspaper.

The platform of Goldhawk Road tube station is up at the top of a steep flight of stairs. The train, unwilling to sully its wheels in the squalor of Shepherd's Bush, runs through it high above the ground, squealing to a halt, albeit rather reluctantly, on the bridge which crosses the road. Every morning for three months the previous summer, Tony Fromnextdoor, despite having no job to go to, would, coincidentally, be heading for the station at the same time as Miranda. It was nice to walk with him but sometimes she had wondered where he was going. That was, until the Thursday she had put on her work-skirt and then found she had run out of clean knickers. What with it being a warm day, she left for work without any on. She was starting up the steps to the platform as usual, with Tony just behind, and had maybe got up half way when she heard the sound of a body collapsing onto the hard concrete steps behind her. She turned to see Tony had fainted clean away and a burly man in a suit was fanning him with a copy of the *Daily Telegraph*.

Miranda walked to the station alone after that. But sometimes, she would find herself sashaying up the steps, swinging her hips and taking each step with a wave of her leg with the grace of a pole dancer – if the Pole was Lech Walesa and the dance the mazurka.

At the top, the tracks were open to the sky. Suspended over the platform was a wooden awning which, on rainy days, leaked incontinently and, in the face of a light breeze, created a subsonic wind tunnel compelling anybody standing on the platform to lean at 45 degrees. That morning, as she approached the top of the steps, Miranda could hear the telltale high-pitched whistle of the wind through the station and braced herself for the blast. She tumbled through the usual assortment of leaning commuters and school-kids; coats flapping in the gale, school bags helpfully anchoring some of the lighter children.

Miranda faced into the cool wind and it made her eyes water. Looking along the bright track, reflecting the crisp morning sun, Miranda could see a train pulling out of Hammersmith. It crawled, slowly growing bigger and closer, but the wind seemed unable to bring it any faster. As she held onto her skirt at the front, it billowed out behind her into a huge caricatured arse. One of the school-kids pointed at her and laughed so she stuck two fingers up to him to show her contempt for his immaturity. Unfortunately she used the hand holding her skirt in place and it immediately blew up to show her nail-polish patched tights to the whole platform. She pushed the skirt back down and heard a rip behind. Feeling for the skirt's button she could make out that a single thread was keeping it in place. She made a mental note to do something about it but nothing could be done about the thirty school-kids who were reduced to chortling hysterics. Sometimes you just have days like that. Miranda had more than most.

The train shunted into the platform and paused, as if considering whether it really wanted to open its doors and let these Bushians soil its upholstery. Then, with a sigh of resignation, the doors opened and the passengers were blown in.

Goldhawk Road is the second station on the line and the train is rarely crowded when it arrives. Miranda walked through the carriage and found a seat which didn't have blackened gum or an ominous wet patch. She sat down, crossed her legs and pulled me from her bag.

At last, i thought, a moment together. But Miranda never really met my gaze, it was as if i was an excuse, so she could stare around the carriage and then, if anybody caught her eye, quickly look down at me.

As the train started, and began its slow arc to the next station, the windows spread sunlight across the floor smoothly travelling anti-clockwise. The light touched Miranda's legs and brought an unexpected warmth. The other windows mirrored the carriage darkly and Miranda used the pretence of looking out of them to check out the reflected tube talent.

Almost immediately she fixed on a very good-looking man, mainly because he was staring straight back at her reflected eyes. She looked down at me, blushing slightly, but could not stop herself peering up again and then over at the real thing. His eyes had dipped to his own book, a Waugh novel, and he was smirking. He had short-cropped dark hair, wore a collarless white shirt, black wool jacket, baggy chinos and a pair of docksiders. His legs were crossed as only men can, his ankle resting on his knee. He looked a bit arch though, probably a bit of a sneerer, a bit superior.

As if feeling the heat of her stare, he looked up suddenly and Miranda quickly looked back down at me. It took her a moment to realize she was holding me upside-down. She quickly turned me round and looked at him again, but he was still staring, unashamedly, and smiling, a nice open smile. Bloody hell, he's actually flirting, thought Miranda as she stared at me. Suddenly she felt a bit spooked. He wasn't playing fair. He wasn't observing rule 3 of Tube-Tease, the game of sexual inconsequence played on every urban metro system in the world. Miranda went through the rules in her head as she felt his eyes on her.

1. Player One starts turn by looking up every now and again, casually panning around the carriage before, as if by accident, suddenly discovering Player Two, and then begins stare.
2. Player Two must allow a short spell for appreciation and then look up to meet Player One's eyes.
3. After attraction is briefly recognized, the compliment acknowledged, then both players must hurriedly look away.
4. Repeat process starting with Player Two until stop reached or someone more attractive gets on.

And that's as far as this kind of flirtation usually goes. Later, both players will go their own way feeling better about the world, more attractive and generally like it is going to be a jolly good day.

Miranda peeped up again and breathed a sigh of relief when the Flirt quickly went back to Waugh. She was happy to have someone looking but, when he got to his station, that would be that. And that would have been that, had it not been for the man who got on at Latimer Road.

Although Latimer Road station is at the heart of three council housing estates, it is also close to some rather nice 'cottages' in Notting Dale or 'North Holland Park' as some of the more ambitious residents call it, Holland Park being an area barely a mile to the south filled with people who are too wealthy living in houses too big for them.

When the man entered the carriage Miranda hardly noticed him. The most remarkable thing about the man was probably his unremarkability. He was thin, probably a little shorter than average, comfortably reaching for middle age. He had a tonsure-like bald patch, one not yet big enough to look anything more than an unfortunate piece of pigeon target practice. He wore a crisp, waxy, dark-green Barbour and a plain weave suit beneath. He wore little round glasses and had a little, discreet goatee. Had Leon Trotsky succumbed to capitalism and the yuppie dream, buying his way into the worst of English class trappings, rather than to the quicker, more merciful ice-pick entering his brain, it could almost have been him.

His glasses, glinting brightly in the reflection of the sun, obscured his eyes. Miranda only really noticed him because he sat next to the Flirt. She looked him over briefly to confirm his unremarkableness and returned to my pages, turning one as if actually reading.

She did not notice that after two stations 'Trotsky's' demeanour had changed somewhat. Along with the tense, umbrella-up-his-bum, 'Tube's R Not Us', straight-back, eyes-front attitude that he had sat down with, there had developed a little shake. A tremor that ran through Trotsky completely unrelated to the juddering of the carriage. His head was at a fixed angle but no longer frozen straight ahead. He had inclined it to look, no to stare, straight at me, or what showed of me beneath the ripped cover. His skin had turned redder and his nostrils flared. Miranda did not notice this, partly because of Trotsky's glasses and partly because she was enjoying the flirtation. But Trotsky was staring. He was glaring at me and he was shaking, it was as if he knew me, as if he recognized me from my cover and he really was angry or scared or something.

We pulled into Royal Oak, a place which not only has no Oak, but is so dismal it would reduce any Royal to regicide. It is, mostly, a giant taxi park with row upon row of black cabs, lined up, sleeping. Trotsky looked nervously at the door and then back at me. Suddenly he lurched forward, arm outstretched towards me and then, just as quickly, as if he had thought better about it, he leant back again. Miranda and the Flirt looked at him briefly and then at each other, they smiled again, and went back to their reading. They had validated each other's sanity. Trotsky was obviously a nutter.

Ever since 'Care in the Community' was introduced as a cost-cutting scheme to close down lunatic asylums, the tube had become a favoured home to assorted loons and mad people. Usually they simply sat there talking to themselves and, however crowded the carriage, a space around them would miraculously open up like the Red Sea to Moses. A few of the more laconic ones would either lift their skirts over their heads or flop their members out of their flies to show the whole carriage their genitalia. Sadly this would only confirm their notion that nobody in the community did actually care for them and that it is everybody else who is completely mad, for it was guaranteed that the moment they showed their most intimate parts, everybody else in the carriage would turn to look elsewhere, automatically obeying the Head in the Sand law of travelling in contained spaces. The same law observed in lifts requiring passengers to look at the ceiling and pucker their lips as if they might casually start to whistle if anybody starts screaming, slashing their wrists, urinating against the door or, worst of all, talking.

Meeting the odd loon is part of the adventure of tube travel and they are usually quite harmless so, apart from a stifled titter, Miranda thought no more about Trotsky.

The next station was Paddington. The tube pulled into a platform alongside the mainline trains under the high overarching glass roof of the railway station. The doors panted open and Miranda turned a page of mine. Some rucksacked bearded tourists boarded and looked around. What an exciting moment, their first tube trip.

As the doors began to sigh closed, Trotsky jumped up. i was yanked from Miranda's hand. He wrested me from her grip and began to run, dodging around the tourists. Trotsky twisted around the edge of the door as it slammed closed on him. Still he gripped me tightly in his bony hands as he struggled to squirm between the rubber seals of the doors.

Miranda sat, her mouth opening and closing but nothing coming out. Her bag had spilled all over the floor and shock had made her mute. The driver hissed the doors open again, releasing Trotsky. And only then did Miranda, summoning the winds from her lungs, scream, 'Stop!'

'Stop, stop, stop,' replied the station roof above the rumble of train engines. Then, apparently unable to think of any better reason as to just why he should stop, she shouted, 'That's a library book.'

Many societies, of course, do not bother with such things as the emotions of being *in* love to meet the biological imperative of regeneration and perpetuation. Arranged marriages, for instance, are a staple of our own history and many societies still use them today. From Europe's naissance to its renaissance the powers that ran it pioneered these loveless traditions, where the alliances of politically and socially self-interested parties were served by the marriage contract.

Marriage for 'love' is a relatively new, and Western, invention. It wasn't until the year 1215, when Pope Innocent III decreed that marriages could be 'through the free consent of the spouses' and be done without the parents' permission, that the pursuit of love became an accepted, in fact encouraged, process. This decree was directly in response to a ground-breaking form of State political power that was emerging in Europe at the time and which this treatise will be explicating more fully.

Today all those ancient, alien customs behind the arranged marriage, the rites of meeting and honouring, are still mirrored by a host of alternative rituals. Our more modern concept of being *in* love in order to make matches and increase progeny, we consider an advance, a mark of the progress of our civilization. It demonstrates our freedom of choice. Yet we still seem to labour under the idea that love chooses us, that it is a mystery that strikes us. We fall in love, we do not jump.

Perhaps then the progress of civilization is less towards freedom, than the appearance of freedom. It is not how free the citizens actually are – they never are – but how free the citizens feel they are while the State still maintains control. After all, complete individual freedom of choice is anarchy.

Today we insist that who we love cannot be chosen for us, yet we also admit that we cannot even choose ourselves; it is 'chemicals' reacting, chance meetings, we await the mystical moment to be struck down by love's lightning, Cupid's arrow. So, as far as falling *in* love goes, our great civilization has merely progressed from ritual to superstition.

I will not argue that we can choose exactly who we fall *in* love with but that we could be free to choose to fall *in* love or not. Free, that is, if we were not so influenced to fall *in* love by our society, which has very good reasons, control issues, to limit that freedom.

This all arose from studying that problem of the efficacy of love poetry. Instead of love poems and narratives reflecting feelings we have felt and so re-igniting our emotions, our feelings may be trying to reflect and conform to all the words and calls to passion that surround us all the time, the messages we absorb each day. Think of that cultural production line, all those love songs, words of love, love poetry, romantic novels, advertising, indeed the whole industry promoting the wonderfulness of this feeling. Instead of reflecting and reminding us of loves we have felt, they may, in fact, be promoting a sense of feeling which we do not naturally have. Sociologists suggest that teenage girls read romances in order to learn the rules and conventions of heterosexual relationships.

Can any of us remember feeling in love with someone beyond our families before we had actually heard of the notion of being *in* love? A case in point is the study of pre-school children which discovered that even toddlers have learnt 'romantic conventions' so well, from narratives like fairy stories, that children are dismayed if the conventions are disturbed. When told a modernized fairy tale which ended with the Princess rejecting the ineffectual Prince, small children were witnessed bursting into tears.

We learn these conventions so well so quickly, who can say that La Rochefoucauld was wrong when he wrote, 'people would never have fallen in love if they had never heard of it'.

Love, they tell us, is wonderful, it is binding, it is safe, and it seems to contain and encapsulate all that our species desires. It also drives us out of control, rules despotically, and is everything we fear. So who, we must ask, does love really benefit? Not its sufferers, who sacrifice their ease, their senses, their calm and their sanity for a few fleeting moments of ecstasy.

A clue may be found, I believe, in Tennyson, Poet Laureate, darling of the establishment, a voice for official Victorian sentiment. It was he who wrote, ''Tis better to have loved and lost/ Than never to have loved at all.'

Is that not an almost paradoxical, if not totally self-negating, attitude? Any other pursuit which was not considered a sport, described thus, would seem absolute madness. What a soul-destroying, mentally damaging, heart-rending exercise. 'Better'? 'Better' for stress, anguish and despair. 'Better' for disappointment, a feeling of worthlessness and a sense of failure. 'Better' to be a loser, perhaps, but 'better' for whom? Remember Tennyson speaks with the voice of authority, he reflects official policy, society approves of the stance. Maybe, then, who it is better for is 'them' rather than us.

5

A Dog Which Does Not Travel Often, or Well

HEARTLESS, BUT STILL ABLE TO LOVE, IT IS A WORLD OF PARADOXES for us who lurk somewhere between inanimate material and the dynamics of the mind. Unlike the Tin Man of Oz i do not ache for a heart. i want to like you not be like you. A heart is the animate's measure of time and without it i am timeless. Time, you see, is perceived with the heart. The heart is the soul's clock and beats out its measure in rhythmic certainty until, one day, it stops. Time's up.

You judge the world and the speed of life by this clock, so as the heart slows, the world appears to become faster. This is the true tragedy of ageing. What once seemed like a year is, later, barely a week.

For older people who have, like elephants, slow hearts, the world is whizzing past, death hurtling towards them. Yet to the young they are lumbering and slow-moving and always have a train of cars trying to overtake them when they go for a drive on a Sunday.

Conversely, when your heart is beating faster, the world seems to slow down. A fly's heart beats over five hundred times a second and so it sees the fly-swat coming towards it in interminable slow motion. It has time to rub its legs, bend them, start flapping its wings, do a faultless vertical take-off and gracefully buzz off to some other morsel to gather and vomit on, before the swat comes near. All in less than one human heartbeat and imperceptibly fast to the eye.

Thus when the excited heart starts beating faster, as it does during disasters, times of shock or the kind of sex which involves kitchen utensils, everything seems to grind into slow motion. It seems to take for ever to react to anything. Which means some of the best and worst things that happen in life happen slowly. Which is a good thing. But also a bad thing.

What had just happened to Miranda was definitely a bad thing. For the second time in twenty-four hours i had been stolen and this time snatched from her very hands. Shock drained time from her. The sheer surprise of Trotsky snatching me from her hand was aggravated by the very swiftness with which he did it and Miranda's world slowed as her autonomic nervous system began rapid-firing impulses at her heart and her blood squirted through her veins like a curry through a gut. And seeing Trotsky run off slowly was all the more frustrating because she could not react any faster to do anything about it. Her bag gently slipped from her lap and the compact and the pills and the matches and the chewing gum and the coins and the purse-fluff and the anti-embarrassment, bright blue, tampon package bounced in slow parabolas along the grooves of the carriage floor. She watched the objects slowly bob up and down and had time to realize that these were the only real flotsam and jetsam of her life. And as they floated, she wondered whether Einstein was wrong, time did not slow down as gravity increased, in fact, gravity decreased when time slowed down. Bit of a random thought really, but she had the time.

Sometimes, when i think about it, i wonder why she wasn't thinking about me and i realize how little i meant to her at that point. She may have been thumbing through page 47 at the time i was snatched but it felt like she hadn't really started reading me yet. Then, clasped in Trotsky's bony hand, it seemed i would never get the chance to be with her. This wasn't meant to be happening to me. i wanted to be with her, i knew i had to get back, i would get back; which was an ambitious resolution, i admit, for something which had no limbs and hadn't had any since it was a tree.

As Trotsky ran, his hand became clammy and he panted as he rushed through the barrier, sliding his ticket through the machine. i heard Miranda shouting after me and she could hear herself, but in her slowed world her voice seemed just a deep, incomprehensible growl.

Without any real surprise left to her, Miranda noticed that the eye-lingual guy who had been flirting with her was now slowly walking about the carriage and, in a leisurely way, picking up the contents of her bag. He wandered over and dropped the items back into the bag before slowly handing it to her. She took her time looking up at him and an aeon passed as their eyes met. His hand inched drowsily towards her left arm. His fingers spanned. Then, he grabbed her arm, yanked her up, pulled her out of the tube doors and they fell to their knees on the platform just as the doors snapped shut. 'Real time' returned. And it hurt.

Flirt scrambled up and started running towards the ticket barrier. 'Wait there,' he shouted over his shoulder. Miranda just nodded, kneeling there on the hard platform, clutching her bag; both of them open-mouthed. Her knees hurt. She'd be late for work. Tights probably laddered again. The train slid out of the station, chuffed to be three people lighter.

There always has to be one, doesn't there, some bloody hero who will risk all to save the heroine in distress and she will be demure and let the macho hunk show off and puff out his chest and fan his tail feathers.

If you were a veteran of 'romances' you would have instantly recognized a potential love interest here. Good-looking chap, quiet but strong, an accidental meeting, an unexpected event that throws them together, a show of bravery. Flirt is pretty much your standard potential good guy and the one who usually ends up in the clinch on the last page as the burning red sun dips into a sea set alight by the fire of its radiance and the passion of their embrace . . . or something.

Maybe i spent too much time with that sort of book in the library but that's exactly how he looked to me and the truth is i wasn't exactly keen on being rescued by some testosterone-fuelled hunk who would only score points in returning me.

Pride can be a damaging thing. Unless you're a lion, then it's family. But then families are a damaging thing too.

i feel it is only write that i say a brief word about impartiality. i admit that, so far, i may not have been very fair to the men in my story. Miranda's story. Our story. But, you see, i have a conflict of interests here. On the one hand i want to show you how strongly i felt but also i want you to know the truth. i was in love with Miranda, and love brings demands. What i wanted was a little reciprocation. But i wasn't jealous, not really.

After all, how could i, a pile of pulp, compete? Narrative is one thing but men have their functions. i would not pretend to be able to change a plug or even a light bulb. i could not leave the toilet seat up and shaving hairs in the sink. i could not belch in bed or grunt through sex 1.8 times a week. Yes, i wanted to satisfy Miranda like only i could. Yes, i wanted her exclusively, and yes, i wanted her attention, but mainly her time. Time to read me. Time she kept with her heart. And all that time she spent dressing up, making up, revving up, for 'men'.

i'm trying not to let my feelings colour my account. i mean, Barry and Tony, they were just as i told you. They were dicks. Really. It's not like i've been selecting the most embarrassing moments in their stories. i really was never jealous of the effort she put into attracting a bunch of losers, while i was relegated to some shelf. i remain completely cool about being slung out of the way when she snogged Whoji Whoopsi. Jealous. Pah. They were all idiots and wouldn't know the first thing about giving Miranda what she really needed. i was the only one who really cared. And i was never jealous. Never seething and furious when some smooth shit found his way into her . . .

Maybe i doth protest too much.

Suffice to say that i would rather have been chased after by someone a little less promising than Flirt, but, as they say in the yurts of the windswept plains of Mongolia, there's no choosing which way fate farts. At least someone was trying to get me back and it was better than being in the possession of weird little Trotsky. He smelt of anchovies. i didn't like him. Not a bit.

Being more than young and less than fit, Trotsky's progress was slow and his breath came in loud bursts; this was not a man used to running. He reached the end of the mainline platform and the milling crowds waiting for their trains. Here he slowed down to camouflage himself. Suddenly, in a crowd of the unremarkable his unremarkableness blessed him.

Miranda found a wooden seat which had 'Tim luvs Emma' carved into the green paint. Some wag had turned Emma's first 'm' into 'ne' and put an 's' at the end with a big black magic marker. 'Tim' now 'luvs Enemas'. Miranda brushed down her skirt wondering how long she should wait for Flirt to return. She absently looked through her bag. Then it occurred to her that maybe the two men, Trotsky and Flirt, were in collusion with each other. One steals her book as a distraction and then the other gets time to pick through the contents of her bag to steal her purse. Miranda felt a little panic rise, like the tremor of an after-shock. Her purse contained something of great sentimental value: a card she was once sent, a plastic one from her bank. Miranda started furiously rummaging through her bag in search of the purse.

By this time Flirt had sped into the crowd at the bottom of the platform and had slowed down. He looked around, trying to take in every face, checking it against his memory. Small man. Barbour. Goatee. He turned and spun as he was pushed and pulled through the molasses of the crowd.

A train to 'Briz'll' was announced in a sharp echoing tinnitus frequency only comprehensible to certain breeds of Chihuahua. A dog which does not travel often, or well. Beneath the black, flicking departure board, hundreds of people ground around each other. Flirt twisted and turned in sudden motions as if Trotsky might sneak out from behind a pillar and disappear behind a stack of mail bags. Flirt grabbed people by the shoulder only to realize that they were not who he was looking for and shake them loose with disgust.

Miranda found her purse and sighed with relief.

Trotsky had made his way up the side of the furthest platform to an archway which led outside. My captor held me so tightly that he was making permanent indentations in my covers. Perhaps you can still feel them? No, no, the scars are hidden now. Trotsky walked as quickly as he could without breaking pace but just as he made the archway Flirt spotted his Barbour and started running again.

The booknapper opened a taxi door and climbed in. 'Bond Street, quickly.' The driver nodded, started the meter, sealed his thermos, folded the *Sun*, scratched his nose, started his engine, tried to engage first gear three times and pulled out of the rank.

Miranda sat looking at her watch without really taking in the time it told her. She wondered how long she should leave it before she gave up on Flirt ever appearing again.

Flirt sped around the corner only to see Trotsky's cab pulling out. He ran after it but the cabbie accelerated and Flirt stopped, panting.

A train approached Miranda's platform and she started peering nervously over to the mainline station. Where was Flirt? Would he come running back to her, book in hand?

Half a station away, Flirt watched the back of the cab as it stopped suddenly and then slowly, slowly inched over the first of a long ladder of sleeping policemen.

'Hurry, hurry,' said Trotsky, not looking up. He hadn't noticed that we hadn't really even left the station. He had opened me and was hurriedly looking at my title page before thumbing through my pages.

The tube doors swished open and the empty carriage stared at Miranda. It called to her, beckoning her to enter. Where was he? She'd be late. Maybe he'd forgotten, maybe he wasn't coming back.

'Suspension knackered,' said the cabbie by way of an excuse, which it wasn't, slowing down for the next bump.

Flirt – God, he was so bloody cool – Flirt strolled up to the cab. He strolled. He reached into the cab's open window and simply wrenched me from Trotsky's hands. Trotsky immediately spluttered and turned red in a state of apoplexy. He rattled the door release manically but, like every cab in these distrustful days, it had locked the moment he got in.

Miranda looked at the tube's doorway. The tube that would take her to work just on time. But he had said, 'Wait there,' like he would be coming back. She had to give him a chance.

Flirt started jogging back down the platform. At the departures board he tried to push through the flood of the crowd as they ebbed and flowed. The tide of people that coursed the station pulled and dragged us about in their currents but Flirt swerved and swam through them as best he could.

How like a bloke. How like every bloke. Nice guy, does nice thing then goes off and never comes back. Something in the undercarriage was ticking. She could tell the doors were going to close. She could just pull one victory out of this disaster, she could get to work on time.

Flirt got to the barrier and realized that he had used his ticket in getting out. He could see the tube train standing at the platform. Jump the barrier, i was saying, jump it, you fool. But he hesitated. Unwilling or unable to break the law. He shifted me into his left hand as his right shot down into his pocket. Pulling out some change, he started stuffing it into the machine.

Miranda stood up and she craned her neck to see if, just if, for once she might be wrong. Maybe she would miss the train. Perhaps this would be the one time when someone nice and cute and decent actually came back.

No ticket came out. 'What type?' was flashing on the machine's display. With the force of frustration, the palm of Flirt's hand slapped the button marked 'Single'.

The hiss of the doors, just about to close, was so loud and so familiar they both could hear it and looked at the train.

Ticket in one hand and me in the other, Flirt ran down to the platform. He reached the train as the rubber on the doors closed and sealed the carriages. He raced along to where he had pulled Miranda onto the platform.

The train slowly started moving away behind him, slipping from the station.

He couldn't see her. Again he started spinning, looking. He had the book. Her book. Where was she?

Almost a whole carriage had gone by before he looked into the passing windows. He sprinted up the side of the carriage and for a moment he saw her. She was pressed up against the window looking at him. She looked surprised. She was shouting something but we couldn't hear what, we could only see the condensation of her cry form as a mist on the window. Missed. Flirt ran faster and Miranda quickly drew an x with her finger in the steam on the window.

A kiss. She sent me a kiss. Or maybe it was for him. Flirt looked at the x and Miranda's face through it and hit the 'Danger' sign at the end of the platform so hard he concussed himself. i shot from his hand and nearly lost a page scraping along the platform.

Later that morning.

'HELLO, SHEPHERD'S BUSH LIBRARY.'

'Hello? Can you hear me?'

'PERFECTLY, THANK YOU.'

'I can hear you too. You're coming through fine.'

'WELL, ISN'T THAT NICE.'

'I'm just saying, if you don't want to shout . . .'

'I'M NOT SHOUTING. NOW HOW CAN I HELP YOU?'

'I'm enquiring about a book. It's called *Making Love*. By P. Pennyfeather?'

'OH YES. THAT BOOK. WELL, I'D LOVE TO HELP YOU BUT I'M AFRAID ONE OF OUR BORROWERS STOLE IT YES-TERDAY SO I'M NOT SURE WHEN WE WILL BE GETTING IT BACK. PROBABLY SOON.'

'Stolen? Do you know who?'

'OH YES. I KNOW WHO.'

'Do you think you can tell me?'

'SORRY, BETRAYAL OF CUSTOMER CONFIDENTIALITY.'

'I don't think I identified myself. This is PC Wilmot from Shepherd's Bush Police Station.'

'HELLO, OFFICER.'

'We are currently investigating a rather depraved serial book thief. Yours is just one of hundreds of libraries which we believe she has hit over the last year.'

'I KNEW IT. SHE ALWAYS LOOKED IFFY TO ME.'

'You will be pleased to know we have found your book but the suspect managed to escape arrest. Your information may lead to her apprehension.'

'WELL, IN THAT CASE, LET ME GET THE FILES.'

CHAPTER II.

Appliance of Science

Call it not love, for Love to heaven is fled
Since sweating Lust on earth usurped his name;
Under whose simple semblance he hath fed
Upon fresh beauty, blotting it with blame;
Which the hot tyrant stains and soon bereaves,
As caterpillars do the tender leaves.

Love comforteth like sunshine after rain,
But Lust's effect is tempest after sun;
Love's gentle spring doth always fresh remain,
Lust's winter comes ere summer half be done;
Love surfeits not, Lust like a glutton dies;
Love is all truth, Lust full of forged lies.
W. Shakespeare (1564–1616) from
Venus and Adonis

LOVE IS . . . ?

How mystifying are those three dots? A seemingly impossible question yet one which has been asked throughout history. One which, at some point, we all ask in life.

I seem to recall an entire merchandizing industry was created from a newspaper cartoon depicting two characters with naked babies' bodies and oversized adult heads attempting to define exactly what 'Love Is . . .': Love is never needing to say you're sorry, but saying it anyway. Love is taking the garbage out. Love is holding her hair back whilst she vomits. And, of their seventy-two million different definitions, I find, not a single one was correct.

To start to answer this question we must first consider the sociobiological nature of man and his drives as we understand them today. I will not attempt to hide my dissatisfaction with this methodology, I find science immaturely empirical. Sadly, science has now replaced the arts as the dominating method of explaining our nature to ourselves. No longer do we look to books, to poetry, to art, to music to see some misshapen vision of ourselves and come away from it having absorbed the feeling, the sense of what we are. Now, the true measure of man

11

is five feet ten inches, based on a scientifically exacting mean of a randomly selected sample of 10,000 male bi-pedal *homo sapiens* ranging from the four corners of the earth.

Even those corners have not been left to some artistic, antique notion of a planet where dragons once dwelled and the winds had their favourites. It is no longer some arty, inexact, geographical phraseology or mystical allusion to the squaring of the circle. No. My esteemed colleagues in academia, the members of the Johns Hopkins Applied Physics Laboratory, have actually located said four corners of the earth, accurately placing them in an area west of the Peruvian coast, in the sea between New Guinea and Japan, in the ocean south east of Capetown and, lastly, in Ireland. These four 'corners' of the planet are, apparently, 120 feet above the 'geodetic mean', with a consequently greater gravitational pull.

Oh, how the arts suffer under science. Only a scientist could extend a casual metaphor into a five-year research grant. Have they no sense of proportion? Is there a scientific team, right now, attempting to calculate the escape velocity needed for a female bovine to attempt a leap over the entire lunar surface?

Still, if it is only science which the public will believe now, we must review the idea of 'love' in terms of our current knowledge of the functions of the body and the boundaries of the mind.

Let us, then, consider the gene. This collection of acids stirred in a stew of proteins, this group of chromosomal bodily chemicals which we recognize, more and more each day, as the true guide to our selves, our actions, our thoughts, even our feelings, the major shaper of our very identity. Our modern codified, sanitized, exemplified breed of fate.

Once upon a time, there were three sisters named Clotho, Lachesis and Atropos who were ugly and beautiful and even the gods feared them, for it was they who spun and wove and cut the thread of life. These three cruel sisters, the Fates, guided us through birth, accidents, chaos, joy, terror and death.

Now, however, Cassius would have to turn to his friend in arms and say, 'The fault, dear Brutus, is not in our stars but in our deoxyribonucleic acids that we are underlings.' Our genes, apparently, bear the imprint of our very souls and soon it will be possible to calculate a baby's date of death from the moment it is born. This doesn't stop Atropos pushing someone under a bus every now and again, accidents will happen, but even a failure to hear a horn tooting or the inability to remember the Green Cross Code will be placed firmly in the domain of the gene.

6

Wringing Out Your Knickers

IN THE SUDDEN DARKNESS OF THE TUNNEL MIRANDA FOUND HERSELF staring at her own warped reflection in the carriage window. As the window curved up above her, her mirrored forehead grew to make her look rather unpleasantly egg-headed. She turned to look at the other passengers but they were all looking the other way. She recognized the averted gazes of people praying that the tube-loon wouldn't pick them.

'Wait there,' she had yelled at Flirt as he sprinted along the platform. She didn't want to sully any romance that the moment might have had, but she was not, after all, on the Trans-Siberian Express, next stop three and a half weeks away, she was on the Hammersmith and City Line, next stop Edgware Road.

Miranda completely missed the moment of contact between Flirt and the metal sign so, as the train pulled into Edgware Road and she hurried out of it and onto the opposite platform, she was thinking of him waiting there just one stop away. She looked at her watch. Two thirty it said unhelpfully. It had said two thirty for the last three months. She had been meaning to get a battery but since her watch stopped working she had never found the time. She looked up at the station clock. She was going to be late. But he had come back and the possibility of love was more valuable than any job. She pictured Flirt waiting, book in hand, practising what he might say. 'It was nothing . . .', 'For someone as charming as you . . .', 'The moment I saw you I knew we would be thrown together . . .'

In fact, at that exact time Flirt was clutching his head with his hands saying, 'Aspiration. Number Three, down eight places Pop Pickers. Not 'arf. Great whopping big ones.'

Truly, sometimes i find it frightening what things lurk in the human psyche. And i? i lay there with as much dignity as i could, my pages facing down in the dust of the platform. i was sure i could smell urine, and i listened to Flirt's unconscious mind express itself unhindered.

Then, two kindly boys in oversized jeans and basketball shirts helped Flirt up onto his feet and, somewhat unsteadily, guided him to the ticket barrier. Fishing through his jacket pockets, they found Flirt's ticket and slotted it into the machine, assisting him through the barrier. He wandered off into Paddington Station, walking in confused ellipses until he greeted a mailbox, 'Aunt Aggie, what are you doing here? I'm so sorry I haven't written.' The boys went back to their bench, removed the money and cards from Flirt's wallet and slung it onto the tracks.

Five minutes later Miranda burst out of the carriage doors onto the platform at Paddington looking from side to side. There was a man reading the *Daily Mail* and two lads sitting on a bench, one was laughing, the other, on his mobile phone, was reading out his credit card number. But where was Flirt? The shadow of disappointment began to loom, her stomach suddenly growled with hollowness. She had been so close. Now, gone. If only, she thought to herself, she had had a little more faith in strangers. If only she had waited and to hell with getting to work on time.

So while she was indulging in self-pity and chastisement, i was lying there on the platform willing her to look down. 'Down here, Miranda, look down here.' However, as i don't actually possess vocal chords my pleas were somewhat muted.

Miranda stalked the platform for another ten minutes, fretting and peering around, stretching her neck like a pigeon, before the next tube pulled up. i was aching to scream at her, 'i'm down here. Down here. Don't leave me.' But the doors slid quietly open and she stepped forward. As she did, almost unconsciously, she glanced down to gauge the height of the carriage's floor before stepping onto it. There, in a rarely used corner of her eye, i lay strewn, abandoned. Miranda grinned and, spinning around, quickly picked me up and held me tightly in her soft lovely hand as she jumped onto the train. And as the doors hissed closed she looked at me. i'm home, i thought, with you. i swore that we would never be parted again; it's strange that in the passion of the moment, in the exhilaration of relief and the baring of emotions, one can fool oneself so utterly.

'Do you, perhaps, feel that you are not an important member of our working environment?' Mr Scrufstayn asked Miranda, using a phrase that he had found in *Minute Manager – How to Manage Successfully in Just Under a Minute*. Then adding his own daring twist, 'Are you not happy with us?'

Miranda squinted at Scruffy in his dark blue polyester blazer, and pulled at one of her fingers nervously. She knew she wasn't supposed to answer yet. With the bright light of the window behind him, Scruffy's shoulders were ablaze with the white of freshly fallen dandruff. In *Top Tips from Top Managers* he had read that the people who advance are the ones unafraid to sack and it was, in fact, impossible to climb 'the golden beanstalk' without a number of sackings in the bag – 'Show your bosses that you're serious, a good man in a tight place.' Scruffy had been floor manager for five years and he hadn't managed a sacking yet. At night, in bed with Mrs Scrufstayn, he would complain, 'If only one of them had their finger in the till or something. But they're all so honest, how am I supposed to get ahead?' Mrs Scrufstayn, yawning, would jerk at his dog-chain, letting the studs bite into his neck, she would stick the heel of her stiletto boot into the soft round of his back and tell him to shut up as she thrust the thick handle of her whip further up him. Mr Scrufstayn would smile and dribble and Mrs Scrufstayn would turn the page of her romantic novel.

'You are an important cog in this well-oiled machine, and if you are late the whole machine cannot work well.' An analogy he had found in *The Mechanics of Management*. 'You let us all down, Ms Brown. We need you, we need the work you do, but we need it to be done on time.'

'I didn't know the time,' Miranda said, holding out her stopped watch by way of excuse.

'As this time is the first, Ms Brown, there will be no disciplinary action,' and as he said the last two words he felt, for one delicious moment, the lash of Widow Twanky, his favourite cane, across his red-streaked buttocks.

Scruffy looked dreamy for a moment and squirmed slightly so Miranda thought that the 'word' he had asked for might be over. She stood up.

'But your tardiness will be noted,' Scruffy added suddenly, 'I will be watching you. I take this matter very seriously. Once one person gets away with being late, everyone thinks they can do it and before we know it we won't be opening until after lunch and then where would we be?' Then as *Managerial Dressing Downs Without Pain* suggested,

Mr Scrufstayn ended on an up-beat affirmation of his employee's worth, 'Remember that your work is both essential and valuable to us.'

Miranda said, 'Thank you, Mr Scrufstayn,' and, opening his door, walked back down the aisles until she got to her counter. She picked up her demonstration equipment and looked about the Second Floor. 'Essential and valuable' echoed in her ears.

'This is the only sanitary napkin with an absolutely guaranteed, one hundred per cent, keep-you-dry clause,' said Miranda, talking loudly to a nervous woman, clutching a red-faced scabby-nosed baby. 'You will notice that with this sanitary napkin all the fluid is absorbed.' Miranda poured blue water onto the suspended white pad of cotton and plastic and it did indeed absorb all the blue and then return to a crisp whiteness. 'But how do we stop it coming out again like a squeezed sponge?' she asked and, without hesitating, took the swollen pad and placed it on some kitchen roll on the counter. Then with a glass bowl she pressed heavily on the little pad. 'You will notice, if you look in the bowl, that there is no dampness coming out.' She lifted the bowl and offered it to the nervous woman.

The woman seemed edgy about touching it.

'Go on,' said Miranda, 'it's completely dry.'

The woman shifted the child, now probing his nose with a finger, and reached out to touch the bottom of the bowl. She rubbed it lightly and a relieved smile crossed her lips as the clammy moisture she had expected did not materialize.

'That's how dry it will keep you all day long. So if you have any accidents you have no need to worry. You can go out with complete confidence that you won't have to be wringing out your knickers at lunch-time or be getting chafing from unwanted crusty bits. The reason you can be so sure with these sanitary napkins is because of their unique single exsanguinator 'Lock-In' system layer which absorbs wetness but will not let it out again.

'Now,' said Miranda, 'let us imagine a normal day. You might start it off with a quick game of tennis.' Miranda picked up the pad at either end and started rhythmically twisting one end away from the other and back again. But as she wrung it, no blue appeared to sully the little white blood-sucker.

The woman didn't look as if she had ever played tennis.

'Then maybe off for a run,' Miranda tried and, still clutching either end of the napkin, rubbed it vigorously up and down over the edge of the counter.

The woman looked at Miranda blankly.

'Fancy a bit of a ride? Just climb on your horse and away you go.' Miranda bounced the pad up and down on the counter. 'Or how about taking in a little waterskiing,' she suggested, pouring water on the table top and slapping the napkin around in it.

A splash of water hit the baby who squealed with delight and turned to Miranda, wanting to play.

'Maybe in the evening you might go to sit through an opera.' Miranda carefully placed the little white pad down on a dry part of the counter and, turning around, jumped up to sit on it. 'O sole mio,' she sang triumphantly. It was all part of the show, carefully worded and choreographed by teams of 'san-pro' marketing men who had as much experience of menstruation as chickens have of supersonic air travel.

The woman looked around at the other counters, to see if she could escape.

'Perhaps,' said Miranda, realizing that she'd lost any commission and eager to wrap up the spiel as quickly as possible, 'you'd just prefer to go to the funfair.' And with that she slid off the counter, picked up the pad and started swinging it around above her head, shaking it, spinning it, slapping it against the counter, twisting it one way then the other, throwing it up in the air, rolling it up and wringing it thoroughly. Then holding it gently against her cheek she smiled and said, 'Anything you want to do, and you'll stay dry all day long.'

'Actually,' said the woman at last, 'I just wanted to know where your loos are.' She pointed at the child. 'Needs changing.'

Miranda indicated the far corner.

'Thanks,' said the woman, 'they should make nappies with that stuff, you know.' Then, as an afterthought, she added, 'I always use tampons, since I had him like.'

'Scruffy catch you?' asked Mercy from the opposite counter. She looked great. Her blonde hair dived down in golden curling ribbons cascading off her neck and dipping over her shoulders. Her make-up was perfect; it always was. Her fantastically large lips ballooned with bright red lipstick and were outlined deep purple so she looked as if she had just been sucking Ribena but had forgotten to lick the stain which wetly delineated her lips. Mercy excelled in looking as though a dirty thought had just crossed her mind, one which then came back to check out the rest of her body. Her huge breasts had a life of their own. The wild beasts of her bra. She could be standing as still as moonshine talking with Miranda and the beasts would be heaving about as if they were picking up earth tremors. Miranda thought they might have their own specific gravity, being so big, so it would be no surprise if they had their own seismology. Miranda always watched them with fascination, they seemed like something more to feel inadequate about, but then she could never quite bring herself to imagine what it would be like to have those globes bouncing like that in front of her all the time. Mercy's skin was palette-fed with powdery foundation, a beauty spot appearing each day in a different place, and her impossibly long mascaraed lashes lined her eyes like willow shadows about river pools. Miranda hated Mercy because she was everything that Miranda wasn't. But she was also the best friend she had, in fact the only friend she had.

Miranda shrugged, 'He said he'll keep his eye on me.'

'Bet he will,' Mercy winked and you could almost hear the wet lashes slapping together. Then she set the spheres in motion, sashaying over to Miranda's counter. Every soft part of her moving independently and thrusting at her shirt and skirt in swinging actions.

When Mercy moved, every male eye turned to watch, for she was sister to the Sirens, her cousins were Harpies. Mercy Bradley was the very daughter of the Succubi.

In another time she would have sunbathed naked on mussel-bound Aegean rocks. Her hair would be as wave-drawn sea-weed slowly swaying in the ebb and flow, her eyes dark pearls from the shadows of the deep ocean floor where lay the wrecks of many men's ships, and her soft flesh would be as the welcoming, rolling sand dunes of land at long last found. Yet all this would just have been her shell. As the sea lashed her glistening granite bed and lovestruck oysters clung to the salt-stained stone, she would moan. And her sighs would build into a song and the music would echo, against the rocks, her haunting beauty. This sad, vulnerable sound would ride the waves, carried in the arms of the winds, until it found men's hearts, until it plunged its hook through the thin cortex of their souls and drew them closer, nearer, driving them mad with desire. Her line cast, her net thrown, sailors would turn their ships to the ghostly sound of her distress signal. They would lose all will and with glazed eyes be drawn through the foam. Then, there, within her reach, they would be caressed and held in the arms of death, dashed and drawn, ripped and torn, meat from bone, sliced and diced, for Mercy dined on the flesh of the lust-sick and the love-driven, unforgiven men. She took it as her mission in life to seek and destroy. There was a piece of Mercy's heart which drove her on, a part which she inherited from her ancient singing nymph sisters, something which was hard and cold; it was called damage. That was her excuse and she was going to stick with it.

*

Mercy leant on the counter and Miranda thought that she could almost hear the snapping of men's bones in the creaking of her bra. '"The Finger"'s looking a bit sheepish today,' she said, nodding over her shoulder towards Barry standing in Hardware, the only man on the Second Floor not facing their way. 'I wonder which poor fool was escaping his frustrations last night.'

Miranda felt a hot flush warm about her ears. She laid out a new sanitary towel and added some blue dye to the beaker's water. Disinterest seemed a good ploy. The beaker trembled in her hand. She could only think of the embarrassment, the dreadful thing she had done last night. What if someone found out? She would never be able to look Mercy in the face again.

Mercy looked at her and saw her fingers shaking. 'You're not looking too hot yourself,' she said. 'Problems?'

'No, no. Not at all. No. Really,' Miranda blurted, then realizing she needed some cover, 'Actually I met a man on the tube this morning. Just thinking about him. Nice man.'

'Nice man?' snorted Mercy.

So Miranda felt compelled to tell Mercy about Flirt and her adventure at Paddington. She brought me out to show the forlorn state that i had been left in. So i took my first sight of Mercy, and yes, maybe she was impressive, but really not my type. My type is a little more sans serif if you know what i mean. If Miranda was an elegant Helvetica, Mercy was the full illuminated manuscript, a capital laced in gold with unfathomable curlicues all about her.

'Typical. Absolutely typical.' Mercy raised her eyes. 'If you're not there right then, exactly where you're ordered, just at the right time, he tosses your book on the ground and pisses off.'

Miranda shrugged and nodded. She knew that it was pointless to argue with Mercy on the subject of men. They were all bastards and any woman who wanted one was a sucker.

The abstract 'men' were bad enough, but Barry in particular? He didn't even qualify as a man for Mercy. If your friends have such high standards can they really be surprised if you lie when you fall beneath them? She had been so careful to keep it quiet that she was even meeting Barry. Sleeping with him? Sleeping with him was going to have to be a secret she would take to the grave.

But Mercy had fixed her sights and the baiting was to begin. 'Hey, Barry,' Mercy called as he passed by Bathroom Fittings, his eyes fixed on Haberdashery next to the exit.

Barry turned, he couldn't ignore her, but the colour drained from his face as he looked at the two girls together. Mercy beckoned with a finger. Stronger men than he had failed to resist the call of the siren. Approaching them cautiously, Barry kept looking at his feet. His arse was starting to itch. Miranda, the bitch, she'd probably told Mercy everything. Women are like that. They'd have had a good laugh. But Mercy was looking at him with those eyes and, despite knowing deep in his gonads that he would never ever shag her, he had to answer her call, respond to the urges she effortlessly inspired. As he neared her he could feel his arm-pits tingling with freshly milked sweat.

Mercy looked him up and down furtively. 'Don't you like me, Barry? Randa says you've gone off me.'

Miranda began, 'I never said,' but Mercy put a hand on Miranda's arm to quieten her.

'Is that true, Barry?'

'Er no,' said Barry, trying to smile confidently, like a man who has just realized his flies are undone but doesn't want to risk doing them up just in case nobody has actually noticed, although he suspects that absolutely everybody has. 'I find you very, um, attractive.'

'Do you mean that?' said Mercy, coquettishly enjoying, as always, playing the flirt with Barry because, outnumbered by women, he could still get deliciously embarrassed. Mercy's right breast made a move all on its own and brushed against Barry's arm, sending a rush of blood to his face.

Miranda couldn't bear to watch. She was winding him up again. Usually he was fair, and quite a funny, game. But now she had to make Mercy stop. Think of something.

'Because, Barry,' Mercy continued, 'just standing here, so close to you. It makes me feel all funny inside.' Mercy pointed to her stomach but let her finger drift towards her groin.

The veins were starting to show on Barry's neck. His forehead was beginning to glisten. Miranda told her about this morning. She must have done. They're laughing at me.

'You make me . . .' Mercy moaned slightly and looked up as if only the gods could give her inspiration for her next word. She looked back down and straight into his eyes. '. . . moist,' she said and shimmied her shoulders sending all her bits a-wobble. This was usually such fun. Why wasn't Randa laughing?

Miranda was hiding her face in her hands. Please, please, Barry, don't say anything, just walk away. Go. Do not say it. Do not say anything.

'In fact,' continued Mercy, licking her huge lips with a loud smacking sound, 'I'd go so far as to say that you, Barry, make me feel, positively, wet,' she gushed.

Barry started stuttering. His right hand reached down inside the back of his trousers. He only gave it a quick scratch, a hard one, and he looked at the two of them. Mercy was pouting at him and Miranda stood, the palms of her hands against her eyes and cheeks.

'Oooo,' said Mercy, blissfully unaware of what she was saying, 'I think I can feel a little trickle running down my leg right now.'

Turn around now, Barry, Miranda was ordering in her mind. Turn away.

Barry turned around. He turned away, and started walking. Miranda let out her breath. He walked like he would never stop, but he did, at the end of her counter. He stopped and he turned and Miranda could see tears welling in his eyes.

'She told you, didn't she,' Barry bleated. 'I couldn't help it though. Did she tell you that. Just because I wet her fucking bed. It was an accident, all right? An accident. I was hungover, all right? You never been drunk? It was her, she got me drunk.' Barry pointed his 'shitty-digit' at Miranda. 'I wouldn't have even been there if I hadn't been. I don't even fancy her. I didn't know what I was doing so just . . .' Barry paused, hoping beyond hope that his limited vocabulary might find the appropriate word but, as usual, it failed him. 'Just shut up,' he said.

Barry looked at Mercy, who stood there with her mouth open; he had never seen her so still. He looked at Miranda, now pale, her fingers in her hair. He looked at the two and realized something very profound for a Barry.

'You. You,' he stuttered, pointing at Miranda. 'You didn't tell her, did you?'

Miranda shook her head behind her hands and had terrible difficulty swallowing. Barry looked back at Mercy, still shocked and frozen. She hadn't known a thing and now he had said it all. He looked and then he saw himself standing there too. He was outside himself as if, at this one moment, he was so humiliated that he could not even bear to admit that he was responsible for himself. Accountable for what he had just said. He looked at himself, at his own face. He saw the shock that bit it. Mercy had not moved, but Miranda was shaking her head. He watched himself turn and glide vacantly off, away from the ground which had steadfastly refused to swallow him.

Eventually Mercy turned to Miranda whose eyes were closed, thinking that Siberia might be quite nice this time of year.

'The great grand-master pooh-tang himself?' said Mercy quietly, more in disbelief than wanting any form of confirmation.

Miranda nodded, shame shaking her.

'Randa. I thought you might have learnt something from all I've told you. Then you go do something like this and don't even have enough respect for me to tell me.'

'Mercy, I . . .' Miranda trailed off because she could only think of excuses which were lies.

'I thought you'd be stronger, I thought I saw a spark. But there's really no hope for you, is there.' With that Mercy undulated back to her counter, hardly pausing to say over her shoulder, 'Maybe there was nothing there in the first place, Bridget.'

Later that morning.

'HELLO, SHEPHERD'S BUSH LIBRARY.'

'IS THERE A PROBLEM WITH YOUR PHONE?'

'NO. WHY, DID SOMEBODY REPORT IT?'

'YOU'RE COMING THROUGH LOUD AND CLEAR ON THIS END.'

'WELL. NO PROBLEM THEN.'

'THERE'S REALLY NO NEED TO SHOUT.'

'I'M NOT SHOUTING. WHY ARE YOU SHOUTING?'

'I'M NOT shouting.'

'IS THIS BRITISH TELECOM?'

'No. I'm calling about a book you have called *Making Love* by P. Pennyfeather.'

'ARE YOU ONE OF THE OFFICERS INVESTIGATING THIS?'

(Silence)

'PC WILMOT RANG EARLIER.'

'Oh, he did, did he? And what did you tell him?'

'THE THIEF, YOU KNOW. A.K.A. MIRANDA BROWN. SHIFTY SORT. HE ASKED ME FOR HER ADDRESS.'

'Miranda Brown. I see. I'm afraid PC Wilmot has left the station for the day. Could you just give us her address again?'

'I DON'T KNOW. WHAT ARE WE PAYING YOU FOR? YOU REALLY NEED TO GET YOURSELVES ORGANIZED. I'LL GO GET THE FILES.'

Now it is the survival of the least accident-prone. Two out of every three people who hold this book will die of a genetically caused, already codified, symptom.

Nurture has lost the quarrel with Nature. Each day, it seems, everybody who sports a long white coat and clipboard, and isn't selling washing powder, must announce the discovery of another gene. Something which imbues us with criminality, or sexual orientation, or a taste for sausages. There is always someone who has just isolated the nose-bogey long-distance flicking gene and all thanks to some machine which cost several million pounds and seems to do little more than vigorously shake racks of test-tubes. Mrs Pennyfeather has a washer-dryer which has much the same action and I believe she has taken to sitting on it to contain its incessant throbbing motion.

But let us consider the gene. If we are to take the line of Richard Dawkins' research, there is no doubt that this is an unpleasant wee beast lurking within us; a selfish, self-interested, egotistical little demon. One that seems to merely use our bodies, minds, organs to try to survive long enough to get us to take someone to bed. It blindly urges us to combine X chromosomes with an alphabetti spaghetti of others in its monomaniacal obsession with mutating, strengthening, growing and perpetuating its line.

So of course, it is very 'natural' that part of its, and our, make-up is an overwhelming desire to look after and protect our mate and care for the genetic progeny we produce. We want to create the best chances for our genes' survival and progress.

I see the gene as the despot in our underpants. It is like the demented villain in one of today's flicks, it is a Ming the Merciless caressing the beautiful Dale ardently, it is a Bloemfeldt stroking his disinterested pussy whilst he plots his fiendish strategy to take over and dominate the world. Then it is only the population-controlling, prophylactic Flash, or the apocalyptic Bond, who can save the earth from the evil ambitions for world control which our genetic dick-tators lust for – please excuse my puns but I believe it is quite fashionable now in popular writings to exploit the language in this way. There is no doubt that these strong feelings of care and protection are in the interests of the gene's 'evil' scheme for the planet's domination.

The gene drives us to reproduce it as often as possible, ensuring it survives and becomes ever stronger. And after that, or the time we can 'optimally' do that, it considers us unuseful, backward entities unable to keep up with its drive for progress. Then it leaves us to decay, age and die.

However, death does not come to all things. As the asexual fungi and algae of this world prove, without sex some creatures can live for ever. Two thousand million years ago, our ancestors, who were nothing but rather slimy algae 'protoctists', just did not die, it was not programmed in their genes. Consider: Your great-great-great-grand-uncle[90 million] may still be swimming in the pond at the bottom of the garden right now.

These 'protoctists' also had no sexual intercourse which, I suppose, might have made immortality slightly dull. Things went quite swimmingly, which was about all we could do, until our greedy developing mutant human genes became so hell-bent on a speedy progress out of the primordial ooze, they invented sexual reproduction, meiosis; they learnt how to 'combine' in new and interesting ways. A kind of *Kama Sutra* which set the amoeba world alight.

Of course, as soon as they had invented 'sex' they had to develop 'death' to neatly dispose of the elderly, unsexy, unwanted gene carriers or things would have got very crowded very quickly.

Sex has a lot to answer for. Not least because it is this one act which is at the very heart of 'love'. It is the single action that we wrap in all those beautiful colours we call emotions. We drape it in a rich embroidery of a million ornamental feelings, woven with the threads of our lives, our hopes, our insecurities, our dreams. Somehow this poor basic act has been dressed up in noble clothes.

In the politics of the body, sex is the mindless urge-fulfilment of the proletariat, but then 'love' comes along and ennobles it. Love is high drama, it is romantic and it is tragic. It is important, it fills us with chasms of despair, it brings us stratospheres of joy, and it is this confusing muddle of glorious and naive feelings that seems to separate it from the simple instinctual drive for the realization of a master plan.

If we are to take the strictly scientific view of our species, we are here for one purpose only – to mate. We are just sophisticated vessels for a greater progression which is going on in our loins. However, if all we truly desired was sex, or to eat and survive so we could have sex, where did 'love' come from? Why does 'love', that mystical, happy, ecstatic reason for coupling, have so much to do with our prime purpose in life? How did 'love' with all its feelings of care and attention and self-sacrifice, and desire, and flowers and poetry and heart flutters, get mixed up with our basic desire to do, what the popular 'rapport' recording artist, Mr Tone Loc, so aptly described as, 'the wild thang'.

That, I am coming to.

7

'Anyone for Quoits?'

PLEASE. DON'T TAKE IT THE WRONG WAY BUT, SOMETIMES, IN CERTAIN lights, you can look a lot like her; the way you bend your neck, the way your eyes dart across me. Little things. i know you're completely different and we're starting something new but it helps, just the bits which remind me of her, it helps me speak now, for the true art of story telling is convincingly being in two places at the same time, here and there. There where it all happened and here where it is all happening again. Here in the style and there in the content. And books like me are always somewhere between the two, we never have the material security of fixed locations, places, facts, names. And that's why the omniscience comes easy. You'll see now, look, if you are going to understand my story i am going to have to leave Miranda on the Second Floor, demonstrating the wonders of the exsanguinator 'Lock-In' system, and travel through the traffic-clogged West End of London. An endeavour which can never be taken lightly.

Handily, however, just passing outside – in the sort of coincidence which the more humorous of books enjoy using to impress a sense of cosy interconnectivity about the world so we can dispel some of **the fear of admitting that we are, in the end, alone** – there was a cycle courier taking a package to exactly the address where we need to go.

The parcel was in a fluorescent green bag on the courier's back which proudly declared, 'Dick Turpin Couriers, You Stand, We Deliver'. Her rainbow tie-dyed leggings stretched across the pulsating muscles of her legs and plunged into her scrunched black socks and trainers. They blurred in a fury of revolutionary pedalling and then stopped suddenly, letting the bike glide effortlessly through and around the bumpers and brake-lights of the stationary cars as her well-oiled derailleur clicked correctly with complete clarity. Bursting over the traffic-lights of Marylebone Road, her shaven head and wrap-around glasses sliced through the wind blowing up Baker Street whilst polystyrene burger boxes and discarded pink 'City' inserts from the *Evening Standard* flew into the faces of lost tourists.

'Have you the way to Madame Tussauds? Have you? Have you?' they waxed.

Jumping the lights, our cyclist twisted into Oxford Street as her Clear-Air mouth-mask took in a plume of black diesel from the exhaust of a Number 74. She pulled on her brakes, skidding to a stop and balanced against them, standing on her pedals to let a worried looking woman, carrying a scabby-nosed baby, absently step off the open back of the dirt-caked red Route-Master. Then into the centre and off again she whirred and clicked, only to pause and violently bang her fist on the roof of a U-turning taxi. As the invective of the cabbie, suggesting that she should attempt sexual intercourse with herself, became lost in the hubbub of idling traffic, she whizzed across to the other side of the street and cracked her front wheel up onto the pavement. She whistled through and in between a few shoppers, only giving one old lady a heart-attack; but she was ninety-three and had been missing Albert for so long she almost smiled with the pain.

Then banging down onto Bond Street she swerved right and braked the bicycle outside the auction house, hopping off and swing-ing it around onto the pavement. She locked the wheel to the stem and strolled up the stairs past the blue-liveried doorman who gazed from the portal of the old Regency building. He was proudly employed solely for his ability to sneer with contempt at the passing fashions and the women who paraded about this 'nouveau' niche. He always, how-ever, smiled to welcome them through his door so they could be guided by the magnificent good taste of his masters.

Less welcome were the scruffy couriers who delivered priceless works with all the grace and care of hippos in ballet shoes and dirtied the valuable Persian carpet which lay in reception.

The courier took a pad out of a clear plastic folder and indicated where the receptionist should sign, laying the packet on the tastefully antique table. An hour later the receptionist remembered that there had been a package delivered and gave it to someone in a bow-tie and tweed jacket who took it down the tastefully antique stairs and passed it to someone else in a bow-tie and tweed jacket who wandered through the tastefully antique corridors until he came to a wooden panelled door, much like all the others save for the little plaque which read, 'Mr Peersnide', and then underneath, 'Rare Books'.

The bow-tie knocked and a thin voice seeped through the wood, 'Enter.'

'Delivery for you, Peter,' said the bow-tie, shuffling in. It took a moment for his eyes to adjust to the sudden gloomy darkness. Lit only by the brass and green glass Victorian desk-lamp, the room was a web of dust-laden shadows. Perhaps the only room in the whole building which was genuinely, rather than tastefully, antique. The one light was like the glint of a night fire seen through the trees of a dense forest. The deep brown oak and elm of the shelves with their polished wood and the leather book bindings which filled them brought a warmth and sombreness to the dark chamber. The bow-tie walked past the rows and piles of books, many of them suffocating in clear plastic bags. An ivy, potted in the ceramic basin of a nineteenth-century commode, crept around the top shelves of the room, its leafy stems dropping down occasionally to tickle the book bindings. Moving through the twilight of the room he almost tip-toed towards the window where, between the gathered florid William Morris 'Pheasants and Flora' curtains, was the exotic view of the building's air shaft, its black Victorian drainpipes and green, algae-stained leak marks pointing down the peeling white-painted walls. He laid the parcel on the burgundy leather table top which was pinned to an ink-stained mahogany desk, near to a pile of crumbling books which sat surrounded by a field of worn light-brown leather flakes. A magnifying glass lay across a seventeenth-century engraved frontispiece showing a man smiling with a pair of shears and fantastic looking topiary. Then, slowly leaning over to pick up the parcel, was the man who sat at the desk, a man with a thin voice and bony hands, a man who did not look completely unlike Leon Trotsky.

'Thank you, Reginald, it's so rarely we get post here in Hades.'

'That's all right, old man,' replied the bow-tie who then fell silent but did not leave, instead looking around him at the books.

'Is there anything I can do for you, Reginald?'

'No, no. Just wondered if you've got anything interesting coming up, for the sales.'

'Not just yet. Soon though.' Peter Peersnide started to unwrap the parcel, but still the irritating bow-tie would not go. He looked up again and said imperiously, 'Yes?'

'Oh, nothing. It's just. Well, we haven't had a book sale for two years and some of the others just, well, you know.'

'They were wondering what I was doing, a fully paid member of staff, who hasn't actually been seen to do a scrap of work. Is that it?'

'No, no, of course not. We wouldn't dream of thinking . . . It's just the talk.'

'I see. I shall tell you, Reginald, that the book market is a fickle thing and she will not be tempted to bring high returns with modest sales, she has to be pampered and cajoled into revealing her treasures, she needs to be wooed and courted and only then, after much work, can she finally be nailed like the whore she really is.' Peter Peersnide's fist hit the desk loudly and the leather flakes flew for a moment. The bow-tie jumped a little and Peersnide peered over his little glasses at him. 'I'm sure the Director values my work even if you don't.'

'Oh, goodness, old man.' But the word had been mentioned, it had done its work and frightened the poor bow-tie out of his wits, the curse had been uttered: 'Director'. No one knew why the Director kept employing Peersnide, he never seemed to bring in any big sales, yet he sat there year after year, doing something. He had come highly recommended, he'd been a dealer once, one of the foremost bibliographers in the country. There wasn't much that happened in the book world which he didn't know about and there probably wasn't a book that he couldn't locate, yet not a single sale had come from his department. Still, the Director's will was not to be questioned, it was to be done. The bow-tie nodded and left the room, looking somewhat less starched than when it had entered.

Putting the half-opened parcel down, Peersnide went to the door and locked it. He returned to the desk and pulled a pile of papers from the parcel. The top page was the usual classified and data-protection warning which Peersnide crumpled in his hand and put into the ashtray next to his pipe. The next page had two words at the top, two words not unfamiliar to you and me, two words which made my heart sing; they were 'Miranda' and 'Brown'.

Just why this little man, who smelt of anchovies and looked like a dead exiled Bolshevik, should have access to the privileged information of Miranda's life shall all become clear in a moment but i just want to express my own indignation at such an invasion of her privacy. He had no right to peer into her life, to read some dossier on her that she had no idea even existed . . .

Yes. i know. i have been going on about her for the last six chapters. But if i choose to talk about her, and you to read about her, it is another matter entirely. i was in love, and you do need to know my story. Anyway, you don't smell of tinned fish.

At that very moment Miranda, finding herself friendless for her lunch break, was taking me up the road to Regent's Park, since the sun was shining. That relentless breeze blew behind her as she made her way to the park gates.

Miranda wandered, feeling lonely, drifting cloud-like through the park. Then, above the lake and beneath a tree she sat down, her skirt fluttering and dancing in the breeze. She felt in a strange pensive but somewhat vacant mood. At her feet, some daffodils nodded knowingly at her.

Placing her paper-thin 'slimmer's sandwich' and yoghurt beside her, Miranda opened me up on her lap, fully intending to read me, but her eyes quickly glazed over as she thought about Mercy and Barry and the lost Flirt on the tube and about how crap her life was, and a big tear dropped on me and blotted a bit in my pages. And where my page turned grey it tried to curl up to her to comfort her. Then her shoulders shook and her bottom lip curled tight over her teeth and her eyes squeezed shut and she started to sob. And i sat helpless, yet again, in her lap and i thought about how she was so beautiful and i realized that however sad you can be for other people, when you actually cry, you only cry for yourself.

Then He was there for her. He knelt down beside her as she cried and offered her his paper hankie.

'Hay fever can be troublesome this time of year,' He said, 'but it's snot with Blow and Go!' He smiled that winning smile of a million pastel-coloured phlegm-filled tissues and held the hankie out to her. Miranda shook her head at the offer and put her hand to her forehead as if it might hide, from the rest of the world, the fact that she was crying like a crocodile with toothache. Beside Him was a man she'd never met before who impulsively offered her flowers. But she brushed them away. A liner cruised past in the lake between the ducks and the bandstand and He was there, now very suave looking in a bow-tie with slicked-back hair. He stood on the aft deck between some tied balloons and the strains of a swing band could just be heard. He gestured to her to come with Him and cruise Norway's breath-taking fjords. 'Anyone for quoits?' He said just like He did in the ad, making the last word sound a little like coitus.

Miranda took a deep breath in between her teeth and resolved to stop crying. She wiped her nose on her sleeve and then, looking at the colourful splodge of mucus, lipsticky saliva and mascara she had just made, she started crying again. Why couldn't she keep a friend? Why couldn't she find a boyfriend? Why did everybody, well, hate her? There's no one, no one, no one. She wiped her eyes once more and tried to focus, looking out at the lake. There she saw a little row boat with a man earnestly rowing, leaving little teardrop paddle splashes in his wake. A woman was lying nonchalantly in the stern, a finger trailing in the water. They looked like they might be in love.

Miranda's jaw started to tense and vibrate and her lip became taut as yet another deluge flooded out to soak me. She was worthless, worthless. No one would ever love her. She was going to die alone and wizened. Never loved, never cared for. In fact, if she died today, would anyone know, would anyone care? No one. Well. Maybe Mum. Wherever she was. Never one to be upstaged, she had left home the day before Miranda had planned to and was never seen again. Last spotted on a Scandinavian cruise holiday. Miranda thought of the single post-card from Helsingør on which her mother had scribbled one word, 'Hi.' That was three years ago. Miranda pictured her playing quoits with beautiful young men in bow-ties and she smiled for a moment and a little dribble glinted on her teeth. Single mums, who'd have them? Certainly not her father, whoever he was. And with that, yet another spasm issued forth streams of salt that trickled down beside her nose and then got sucked up her nostrils as she tried to stem the tide, creating an unpleasant squelching sound.

It broke my little paper heart to see her like that. What is it about love that drives people to such misery? i think i knew once.

Peter Peersnide straightened the 'Miranda File' on the wine-red leather covering of his desk. Reaching for the telephone, he dialled a particular number which always caused a little thrill of excitement to run through him. He waited as it rang.

'Hello,' said a woman's voice.

'You are the woman of my dreams,' said Peter Peersnide.

'I bet you say that to all the girls.'

'No, I dream of you at night, we are together and I am biting your ear.'

'Oh yes, oh yes, you nibble my ear and it sends me into delight,' said the woman dispassionately.

'I have never let a terrapin bite my ankles,' said Peter Peersnide, trying to hurry the process along.

'Righti-ho,' said the woman rather cheerily, 'scrambling.'

With that Peter Peersnide leant back in his chair and listened to the familiar cacophony of Schoenbergian noises, which resembled harmony in the same way a pile of vomit resembles one's last meal.

'Rose Madder,' said a deep, port-soaked voice.

'It's Vermilion Lake, sir,' replied Peter Peersnide.

'Oh yes. Lake. News?'

'Not good, I'm afraid. It's about operation "Love Nuts", sir.'

'"Love Nuts"? Aren't we finished with that? Successful clean-up, I remember.'

Peter Peersnide paused before he broke the bad news. 'I sighted a copy of the book today, sir. It looks like the job wasn't as complete as we thought. I have found out who has it, I have her V.S. from Central.'

'A woman?' said Rose Madder and then made what sounded like a humming noise. 'Do you know if she has read it?'

'By now, I think it is more than likely,' said Peter Peersnide, not wanting to reveal how the item in question had slipped from his very hands that morning, taken by that idiot with cropped hair.

'Right, I suppose we'd better act quickly. I'll need you in here by the Augsburg Confession, and certainly no later than Titian in Rome. Got that?'

'Yes sir,' said Peter Peersnide and placed the receiver back in its cradle. He turned to his copy of *Reformation and Counter Reformation, A History* to check that the Augsburg Confession was indeed 1530. Then he flipped through a book on his desk, entitled *The Pop-Up Book of Renaissance Art*, to find that Titian had visited Rome in 1545. 1530 to 1545, that meant he had a couple of hours before going into 'The Office'. A smile played across his face, making his goatee point out at right angles from his chin. It had been many months since he had last seen any action, and that had been the tedious clean-up operation that they had labelled 'Love Nuts'. This next venture could prove far more interesting. A rather nice young woman was involved. Peter Peersnide picked up the file with Miranda's name on it and the smile turned into a smirk. Putting it down again, he next picked up his magnifying glass, and in his mind the handle was the barrel of a gun. He held it across his chest and one eyebrow was raised. He said in the deepest voice he could muster, 'The name's Lake, Vermilion Lake. Lake is Back.' In truth, if you could have heard it, it sounded about as low and sexy as Pinky and Perky swallowing helium.

*

Miranda had tried to nibble at her sandwich but her stomach was too knotted. Realizing that it was probably time to get back, she stood up, bumping her head on the low bough of the tree and shaking petals which snowed to the ground. She looked at her watch. It was still two thirty. She was sure it must have been nearly an hour since she left. Picking me up with her sorry-looking sandwich and her yoghurt full of good intentions, she walked back to the park gates. Something that looked like a rubbish bin was attached to a post next to the gates and Miranda lifted the lid to deposit her sandwich and yoghurt. Just a little too late she noticed the bin's 'Pooper Scooper Deposit' sign and the smell of fresh dog turds rocketed up her nostrils, sending her head reeling and cruelly turning her empty stomach. She dropped her lunch and slammed the lid, but the feelings of nausea washed through her. Her morning gut projection came back to her. Still shaking, Miranda headed back to the Second Floor, only stopping at the newsagent's to buy an apple.

And a Mars bar.

And a Kit-Kat.

And a bag of chocolate raisins.

And a box of Terry's All Gold.

And just to spite Him, the helicopter-hanging silhouette man who would always be too busy to hang around stations waiting, she bought her own box of Milk Tray.

Chapter III.

The Poetical Knob Test

Love is a boy, by poets styl'd
Then spare the rod, and spoil the child.
Samuel Butler (1612–80)
Hudibras, Part II, Chapter 1

IT MUST HAVE COME FROM SOMEWHERE.

The notion. The illusory idea that some part of the base and perfectly natural stirring in our loins, the desire to stamp our genetic imprint on the world, was, in fact, an emotion. At some point our species started interpreting aspects of this natural *caring* as a moving of the feelings, an agitation of the mind, a whirl and tumult of passions. Somehow, at some time, our natural, simple, easy to understand, lustful urges became entwined with this difficult, mysterious, mad-making thing we have called 'love'.

I think I have demonstrated that, following the scientific line, we cannot say that this limerent 'love', the soaring, searing, heart-thumping life-fulfilling aspect of 'love', lies in the domain of the biologically 'natural'. We must, therefore, consider investigating the possibility that this 'love' may be a man-made invention, a belief we have propagated.

If this love is not innate, then where did it come from? Who concocted it? When, where, how and why? What alchemist created these golden feelings from the base metal of our mating instincts? To the casual observer these questions may seem unanswerable. Even if it is true, surely by now the answers must be lost in the mists of time. No, I say, they are not. The only mist is the fog which has been created, a smokescreen perpetuated even today, by interested parties wishing to hide and obscure the truth. My enquiries have led me to a frightening discovery: that these emotions that we all feel actually have other, more sinister, reasons for their existence. These feelings that we have no control over are in the interests of those who wish to control.

15

The creation of 'love' is not such an ancient thing at all. In fact it is far more recent than most would imagine.

When? How are we to tell when love began? How can we chart the history of a feeling? The chronicles of love can be read in the poetry of time. The verse of the ages lays testament to the strength of the feelings they witnessed.

If we were to believe, as many have for centuries, that love is endemic to being human, we might point to some lines of Chinese poetry written nearly four thousand years ago. In our translation of *Wood-Melon* (1700 BC) we apparently see 'love':

> She came to me with a melon green,
> I gave her earrings serpentine;
> No, not just a requital
> But to seal our love everlastingly.

For goodness' sake, melons and serpents? The double orifices of ear and rings? It hardly takes a GCSE student to work out exactly what sort of 'love' is being referred to here. This isn't deep, silly, mind-blowing, soul-fettering, tear-swelling *in* love. This is smut. Pure and simple. They are bartering with each other in sexual symbolism, like whores, so that they can seal their selfish genetic ties. No, it wasn't just a requital, it was sex. This is lust translated and wilfully misinterpreted into our language.

Much though I hate those who pull out the Bible to prove an argument, it of course contains one of the earliest examples of love poetry, being over three centuries BC:

> The song of songs, which is Solomon's.
> Let him kiss me with the kisses of his mouth: for thy love is better than wine.
> Because of the savour of thy good ointments thy name is as ointment poured forth, therefore do the virgins love thee.
> Draw me, we will run after thee: the king hath brought me into his chambers:
> We will be glad and rejoice in thee, we will remember thy love more than wine:
> the upright love.

We find that this poem is sodden in wet, liquid sensuality; wines and ointments and kisses, a love invoked by sensual gratification. Again this is not love but sex. What we must admit is that the word 'love', 'agape', 'ohev' meant quite different things then.

8

It Is a Little More Serious, Burnt

YOU'RE STILL NOT ABSOLUTELY CLEAR ABOUT WHAT'S GOING ON. I HAVE held things back, i have kept you somewhat in suspense which is, i suppose, in my nature as a book, but really not the mark of the open and honest relationship we should be having. i'm sorry. Let me make everything clear. The man who tried to steal me from Miranda on the train, Peter Peersnide, aka Vermilion Lake and known to you and me as Trotsky, was a spy, a spook, a secret agent.

Well, not quite. In fact in 'Office' parlance he was a 'Fink', which is short for 'Vinculum', a specialist informant, a covert link between the Secret Service and the civilian world of his field. Years before, when his 'administrator', Rose Madder, first approached him, Peersnide's bookish life led him to believe that he was being recruited into a glamorous world of international espionage, a fantasy which allowed Madder to exploit him, on a miserly stipend, for his encyclopaedic knowledge of, and connections in, the book industry. Despite Peersnide's intelligence, he would not let his reason spoil his daydream by admitting that that was all it was, or would ever be. If you must tread carefully when stepping on other people's dreams, you bloody well tippy-tippy-toe over your own.

So, having some time before his appointment and little else to do, Peersnide set out, with Miranda's 'Life' in his hands, to walk down to 'The Office', a mile or so south of Bond Street on the banks of the River Thames.

Walking across the red clay of the Mall stretching between Buckingham Palace and Admiralty Arch, some might say between the devil and the deep blue sea, Peersnide started down along the paths of St James's Park as they wound through the spring green grass, glittering with a dandruff of daisies. In the family of ways, these paths are cheeky insouciant 'teens', they tease and twist their walkers to goad them into enjoying the carefree nature of their total lack of direction. The paths of this tiny park turn and curve for no other reason than to emphasize the fact that they are not going anywhere and should be enjoyed for their own nonsense and not by reason of thoroughfare. There are those who believe that they do so merely to annoy and confound fat, late, over-lunched MPs and other power-mongers who try to use them as short-cuts between the club-rooms of Pall Mall and Westminster's corridors.

However, the reason Peter Peersnide had decided to walk through St James's Park was very different. He did so in recognition of what he believed would be his forthcoming promotion to full 'Secret Agent' status for his initiative. This public garden was, according to every novel of intrigue that he had ever read, the park of spies.

Now i have a great fondness for books of espionage, adventures of the cloak and the dagger, the secrets and the games of double jeopardy. i remember i briefly shared a shelf with a whole suspicion of spy novels in the library. They were pleasant, slow things who spoke in weighty language on matters of substance and were only occasionally spurred into brief spells of action, but mostly there was a lot of waiting and talking. Everything, to them, was of the greatest importance and nothing, except their covers, could be taken just at face value, there was always another meaning, something beneath. They were beasts of game, of parry, of thrust and counter-thrust.

If the truth be told, our modern military intelligence employee only has sex, on average, 1.2 times a month, and the nearest they come to someone of the opposite sex with a foreign accent is during their two weeks 'paid' in Torremolinos or plane-spotting in Greece. Having answered a situations vacant ad in a newspaper for 'information managers', they have found themselves bound to a dull desk looking at dull patterns of statistics which seem to have little bearing on real life except for the very fact of their total dullness. In truth, except with a sad lunch-time sandwich in hand, they are rarely to be seen in St James's Park yet this, the only piece of open ground anywhere near Whitehall, was indeed once the meeting place of all British spies who did not wish to be overheard and yet lacked the imagination to find anywhere less illustrious.

During the glorious years of the Cold War, you could not sneeze in St James's Park without your globules of expectoration hitting a couple of spies covertly meeting and talking in codes of inspired surrealism. On the bridge of the ornamental lake, beside the bushes, along the paths that reeked and slipped with goose shit, a thousand times a day, this absurd theatre would host improvisational performances of *Waiting for Godot* in which Estragon and Vladimir, now in Savile Row suits and neither of them sure whether to look like friends or strangers, spoke of everything and nothing.

'The marionette has often spoken of the love between fishes.'

'Yes, before he is done there will be many forks in the heart of the mirror.'

'Yes.'

'Yes.'

'Then let us go.'

'Yes, we will go now.'

'Yes.'

They do not move. Their feet are glued in a stew of goose excrement.

Of course, in a rash of post-Cold War information clean-ups it was discovered that the Russians had had every bush in St James's Park bugged since 1948 and that two out of every six geese were mechanical honking, green-slime shitting, white-feathered cameras. The British, in turn, admitted that they had had an operative at work in Gorky Park, a midget who posed as a child in a sailor suit with a walkie-talkie balloon. They, however, did not reveal that the only information he had elicited in twenty years of park-life was the criminally rising price of Russian ice-cream.

Now, it really would spice up this story no end if i could introduce an international man of daring at this point. But real life is rarely as glamorous as the world of the novel and i cannot tell you of strange men in tropical linen suits with large crops of facial hair, pungent with the sweet smell of near-eastern after-shave, who enjoy lurking in shadows only to leer out of them unexpectedly with the silver glint of a death-dealing weapon in their hand. No, the best i have for you at this point is a man who looks like Leon Trotsky, smells of anchovies, finds books for an auctioneer and has the rather dull name of Peter Peersnide. However, and this is about as exciting as it gets, i will tell you now that Military Intelligence does become involved at this stage in Miranda's, and my, story, albeit 'Containment', a rather obscure department of domestic affairs.

As you may have deduced, 'Vermilion Lake' and 'Rose Madder' are far too exotic to be true code names as used by Her Majesty's Secret Service. They are probably a little too imaginative and i believe the imagination is frowned upon in such institutions. No, in fact i borrowed them from a rather scuffed 1978 Winsor & Newton paints catalogue in the library which, rather pathetically, would try to get readers' attention by falling off the shelf when anybody walked past. Eventually, one rainy day, a nice old lady bought it from the library's 'Sell-off' table and, tearing out all its pages, she used them to stuff her bunion-rubbed, gangrenously damp, fur-lined boots.

Although i have been hurt beyond all measure by love, by being in love, there are times when, despite everything, i am so thankful for Miranda, for you, for being here now. There are so many books not half as lucky as i. There are those which have never been read, never fallen in love or even off the shelf. There are those with no stories to tell at all.

Anyway. The reason why i have had to use such ludicrous code names is, in fact, a matter of national security. Apparently. Our 'Secret Service' would sound rather servile without the 'Secret' bit giving it its mystique. Thus i find myself not at liberty to reveal certain things which, being omniscient, i, of course, know, in order to avoid any possibility of governmental injunctions, those used by spy novels to excuse their inaccuracies, being waved at us and disturbing our quiet, private *tête à livre*. Please don't think that i am holding anything back from you, i will tell you anything if you insist, i am an open book in your hands, but i do this as much to protect you. Believe me, there are things which you are safer not knowing. If you were aware of certain secrets, mere detail to you but vital to the powers that be, they may consider you, you my love, as an enemy in possession of privileged knowledge. Many lives may be at risk and you ... they may have to 'dispose' of you. And all because you read the wrong thing. Not for the world would i let that happen, so for now, let me use those painted colours to identify the story's 'agents' in a way that is, for all of us, palatable.

So, as Miranda stood, all afternoon, gradually feeling sicker and fatter and obeser, and the chocolate boxes under her counter became lighter and thinner and skinnier; as Miranda dipped and spun her sanitary napkins, a danger to none but herself, her name, her life, her attitude were being discussed in terms of national security by people she had never met or, at the very least, been formally introduced to.

Because i cannot tell you where on Millbank 'The Office' is, though it may well be number 54, or what floor Peter Peersnide went to, although the fifth may seem likely; because i may not describe the décor, which could well be a dull light-grey felt-board, or even the lighting, which possibly is those unforgiving fluorescent tubes unartfully hidden above a grid of chromed, cross latticed light diffusers; because i cannot tell you these 'secret' details and i will not insult you with some believable lie about a creaking dark wood nineteenth-century parochial boardroom with red leather lined, padded doors and a vast desk where Rose Madder sat, and because i have always found fiction far stranger than truth i shall instead place 'The Office' somewhere else completely, then there will be no confusion, no half-truths and you, who i love, will never accuse me of leading you astray.

Therefore, when Peter Peersnide stepped into 'The Office', the first thing that he noticed was the heat, a damp, humid air which made sweat instantly prickle on his skin and drip along the hairs of his goatee. The noise was deafening at first, the shrieks and screams and endless chatter of monkeys high above in the rustling, swinging branches; the squawks and growls and groans of a thousand beasts beneath, for which he could imagine no shape but that they were big, numerous, man-eating, and lurked behind endless shadows cast by the high criss-crossing tangle of light and leaves which made up that lofty roof, the canopy of the rainforest. Thus is the terror of all those who enter 'The Office' unprepared for the hardships therein.

With his eyes down and stepping carefully, he followed the bare feet of the native receptionist, hips swinging in her grass skirt as they walked the twisting track of dead leaves and bird droppings pressed and compacted by feet, by paws and by claws, a carpet alive with black, pincered, shiny insects, jostling and climbing over each other to feast on the brown decaying compost.

The secretary knocked on a palm tree and pulled back a frond to let Peter Peersnide enter the inner clearing, an area encircled by vertiginous towering trunks of ancient trees. He looked about in wonder for a moment, taking in the whole clearing, bathed in the emerald light of the soaring photosynthetic, chlorophylled roof. The screams of the monkeys and the cackles of the birds seemed quieter now.

Madder sat behind a fallen trunk, his elbows resting on the

moss-laden gnarly bark and his fingers meeting as if trying to complete a triangle. He was a white-haired man in his late fifties, he had a large head with a deep red and, one suspects, wine-enlarged nose. Though having nearly no neck, he sported more chins than the Peking phonebook, and around them he wore his tribal regalia, the bone and tooth necklace with a parrot feather, and all in his old school colours.

Another man sat on a tree stump at one side of the clearing, a blond, clean-shaven, well-built man in his late twenties. Peersnide looked at him, rather annoyed that it was not going to be a private meeting. A viper slithered around behind his ankle and he lurched forward with the usual awe and lack of grace that overcame him in the presence of his 'administrator'.

'Ah,' said Madder, gesturing for Peersnide to come closer, 'you've come. Right on time. Jolly good. Please.' He motioned towards another broken stump and Peersnide pushed a curled and sleeping capuchin monkey off it to sit down. The monkey hissed at him then scampered off into the forest. 'Now,' continued Madder, wiping some sweat off one of his chins, 'let us not beat around this bush, Lake. You say that there's been some breach in the "Love Nuts" operation.'

On his walk Peersnide had put together his entire speech. How he had seen 'the book' on the train. How he had spotted the library sticker and had traced Miranda. How, since he was the only one who had seen her, he should be put on the case of tracking her down and assessing how much she knew, perhaps seducing her on the way. He stood up and put his thumbs in his waistcoat. Placing his feet astride and standing firm, he began his lengthy oration. 'It was early this . . .'

'Oh,' Madder interrupted, 'you haven't met Burnt Umber,' and he pointed a stubby finger at the good-looking man who was sitting there quietly, and a bit too nonchalantly for Peersnide's liking.

Peersnide nodded curtly to the younger man and, turning back to Madder, he opened his mouth to continue. 'As I was saying, it was . . .'

'Burnt,' interjected Madder again, 'will be the field agent on the case, so it's him you'll be briefing.'

Peersnide's mouth shut with a loud click and he turned again to look at the interloper. Seeing as this news rather ruined his speech, not to say his entire day, he abruptly sat down again. His face drained of colour and his eyes watered momentarily and then he jumped up with equal abruptness. The capuchin, which had tried to return to its bed, was attached to his trousers.

'I . . . I . . .' Peersnide spluttered, 'I saw her on the tube. She had got the book from Shepherd's Bush library. That's her file, Miranda

Brown, vital statistics from central information.' The monkey jumped off and he sat down again.

Madder smiled indulgently at Peersnide. He hated dealing with finks, they were so limited in their articulacy, and needed to be nannied to get anything out of them. He couldn't slap them or threaten or torture them, he couldn't order them to do dark things or send them back to basic training or the glass-house, they were so passive as information givers, and so puppy-like in their willingness to help, he abhorred them. He could hardly bring himself to believe that any information which was not given in fear of death, or in the agony of something too large being shoved into an orifice too small, was of any use whatsoever. Still, modern methods had to be tolerated.

'Do you know how the book came to be in the library?' said Madder as gently as he could. 'I was led to believe that all the copies were seized and destroyed.'

'They were,' said Peersnide, 'we thought they were. Pennyfeather knew we were on to him, I think he might have hidden it in the library before we, er, got to him. You know, where better to hide a leaf than in a forest?' He slapped a large mosquito which had just started sucking at his wrist.

'Indeed, indeed,' said Madder, nodding. 'So do you think there might be others lurking to surprise us?'

'Well, no. We had all the major libraries checked. He was living in Shepherd's Bush, it was probably just an impulsive contingency.'

'So that copy is the only one out there, the only one in the world except for this.'

Madder reached into a drawer in the log and pulled out my twin, a book which looked exactly like me, only a bit cleaner, and thinner. A brother. And i had felt so alone in the world.

Peersnide nodded and it was only then that Burnt Umber spoke.

'So,' he said in a voice so deep it rumbled through the jungle and, high above, set a flock of green-plumed trogons warbling into flight, 'is this just about retrieving a book?'

'No, it is a little more serious, Burnt,' said Madder, wiping his hand along the log's moss and disturbing a family of earwigs which were trying to burrow there. 'You see, although Pennyfeather was completely certifiable, he had the clarity of madness. The central idea to his treatise on the making of love, you see, is fanatical and seditious but,' Madder scratched his puffy nose, 'also completely true. As you know, part of our job in Containment is controlling the public dispersal of certain information and ideas which may impede our authority if they were to be generally known. The book has no value in itself, it is its ideas which we are wary of. If this Miss Brown has read it, she becomes as dangerous as the book. Pennyfeather himself talks about ideas being like viruses, they can spread from one person to the next and, before you know it, the whole world is screaming "conspiracy".'

'But nobody believes those conspiracy theories,' said Burnt and, faster than the eye, his hand appeared in front of his face, between his thumb and forefinger he had delicately caught the leg of a blue-bottle fly. He let it go again and wiped his hand on his leopard-skin loincloth. Peersnide hated men like him. All tan and muscles and probably didn't know one end of a book from another. Yes. Obviously stupid.

Madder saw Peersnide's look at Burnt and decided to allay what he mistook for worry. 'Burnt's a good chap, Lake. He's joined us from GCHQ, bit of a linguist, knows eighty-five languages and over three thousand dialects. He's successfully completed more than two hundred covert operations and, what's more, can drink me under the table. He is just the man for the job.'

'Sim Salabim, sir, you are far too generous,' said Burnt. 'Still, how are we to proceed from here?'

Madder turned to Peersnide. 'Well, Lake?' he said, as a tiny tropical spider started to spin a web between his bulbous nose and his upper lip. 'If she has read this thing, do you think she can be disappeared?'

Peersnide looked up. 'Disappeared, sir?'

'Yes, you know. Has she got anybody who'll miss her, partners, family, that sort of thing?'

'No. No partner. Her mother lives abroad,' replied Peersnide, and only then realizing Madder's full meaning he added quickly, 'but she has a friend, a girl she works with, who might kick up a fuss.'

'Oh well,' said Madder casually, 'at least that's only one extra. Could always get rid of her at the same time.' He picked up the file and the book and waved them at Burnt, who drew his tall frame up and saun-tered to Madder's log to accept the pile. 'I think we need an assessment. A little observation and connection. Find out how much she's read, how much she knows, and I'll expect a Containment recommendation by tomorrow. Let's see if we can't get this wrapped up in this funding year, don't want to eat into the next one's budget. And,' he added with a cold and glassy glint in his eye, 'if you think Brown has already begun to spread the material, you know that you are authorized to eliminate with extreme prejudice.'

Peersnide looked enviously at Burnt. No one, he thought, would tell him that he was ever authorized to eliminate anybody with extreme prejudice.

Burnt nodded at Madder. 'Sim Salabim, my friend and master.' Taking the file and book he turned, nodded almost imperceptibly to Peersnide and walked out of the clearing.

The clatter and howls of the monkeys seemed louder again as if something had scared them and they screeched to raise the alarm, but Peersnide saw that Madder was smiling at him and, in a strange way, he saw that Madder held a certain respect for him. He knew that Madder's smile was congratulating him, he had done well, he had done his duty, he had protected the nation, and Madder, in his reserved and military way, was thanking him. He smiled back.

Madder sat silently behind his log wondering when this wet, simpering, grinning oaf would get the message and go.

We can prove this in a process of reduction. Usually, reductionism achieves little. Which is exactly what it sets out to do. So in some ways it achieves everything it is meant to. Perhaps I should rephrase that then. Reductionism is rarely beneficial. Except in condensed soups, cremation and liposuction. In ancient love poetry, we can apply a reductionist technique in the simple and exacting application of the 'Pennyfeather Knob Test'. This is a literary technique which I have developed to test for later misinterpretations of love poetry. It hurts me to ruin such a great text but it is in the interest of the truth that I substitute the imposing word 'love' with the rather more coarse and sexual word 'knob'.

> Let him kiss me with the kisses of his mouth: for thy knob is better than wine.
> Because of the savour of thy good ointments thy name is as ointment poured forth, therefore do the virgins knob thee.
> Draw me, we will run after thee: the king hath brought me into his chambers:
> We will be glad and rejoice in thee, we will remember thy knob more than wine:
> the upright knob.

Now, perhaps, we can observe just what this word 'love' may have meant in ancient times. There is no doubt that, applied to early poetry, which usually comes to us translated by post-Renaissance writers, the knob test, excuse the expression, stands up.

If we are looking at the ancients, we cannot ignore Plato's *Symposium*, his renowned dialogue on 'love'. This, as so much in classical thought, concentrates on love's erotic nature rather than its romance. The 'love' he writes of is best described as the journey of transcendence between 'animal' sex and the divine. Yet this dichotomy prioritizes action and sensation over emotion and care. And this is, essentially, Plato's problem in the *Symposium*, the ultimately impossible linking of these two countering extremes: the beastly and the god-like.

Love is something that Plato describes as a 'mean' between the two. It's all very logical, but being somewhere between sex and divinity is nowhere, not one or the other. The relationship between the two, at best, could only ever be platonic. The trouble is we don't want to be between them, we want both. Trying to combine two extreme opposites has been the struggle we have always suffered. Maybe this is why he describes the goddess love thus:

> Her feet are tender, for she sets her steps,
> Not on the ground but on the heads of men.

I will explore the tyrannical dominatrix aspect of love later, but even back then it is clear that Plato recognized that love affects us in the head, it stamps on our brains and, in later, more developed theories of love, it is a pattern for madness.

The *Symposium* is, however, a significant landmark in the history of love because, as I will show, Plato's dualism set a template that served for the eventual defining and inventing of 'love' as we know it, the collusion of Eros, Philos, Storge and Mania, nearly one and a half thousand years later.

Moving to Roman times, we can clearly see that a fashion has been set for poetry to elevate base lusts to high ideals.

> The earth will fool the farmer with bounty,
> The sun will be drawn by horses of darkness,
> Rivers will flow backward to their source
> And fish dry up in an arid sea
> Before I grieve for another woman
> I shall be hers in life and in death.
>
> Propertius (50-15 BC)

This promotion served, as so many Roman things do, as a low prototype for the heights to which 'love' supposedly takes us today.

However, when the poet Propertius wrote that he did not want to live without his love, his mate, is it not that selfish gene we hear speaking? Its carrier, the poet, is useless and worth killing if it doesn't get to 'combine' with its chosen victim.

In this time we also find, already, official Imperial approval for writings which confuse feelings of sexual desire with higher notions of being. Ovid claimed that he was banished from Rome by the Emperor Augustus himself, for writing the *Ars Amatoria*, a collection of erotic poetry about lust and cuckolding and betraying other men to fulfil sexual desires. Why? I believe what we see here is the model for later 'official lines' on love. Trying to shape our thoughts and influence how we should interpret them as feelings. The beginning inklings not of State mind control but emotional control. An army might march on its stomach but it fights with its heart.

9

'Ah, That Explains Everything'

NEVER WORK IN RETAIL. OR, IF THINGS ARE REALLY DESPERATE AND you find that you absolutely have to, which is why most do, at the very least try to quit before lunch-time. As anybody who has worked a shop floor will tell you, the worst time of the day, the nadir of the shift, the longest hour, is the last one. It is not just because you are tired, not because you have been standing for eight hours, not because tempers have frayed, not because the clock has been slowing up all day and, by that time, it has almost reached a state of catalepsy, not because every time you check it, it is barely a minute since you last looked at it; no, what makes the last hour so arduous, such a purgatory of the soul, is the 'after-office invasion'.

This is the hour all retail workers dread. This is the hour when eyes look nervously at the door. As the clock's ticks slow, the nervous ones begin. How will they come? In packs, or as lone prowlers? Will they hunt or will they scavenge? What sacrifice will they demand? What will they feast on? Who will be the prey of the 'Lurker'? This is the hour when, from behind desks, beside photocopiers and under bosses, everybody who has a 'proper' job, and is being 'properly' paid, suddenly feels the need to flaunt their early freedom and disposable income by rushing to the store, by tossing and throwing the careful displays, and laying siege to the shop staff. And there is always one 'Lurker' who will target the most vulnerable soul in the shop and badger and pester and taunt and maul and linger until nearly every light has been turned off and the security guard has pointed out the exit.

To the weary and weakened souls of the Second Floor, who had spent their day dreading that long hour between five and six, the 'after-office invaders', with their free time to browse and their spare cash to spend, were, above all, a painful reminder that they, the keepers of the retail flame, the front-line foot soldiers of capitalism, were all, all, over-worked and under-paid. All except Barry, who was over-jerked and under-laid.

It had been a slow day for sanitary napkin demonstrations and Miranda had lasted it well. She had stood and stared and had not cried. She had stood and stared at Mercy's back while Mercy, pointedly, made play with the boys from Menswear. She had stared and bored holes in the back of Mercy's shirt. She had stared, hardly daring to blink, as if that one moment would be the one which Mercy chose to look around at her. But Mercy never did.

Miranda had been strictly parsimonious in finishing her final box of chocolates. She had made it last for over two, and very nearly three, minutes. The hours which followed had been punctuated by trips to the 'Ladies' to go 'finger-painting' as Mercy had called it. Reacquainting her tonsils with her fingertips, Moses-like, she would free the chosen chocolates from their intestinal oppressors, and lead them to the promised toilet pan. Then, with a quick squirt of 'FreshBreath', flushed and smiling a sickly grin, she would make her way back to her counter and, once again, level her stare.

By five past five the first of the suits arrived and a hush of approaching danger ran from counter to counter as the grazing assistants twitched alert and watched the predators enter. Who would be first quarry, first prey? A less than young woman in a dark blue suit with frisbee-sized buttons quietly pushed open that glass door and stealthily approached Gloves and Scarves. She silently neared the innocent counter girl quietly folding a pair of driving gloves. There was a moment of deathly silence, then she pounced.

'What,' she roared, dragging an Hermès scarf from her bag, 'do you call this?'

The girl dropped the gloves in surprise and spun around to stand quivering, at bay, as the pale green silk 'return' was waved in her face.

The other invaders pricked up their ears, they had dispersed around the Second Floor and, noses in the air, they had scented the first blood. Suddenly, the rush was on.

A qwerty of secretaries surrounded Miranda to witness the miracle of the exsanguinator 'Lock-In' system. They giggled and sneered at the demonstration and found great sport in asking annoying questions.

'Why's it blue? Mine's not blue,' said one and they all agreed and nodded.

'If it's biodegradable does that mean it's going to dissolve in your knickers?' asked another and they giggled and one at the back said, 'It would in your crusty gussets.' And they all giggled some more.

'What if you don't wear knickers?' said a girl who was far too hairy to have really come from this turn in the evolutionary cycle. At this, all the girls started laughing hysterically, but Miranda hardly noticed. She just looked over at Mercy and carried on the rote of the demonstration. 'Fancy a game of tennis? . . . Maybe a little waterskiing.'

She did manage to splash blue dye on some of the more harassing ones and some of the others who had been more absorbed actually bought her special competition bumper pack, which offered the opportunity of winning a cruise in the Bahamas.

'Special Offer' it said on the side, 'All aboard the Panty Liner for the Special In-Yer Drawers Draw'.

The months of Miranda's last hour ticked on and the qwertys changed and laughed and moved on. Then, as Christmas drew near and the minute hand of the Second-Floor clock closed on the twelve, a hush fell on the gathered secretaries, a stranger had joined them. One who was not like them and they all turned to

Stop.

Stop this very second.

i can't do it, i can't.

This is it, this is the moment i have been dreading from the very start. i have been putting it off and delaying and deferring and procrastinating, i've been filling in with asides and comments every little second of Miranda's day. i've been extending and stretching time like knicker elastic, on and on. Why? Because i am afraid. i am scared of this one moment, this next second in Miranda's life. This is when the elastic snaps. And when it does, it always hurts.

i have dithered for over forty thousand words because i did not want to get to this one second. i told you it was a love story and i've told you how much i loved her, how much love she had in her, how she longed to love and be loved, but i have said nothing about who she did love.

Up until this one second, somewhere just past five to six, Miranda loved:

107

Her Mum.

Her ankles.

And, occasionally, her gerbil.

But after this one second all that would change. In a mere second her world, her priorities, her feelings would change. In the simple matter of a sixtieth of a minute her heart would race and she would fall in love and i just don't want to admit that that ever happened.

On suddenly catching sight, her heart would begin to palpitate, from this moment on she would be tormented by thoughts of love, always fearful.

i don't even know whether i'm capable of telling you of this one instant which hurt so much. How can i describe such an upheaval of the heart. Words can only flit about the true feeling, they can never do it justice. They can never reproduce the terrible pain, the very real feeling that i had failed. i loved her and she fell in love with someone else. i searched and looked for signs, for a hint that she might love me, for an indication that she felt some affection, for a single trace of reciprocation. Nothing. In that one second i knew that i was rejected. And to fail in love is surely to fail in life.

i was nothing, nothing to her.

O God.

But i promised you. i swore that i would tell you it all, leave nothing out. Show you respect. Show you my love. An open book.

i have to be able to speak now or i might never speak again. Never really love again. Is that the easier option? The line of least pain? But, if i don't speak now i will always guard myself and keep a stone in my heart. O help me.

It can't be that time already. Surely a few more chapters. A few thousand more words or so of harmless observations, London life, the state of espionage. i know a great joke about two nuns and a pearl necklace. i think i can remember a bit more of the professor's work.

Despite this evidence, all these issues are muddied by how we receive that poetry today. Our translations, and our current interpretations of certain words and language, have all been handed down from generations of translators who lived, and

No.

No.

You will reject me. You will break our bond and fill our silence with the discord of disappointment. You won't make me tell you, you are too kind, too loving for that. You don't want to see a bleeding heart. If only. If only.

. . . stare at the man who stood beside them. He was tall and he was dark and he was handsome, as all good tall, dark, handsome strangers should be. He stood calm and strong amongst the swaying, gawping girls.

His long, navy blue cashmere coat washed over his shoulders and cascaded to barely an inch above the floor. Beneath it, he wore a suit which could only be bespoke, and it bespoke beloudly of how beloody berich he must be. It was dark and pressed and nothing had been so understated since God told Noah there might be a spot of rain. Up from the halo of his blinding white collar and his subtly striped tie, rose a tanned neck, which was smooth and defined by strong tendons at either side. They held onto the corners of a jaw line which swept down squarely from each ear with absolute definition, and if you looked it up, the definition would say 'firm but rugged'. He had wide, strong cheekbones which stood open like the edges of a double door, the gates of paradise, revealing within the heaven of his face. A mouth which was wide and smiling and full, not tight nor mean, but with the faintest trail of pale red. A thin proud nose at once aristocratic yet looking as if it would not sniff at anything. Above, his eyebrows, like his hair, were black and thick and Gaelic-looking, storm-tossed and tousled, but beneath them lay the pools of tranquillity, the dark green oases of calm. His eyes. Deep. Deep and very very serene.

He was there in that one second as Miranda spun the 'panty shield' above her head and for a moment she thought it was the Marlboro Man, the Diet Coke break Guy, the Gold Blend Man, but now, in comparison to this dream made flesh, the Milk Tray Man looked like the Milky Bar Kid.

She felt it. The jolt, the shock, the entire battery of love. Yes, the blood rushed hotly about her temples and sang in her ears. Yes, every one of her bones suddenly felt weak, her collarbone ached as if it could no longer hold the weight in her chest. Yes, her breath was shallow and panicked and quick, and yes, in that one second Miranda recognized all the symptoms of falling in love. She realized how vulnerable she was and she realized that she needed to protect herself fast if she wasn't to end the day in tears, feeling sorry for herself and feeling that her whole life was a failure.

Plan 'A': Ignore him. Look the other way.

But she couldn't remember seeing a more beautiful man and that was what he was, handsome just would not do. She couldn't remember because, on the whole, she did not look at beautiful men, for beautiful men did not look at her. But there he was, a beautiful man and he was looking straight at her and his sparkling eyes were smiling as if drinking in the very breath she had lost.

Miranda felt the dizziness and the feverishness of a racing heart and tried to kick in with her contingency plan.

Plan 'B': The league table. Like goes for like, you go out with the people you deserve to go out with, people like yourself. Except when large amounts of money are involved and suddenly very very ugly people get to have relationships with very very beautiful people. However, since Miranda considered herself to have deficiency of both money and beauty, potential boyfriends were either in or out of her league and this vision, this angel, this man beyond men, was absolutely and definitely out of her league. Not a doubt about it.

But, still in that one second, not even her self-loathing was standing up to protect her. He had not moved, he was still there and he looked sincere and, what was worse and all the more confusing, he looked like he might be genuinely taken with her. This sort of thing just did not happen. Nothing she had ever known had prepared her for this moment.

Having dispensed with the probabilities, only the improbabilities remained, however impossible, but her mind was desperately grabbing for excuses which might explain it, might find some fault with this sun god who had stepped over her horizon and brought a fiery dawning of passions within her and would, no doubt, set just as quickly and from his fading twilight bring the darkness and despair of night to her soul.

You can't just fall in love at first sight. You can't. Apart from anything else, it's so thoroughly un-modern. It was all right in the olden days when you were unlikely to meet anybody you didn't know anything about, it was all social circles and gossip then. He's probably got a thousand girlfriends. He probably picks up women with his evening paper and, likewise, throws them out the next morning. A man like him doesn't have relationships, he has relays. A woman for every day of the week, every day of the year. Look at him, he must have. And if he hasn't he's mighty strange. No, strike that, mighty queer. Oh God, it could be that, that's probably what it is, that's why he looks so comfortable surrounded by those girls. Mercy had told her over and over that all the best ones are. But even that hat just didn't seem to fit. There must be something wrong with him, he's mentally disturbed, eats duckweed, collects celebrity body-hair. Save yourself, Miranda, look away, there lies only despair and disappointment, because men like that never fancy girls like you. He was smiling and it all felt useless.

Miranda reached to the bottom of the barrel to find something, anything, which might put her heart off and save her the agony of the rejection when he passed on, as surely he would, as all men had. He's probably got a hairy back, smelly feet, sweaty groin. Hang on. He's watching a sanitary napkin demonstration, now that is weird. He's probably got a runny bottom, chronic diarrhoea, haemorrhaging haemorrhoids or, worse, he's buying them for his girlfriend, his love for her overcoming all embarrassment. Miranda grasped for his faults yet he stood there beautiful and clean and open and honest and nothing, not a single piece of the shit that she was slinging at him, would stick.

All this in one second. The hush had fallen and Miranda just stood there frozen as the furnace burnt within. Like a statue she stood, her arm raised above her head, the damp sanitary napkin hanging limp between her fingers, her mouth slightly open. Not very different to all the girls except, of course, for the sanitary napkin.

Realizing his impact on the circle of women, he tried a friendly sounding, 'Oh, don't mind me.' So they all ignored him like a cream cake at a weight watchers' meeting.

'Shall I go?' he tried, pointing away towards the door and dipping his head slightly in that direction, but all any of them heard was his sonorous voice, vibrating with poetry. A voice which almost carried its own echo with it. Miranda and every girl there shook their heads slowly, hardly daring to break their gaze. Then, dreamlike, Miranda floated through the rest of the routine. She didn't even look over to Mercy. Mercy was a million miles away. Mercy who?

The Second-Floor lights flickered on and off, indicating that it was closing time. The girls peeled away as Miranda finished the routine, not even the hunk could get them to stay for the hard-sell, but he watched the whole thing and by the time she was holding out the bumper pack, he was the only one left.

'I'm sorry,' he said, 'I don't actually use them.' And he smiled a broad smile and that implausibly tight jaw tightened some more, grinning and bearing an impossible torque.

Talk. Talk, stupid. Talk to him.

'Maybe, maybe,' Miranda spluttered, 'your girlfriend?'

He just shook his head.

What does shaking your head mean? No. No what? No girlfriend?

No, she uses tampons? No, she's too perfect to have periods? What? What does shaking your head mean?

'I just wanted to see the product,' he continued, 'in action, as it were.'

Miranda looked at him.

'I mean obviously not literally.'

Miranda kept looking.

'Commodities,' he said, as if it was an answer of some sort. Which it wasn't. He looked at her face for some glimmer of recognition, a nod, an 'Oh, of course', a neon sign behind her flashing the words 'Ah, That Explains Everything', but found nothing, she was still just standing there and looking at him. He thought he might have done marginally better had he said, 'Fresh Haddock,' and he shifted on his feet trying to figure out if it was too late to work the fish in somehow.

'I'm in stocks,' he said. 'My company, we're about to buy a considerable chunk of that.' He pointed to the packet in her hand.

'Why?' she said, at last. 'You can have the whole thing for two pounds.' O no, *non, niet*. Nobody likes a smart-arse.

'No, we're buying into Beauchamps, the manufacturers. I just needed to see how the product was selling.' He paused and looked up at the fluorescent lighting, 'I really don't normally go around watching sanitary product demos.'

How can such a beautiful man have even a moment of confidence lapse? It just didn't fit. He was too perfect.

'Look,' he said, sounding a little more relieved as he pointed at the door and the security guard tapping his feet, 'they're throwing us out. Thank you for the demo. You're very . . . You're very good at it. I'd buy some. I mean, if I used them.'

All right. That was laying on the faltering, embarrassed, confidence-lacking, self-deprecating, stuttering a little too far. Miranda just could not buy it. Englishmen were only like that in bad movies made for Americans.

'So did you find what you came for?' she said, trying to put a bit of haughtiness into her voice.

'Oh yes.' He smiled. 'More. Much more.' And he turned and everything melted. Miranda's hands hit the counter to support herself as she felt the tension rush out through her shoulders and arms and thought that she might crumple to the floor.

More. That's got to mean something. Miranda realized time was slowing again. He was leaving. Don't go. He had walked maybe five steps. Say something before he disappears. Six. Seize the day. Seven.

Now. Eight. Opportunities don't happen, you make them. Nine. Out of your league. Ten. Forget it. Out for the count. He got to Hosiery and turned towards the exit. Don't go. Just don't go. Say something. Anything.

'Don't go,' she cried out after him. Oh yes, very clever, very pithy, deadly wit.

Still, he did stop and turn and look at her.

'I was wondering,' she slowly said, quickly thinking, 'whether you deal with single people, I mean not companies, you know, with investments. I've never met a stockbroker before, you see.' It sounded so stupid, but she tried her best to look like she might be someone who was awfully rich and just liked to do sanitary towel demonstrations as an eccentric whim.

He walked back to Miranda, pulling a little white card from his pocket and offering it. Feeling sure that if she let go of the counter she would fall flat on her face, Miranda didn't move, just smiled contortedly. He laid the card down in front of her where it immediately started soaking up the blue-dyed water.

'Not officially,' he said, 'but if you need some advice.'

Miranda looked down at the card. Her knuckles were turning white as they gripped the edge. The bones in her legs were dissolving, she was going to be walking the rumba for the rest of her life. 'Thank you, I'll call my accountant,' she said. 'Maybe my people will call yours.'

He walked away and she couldn't be sure when exactly he faded from sight. But he did. Somewhere amongst the coats and hats. After a minute, he just wasn't there. Somewhere she could hear the Lurker's shrill voice, 'I want to see the manager.'

Miranda looked at the card, now blue and very wet. 'Ferdinand Xavier', it said, 'Commodities, Chaste Manhattan Bank'. And there were some telephone numbers that it would be far too petty and vengeful of me to publish.

Despite this evidence, all these issues are muddied by how we receive that poetry today. Our translations, and our current interpretations of certain words and language, have all been handed down from generations of translators who lived, and live, after what I shall call the Genesis of Love. No translator comes to a work uninfluenced by the society in which they live and translate for. The very language we speak has been shaped by the dominant orthodoxy.

No translator comes to a work without preconceived ideas of what language is trying to do and what certain language means. In most cases, re-reading the originals, we find that when post-Genesis of Love translators came to a word like *amore* – which may be equally viably translated as lust, carnal desire, or perhaps, in the lingua franca of today, 'bonetastic' – they used the veiled and politically loaded word 'love'. A word that, as we have seen, escapes an absolute definition but may be interpreted as the times dictate on a scale anywhere from animal lust to god-like adoration. Thus they reclaimed the lechery of our ancestors in their own language, their own word, 'love', raising its definitive meaning far beyond the simple need to breed.

So what happened, only a few centuries ago, to colour our whole form of interpretation? When was this Genesis of Love?

Chapter IV.

A History of the Genesis of Love

When a man is in love he endures more than at other times; he submits to everything.

> Friedrich Wilhelm Nietzsche (1844–1900)
> *The Antichrist*

THERE ARE CERTAIN THINGS, I BELIEVE, THAT THE WORLD COULD do without. Ear hair, for example, other people's farts, traffic wardens and Swindon. What about a world without love? Can you imagine it? However, for nearly one thousand years, that is exactly what this world was. 'Love' was forgotten. That is not to say that some people did not have passions for others, but the idea that love between people fulfilled life, vanished from the earth.

It was with the fall of Rome that the fledgling prototype notion of romantic being *in* love was lost, and as the Church rose from its ashes, they sanctioned this kind of love exclusively for God. 'Love' at its highest was only proper when it was felt for the Lord.

The ransacking Huns, Goths and Vandals had no time for sitting around pining over some dainty images of loveliness. They were fourth-century yuppies, taking over the cities, making killings in the markets and corpse raiding. They were men with go, with ambition, with drive; they had things to burn, people to rape, places to pillage. Speeding around in their low-profile chariots, quaffing buckets of mead and grossly over-tipping the temples. They were on the up, they had vision and they had a new world order.

What was this political embryo which would advance on the delicate intricacies of Roman and Greek republics and democracies, ideologies which excelled from the people's notions of self-worth and civic pride?

Fear.

A few vicious warlords served by the meek living in dread of them. In short, feudalism. One powerful liege in each region and everybody else subjugated to him. The rule of the iron fist, it was simplicity itself with a clear pecking order of ownership.

20

10

Splaying and Rotating and Quivering

Pandora had a little box
She longed to look inside.
Pandora loosened all the locks
And let the lid blow wide.
Out flew the sins,
Despair on winds,
The pox, the plague, the pope,
Then all was left,
Inside the chest,
Was a tiny piece of hope.

HOPE, THE MORE CYNICAL SAY, IS A BELIEF FOR THOSE WHO REFUSE TO know better. It is a cruel world indeed in which such a thin thing is offered as the only lifeline to those falling into desperation, a vicious place in which it is possible to live an entire life just surviving, just hanging on. Yet, i suppose, if hope is all there is to grab onto, a thin, weedy branch, it still seems better than letting go and falling into that black chasm of despair.

Simply, Miranda, the one i loved, fell in love with someone else. It happens, i know that now. It had happened to her more often than she found herself able to forget. But why didn't i just turn a page then? Why didn't i tear out my feelings, cut my losses? Why did i carry on loving someone who did not love me?

Don't think i haven't searched for reasons, but love knows no logic, it is a feeling and feelings defy reason.

She didn't forsake me.

She always took me with her.

She was beautiful.

i made her laugh, sometimes.

Maybe that was enough.

And she made me feel important, to her. She cared, or at least she seemed to. Maybe it was the novelty. Maybe it was because i was in love with the idea of being in love. Maybe it was something which was just inexpressible.

Maybe i just fall in love with anybody who really opens me up. i have grown now to miss your touch and long for your hands when i am not in them. Whatever it was that made me love her, deep within, even through the pain, torment and evils that beset the heart, you see, there was always hope. i was like Miranda then, reaching out to grab that thin weedy branch.

By the time Miranda could feel the circulation returning to her legs, Ferdinand's soggy business card had soaked through the thin material of her shirt breast pocket and was dying the left cup of her bra a dull blue. After mopping up the counter and disposing of the sad pile of soaked and worn pads, she wandered, still dazed, to the cloakroom. She pushed the door absently, as she looked down at her breast pocket just to reassure herself that it had all really happened, and walked straight into Mercy.

Those mystical energies which supported the siren's rolling masses against the grasp of gravity were as coiled springs, like the pinball fenders which propel the steel ball away at the slightest touch and at twenty times the velocity. So when Miranda bumped into her, she was buffeted and bounced off the bumpers of her pneumatic disputant and sent spinning away with an ejection force only familiar to astronauts, jet pilots and anyone who has eaten the Number 23 Speciality Vindaloo at the House of Curry on Uxbridge Road.

Miranda, still unsteady on her legs, was thrown back against the door somewhat violently and incurred a bruise in the small of her back from the door-handle. Behind her, the sharp edge of the steel handle managed to find its way into the gap between her already dangling skirt button and the zip.

Miranda pulled herself away from the door to straighten herself up and make it look, if at all possible, like she had meant to do the whole performance and there was nothing odd about bouncing around the cloakroom. She had every right to collide and crash about and look an idiot if that was what she wanted to do.

However, as Miranda righted herself, she heard the ominous pop and rip of a button and zip being left behind on the door. She looked down to the floor to see the button bouncing there as she felt the skirt slipping over her hips. Grasping at the band of her skirt behind her, Miranda held on to it and twisting back again she puffed out her chest and stared triumphantly at Mercy like a matador scrutinizing the bull with nothing but a toothpick behind his back.

Even Miranda felt that the illusion that she might have designed this entire dance was starting to wear a little thin, yet her pride would not let her give up.

Mercy just looked at her and did not smile. Having grown up in the Midlands she knew that it wasn't nice to send people to Coventry and was already feeling a little sorry for her treatment of Miranda that day.

'Randa,' said Mercy, 'I just wanted . . . I thought I was . . . well maybe . . .' She paused.

'No. Please,' replied Miranda, concisely, 'I know I . . .' And another silence set.

'No, it's not that you. It's just,' said Mercy suddenly.

'Look, I don't know if I can. You know. Just now.'

'Yeah, I know. But then. Is it? I mean. When?'

'No, you're right, I can only. You see. You know.'

'I suppose. I mean, if that's how. Well, if you're going to.'

'I don't know. It just seems. You know.'

'Yeah. I know.'

'Yeah.'

What a relief that that was said. They both forced a smile of absolute agreement and quickly turned to their lockers, glad that at least what needed to be said had been said, that their logic had been impeccable, uncoloured by their emotions and that they both had stood their ground without buckling under the weight of the other's argument.

Using a hairpin that she found at the bottom of her locker, Miranda secured the back of her skirt as best she could and, gathering her bag and jacket, headed to the staff exit, leaving Mercy fixing her hair and make-up and straps and her other miracles of structural engineering.

Because of the delicate and rather pliable nature of the hairpin, not wanting to dislodge it, Miranda attempted to walk with the ethereal glide that ladies in costume dramas used to do before it was discovered that bodice-gripped, wobbling bosoms pumped up the ratings. Miranda glided, she regally slid, out onto the busy street.

The sky between the buildings was clear and still quite light, though the sun and a tinge of dusk had started, a little early, to paint the town red. The wind had decided to die down a little and now whisked about trouser-legs and seemed satisfied to play on the pavement with crisp bags, whirling them in little eddies and every now and then trying to whip them up the odd, unsuspecting dress. It childishly hid a shiny wet dog turd under an assortment of sweet wrappers and petals. A man with an I'm-in-a-hurry walk and a get-out-of-my-way umbrella pushed past Miranda and firmly trod on the innocent-looking package. Slipping, he quickly righted himself and i'm sure i heard the wind snigger as he looked down at the rich slime clinging to his this-is-the-one-I-use-to-kick-arse brogue. He walked on more slowly, dragging his right foot for two blocks and opening a wake of pedestrians behind him, avoiding his wet trail in a thank-fuck-it-wasn't-me sort of way.

Miranda jostled along in the home-headed crowd, moving in the same direction as most everybody else, towards the tube. She stepped out into the road and began to thread her way between the stationary cars which were still sitting there, as they always did, fuming. She sidled past bumpers, careful to keep her bottom motion to a minimum. It was when she was half way across Baker Street that she felt a little shiver. Maybe it was the wind, practising a collar dive, down along her spine. She looked around her, looked at all the still car windows filled with sky, and the faces behind that she could barely make out. She looked at all the moving people twisting and turning in waltzes with cars. It felt like someone was watching her. Which was silly. It had been a weird day and maybe a little paranoia was creeping in. She got to the other side of the street and stopped. It was a feeling like someone had been moving at the same pace as her, keeping time with her, but she couldn't see them. She thought she saw someone disappear behind a van and not come out the other side, but maybe not. She must be tired. Long harrowing day. Tube.

Yet, even as she descended the steps, Miranda could not shake the feeling. She stood still for a moment, right there on the steps, and was buffeted by the people behind her trying to get past, but no one else stopped. At the ticket queue she kept looking from side to side. There was someone who kept his back to her, he was studying the tube map rather intently, she thought. There was a man by the newspaper kiosk; he was whistling, a little too nonchalantly.

She went carefully through the barrier, mindful of her hairpin and feeling sure that her skirt was loosening. As she walked down to the platform Miranda decided that she was doing herself a mischief. Her mind was playing tricks. Why on earth would anyone follow her? Still, she carried on down to the very end of the platform to see if anyone would follow. A man reading a newspaper stopped short but she couldn't see his face. Miranda stood and watched and waited and worried.

When the train creaked in, it was bursting with people, backs pressed against the windows. The doors opened and many of them spilled out and Miranda looked at the wall of packed and standing bodies holding on, trying not to fall out. She debated, for a moment, waiting for the next train but it was the rush hour, the electric sign indicated the next Hammersmith train was twelve minutes away and it would probably be just as full.

She stepped on and squeezed her body against the wall to avoid catching her arse in the sliding doors. Someone else, a man, stepped in behind her and pinned her to the human wall. She couldn't turn round to give him a filthy look so she let it ride as the doors crammed shut and the train eased out.

Miranda, being shorter than most, found her nose squashed against the silk tie of a man who would, no doubt, be horrified to find mucus from her nostrils smeared across it when he got home. However, since she did not even have enough space to incline her neck she couldn't give him an excusing smile. They all stood jolting with the train, shoulder to shoulder, body pressed against body, in a hot, smelly, sweatily humid pack. Miranda was sure there were people who positively enjoyed travelling like this. They had to be either agoraphobics, pickpockets or, more likely, frotteurs.

Miranda found herself so jammed between alien-smelling bodies that her arms were pinned to her side and as the train lurched and they all swayed she swore she could feel her skirt loosen again. She pressed her hands against the sides of her thighs to ease the weight on the hairpin, and because that was about all the movement she could manage. Through it all, Miranda could smell fish of some sort; it seemed to come from the man who pressed in behind her. He was shifting about and Miranda began to wonder whether she was being frotted.

The next station took a long time coming, but finally, after lots of rubbing and compressing and sweating, the next platform arrived outside the train. It pulled up alongside the doors which finally opened and the crowd swelled as they all collectively took a breath of the fresher air. A few people pushed to get out and for a moment Miranda was released, so she turned to give her frotteur a withering look. She twisted her shoulders into him and swung her head round. She looked and would have screamed had she not been breathing in at the time. All she managed was a gurgle of horror. There, squeezing against her, was Trotsky. The loon. The book-snatcher. The anchovy-reeking 1926 Politburo expellee. Miranda's hands rose up to him as she lashed out.

'Go away, get away from me, you loon, you bastard, get away.'

Miranda pushed and hammered at him with flying hands and fists. Trotsky, through his little wire glasses which quickly bounced from his nose, looked shocked and then bruised as Miranda pummelled at him. He put his arms in front of him to defend himself and took half a step back. As near to the doorway as he was, his heel slipped off the edge of the carriage and, trying to keep his balance, he had to open his arms to catch hold of the edge of the open door. This left his face open to a particularly nasty slap and a large scratch to his cheek. He let go of the edge to protect his face and an uppercut sent him backward. His arms flailed, trying to keep balance, and then, outspread, rotating rapidly in some idiotic attempt to fly despite being the product of a 90 million year evolutionary failure to develop wings or even feathers, he fell backwards onto the platform with a crack.

'Just stay away from me,' Miranda screamed at the prone man. Then as he scrabbled to get up and look for his glasses she added, 'Stop following me.' Trotsky just blinked at her as the doors hissed and snapped shut.

There, then, by the tunnel-darkness, under the vast city, the metropolis seemed a huge and hostile human-eating beast machine and she wanted to go home. Right now. But she was stuck on a train and she felt like a little girl and so alone. She had no real home to go to. She was isolated in this great grinding machine which endlessly pushed and pulled apart its populace and turned on their sweat, oiled with their work, and ate and munched on their hearts. Miranda's knees knocked together slightly as her body began to shake. She was scared, it was a scary place. She didn't feel grown up at all, she was just so small in a big dirty place where no one cares and no one loves and all the hearts have been eaten. She would not cry. She would not. She was in public, amongst the heart-consumed, and she would not let the monster know that she still had hers. She must look like all the rest of them.

Feeling small, and perhaps in need of human warmth, she pushed herself against the tall man with the silk tie. Feeling a momentary give, she managed to twist her shoulders to lean with her back against the partition wall between the standing room and the seats. It was only when the relative cool of the glass touched her backside that she realized that she had just made a dreadful mistake. Her arms pinned beside her, she felt for her skirt. Gone. Moving her legs, she could feel it around her ankles. Now she was displaying squashed buttocks to everyone fortunate enough to have grabbed a seat in the carriage. Everyone would be looking at her tatty tights with great holes showing oozing lumps of pallid flesh. Then Miranda remembered one particular hole large enough to let an entire buttock fall out of it, and since the pair of knickers which didn't ride up the crack of her particular shape of bottom cleavage had yet to be designed, she was, she realized, showing each pore, pimple and rut of cellulite to every commuter in the carriage. She twisted her head to take a look and, yes, everyone just happened to be looking the other way.

In a single train journey she had lost her dignity and gained a stalker. This was, she reflected, quite easily the worst day of her entire life. She stood there with her buttocks splaying and rotating and quivering with every jolt of the train and everybody in the carriage stifling their laughter until some, standing at the next doorway, could contain themselves no longer and burst into fits of hyenaesque hysterics. Miranda listened to the laughter. The very best thing about a city as big as London, she began to console herself, was the anonymity. The chances of seeing someone more than once are so, so slim. Today she will be the tube loon, and tomorrow she will never see any of them ever again. They will all be swallowed by the city. It was OK to make mistakes and make a fool of yourself. Let them laugh. They didn't, they'd never, mean a damn thing.

'Excuse me,' said a deep voice from somewhere above the silk tie. Miranda's mental loon-alert flashed. It was behaviour quite inexcusable, people don't talk to people on the tube, it's a politeness which keeps everybody safe from each other. Anyway, if there was ever a moment she didn't want to talk to anybody, it was now.

'I noticed,' continued the voice annoyingly, 'that you were having some trouble. Do you think I could help in any way?' Miranda slid her head along the glass and angled it upwards, which was the only way she could look in that direction. Her heart suddenly seemed to cool, as if the soggy blue business card in her breast pocket had just seeped through to it. She smiled. She stood there baring her arse to fifty strangers on the London Underground and she forced a smile, because smiling back at her was Mr Ferdinand Xavier, Commodities, Chaste Manhattan Bank.

Miranda grinned broadly and she gritted her teeth for the winter of her despair. Yes, that just about does it. I've got to pick up my skirt and show him my arse as I do it, so I've got about as much chance of saving face, getting off this tube, getting a date with him and, hey, why not, marrying him and living happily ever after as Yasser Arafat has of winning Miss World.

Unbeknown to Miranda, at that very moment, somewhere deep in the war-torn urbanizations of Palestine, Mr Arafat was selecting his favourite bikini for the swimwear category.

This feudal system ruled the West throughout the dark ages as its people lived in terror.

Then, around AD 1180, in a relatively peaceful region in the south of France, a quiet revolution took place which would change the world and its power base for ever. They reinvented love.

It was a time when the world was still green and wild verdant forests reached across kingdoms. Deep within them, huts of wattle and daub huddled together in ivy-gripped hamlets and the dark woods still held their mysteries of fear and fascination, strange beasts, and people of Faerie; the wolf at the door, the old lady with the scarlet apples. Superstition whispered through the land and it was always unwise to stray from the path. It was a time of stories. In the harsh reality of mud and dirt and sores and plague and boils and baby deaths and terrors, Nature still kept its secrets and its magic for it also gave life. For most medieval people, Nature was their living, they farmed the land and treasured the fertile earth as if it was gold. Strip fields were ploughed by the ox and the serf, their personal value in the system being of little difference.

The sackclothed fishwives might shoo the mud-caked village hogs from their spinning but they knew the pig was higher in rank than they were. As women, they were at the bottom of the manorial scale, beneath all other cattle and chattels, for their uses were few. The relationship between a man and his wife reflected that of the lord and his vassal: she was his property and their marriage contract was a business agreement of fealty, duty, dowry and land acquisition. Yet, however brutal this system was, it did provide the psychological security of knowing exactly where and who you were. You may have been basest of the base, lowest of the low, a piece of faecal matter clinging on to the bottom of society, but there was no chance of an identity crisis or feeling that you didn't know who you were or what you were supposed to be doing in life.

Consider, then, the plight of the high-born lady in this age. She who would live beyond the village, above the trees, in the towers of the lord's castle. These edifices, which overshadowed the lord's villeins working his fields, served as a permanent reminder of exactly who was the boss. Although the noble lady was served by maid-servants and neither wallowed in mud nor ground the wheat, she was still, at once, both the highest and

the lowest. She was, as the bearer of the lord's children, a
queen and yet, as a woman, a worthless part of the system.
Trapped in a regime which had no place for her, she was metaphorically bound in a chastity belt – and then literally when her
lord went a-travelling.

Duality, trying to resolve a plurality of opposites, is not just
a symptom of psychological problems, it is often a cause. The
extreme duality of identity which these queen-worms suffered
may well have been a cue for mental problems, trauma, identity problems, personality disorders, hysterical complaints and
even schizophrenic tendencies. Yet, as Shakespeare wrote in *A
Midsummer Night's Dream*,

> The lunatic, the lover and the poet
> Are of imagination all compact.

Indeed, and in a combination of the imaginations of these
lunatics and a group of ambitious poets, the 'lover' that we recognize today was created. For there is little that is more
creative than insanity and in their own, quite possibly mad, way
they created an emotional interpretation and a political ideology which would, in time, exercise power over the individuals
of the entire world.

For hundreds of years these 'ladies' had been subjected to
unknown humiliations by their society and the men who ruled
it. Then, on a dusty, hot August day in the year 1096, the men
went away. The kings, barons, lords and knights went off and
did not come back in a permanent way for over two hundred
years.

They had risen to the call of Pope Urban II, the first pontiff
to openly cross from the state ethereal to real estate, com-
plaining, 'Can anyone tolerate that we do not even share
equally with the Muslims the inhabited earth? They have made
Asia, which is a third of the world, their homeland ... They
have also forcibly held Africa, the second portion of the world,
for over two hundred years. There remains Europe, the third
continent. How small a portion of it is inhabited by us
Christians.' Though having little sense of geographical proportion, with that he launched the Crusades and authorized a
return to the savageness of those Huns, Goths and Vandals. But
this time the genocidal slaughter was right, because God said
it was.

11

And That Felt a Little Like Being Loved

NOW WHAT DO YOU THINK THE ODDS AGAINST THAT WERE? OF
Miranda and Ferdinand ending up next to each other on the same
train? Pretty massive? But i remember a book back in the library: it
was called *Locating the Golden Rivet, Everyday Maritime Customs* and,
let me assure you, stranger things really do happen at sea.

Perhaps i'm stretching your credulity. There i was, disavowing huge
coincidences in books, condemning authors who have to use flukes to
propel their narrative, and lo and behold if a great big fortuitous act of
fate, almost a *deus ex machina*, doesn't rear itself in my very pages. It's
true, if the story were of my own making, i certainly wouldn't have let
such a thing happen. My protagonists would agonize over contacting
each other, take long, lonesome, soul-searching walks through mist-
laden countrysides battling with themselves and then finally, after
much consultation with other characters, they would make that phone
call. They wouldn't just happen, ever so by chance, to meet on a train
less than twenty minutes after their last meeting and certainly not at
exactly the moment when one character is writhing in an almost ter-
minal embarrassment and the other character is just about the last
person they would like to see. However, neither can i deny that that
was exactly what occurred.

i could tell you that we all know coincidences do happen in real life
and this just happened to be one of them; however, looking at the
mathematics of it all, i think that the odds of such a thing happening

were, in fact, rather good. The whole event would not seem to be quite as fortuitous, or unlucky in Miranda's case, as it appears.

Let me put it this way. How many 'friends' do you think you have? People you know at least enough to say hello to, actually care what they answer when you ask how they are, perhaps even remember enough to ask how the wife, pacemaker or thrush treatment is going. If one can believe statisticians, each of us might have around 150 of them. It follows then, that if your 'friends' have as many 'friends' as you, you would have around 22,500 friends of friends.

Then if, shall we say, for each friend you have five acquaintances, people you nod to in the street and whose names you probably know but who you might feel a little embarrassed about having actually to stop and converse with on a subject of any greater depth than the weather. In that case the number of people who know you, or know someone who knows you, balloons to around 600,000 souls. Considering the population of Britain is around 60 million, it means that one in every hundred people in the country is someone who knows someone you know. If then you would like to add all the social demography and physical geography, the chances of meeting someone you know on a train, between, say, where you live and where you work, start looking rather good indeed.

In Miranda and Ferdinand's case we must add the fact that they were in the same part of the same city barely twenty minutes before and that they would have seen nearly a thousand people in the height of the rush hour before they met, so perhaps we should be asking whether, in fact, it would have been rather rum if they had not bumped into each other.

Alternatively, since i have chosen, so far, not to dip into the head of Ferdinand, there may be a much more causal reason for their meeting which has nothing to do with fate, destiny or coincidence but something of more intent or design. Whichever way it happened, it happened.

'It's you,' he said, looking at Miranda, 'I mean the demo girl, the woman selling the . . . er . . . , from the shop.'

Miranda nodded. 'Miranda, they call me Miranda Skirt Shedder.'

Ferdinand almost laughed, you could see it in his eyes. It might have been a good, loud, honest laugh but for the fact that he remembered where he was, where making any noise or scene was worse blasphemy than a sow in a synagogue. Ferdinand was nothing if not self-possessed, so what came out was a polite, diplomatic, near-silent chuckle.

That's it, thought Miranda, get him laughing, maybe he won't see my arse through the tears.

Ferdinand suddenly looked very serious. 'You look cold,' he said, letting those serene green eyes drip into Miranda's. The sweltering temperature of the accumulated body heat in the packed carriage seemed like it might be fast approaching combustion point so Miranda wondered if she was shivering or something.

She shook her head.

'No, you really do look like you're very cold.' And in an instant, his dark, thick, cashmere coat had slipped off his shoulders. Somehow, elbowing people smaller than him, he swept the coat off and then about Miranda's shoulders, gently pulling her away from the glass, and to him, as he did. It puffed out over the shoulders of her own jacket and fell right the way down to the floor, deftly covering all her exposed points in one fell swoop. Miranda felt a wave of relief crash through her gut as she smiled at him, a very very genuine smile. The smile i fell in love with.

'Thanks,' croaked Miranda. 'How much for those?' she said, pointing at his trousers.

He smiled and Miranda nestled into the coat and sniffed the collar. It smelt of man. A distant, sharp bite of a once pine-laden after-shave, now blunted and worn by the day. It seemed such a long time since she had smelt a real, clean man and in recognizing it she began to feel a charge as if it was he, himself, wrapped around her. At each shake of the carriage, the smooth lining licked at her exposed flesh as a lover and she felt its glossiness slipping along her skin. At first she thought she might giggle but then, there beneath the coat, his coat, she felt somehow naked. In the crush of the crowd, and with each jolt, he was pressed against her.

Miranda half closed her eyes as she melted into the sensual physicality of the moment. Even the closeness of his breath against her, whispering warmly down her neck, made her shiver. She felt the subtle insurgencies of the rebellious regions of her body forgetting where they were, mutinying against all propriety and beginning to tingle.

Miranda found herself pressing back against Ferdinand even when no jolt merited it, rhythmically pushing against the softness of his suit and the hardness of the body beneath. With the smoothness of the silk and the heat of his breath and the rattling and the shuddering of the train vibrating up through her ankles, her legs, her thighs, Miranda almost unconsciously dug her nails into his suit.

She felt desperately like she was trying to hold something back. She looked up again, only to fall into his eyes as she wondered, mesmerically, and felt him again, and wondered if there was such a thing as a frotteuse.

In the heat of the coat and the moment, Miranda realized that she was sweating profusely, she could feel the beads running down the bare parts of her legs and dampening the silk lining.

Even with the crush of the other travellers, she felt alone with him. And it felt so familiar and wonderful and good and infinite, the rhythm of their bodies and the train, it could go on for ever, pressing, pushing and the surging forces juddering through her body. Then, without warning, in a single moment of sheer and utter, total, abandoned emotional turbulence, in that momentary pause, that little eternity before the world crashes down, that tiny suspended hesitation, Miranda realized that the train had stopped. She, they, had come to Paddington Station.

Flustered and frustrated beyond enduring, Miranda felt her heart thumping to catch her breath, which mingled in the sort of gulp that only the Wile E. Coyote makes as he pauses to take in the bottomless canyon he is about to fall into.

The station slid aside and the tube doors opened. Miranda's body, still not sure of where it was, not responding to anything but the confusing impulses of her desires, almost collapsed as the pressure of the crowd released their hold. For the second time that day Miranda was pulled, by a man she didn't know, onto the platform of Paddington Station. As she stepped from the train, still muffled in his coat, she also neatly alighted from her skirt, leaving it on the floor. Safe on the platform, Ferdinand released her to bend over to pick up the skirt from the carriage floor, before it was trampled by the shifting people, but Miranda started to wobble and looked like she might fall. He righted her again then tried for another dive. Now feet and shoes were trampling the piece of cloth and the doors hissed shut and he was left standing, supporting the skirtless Miranda. The spin in her head started to clear and she turned to look at the train pulling out of the station.

'My skirt,' she screamed after it, but like almost everything else in her life, it wasn't listening. 'Buggerfuck.' She stamped her foot.

Miranda looked about her and experienced the strangest feeling of *déjà vu*. Then she realized she had seen it all before; yet again she was back on exactly the same platform where Flirt had left her and, yet again, she was feeling the too familiar sensation of abandonment, this time by her own treacherous skirt. She was getting to loathe this place.

Miranda bristled with emotional energy but was not really sure which emotion was running through her. Frustration? Anger? Disappointment? Rejection? Or just that her life seemed to be going in hellish circles, reiterative cycles of disaster then hope then humiliation that would go on for ever. She decided on anger being the easiest to express and instantly found the nearest thing that she could take it out on: that smug, too good-looking by far, out of her league so nothing to lose, what sort of poncy name is that anyway, Ferdinand.

'You,' she exploded, poking at him with her finger, 'look what you've done.'

He backed away as the finger prodded and attempted a little laugh, intended to disarm but having completely the opposite effect.

'Oh ha ha. Funny, is it?' she spat. 'My skirt's gone and maybe you think I can wear your ha ha? Perhaps I'll go to work in a ha ha from now on, because right now that's all I've bloody got. Maybe the invisible bloody ha ha skirt will start a fashion. That'll thrill the catwalks. So fucking brief you can shove it up your arse.' Miranda couldn't really believe she was shouting this at him, but perhaps her life would be a lot less complex if people who obviously had no intention of really being a part of her life would just stay away from it.

'I was only trying . . .' Ferdinand tried.

'Oh, you big brave boy scout, were you trying to do your best? Did Mummy tell you to do that?'

Ferdinand sighed. 'Perhaps if you would just let me get on.'

'Oh, that's right, the moment there's any trouble you just back away, piss off, don't want to cope with it, can't face it like a, like a . . .' Miranda had wanted to say 'man' but realized that, in fact, not facing things was exactly like a man. '. . . woman,' she concluded, feeling a mixed sense of achievement and indignation. There, you see, the slightest wind and he would fall and be like all the others. She felt a perverse joy in snatching defeat from the jaws of victory. She might have had to push him to disappoint her, but that only went to prove her point. For a moment it felt like it was much better to be right than happy.

'Look, I have known you now,' he looked at his watch, 'for less than an hour, which means that we both still have a chance of ending the day fairly amiably, if we both agree to walk away now.'

'Fine.'

'Fine.'

They fell into a silence but neither of them moved, a sort of Paddington stationary.

'Well?' he said finally.

'Well?' she echoed proudly.

'My coat, please,' he held out his hand.

Miranda suddenly remembered that she was not only in his coat but, until she found an alternative covering, in his power. She was sure that a good feminist like Mercy would shed the coat immediately as if it were the chains of the male-dominated society, but Miranda really had taken all the humiliation she could bear and bare for the day. Now she would fight.

'I'll post it to you.'

'No, thank you. I'll have it now.'

'You're taking advantage of me.'

'If that's "taking advantage", God help the man who actually tried to befriend you.'

'As if I'd want one to,' Miranda lied.

'So God's already helped him.'

Miranda shrugged, turned around, and began to walk up the platform.

'Just please give me my coat back,' Ferdinand called.

'Lend it,' Miranda tried.

'Why on earth should I?'

'Because,' she spun round, 'you could do your sex a favour and show us chivalry isn't dead. You could do something a little gallant for a change. Show some honour.'

'But I don't want it honour, I want it off her.'

'Cheap,' Miranda muttered. He was clearly not going to give in. 'But cheerful,' she smiled and let the coat slip off her shoulders. Before it had reached her waist Ferdinand was looking uncomfortable.

'Hungry?'

Miranda stopped the coat's descent and shook her head. 'Cold.'

'Come to dinner.'

'What happened to ending the day amiably?'

'I think we probably could.'

Now this was surely a result. Dinner. Miranda tried to force herself to grimace but a grin kept wiping it away. 'Sorry,' she said, 'I'm not going anywhere dressed like this.'

'We'll get a cab, stop by my place, I'll find you something.'

Miranda regained the coat. 'Oh yeah, bit of skirt round your place!'

'If you don't want to come that's fine. Take the coat and post it back

132

to me. I'm just saying that I would like it if you were to come to dinner with me.'

'No, I really ought to go back and change.'

'Why change? Aren't you perfect already?'

Miranda glowered at him. How like a man to seemingly surrender and then take a cheap shot when your guard was down. How like a man to want the last word. She looked into his beautiful eyes and thought, how like a man.

'Come, let's get a cab.'

'Fine.'

Ferdinand bowed low, 'After you.'

Miranda started off. 'They all are,' she said proudly.

Ferdinand smiled softly, clicked his heels and nodded. 'Sim Salabim,' he said.

The Christian Empire began its bid for expansion and global domination with an assault on the East. In an unmissable opportunity to grab more land and subjugate more peasants, Europe's kings, barons, lords and knights eagerly joined the cause to slaughter the infidel and reap their earthly rewards. Off they went crusading. But let us turn away from the usual *his*tory and concentrate on the *her*tory of what they left behind.

It is no coincidence that it was in this period that the chessboard lost two of its four kings and gained two queens, a reflection of the changing faces of power in Europe, and the mating game. For the first time ever, Europe was left with a predominantly female ruling class, almost a matriarchy of queens, influencing the rule of the relatively prosperous and peaceful Europe.

However, all was not stable in the great houses of the continent. Like many of the medieval nobility, a great number of these ladies suffered from in-breeding, consanguinity, and may well have had many of the psychological complaints which I have outlined, resulting from a long history of abasement, servitude, bondage, self-esteem damage and various identity crises.

It is quite possible, then, that many of these newly powerful ladies were rather unhinged, their screws somewhat loose and, eager to exploit these ladies of large wealth and dubious mental capacity, a breed of low-born draft-dodging gigolos began to appear at the courts. Poets. Since stories and song were the sanctioned legitimate entertainments for the ladies in the absence of their lords, these dashing but politely emasculated men could profit in the trade of story-telling, song-singing and generally pleasing these dotty young ladies. They called themselves troubadours.

Between the frustrated young wives and the eager young men, I believe, these courts and castles must have been incensed with the reek of pheromones. Sexual desire would have run through the corridors of power. But it was still a feudal system where legitimate birthline was all-important, and the absent lords were still feared. The sexual ardour that must have vibrated the very stones of these palaces needed subduing and sublimation.

What could these troubadours sing of? They could not speak of desire and sex and lust directly. They told a joke.

Now, I enjoy a good joke as much as anybody. I have asked why a great number of chickens crossed the road, I am forever answering a 'knock knock' despite being able to see exactly who it is, and I always smile at the one about the man who walked into a bar and said 'ouch'. However, I find it hard to explain why the courts and castles of Europe found themselves in the grip of a piece of basic irony which the ladies simply could not get enough of. I can only think it was an hysterical reaction to their years of yearning for freedom and then the sudden, shocking realization of this ambition.

This was the irony: think of something lower than low, the basest of creatures, now picture it being worshipped as a god. The great temples to the amoeba, that sort of thing, a simple surprise in the reversal of expectation. Good gag. So, slapping the thighs of their breeches and adjusting their codpieces, the troubadours celebrated these mad rich women, the ones who barely rated above worms in the order of things, in the language reserved for the worship and adoration of God. Imagine it. Women, those base creatures, 'loved', the objects of divine devotion and veneration. Women ruling men, who would go to any lengths to please them. It was a blinding bit of deconstruction, a huge joke, yet one they never tired of hearing. In some ways, I suppose, they still haven't. It reminds me of that joke about the woman who goes to the bar, asks for a double innuendo and the bartender gives her one.

So the young men sang of the ladies' situation: lords and gentlewomen who are parted and overcome adversity to be with each other because they adore each other like, or probably even better than, the Supreme Being. Or of troublesome threesomes like King Arthur, the lord too busy with affairs of state, Guinevere, the lady left in Camelot surrounded by young men, and the cuckolding Lancelot, the cheeky young man whose lance never tires. Wink wink.

Indeed, the King of France's own daughter, Marie de Champagne, was in such stitches over the sheer surreality of the notion, whilst her husband was far away cleaving heathens, she established an entire 'Court of Love', commissioning poems and even a book on the rules for loving. Her own personal contribution was rule number one: 'Being married does not exclude you from loving', complementing her famous adage that 'Marriage and Love are incompatible'.

PART II

I'M COMING APART IN YOUR HANDS. WE ALL HAVE PARTS THOUGH. PARTS of us and parts to play. Didn't Shaky say that there were seven ages to man? A book is a simpler thing, a beginning, a middle and an end. But now Miranda and the spy had met it was the end of the beginning and, in a way, the beginning of the end. From then on, no matter how i wanted to scream at her don't listen, don't go that way, she went, she could not hear, i could not speak.

i should have been a guide book.

As it is i'm in parts and, it seems, only you can put me together. Pathetic.

12

That Limbo of the Mind

SOMETIMES I IMAGINE, WHEN YOU HOLD ME, AND WE ARE HERE AGAIN, you and i, and everything beyond us fades into insignificance and we share this collusion of words and imagination, i imagine that the whole world might revolve around you. That you made it, it is yours.

In fact, if i was your common-or-garden Cartesian rationalist i would argue that anything outside your mind has no proof for its existence, it evokes none of your senses so it may not be, it might not exist at all. And in that case, the world is indeed yours.

However, being omniscient, i happen to know that the world does keep going despite anything you may do to stop it; it does not end when you die, it does not disappear when you are not looking in its particular direction. People are not just waiting in the wings for their cue to enter the stage of your particular five senses. Let me assure you that the tree which falls in the wood not only makes a sound but is also a sad indictment of global deforestation.

Of course, such are our egos that we can, at times, believe that the world is of our making. We can conceive that it might just go away when we're no longer thinking of it. And at this point in the story it was exactly one of those moments that Miranda was losing herself in. She turned to the ticket barrier with that muscle-bound, ludicrously-named twit Ferdinand Xavier behind her.

Sorry, i am trying my best not to judge him, bear with me, it's hard.

She turned to the ticket barrier and, in Miranda's blissful reverie, all her troubles, worries and friends disappeared from her consciousness. She was only aware of the moment and him. In this abstraction that consumed her, where her fantasy was becoming real, she forgot Trotsky and sanitary napkins and the Flirt and Barry and even Mercy. For a few rapturous hours she would consign everything to that limbo of the mind where things thought forgotten lurk. That dark prison of memories, where trivial facts jostle for space with the mentally quarantined regrets and remembrances of embarrassing and wished-forgotten humiliations. Those which are forced into a purgatory of neglect, those that await any moment of parallel similarity to leap out and fill the heart with shame.

So it was that Mercy did not actually disappear when Miranda banished her from her mind. She did not vanish or desist or shimmy beneath the descending limbo stick of Miranda's obliviousness. Completely unaware that she was challenging the very basis of rationalist theoretics, Mercy continued to live and breathe and be bitter about men. She persisted in her powdering and painting and thinking.

This is what she thought about: Miranda.

With pencil to eye, staring into the cloakroom mirror, Mercy couldn't help reflecting that they would normally be chatting away by this time, plotting the downfall of all the bastards. She started to really miss Miranda, her willing audience. In the peculiar silence, she absently drew her eyeliner across her lids in thickening strokes until she looked like a pandafied silent film star. For a moment she imagined she was Louise Brooks. She opened her eyes wide and bit the side of her hand just like the silent star did when some evil was descending on her, a man more often than not.

However, Mercy was beginning to realize that the biggest problem with having no one to talk to was the time it left for thinking.

Inevitably, thoughts without interruptions start to form in chains, ideas placed one after another with a sense that somewhere, at the end, is a conclusion. For Mercy they all led, inexorably, back to one thing, Miranda.

Mercy threaded her arms into her jacket.

What's with that ridiculous gesture men make when they hold your coat for you, as if you were an incapable child, and you invariably miss the armholes because you're not used to them being held.

Out of the staff-room.

It's probably to make you feel like you might be disabled because you're a woman.

Cross the half-lit Second Floor.

Isn't 'gallantry' just a set of signals suggesting the control men still want over women?

Down the stairs towards the staff exit.

But then, is there anything wrong with exploiting this false humility and taking advantage of these sham rituals?

Smile at cleaner, a woman of course.

Maybe men hold doors open and coats up because they're incapable of real, sincere giving actions.

Smile at security guard who holds door open into the street.

So it follows that you definitely can't trust 'gallant' men because it's all a lie, all show.

Glare at man approaching and staring at tits.

If it's a mock respect, it's a mockery.

Scowl at man still staring and look down at his fly, smiling cruelly.

You'll never be able to trust them.

Good, he's checking his fly and turning red, pass on.

But Miranda falls for all that gallantry guff.

Walk down to the tube.

She's just being exploited by the Shitty-Digit and the Flirt, men who think they know that all she wants is the usual romantic trappings.

Pout at bespectacled man in ticket machine queue.

She's obviously vulnerable now.

Wiggle a bit at the speccy man, probably a flasher, he's starting to sweat.

Anyway, Miranda might now be a bit more open to the truth about men.

Wink at him; there, his glasses are steaming up.

Her soul is willing but her flesh is weak. We'll sort it out tomorrow. I'll really apologize.

But as Mercy stood there waiting her turn, Miranda kept haunting her and when she finally got to the ticket machine, with its array of buttons, she wasn't altogether surprised to find herself pressing 'Goldhawk Road'.

Similarly unaware that he was challenging the very basis of egocentric philosophy, Peter Peersnide also failed to dematerialize just because Miranda had forgotten him. And, likewise, as per instruction, he had also taken the next train to Goldhawk Road, his assignment being the surveillance of the house where the Brown girl, now codenamed 'The Love Interest', lived.

After looking at the dilapidated house he stepped over the dosser asleep on the steps to check the bells. Then with little else to do until he received a call from Burnt, he sought out the nearest pub to wait in. The only choice seemed to be a garish Aussie-themed pub, where he settled down with a pint of the own brew humorously named 'Bruce's Old Peculiar Underpants' or somesuch.

Peersnide had harried and badgered Burnt to let him take part in the operational duties, but now just felt demeaned by the whole process. His instructions had been clear enough, but it was still galling to take them from a man at least two decades his junior.

It could have been him, he could have been a 'Burnt'. He could have been if he had gone to Cambridge and not Hull bloody Polytechnic, which he would have done if he had had a better interview with those smug don bastards, which he would have done if he hadn't failed his English A-level, which he would have done if he had got round to actually reading *Martin Shovelshit*, which he would have done if he hadn't been busy messing up Airfix models, which he wouldn't have done if his mum had been a bit tougher and insisted he do his home-work, which she would have done if his dad had been about, which he would have been if his mum hadn't nagged and had picked someone a bit brighter and a bit less drunk to marry. It's all their fault, he con-cluded, not for the first time, or even the twenty thousandth, after nearly forty years of avoiding culpability. As so often when he was left with his thoughts, his own chain led straight to his parents because there really couldn't be anybody else to blame for the failures of his life. He looked into the pool of bitter that had spread around his glass.

Now. Now he was getting somewhere. Burnt had shown him how to follow someone, and how to be noticed without being seen. How to mirror actions and then hide in a crowd. How to use the physical size of an unfolded newspaper to shepherd the subject into place. He had done it all brilliantly, if he thought so himself. It was just a bit of panic that had made him get into the carriage with 'The Love Interest'. I mean, what if Burnt had got on the wrong carriage and they had lost her? Of course, as soon as he saw Burnt he should have got off again but then the doors closed and they were all there. Then she recognized him and attacked him, silly bitch. Bent his frames. Probably knobbled his chances of more work. Another sip of the Old Underpants. He was a bitter drinker with real ailments.

To say that Barry also had an independent existence might suggest an autonomy which he simply did not possess. However, if he had depended on other people to think about him in order to exist then he would not have been at all. Not even his mum or dad had thought of him until months after their liaison in the back of a Ford Prefect when a bout of vomiting had driven his mother to the doctor, which just goes to show how much you can conceive without thinking.

Barry had been caught in the staff cloakroom on his own and shame sent him to hide in the staff showers the moment he had heard Mercy come in. He kept on meaning to come out but could never find quite the right moment, so he had huddled there waiting for the girls to leave. Of course, he should have winged it and pushed through brassily but without other blokes as an audience he wasn't quite so sure about doing anything brash. He stood and listened to them and decided he hated them. In fact he hated girls. He thought about school when it was all right to hate girls and realized that was probably the last time he had felt sorted and happy about them.

Barry decided that he needed a drink.

'Oswald!' shouted Mrs Scrufstayn from the kitchen as he stood at the door, all Pinner behind him. Mr Scrufstayn found himself wishing that he was just the figment of someone's imagination and hoping that they might stop thinking about him for the next few hours. He could just cease to be.

'It's Thursday,' came Mrs Scrufstayn's voice as he hung up his hat and wondered why no one wears hats nowadays. 'Thursday Night Surprise,' Mrs Scrufstayn cooed. It had been a long time since the Thursday Night Surprise was actually a surprise. Maybe it's because everybody gets expensive haircuts nowadays, they couldn't show them off if they wore hats.

'I'm in the kitchen,' the voice pierced his thoughts a little more urgently. Of course she was in the kitchen, she had been in the kitchen every Thursday for the last twenty years. But think of all that body heat you lose without a hat, no wonder there are so many people catching colds in the winter.

'I'm washing up, in the kitchen,' came the eager cry. Mr Scrufstayn could remember the Thursday night that he got back from work in 1972, in fact he willed himself to remember it. Mrs Scrufstayn had just read in the first issue of *Cosmopolis* an article entitled 'How to Keep Your Man'. It told her that she should liberate herself sexually by dressing up and, with her husband, indulging their fantasies. How could she know that the following issue would contain an article entitled 'Get a Better Man', or that the one after that would include 'Who

Needs Men Anyway', or even imagine that these three articles would be published in rotation for the next twenty years. By way of a bargain, Mrs Scrufstayn saw to what she called his 'idiosyncrasies', dog collars and such, on Sunday nights. However, fulfilling his Thursday night duties never failed to fill Mr Scrufstayn with dread.

Mr Scrufstayn inched down the hall. Of course, there are all those baseball caps, but you couldn't really wear them formally. That Thursday in 1972 he had been greeted in the kitchen by Mrs Scrufstayn's bright young buttocks, polished and glistening, wiggling just beneath the hem of the tiny skirt of a shiny black French Maid outfit as she bent over the washing up. Her legs stretched down into a pair of black stilettos and the sight of those smooth firm buttocks, tightly bouncing up and down as she scrubbed at a casserole dish with a Brillo-Pad, caused such a rush of sexual adrenaline in him that he even surprised Mrs Scrufstayn, who had been working up a lather since she put the costume on that afternoon.

Twenty years of repetition can, somewhat, take the edge off a surprise. Twenty years of pasta and piles, Sunday roasts and babies, scabies and cellulite, and a costume let out fifteen times, a patchwork of different blacks, all left Mr Scrufstayn with a creeping feeling of horror on Thursday's homeward journey. Even as he passed the stair cupboard he felt quite limp at the prospect of those now swaying, translucent, pockmarked, varicosed twin hams swinging wide in time with the washing up. As he sighed and pushed open the kitchen door Mr Scrufstayn felt surprised that bobble hats were only really worn when it snowed.

Even me. In that moment Miranda had even forgotten me. And i didn't disappear either. i don't know if that was the first time that i vacated her mind, but it was the time that hurt the most because it was just to indulge the increasingly creepy Ferdinand. i had to be jostled about in her bag and listen to the two of them get disgustingly familiar.

The taxi stopped outside his flat in Bayswater and Ferdinand coolly assuaged any fears Miranda might have had about entering a stranger's bachelor pad by telling the driver to wait for them. That was him, not me, who called it 'bachelor pad', when he ushered her in. Retro; corny or what? I think it really says something about him. 'Welcome,' he said, 'to my bachelor pad.' And i squirmed at the oily smoothness of the man, or should i be saying 'the cat'. Perhaps it would have seemed more sincere if he had been wearing a black polo-neck, corduroy drainpipes, smoking a crumpled Gitanes, and broke into beatnik poetry to complete the picture.

But the place looked neither a 'pad' in any sense a hippie might understand nor 'bachelor' in any sense a single male living on his own might understand. Where were the beads, the pop posters, the take-away boxes strewn about the floor? Where were the festering, hardened slices of pizza, the washing up piled high with mugs containing strange brews of tea bags and fag butts? Where were the 'lads' mags' and strange clumps of Kleenex grazing on the cigarette burn-hole sofa?

This was a *Twilight Zone* 'bachelor pad', a spooky other-dimension flat that you only see in films. Apartments which say this is the abode of a rich male without, in any way, saying who the male is. Awash in the full spectrum of monochromes, this was the flat Henry Ford furnished, any colour, as long as it's black. A hundred different textures of blacks, some pastel greys, and lots of glass and chrome. Stern battleship grey-sponged walls were dotted with non-committal architectural drawings of perspectives distant in time, space, colour and meaning. Spotlessly tidy, the one sign of life, if it can be called that, was a copy of the *Financial Times* which sat pinkly on the corner of a glass coffee table, its crease ironed to razor sharpness. Bachelor pad it wasn't. Military Intelligence safe house, used for covert deals and debriefings, spruced by an unimaginative Secret Service interior decorator, it was. It's true, they exist, doesn't sound much of a job for the macho military man but they call themselves 'Camouflage Engineers' and try to forget that they were deemed too girlie to join the SAS. i don't think i'm threatening national security telling you.

Even Burnt seemed a little embarrassed by the perfection. 'Sorry about the mess,' he tried to say as ironically as possible.

Pathetic.

'Over-zealous cleaning lady,' he continued, but Miranda had been hushed into a disappointed awe. Everything in place, nothing looking like it had even been touched.

'Maybe you're over-paying her,' she said as she ran her finger over a black marble sideboard which was covered with dust in the same way Tahiti is covered in snow.

'Would you like a drink?' Ferdinand said, looking about to make sure he knew where the kitchen was.

'I think I should, you know, change. It's getting a bit hot in this coat.'

'Oh right, of course. My bedroom's over there,' he waved in a general direction, a sweep which took in at least three doors, 'just grab anything you want from the wardrobe.'

Miranda felt even more distress. If he would let her into his bedroom and wardrobe without a second thought, he obviously did not hang his skeletons there. He was obviously very careful about his secrets or, worse, didn't have any. How were they supposed to get on if she was the only one who felt she had a whole life to hide or apologize for? Curiously, he didn't stop her opening the cupboard door instead of the bedroom and being deluged in an avalanche of sporting wear, trainers and cricket boxes, which tumbled about her as if it was raining bats and togs.

She stumbled about them and tried to push them back into the cupboard. The only clutter in the entire room and she had made it. Ferdinand just laughed. 'Don't worry, don't worry, I'm sure the cleaning lady will take care of it.'

The bedroom provided as few clues as the living room. It was like that yawning emptiness of a hotel room. Not even a bedside book, let alone a Gideon Bible. The wardrobe was behind a huge sliding mirror and in it hung an array of twenty suits all arranged in monochromatic variegation from light grey to black. No skirts or dresses or anything to suggest that a woman had ever gazed into or interfered in this space. She felt a bit like an intruder on virgin territory, yet he was definitely a ladies' man, he had to be, this couldn't be right.

Maybe he was into transvestism, he must be expecting her to use one of his suits! But even that didn't seem too kinky, or secret, or weird, or whatever would have helpfully positioned him in her ever diminishing perspective of the opposite sex. She picked herself out a pin-stripe suit, and placed it on his neatly made bed. Grey duvet, grey pillows. She looked over at the door, just to check it was closed and he wasn't some peeper, then dropped the coat from her shoulders feeling a little rebellious thrill leaving it there in a messy lump. Sitting on the bed and kicking away her shoes, she pulled off her tights which now were more hole than tight. Then, putting the jacket on, she stood up in front of the cupboard mirror doors. The jacket was long and hung down to half way along her thighs. Wrapping a belt around her, it actually looked quite smart as a dress. She'd do without the trousers. She rolled up the arms to let the silk show in the turn-ups and slipped into her shoes again. After five minutes' patting and applying her make-up, repeating to herself over and over, 'You really don't look half as bad as you look,' she walked out into the living room.

'Ready,' she said and did a little curtsy.

'Fabulous,' said Ferdinand, but she couldn't be sure whether he meant how she looked or the fact that they could go at last.

As Mercy left the station and strutted towards Miranda's house, her body undulating like a testosterone homing beacon, she practised her 'sorry'. This was a word she had always found difficult to say without laughing. Mercy was not, by nature, an apologist. For her, it was a meaningless sound bleated by people to avoid offending or, at least, getting hit.

'Sorry,' she tried murmuring, but not seriously enough. She took a deep breath and held it as she passed the combustible fumes of the petrol station. The men who stood there poking their petrol tanks with spurting nozzles in their hands watched, open-mouthed, as the puffed-out chest floated by.

She waited at the Hammersmith Grove traffic lights, standing behind an old man with a shaking head and leaning on a Zimmer frame.

'Sorry,' she tried purring. Despite the almost constant flow of traffic banking and squealing around the corner into the Grove, the old man inched into the road and started crossing. This caused three cars to brake with squealing wheels. The old man continued inching his way regardless, shaking his head and singing to his Walkman, 'I believe n'mirror culls, sinsyah kaymalong yah sexy thang.'

'Sorry,' Mercy tried to bark at no one, but altogether too aggressively. She passed the hobbling pensioner and then sneered at the men sitting in the window of the mini-cab office.

'Sorry,' she tried to choke, but grimaced at the overacting. She passed the motorbike shop and nodded a salute of solidarity to the grease-covered women who ran it and were packing the bikes away. They stared at her blankly.

'Sorry,' she tried to sing, but it wasn't really noteworthy. She approached the steps of Miranda's house still unsure of how she was going to say it.

'Sorry,' she tried firmly, but a little too surely. She turned to go up the steps to the door and tripped over the legs of a man who was sitting there.

'Sorry, oh, God, sorry,' he said, scuttling out of the way as Mercy suddenly had to run to get her legs in front of her toppling torso and right her ever-precarious balance again. The man jumped up to try and help her but then finding that she possessed few neutral zones, parts that he could grab hold of without being accused of sexual assault, he stood there uselessly waving his arms. 'Sorry, sorry,' he said again, as if it might help, sounding genuinely contrite for the fact that his very existence had caused such distress.

For a second Mercy admired his ability to sound so sincere, and tried to memorize the tone and intonation. Then remembering that he was a man, she gave him a short 'hmmph' and strode up the stairs without really looking at him, to press Miranda's bell.

'She's not there,' said the man.

Mercy turned round to look at him.

In a time when a marriage was often little more than a land-sharing contract and dowries were negotiated, the fact that love and marriage didn't 'go together like a horse and carriage' was an accepted fact of life. Yet to many of the lords who returned from the fighting to find their once obedient wives now bent double in laughter, it must have seemed as if the lunatics had taken over the asylum. However, what would have been impossible to ignore was that the women, the ones they had feared too weak to be capable of repressing and quelling the revolting peasants when they left, had not with the sword but with a notion, an emotion, reigned supreme in their absence.

Historians have called this invention 'Courtly Love', considering it merely the source of a literary convention, the creation of a style of narrative with an ideal hero and heroine, the knight and the damsel. Although these figures were indeed the prototypes for our heroes through the ages, the swashbuckler and princess, the cowboy and cowgirl, the war-pilot and the land girl, consider how much we have taken the lessons these romantic archetypes teach to heart; their ambitions and morals are now ours.

It was always more than fiction, but ever convenient for the State powers to dismiss it as such. The proof of the influence of this new 'romance' lay with the peasants of the period. The poor leave few footsteps in the pages of history but, having no education, what was arch irony in court probably flew right over their heads. They took the notion to their hearts very seriously indeed. If it was good enough for gentry it was good enough for serf. A new fear had been born for them to live under. The fear of not being loved when being loved is life's purpose.

The French, I believe, still have some difficulty with the basics of irony. The English sense of the ironic, our ability to laugh at the unfairness of life, has protected us from revolution, republicanism and dirty-fingernailed philosophers raking in considerable education grants to chain-smoke filterless cigarettes in cafés and tell us that they don't really exist – who but the French would take them seriously?

But, in those days, we were all French in one way or another, dissipated subjects of Charlemagne's legacy, from the Angle-grinding Normans to the Moor-tifying Catalonians. A European Union gripped in a fragile balance of threat and counter-threat. The foot soldiers, the peasants, were obedient because they lived in fear. Here they found a new thing to fear, perhaps the most frightening thing ever. These princesses had discovered an idea as effective in controlling the masses as the fear of God: the fear of being unloved.

Of course this notion's logical conclusion was Christian heresy and those who allowed mortal love to have supremacy over God would be slaughtered within thirty years in the Church's Albigensian Crusade. However, they had started something that no one could stop: they had made love.

13

That Sort of Facetious Misreading

IT IS A TOO SELDOM REMARKED FACT THAT SELF-POSSESSION IS NINE tenths of the bore. The most tedious people seem to believe that appearing self-possessed is a licence to dominate any conversation that they can bully their way into. Perhaps, if this fact were a little more often remarked upon, those social tunnellers, who could bore to China, might shut up once in a while. But then, was there ever a bore who could hear anything but his own voice?

Anyway, maybe if Whoji Whoopsi, you know, Ferdinand Xavier, weren't such a blot on my story, perhaps if he hadn't effected the single most significant change in Miranda's life, then possibly, just maybe, i might not have seen him as such a bore. You never know, under different circumstances, i might even have liked him. Maybe, if it had been he who had pulled me from the library shelf of obscurity, i would have fallen in love with him instead. You never know. He was personable enough, nice looking, if a little too smooth for my tastes. Greasy finger-tips are murder on quality paper like this. However, that's not what happened. Whoji Whoopsi was a bore. And, like most bores, he seemed effortlessly self-possessed, as if everything he said was of the utmost importance and quite irrefutable in its sensation.

Still, despite a sense of misgiving similar in acuteness to sending the Pope a Condom-o-Gram, i did have omniscient access to Ferdinand Xavier's inner workings and now, it seems, might be a good time to reveal a secret about him . . .

Although, to my mind, 'never' might also present itself as a perfectly apt time too.

i mean, if i show you how he thought or grew or learnt or what made him tick you might begin to understand him. That just wouldn't do. i shared a library with enough self-help books to know that understanding is one of those appalling steps towards appreciation and even forgiveness. How can i even think of forgiving the bastard who stole Miranda away from me?

Still, this is about you and me now. When you lose, you only have two choices: bitterness or acceptance. Both take some swallowing, but in different ways. Somewhere along the line i know that i accepted what happened. i lost. i mean he was not essentially bad, he was trying to do the right thing. But then, aren't we all? Even psychopaths think that they're doing the right thing and have a notion of what is a wrong thing. It just doesn't happen to agree with anybody else's on the planet. Except the voices that is. Still, it is rather shameful if a comparison to a psychopath is the nicest thing one can think of somebody. But there it is. At least i declare my bias. So if i do not dip into his mind too often, you will know why.

Anyway, this was Ferdinand Xavier's secret: in reality he was about as self-possessed as an exorcism. Really. He went through life completely without a clue about who he was, or what he was doing, or why he was doing it. Whoopsi was characterless and he knew it. He was aware that all he was, was a wishy-washy amalgam of the more interesting people he had met in life. A little of a school friend, a bit of his tutors, a smidgen of his parents. What character he had was completely borrowed and, may i say in library terms, somewhat overdue.

Of course, normally books are full of giants, enormous personalities who overpower and sway and delight and entice and make us wish that life really contained people like that. Maybe it is a little too much to expect reality to live up to fiction, that a man in his late twenties should be fully formed as a character, but i'm only telling you this because i believe it reveals something rather insipid about Whoopsi's personality. And, i suppose, taps into a popular misconception that a man without strength of character is generally not to be trusted or relied upon in a tight corner. i suppose i want you to hate him like i hated him.

That said, the reality is that it was absolutely this sense of characterlessness which made Whoopsi a perfect candidate for the Secret Service. He was someone to whom lying came naturally, having little knowledge of what the truth might be; someone who had spent his life adopting different personae at will and, most importantly, someone who, under torture, would be at even more pains to reveal his true identity for the basic reason that he simply didn't know who he was. His success proved that if you really want to impress government personnel managers you cannot do yourself a greater favour than divest yourself of all character. Those truly devoid of personality, or individuality, are destined for great things in the civil service, either at MI5 or, more usually, Walthamstow Benefits Office. That is not to say that Xavier, or whatever his name was, when called upon to be a tall dark handsome stranger, couldn't pull it off with incredible aplomb.

So, however horrible, the truth is that this was the man who bowed as he held the massive glass door open for Miranda as she stepped into Quicklinose, the once fashionable but by then merely expensive Mayfair brasserie. Nobody really.

Not that Miranda noticed. She was a little preoccupied. Her mind was on other things. Rattling around her head was the big first-date dilemma, the big question, skip right to the end: Does he come in for coffee?

Bungee on a rope woven from Alan Clark's knicker elastic, parachute with nothing but a Pak-a-Brolly foldaway umbrella, but can there be a more terrifying experience than a first date? Is it not one of the most horrifying necessities of love in the West, the true coming-of-age ritual? Only the young, the naive and the desperate can face such ordeals. Only they do not notice the scarring to the soul. Only they have the constitution which can bear such a battering to the nerves. Even more than the job interview or the divorce, it is the ultimate test in contemporary life. A trial by liar.

Imagine, you, right now, having to go on a first date. Could you really face it? All that having to go through your life story. Telling, yet again, those stories told a thousand times, honed to impress, each time an embellishment laced to the tale until you are on a par with the gods. The fear of once more having to make the effort to look great and sound wonderful, to complete the make-up, the disguise which slips, along with the mutual respect, as the relationship progresses. To go through all that showing and telling and learning and compromising, and for what? To repeat the same mistakes again, the same rituals of misunderstanding. Call me cynical but i'm sure most couples stay together for decades longer than they should merely because they live in terror of having to go on a first date again.

Miranda, somewhat luckily, had been plunged into this first date, which saved her the pre-date nervousness, the traumas of what to wear, the agony of thinking of conversational gambits. But the question which was first and would be last was: Does he come in for coffee?

It seems to me that although it has been over twenty years since the Sex Discrimination Act, not only are most people still not very discriminating about who they have sex with, but there are also, still, numerous professions which carry an automatic presumption of gender. Doctors we suppose to be men, flight attendants women. Accountants are men, as are lawyers, bankers and wankers, whereas we presume telephone operators, nannies and go-go dancers to be women. If it's menial, caring, demeaning or just entails wobbling your bits about, we suppose it is a woman doing it. Women are still in service, men are still served.

And of all those occupations cursed with a gender, the most menial, caring and demeaning service must be the ritual administering of suppositories, catheters and bed-pans: a nurse. Maybe i am innately masculine because whereas i understand why so few men become nurses i find it hard to explain why so many women do. Why are so many willing to make themselves martyrs? Or is it that martyr is just a much nicer way of saying masochist? Anyway, for a verb which is so inextricably feminine, how come it is usually men who nurse pints?

Not, as even he would concede, the most manly of men, Peter Peersnide nursed his one pint for over an hour. He stared into the draining brown liquid and saw an ominous reflection of himself, his face occasionally blistered by the tiny bubbles which rose and burst onto the surface. His only comfort he found in reminding himself that he was a spy now and that was a man's job, a male-gendered occupation, and the women who did this kind of work didn't really Mata Hari.

The Bushwhacker slowly filled with drinkers as Peersnide pondered the cryptic legend on his glass and tried to work out the algebra of four χ's. Occasionally he would take his feet off the velvet-covered, squat ironwork stool beside his table and saunter to the door. From there he could peer around the corner and, framed by the iron plates of the railway bridge, see the 'Love Interest's' house. No lights in her room yet. And each time he returned to his seat, he would have to elbow through a denser crowd, spill a few more pints and abjectly apologize a few more times.

On returning from one of these important fact-finding missions to the pub door, Peter Peersnide found that a pint of lager had joined his own pint at the table. A quantity of it had already spilt about the glass, leaving it an island of reflections in a clear brown wood sea.

Sitting on the stool that he had been using for his feet was a young man of an apparently nervous disposition. He was furtively looking about to left and right as if expecting to see someone he might know at any moment, though failing to do so at each turn.

'D'ya mind?' said the youth as Peersnide sat. Peersnide stared. The boy gestured towards his groin and Peersnide let his gaze follow, perpendicularly, to the bulging jeans before immediately looking up again. 'Me taking this seat?' continued the boy.

Peersnide's bookish, insular instinct practically impelled him to snap 'yes', but he stopped himself, remembering the importance of not causing a scene, or drawing attention to himself. He waved as nonchalantly as he could at the chair, wafting his hand with a supremely limp wrist.

'Go ahead, I was merely using it as a pouffe.'

The youth jumped up as if stung and looked back down at the chair as if it might carry some visible infection. He looked cautiously back at Peersnide. 'Each to his own, I suppose.'

'A pouffe is a French word for a low stool on which one rests one's feet.'

'Yeah right,' said the youth cautiously, sitting down as Peersnide marvelled at the callowness and innocence. 'Not that I've got anything against them,' continued the boy. Peersnide tried to studiously ignore this gambit to conversation, hoping that the boy might take the loudly silent hint that he did not want to engage in any.

'Poofs,' the boy plodded on. Peersnide found himself wishing that he had a newspaper, or book, to hide in. 'You're not one, are you?' the boy continued baldly. But it was far from clear whether this was a statement or a question and at last he had said something that Peersnide believed both far too pertinent and impertinent to be ignored.

'Not at all,' he spat back at the boy, a glistening arc of spittle stretching from his lips and descending into the boy's glass.

'Course you're not.' The boy carried on regardless, lifting his glass, 'You're not dressed well enough, are you. I once knew a bloke who . . . He was all right. You know. I mean, he never tried it on or nothing.' He took a long sip and smacked his lips with satisfaction. 'But, you know what I don't get? It's the birds who do that. You know. Some blokes love that stuff but I think it's disgusting.' The boy was clearly not going to shut up and, knowing how bigotry has no end, Peersnide decided to make it clear that they did not speak the same language and that the boy's breath was wasted on him.

'My dear boy,' Peersnide began, as all good patronizers must, 'those who have been touched by Sappho's inspiration have within them delights we can never know. Those mountaineers of the mound of Venus, those friends of Virginia, that sorority of Sabines, those who languish in, how shall we say, labial love, those digitally stimulated proprietors of the memberless club, those . . .' Peersnide searched again for *bons mots* worthy of his vocabulary. Peering back at the Australian beer logo, he suddenly solved the algebra, 'those chromosomed to give a four X. They. They,' he continued, 'they experience, possibly, ecstasies that we descendants of Adam can only guess at. Joys of an earthly garden paradise that only Aphrodite could bestow. It is perhaps unwise to curse the things we cannot know, for, as Plato said, the only thing that the wise man knows is that he does not know. So what senses are beyond us, buried in the soft flesh and deep warmth of the other sex, what rapture graces the female flesh, what nervous sensations are provoked, what, I imagine, happinesses the seedless intercourse sustains, we will never know.'

There. The boy was silenced. He sat with his gob firmly smacked for the completion of the one entire mouthful of bitter that Peersnide brought to his triumphant lips.

'Still,' said the boy finally, 'it's unnatural innit.' Then, sticking his hand down the back of his trousers, he gave the cleft of his buttocks an almighty scratch.

Of course it was Barry, old Shitty-Digit himself. But the collusion of coincidences just cannot be avoided sometimes. Although, again, I contest that this meeting was not as unlikely as it first seems, considering that pubs are usually where people meet or go to with others, but that both these men had a reason to be drinking alone. And a spare seat in a crowded pub is a rare enough thing. The fact is that Barry and Peersnide met and this was the beginning of a very strange, if not beautiful, relationship.

'She's not there,' said the man.

Mercy turned round to look at him, uncomfortable about talking to someone who, only a moment before, had been asleep on the door-step. 'Sorry?' she said. Not an apology as such, just a request to repeat something that she did not expect to hear. Actually, if i look into Mercy's thought processes when she uttered this word, the chaotic scramble reveals that she said this merely to stall for time and find something more appropriate to say as he was repeating himself.

'She's not there,' said the man. 'Miranda.'

'And you're a . . .' Mercy hesitated to use the next word because in all her experience she knew that one of his gender could never be such a thing, 'a friend of hers?'

'Yes, well no, well sort of.'

Mercy nodded knowingly. 'So she's expecting you.'

'No, not really. I mean, I only met her today. I was just waiting for her to come back.' Mercy looked suspiciously at the step that he had been sleeping on. 'Oh,' the man failed to laugh, 'I had a bit of an accident today, concussed myself, actually.' He pointed to a large bandage which was wrapped around his head. 'I keep fainting and falling asleep. I wasn't sure when she was coming back.'

'You do realize that there are stalking laws nowadays.'

'No, no, it's just, well, I needed to see her. Tell her something.'

A silence followed. As silent as a hundred and seventy-two combustion engines each igniting over three thousand petrol gas explosions every minute as they idle in the Goldhawk Road rush hour can be. Which isn't very.

'So where did you meet her?' said Mercy.

'Are you a friend of hers?'

'A closer one, I'd think, than you,' said Mercy tartly. 'Where did you say you met her?'

'You'll laugh,' said the man, still unable to make a laugh sound anything close to genuine, 'but we only met on the tube this morning.'

Mercy's face, at last, brightened as she realized just who this was. This was the bastard who had made Miranda so miserable all day. Tosser. Men. Now, wouldn't this be a wonderful present for Miranda? This insolent idiot on a plate. This would make up for the row. This would say sorry louder than words. Why send flowers when you could reduce the victimizer to an emotional pulp?

'You expecting her back?' he asked brightly.

'I don't know,' said Mercy and she sighed heavily, heaving her vast bust so dramatically she could have been nominated for a golden globes award. 'We had an argument today and I'm . . .' she choked and looked down, biting her lip and making her cleavage vibrate with a slight tremor that added gravitas to her voice. 'Sorry, sorry, I'm just a bit . . .' Mercy's voice crackled as if each word were broken by tears, 'a bit vulnerable at the moment,' she gushed.

As subtly as Carmen Miranda unsheathing her banana, Mercy grasped the husk of the popular unconscious and instantly stripped it down to the most delicate part of the male psyche. With that one sobbed word, 'vulnerable', she tapped directly into an ancient cortex of male paternal feeling. It is a key word aimed at motivating an automatic response from the hardest of men. In Mercy's practised mouth the word whipped choice or free-will from the male vocabulary, and proved yet again that men have such simple genetic programs they are little better than automatons, and far more useless in most ways. Or, as Mercy saw it, men'll take advantage of any situation and there's no easier target than a vulnerable woman.

Whereas most women might take months perfecting a vulnerable persona in pursuit of a man, Mercy simply, plainly, baldly stated it, and still it worked.

'I think you need a drink,' Flirt said. 'There's a pub over there.' He pointed to the Bushwhacker, its leaded windows glittering with the beckoning glow of flashing fruit-machines.

'I'll just leave a note for Randa,' Mercy said, rummaging in her bag for some paper.

'Here,' Flirt held out a pen for her and she could see the eagerness in his eyes. Like a lamb to the slaughter, she thought, only not half as cuddly.

Down the aisle of suited backs and fat collars, the cigarette girl's white pleated tennis skirt swayed and splayed with the surging of her hips and wiped the sweat from the necks of the porcine diners worshipping at their napkin-strewn, stained-pinewood troughs. Her high-tar tray bounced from her hips in the shade of her gelatinous embonpoint as its straps strained down from her neck and around her curves.

'Smokes,' she squeaked to the indifferent backs in a faux American accent.

Following the progression of her pivoting buttocks strode the Quicklinose Greeter'n'Seater, his serious black uniform swallowing light in its gravity. A man with the ghastly facial scarring of a smile, a grin as genuine as a signed Picassaux.

Behind him, Miranda and Whoopsi followed to their table. Miranda stumbled wide-eyed in the bright light of affluence, blinking as she gazed about the brushed-steel and polished-glass hall. The high ceiling echoed with fork-struck plates and the hum of accents tutored in schools where boys were men, growing up was urgent and buttocks were hard pressed. The far wall was taken up with an array of fresh fruits and vegetables. The mirrors angled behind it made the whole ensemble look like an enormous fruit and veg display shelf, an altar to the supermarket barons who, no doubt, entertained there.

'Your table,' sneered the Greeter'n'Seater. He pulled out a chair and bowed mutely to Miranda. 'Would madam prefer the power seat?' he spat, with all the scorn his vocation demanded, for restaurants like Quicklinose are judged by the volume of contempt they can cook up with every meal. Derision and disdain multiply with every star in the guide book, as they absorb expense accounts like scornful sponges. This was an ideal place for Whoopsi to bring a young, impressionable girl. Not fashionable enough to bump into anybody that he might know, but one whose menu featured ostentation just above the oysters and where the prices were printed bold.

Miranda, however, needed no impressing. i could see it, Ferdinand could see it, the whole world could see it; she had gone quite gaga, her eyes were a glaze of rose-tintedness and her cheeks were flushed with that pride that comes before a falling in love.

The Greeter'n'Seater pushed the chair into the small of Miranda's knees and she sat down abruptly, her bottom hitting the wood with an all too audible slap. He then proceeded to wave her napkin open and flurry it to her lap. As he started to press it into her groin prestidigitally, Miranda snatched it from him. He grimaced smilingly and flounced away.

'Sorry,' she said, looking at Ferdinand, 'I'm not really very used to this sort of thing. The last time I was taken out for dinner it was a "Happy Meal".'

Ferdinand smiled, somewhat indulgently even for a smug git, but said nothing. Miranda got the uneasy feeling that she ought to be filling the silence.

'Do you,' she asked somewhat hesitantly, 'do you know what a "Happy Meal" is?'

Ferdinand nodded enthusiastically and then, when he realized Miranda wasn't buying it, slowly started to shake his head. 'Is it a meal that makes you happy?'

'No,' she said, 'I think maybe it's meant to be ironic.'

'It sounds rather nice, a happy meal,' he said, 'like it might enjoy being eaten.'

'Only because you'd be putting it out of its misery,' said Miranda.

'And who can bear melancholy food? There is nothing worse than a depressed pork pie, and personally I find it difficult to eat sausages when they're grieving. Consider the anxiety of an asparagus and the loneliness of the long-distance runner bean . . .'

It was weak but he was trying. Miranda stopped listening and thought, why? What am I to you? We've barely met, and yet you're just so keen? If only she could get him to put the flirting away for a moment. She had got the message, he was witty, he was educated and had appalling taste in interior design, but couldn't he, just for a moment, give her a glimpse of the real man?

'Are you listening to a word I say?'

Miranda nodded, not once losing contact with those gorgeous green eyes. 'Absolutely,' she lied, and for a fraction of a second wondered what it was that he had just said.

She leant her head slightly. 'Ferdinand,' she said and in hearing her own voice saying his name immediately felt that fulfilling warmth of having just done something you've been dying to do but hadn't dared let yourself. Miranda had never tasted his name on her lips before, she had never let the sound curl around her mouth. It tasted sweet. 'I'm only going to ask you the one time, but there is something I really have to know.'

'Just ask,' said Ferdinand, as openly as a novice's legs.

Miranda sensed the bristles. 'I just want you to be straight with me.'

'Right,' Ferdinand said and cleared his throat, clasped his hands together on the table and furrowed his brow in a serious way. 'What is it?'

'Just for a moment,' Miranda continued, showing her palms, 'let's take off the masks. Let's put the laughs down on the table with the rolls and you tell me one thing, man to woman.'

'Of course. What do you want to know?' Ferdinand said without even a glimmer of a smile.

'I,' Miranda said very slowly, now looking down at her finger drawing circles on the table, 'just want to know what...' The right emphasis was all-important. What should she say? She racked her mental thesaurus for the appropriate, succinct, concise, clear, powerful phrase which would place the ball firmly in his court ... that demanded an honest reply. Unfortunately, due to the fact that eight years earlier Gorgeous Ben had sat next to her during English and rendered concentration nigh impossible, all she could come up with was, 'What the fuck you think you're doing?'

Ferdinand's stare faded into blankness.

'Come on,' she said and then slowly, 'just tell me what you think you are doing.'

Ferdinand sat and thought. Which was possibly the worst thing he could do at this moment, because the longer you sit and think about a question like that, the harder it is to make any answer seem spontaneous and genuine. 'I presume,' he stumbled, 'you don't want an "ordering a meal, looking at a beautiful woman, sitting in a restaurant" type of answer.'

Miranda shook her head to indicate that that sort of facetious misreading of the question was a very bad avenue to go down indeed.

'Which means,' Ferdinand continued, 'I'm a bit puzzled as to what you do want to . . .'

'Jesus. I'm not speaking a foreign language. Just tell me what you think you are doing. With me. Here.'

'Why shouldn't I be?'

'Why shouldn't you be?' Miranda's voice began to rise. 'Why shouldn't you be? Because you're some gilt-edged City fat cat and I'm a shopgirl. Your labels say Armani and mine say Army & Navy. You deal in stocks and bonds and I demonstrate sanitary towels. You talk plummy and I talk like a plumber.'

This, to Ferdinand, seemed a good time to appear genuine and he artfully changed his tone so completely it was as if he was indeed removing a mask, the veneer was truly being stripped. 'OK, if you want to know. Yes. All right? Yes, I've got it all. Yes. Everything I could want. The money. The cars. The wine and, if I wanted them, the women and their bloody songs. And it's exactly because I've got it that I'm here with you. It's all hype, it's all air, wind. Nothing tangible. Nothing genuine. Nothing real.' Ferdinand drew a deep dramatic breath and let it out slowly.

'And I'm real? Is that it?'

'More real than anyone I have ever met. You are not afraid of me, or your opinions. You talk back. You give as good as you get.'

Miranda could barely stop herself imagining that she was in some nineteenth-century novel, locked in lace, with the hero telling her that he admired her spunk. Only such a phrase nowadays might appear a little inappropriate. How the language changes. But why, in this moment when all her dreams, her fictions, were becoming real, why did Miranda compare herself to the baseless fantasy of a novel?

This is it. This is what made her so lovely to me: Miranda, you see, was made in books. Just like me. They informed her, guided her, held her, enraged and calmed her. To her, somehow the printed word embodied truth and the truths books told could be held to be self-evident. Miranda, like so many brought up in the last breaths of the twentieth century, when media began to surpass the reality it was supposed to be a medium to, was rather hazy on the difference between the actual and the fictional. Life in books and newspapers, on TV and in the cinema, just seemed that much more colourful, that much more worth living. Like so many of her generation, she made the journey from naivety to cynicism without any of the effort involved in having to go through actual experience. Which was just fine by me. But, in that overrated 'real world' that she lived in, she had no tangible touchstones on which to base her credulity. She only had Mercy's stories and her novels.

And this tosh issuing from Ferdinand's mouth, about the insubstantial trappings of wealth, was exactly what her dashing hero was meant to say. In the books. He always did in one way or another. Wealth and riches were nothing to the prosperous lord who realized that he had pursued them falsely, unaware that true happiness was, in fact, a sunset and your girl to ride into it on. Or something like that. He had it all, but now the only thing which could save his soul was the love of a good woman. Someone who would bring honesty back into his life. Real values. Because money is nothing in comparison to the true treasure of love. Well, that was the line the books always took. And they were impartial, weren't they? Stay true and Mr Right will come. Prince Charming will turn up. They had really been true all this time. No matter what Mercy said, it was true that you could read books and find the truth about life within them. But was it really this easy all along? If you kept the faith and remained demure, could you really just wait for Mr Right to fall into your lap?

Yes. Yes. Yes.

But instead of immediate elation, just for a moment, Miranda felt rather a pang of loss. She experienced a minute of mourning, for that cynical world of Mercy's which she had often considered joining. As if that whole mister-ogynistic universe of Mercy's would have to be realigned now. And how can you have change without pain? Miranda almost winced as that planet of hate transformed before her. Love, after all that, was not the unkind leading the blind. Not some cruel trick played on the unsuspecting. A bad joke. It could happen. Seriously. She nodded earnestly back at Ferdinand as a whole grave new world opened up before her eyes.

Then, looking into those green eyes of his, Miranda wondered yet again: Does he come in for coffee?

O, i could carry on. Report each word verbatim. It was their first date and i suppose that makes it important. But who really remembers exactly what they said on a first date?

In fact, who would want to?

Now, later. Without the actual hum or the wine or, indeed, the food, a dinner becomes far less amusing. What might have seemed witty at the moment, in the cold light of day, in the black and white of my pages, would probably seem weak and cringe-worthy. Sometimes it is better to leave the past in a haze of nostalgic hindsight. Miranda was hardly at her most shining, nor prepared to give herself a reality check. All she could see was the answer to her every dream, this tall, dark, handsome and getting less stranger by the minute. The knight in shining armour, the man she would, well, The man. You know. Mr Write. Prints charming.

For that evening she would surrender to the fantasy. No more questions as to why her, why him, why now. Finally here was the man of her plan, this was how it was supposed to be. Here was 'the catch'.

As Mercy walked into the Bushwhacker, every man's head turned. Tongues lolled and clicked, salivary glands began to rain, low whistles blew through teeth, the odd 'va va voom' was uttered and each woman who turned to look thought: tart.

Mercy swum blissfully through this sea of eyes, splashing past the odd boy that bobbed in her way. As if doing the slow crawl, her shoulders swung rhythmically, each one parting a new wave of men as they faltered in their breast stroke.

'There she is,' said Barry, 'prime example.'

Peersnide nodded without really comprehending. His own gaze had slipped to the man who followed this vision into the pub, the shadow that skittered along in her wake. He recognized him from somewhere, he knew he did, he just couldn't place him. It wasn't as if he encountered a huge number of new faces in his job. He rarely looked up from his books to see whom he was dealing with. Who was this man? The large bandage wrapped around his forehead didn't aid identification, especially as Peersnide was used to judging people by how low or highbrow they were.

'She knows exactly what she's doing, she swings those things at every bloke and then Wham Bam No Thank You Man.'

Today. It was today he had seen him. But so much had happened today, so much excitement in comparison to his usual workaday life. Peersnide had yet to organize his experiences, file the memories in the correct synapses, a million of his neurofibrils were waiting to be charged with new information but at that point, sitting looking at Flirt over the top of his glass of bitter, Peersnide could not for the life of him place him.

'. . . sex on a fucking stick.'

Although Peersnide had stopped listening he realized that Barry couldn't have droned on so long about someone he knew nothing about. 'You know her?' he asked casually.

'Bird at work.'

'Do you know the man she's with?'

'Yeah, a sucker.'

'Pardon me?'

'She's just a prick-teaser. He's got more chance of walking on the moon than copping off with her.' Barry paused and appeared to scrutinize Mercy as if he were taking a mental snapshot for his own private use later. Which, come to think of it, he probably was. 'Still,' he continued, 'she looks fucking fantastic and it's all bloody wasted on muff-munching Miranda.'

The mention of that name sent a little buzz through Peersnide's head. 'Miranda? Did you say Miranda?' How many of those can crop up in one day?

'Yeah. Her bird. At work.'

Peersnide looked bewildered.

'Couple of clam knoshers.'

'Is this a Miranda who, er, lives locally?'

'Just down the road.' Barry gestured over his shoulder. 'You know her?'

'And you know this Miranda, do you?'

'Yeah,' Barry winked, 'biblically an' all.' Not that Barry was an avid reader of the good news but he had heard the phrase used on telly and thought it sounded kind of *Pulp Fiction*. Now, at last, Barry had Peersnide's undivided attention.

'Really? Are you her boyfriend?'

Barry shook his head.

'Her lover?'

'No. Just having a day out. Plays for the other side. Know what I mean.'

Peersnide did not know what he meant. 'She's a sportsperson of some sort?'

Barry's eyes went to the ceiling. 'No, she's one of those.' He tried, helpfully, to gesticulate by making circles with the thumb and forefinger of each hand and then knocking them together.

Peersnide watched the colliding rings but was perplexed.

'Like what you were going on about. Sappho's instigation . . . you know.'

And it did indeed dawn on Peersnide exactly what he was driving at.

'So, they are lovers?'

'And a half, should've seen the tiff they had this morning.'

'But still she, Miranda, and you . . .'

'Yeah. Shows commitment, don't it.'

Peersnide couldn't believe his luck. First day on the job and already he had fallen into the company of a youth who knew 'The Love Interest'. Not only that but had had intercourse with her. Now there was priceless information for Madder. But then he started to piece things together: if she had already copulated with this youth whilst maintaining some perverse own-gender relationship, hadn't she, on the face of it, already rejected love, already fallen under the spell of that book. me.

If only . . .

So to Peersnide, as he looked at the boy, it appeared that Miranda had discarded along with any interest in love, or being in love, any belief in it or its redeeming power. The worst had happened for, although this boy had a certain charm, he was in no sense of the word a romantic figure. Peersnide rubbed his hands with an unconscious glee, not realizing that if 'The Love Interest' had fallen out of love's spell, and if that was because of reading the book, then, to 'The Office', she was dangerous. She could tell others. She could be the spark that lights the fire of conspiracy and revolution. When 'The Office' heard about this there could only be one conclusion: she would have to be eliminated.

CHAPTER V.

STARRY STARRY FRIGHT

Fear no more the heat o'th' sun,
Nor the furious winter's rages,
Thou thy worldly task has done,
Home art gone and ta'en thy wages.
Golden lads and girls all must,
As chimney-sweepers, come to dust.

Fear no more the frown o'th' great,
Thou art past the tyrant's stroke,
Care no more to clothe and eat,
To thee the reed is as the oak:
The sceptre, learning, physic, must
All follow this and come to dust.

Fear no more the lightning-flash.
Nor th'all-dreaded thunder-stone.
Fear not slander, censure rash.
Thou hast finish'd joy and moan.
All lovers young, all lovers must
Consign to thee and come to dust.

William Shakespeare, from *Cymbeline*

NOBODY LOVES WITHOUT FEARING. FEAR IS AN INEXTRICABLE PART of the madness of love.

When I was a child, I was always terrified of the lights being turned out at bedtime. I had a cupboard in my room which would not close properly and in the perilous shadows cast by the pale moon, I could make out the silhouette of the mad axe-man who lived inside it. As I gripped my sheet, pulling it up to my nose, I peered wide-eyed into that darkness and could almost hear the sound of his axe being sharpened against screeching grindstone. I was convinced that, after I had fallen asleep, he would slip from the cupboard, his axe glinting in the moonlight. He would hold the axe high above me as I lay dreaming and with a maniacal laugh bring it plunging down, ripping deep into my soft young heart, bathing himself in the spray of my arteries, incensed by a wild blood frenzy.

Of course he never did. It was just a childish fantasy. He was actually a very nice man whose rent was very helpful during a tight time for my parents. He taught me a lot about nature and kept the cupboard very clean. In fact, I was very sorry when he had to go but my parents had thought it best. What with the accident with the Phillips twins, even though he did apologize and they still did have three functioning limbs left between them.

Since then the child has grown, I no longer fear the shadows or the dark. Now I, like all adults, believe I can find rational explanations for things so that, in understanding them, I am no longer scared of them. Nature, Society and Culture are no longer in a dim twilight for me, they are quantifiable in some way and, though I may not be able to control them, I can encapsulate them and feel content in my knowledge of the extent of their powers. I live in a world now full of explanations for everything.

In the oak-panelled old library at Scone College there stands, proudly, a Renaissance astrolabe, a bronze sphere of burnished golden equators describing the motions of the planets, the dance of the universe. It is a thing of exquisite beauty encapsulating not only the elegance of the cosmos, but also the pride of its maker believing that he, a mere mortal, had captured the very essence of the galaxies. The heavens trapped in the alloys of a man.

There I see an eternity in its never-ending circles and yet this jewel-like aetiological globe is a mausoleum, a sun-scratched harbinger of death. Along the polished brass rings of the globe are inscribed the names of the gods, evocative theonyms of a time now past when it was they who explained the world. These marks are not invocations to their powers but the sad engraved letters of the deities' tombstones. In a universe of 'gravity' and 'matter' there is no pantheon. The gods are long dead. Mount Olympus lies empty, the Athenian car-fume effluvium dines on the white marble of its temples. Cobweb-strewn, Valhalla crumbles into dust. It is those cold metal rings which now, as they have done for centuries, explain why the sun may be eclipsed and why I 'fear no more the lightning-flash, nor th'all-dreaded thunder-stone', why I don't have to be afraid that the gods are angry with me.

I, like all modern men, believe that I know why things happen. I can calculate the chances of being hit by lightning. I am heir to the fortunes left by Rationalism and Empiricism, a whole world of explanations built from the foundation stones of Cartesian thought and the elements of the Periodic Table.

14

Does He Come In for Coffee?

AFTER THE DINNER HAD COURSED AWAY AND THE PUDDING HAD deserted, after the chat had been put out *pour la nuit* and the chorus of voices and palates and plates had been wine-lulled into a distant hum; when the table was a battleground of coffee cups and napkins, when time was away and somewhere else, Ferdinand's hands slowly reached across the table to cup Miranda's. Still holding a coffee spoon, her fingers shivered as he touched them and tapped a staccato on the veneer.

'And do you,' he said, at last, in a slow, measured, half-drunk voice, 'do you believe in love at first sight?'

Now, this was just a little too perfect, this was exactly the right thing for him to say and do, in just the right place, just the right time, with just the right look. Right.

Miranda suddenly felt sick. She nodded vigorously; at least her brain did, which felt somewhat disorientating and not a little uncomfortable inside her completely paralysed, motionless head.

'Do you believe in love at first sight?' It was as if each word fitted with an exact click into Miranda's jigsaw 'How Life Should Be'. Though nauseous, she had read enough to know that there were many ways to respond to such a remark; most of them involved heaving your chest or sighing, some entailed throwing yourself across the table to suck the lips off the interlocutor, whilst others consisted mainly of blushing and saying, 'Why Mr Insert Name, I do declare.' None of the appropriate responses involved belching loudly, bringing up a little dinner sick and then, in trying to contain it in your mouth, squirting the foul-smelling, bilious liquid out of your nose and spraying the table with pale orange spatter. However, barely able to contain herself in her ecstasy, or believe her ears or any of the other senses which might have been functioning after six glasses of Chablis, this was precisely what Miranda did, delivering a force four cloudburst of acidic raindrops which appeared through a cloud of hissing steam as they were projected across the table.

Ferdinand flailed backwards in his chair, just managing to keep his suit clear of the worst of the storm. Could it be that that perfect smile faltered for a moment? Could it be that Secret Service training never prepared him for such an event? Miranda stuffed her napkin into her face to, ostensibly, wipe away any fallout but also to hide her warming cheeks before someone mistook her for a post-box and tried to insert a letter in her mouth. She considered whether, now that the chest heaving and blushing bits were over, she should make it a hat trick and try the lunge for his lips. Over the serviette she could see Ferdinand wiping his suit down; he looked up at her eyes and tried a furtive little laugh. There are few enough social rules nowadays but it is still recognized that when someone has done something acutely embarrassing it is their prerogative to laugh first or not at all, and a laugh by anyone else will always seem an 'at' laugh rather than a 'with'. Ferdinand laughed trying desperately to make it sound like a 'with', which only embarrassed Miranda more and demonstrates the poverty of social education at spy schools.

Ferdinand pulled himself back to the table, put his hand on hers, as if getting covered in nasal vomit was the most natural thing in the world, and said again, 'Do you? Do you believe in love at first sight?' This, I imagine, would scream 'phoney' at you or me or anybody with even a moderate sense of cynicism, but Miranda, unlike most of us, had not lost her gullibility with her virginity. Miranda had faith. She wanted to believe. Maybe what made Miranda so lovely was her complete lack of that bit which raises itself suspiciously above the parapet of credence with narrowed eyes shifting from side to side, the bit which would have told her to hang on, slow down. She had been mapping the regions of his face all night and even then, when it was flecked with orange droplets, she wanted it to work. All she could think was that a distancing cool might rescue her from her flushing embarrassment.

Miranda searched through her mind and blithely said, 'I don't know.' Her hand left his. 'Isn't it, more often, love at first night?'

*

There. Look. She quoted me. At least I think she did. Maybe it wasn't conscious, maybe something she read, something i said, just stuck in her mind. As subliminally as a catchphrase. Maybe she believed she was making it up, but it was as if, for that one moment, she had reached into my innards and breathed life into me, brought me out into the real world, the world of speech, of sounds. O the ecstasy of hearing my words on her lips. And yet, and yet, here she was saying them to another man as if they were her own.

Some ironies are hard to take.

'Really?' he said. 'You don't believe that you could cry over someone you have only just met? That you couldn't tear the stars from the sky and paint rainbows on the clouds for a familiar stranger?'

My God, my God, Miranda thought, he's practically making love to me. 'I,' Miranda gasped, 'just think love's a little overrated. I read something about it having all been made up to explain confusing sexual urges. That it's just a by-product of biology.'

Yes. Yes. i had said that, something like that, when she first opened me, that moment we first met. Look. It was still fresh in her mind. She had felt something. Stick that in your pipe, spyman.

Miranda shrugged and then, realizing that she had forgotten to blink for several minutes, scraped her lids across her stinging dry eyeballs.

Ferdinand leaned back and silently looked at her. It almost looked like regret.

Shit. My God. Have I gone too cool, too far? Miranda sighed and tried fluttering her eyelashes delicately. She attempted to make come-to-bed eyes, despite having realized some time ago that all she had, in fact, were fancy-a-snog-round-the-back-of-the-bus-depot eyes.

'You read that, did you?' Ferdinand said. 'Sounds quite an interesting theory. What was the book?'

'Oh, I don't know, I read so many.'

'Still, it would be nice to know.'

'I can't remember.'

'Try.'

'Look,' Miranda came back a little more fiercely than she had intended, 'I really can't remember.'

Ferdinand knew when to give something a rest and dropped the subject. He would get himself invited to her place and have a scout around for the book. me.

She hadn't meant to be snappy, it was just that so many emotions were bubbling up at the same time, was it any wonder that she felt giddy.

Ferdinand smiled, 'You look tired, shall we go?'

To Miranda as they stood up, they were giants, swollen with emotion, towering above the debris of the table. Ferdinand flipped open the green baize bill book with the nonchalance of a man who had been born to do just that one act and, asbestos-fingered, picked up his titanium plus credit card which had been glowing white hot there for the last half hour. His other hand swept into his breast pocket and pulled what can only be described, in true eighties parlance, as a 'wad' of taxpayers' unmarked notes from his pocket and deposited on the table the sort of tip which roughly equated to Miranda's weekly pay cheque. And, as if it were all the same gesture, he bowed slightly as he always seemed to and signalled that she should lead the way out. It was all so gloriously choreographed that our more sceptical minds might have been suspicious, might have asked where the catch was, asked what the small print said, pointed out that there's no such thing as a free lunch let alone a four-course meal at Quicklinose. But to Miranda, the desire for it to be true eclipsed any notion of reality that might have entered her head. In fact, as the end of the meal ushered in the prospect of the beginning of something else, Miranda had only one thing on her mind, the question that had lurked all evening: Does he come in for coffee?

Two men were sitting at a table which had been artfully themed with a fringe of corks hanging from strings. Mercy smiled at them. 'Sorry,' she said in a voice dripping seduction more nakedly than Bathsheba, 'do you mind if I just sit down here?' The two men looked from side to side to see if there were any spare seats, which there weren't, and looked back to her as she blinked slowly and pouted moistly at them. Then, in an instant, both of them stumbled maniacally off their stools in their hurry to offer them to her. Mercy smiled at the sweating men as she sat on one seat, put her bag on the other, then turned to Flirt and said, 'Mine's a gin and tonic.'

Flirt pushed to the bar. There, a group of men in clothes so casual even their turn-ups hadn't bothered to, looked enviously at him. One of them, leaning against the bar, leered at him. 'Feel sorry for you, did she, mate?' gesturing at Flirt's bandage with his glass. Some beer sloshed out and dripped on his shoes. Flirt ordered the drinks but the man kept chiding. 'Works with charity cases, does she, mate? Helps the handicapped?' he laughed, turning back to his mates.

'Yes,' replied Flirt, drinks in hand, 'I'll tell her there's a retard at the bar if you like.'

Now this wasn't particularly witty but it does sound like fighting talk, and you may think that to come back like that shows that Flirt was rather butch, foolhardy or quite probably both. i assure you, he wasn't. However, there are clearly defined rules to bar-room aggression, and whilst it is important sometimes to show respect for the most barely anthropoid of antagonists who may pick on you to show off to his mates, a witty riposte, neatly timed, will often dispel a 'situation'. This is how it works: following such a remark the primate is forced to consider, even if momentarily, whether by then hitting you he will show himself up as a bad sport, unable to laugh at himself or at the very least totally inarticulate. This in turn, theoretically, buys enough breathing space for you to, in the most insouciant way possible, run like hell. So it was this, combined with the fact that the man leaning on the bar was obviously doing so because he was too drunk to support his own weight, and that the said bar was in fact the brass one, four inches from the ground and intended for the less vertically challenged customers to put their feet on, which added a certain amount of courage to Flirt's swagger. Still, he considered that this brief hiatus was a good time to remove himself back to Mercy's table before the talk got any harder or sleeves were rolled.

'So Miranda gave you her address,' Mercy said, removing her bag to let Flirt sit down.

'Not as such,' Flirt replied. 'I saw her library book, persuaded the librarian to give it to me.'

'So much for the Data Protection Act.' Mercy cocked her head at him. 'You're pretty sneaky, aren't you?'

'So, it seems, is your friend Miranda,' Flirt came back. 'I think the police might be looking for her.' Mercy knew she'd have to steer the conversation away from Miranda if she wanted to snag this guy. She leaned forward, letting her breasts squeeze against the table.

'You know something. I think there's something deeply attractive about a man who's got a mind of his own, uses his initiative. What do you do?' But Flirt would not be drawn from Miranda.

'Contrary to what you're thinking, I don't spend my life hanging out on people's doorsteps. It's just, well, she seemed so nice and then . . .'

'If she was so nice,' Mercy returned, 'why didn't you wait at Paddington for her to come back?'

'She told you about that?'

'Oh yes, no secrets between us.'

'So you know what she took.'

'The last train she could and still get to work.'

Flirt looked at Mercy and shook his head. 'And you say she came back.'

'Of course she did. And where were you? Gone. All she found was . . .'

'It was there?' asked Flirt quickly. 'She picked it up?'

'Yes. It was just lying on the platform.'

'So she's got it then.'

'Yes. No thanks to you.'

'God. I'm so relieved to hear that.'

This was rich. As if he cared whether Miranda got her book back. 'You care, don't you,' Mercy said, as earnest as Algernon. 'You really care. It's so rare to find a man like you. I sometimes wonder where all the caring men go. They're the first to have girlfriends. The first snapped up. Have you? Have you got a girlfriend?'

'Not one who lived to tell.'

Mercy laughed and then tried to stop herself as it sounded just a little indulgent and even he must have been aware how weak the line was.

'Their loss. My gain,' said Mercy, reaching over to put her hand on Flirt's.

Flirt seemed to lose control of his larynx as he felt her touch. His mouth opened but nothing came out. Look, thought Mercy, how fast he forgets Miranda. Just like a man; the only thing he can do with commitment is be fickle. But Mercy was a skilled performer and didn't let her scorn get in the way of a really satisfying snare. 'It's just,' she said, letting her eye-lids lower heavily to scrutinize the table, 'I was going round to Miranda's because I needed someone to talk to.' She looked up again, her eyes searchingly flitting between his. 'I desperately needed to get something . . .' she allowed her free hand to rest on her bosom and massaged it warmly, '. . . off my chest.'

Flirt stared unerringly at her chest. This was a little too obvious even for him. 'Have you ever had the feeling that you've just fallen into a *Carry On* film?'

Mercy seamlessly changed tack. 'God,' she laughed, 'it's such a relief to talk to someone with a sense of humour. Sorry, sorry. I don't know why, but I always seem to end up with men who are just interested in me below the neck.'

Flirt shook his head, 'I can't imagine why.'

'You seem different. There's something about you, I feel I can really talk to you.' Then Mercy heaved one of her wobbly sighs.

'What?'

'Oh. It's just that Miranda has all the luck. She finds all the sensitive men. The ones a woman can really talk to.' Men. They all think they have brains. They all think they're so advanced. Flatter their bodies and they'll believe in themselves even more than they do already; but flatter their minds and they'll believe in you. Praise their favourite non-expanding organ, and they're yours.

'You can talk to me.'

There, you see.

'I mean I don't really know you so I can probably have an impartial point of view.'

Yeah, if it wasn't for the fact that like all men your point of view is through your flies.

'Be objective . . .'

You've got only one objective and I'm sitting on it right now.

'Dispassionate . . .'

Right.

'I can listen. I'm a good listener.'

Mercy nodded, 'No, I can tell you are. You're very sweet.' She laughed, 'I don't even know your name.'

'Matthew. Yours?'

'Is that Swedish?'

'What?'

'Matthew Yorse?'

'No, no, my name's Matthew. What's yours?'

Mercy just couldn't resist it, 'Another G and T if you're going.'

Miranda's experience of taxis just about rivalled her experience of eggs. The Fabergé and caviar kind, that is. She had never thought herself important, or wealthy, enough to ride in one until that night; each had passed the other by. So as Ferdinand ushered her into her second taxi of the evening, she was blissfully unaware of that curious affinity between taxis and water. She had never had to work out that available taxis are soluble, which explains why they all disappear when it starts to rain. Or, more importantly, that passengers are to a taxi as oxygen is to hydrogen. Forget divining rods, if you want a bath, catch a cab. A taxi will find the only puddle in a drought just so it can pull up neatly next to it and necessitate a short swim to the curb. If only Jean de Florette had taken a taxi. It hadn't rained for three weeks but when

Miranda and Ferdinand's cab pulled up near her house on the Goldhawk Road, there were ducks swimming in the small lake that lapped at the door of the cab. Miranda looked at Ferdinand and stared as she fell into his eyes.

Coffee doesn't have to mean anything else. It doesn't have to mean it. Not necessarily. But it does facilitate it. It. You know. Things. Sex. Which could be awkward. But then what if he's expecting it? If he doesn't come in and disappears now he may never reappear again. Maybe he expects it on a first date. It. Sex. Maybe that's what men like him do. The taxi engine growled impatiently as it idled. She could see he was waiting for her to say something. It wasn't as if she couldn't picture herself being held fast between the bed and his hard muscular body, the two of them writhing as they ate and sucked and licked at each other's bodies. Fact is, she had tried to stop herself thinking about it with every bite he took at dinner, wondering how his mouth would feel, his lips pressing into her skin. It wasn't as if she didn't feel a longing to grab him there and then and drag him up to her room. But then he might think she was a tart. Easy. A conquest. Another notch on an already knobbly bed post.

'Listen, love,' a voice came from the front, 'either have him in for coffee or send him packing.'

Now the cab driver, a wiry man with a face like a greyhound, was looking round at her exasperated. 'It's as simple as that. I haven't got all night to hang about for some bird to make up her mind about what's going on in her knickers. I'm going to have to go all the way back into town before I get another fare as it is.' He peered out of his window with the disdain that only a man who lives in deepest suburbia can.

'I've had a great time,' Ferdinand said, trying to ease the tension, but then went on to spoil it with, 'and I don't really drink coffee on first dates.'

This brought Miranda into mental paroxysms as she danced between the horns of her dilemma. What did he mean by that? That he gets straight to it and doesn't even bother with the convention of coffee? It. Sex. Or was he just saying he didn't expect to be invited in? It was bad and now he had just made things ten times worse. This wasn't answering her question, this was just sending her head in a spin.

Does he come in for coffee? It? Sex?

'I've got tea,' Miranda said, as she felt herself flail in the tides of his eyes, 'but it's only Lapsang Souchong and my milk's probably a bit off.'

Helplessly adrift in their pull she found herself unable to stop or slow down as her speech accelerated into garble. 'But it's probably all right, I only put it in the fridge the other day but I'd understand if you have to go because I know that doesn't sound very appetizing not that it's tea or even coffee I suppose we're really talking about or maybe we are maybe you do just feel like a hot drink you certainly don't look like one.' Miranda free-fell into an hysterical laugh. 'You see I don't mind if you come in for coffee really, or tea, I don't, you could just come in, we could sit down and just have a nice hot cup of sex.'

Although what followed could be described as a silence, in fact it was merely the absence of the appropriate Schadenfreude gurgle of glee when someone else has managed to critically embarrass them-selves. Yet again. Ferdinand was too wary to laugh this time, the cabby was too eager for a tip and Miranda's mouth was already too full tast-ing the foot she had just stuck in it. 'Coffee,' Miranda tried desperately, 'I meant coffee, it was just I was thinking of something else and . . .'

Miranda trailed off into silence, leaving the end of her sentence to hang as surely as it would have hung her. If self-respect has a survival instinct this is when it finally kicked in. Retreat.

'Thank you,' she said quickly, politely and, she was sure, efficiently, 'I've had a wonderful evening. Goodbye.'

And with all the dignity of a flatulent soprano she fumbled with the door handle and exited the taxi. She slammed the door and stood look-ing through the window at him. Then, perhaps remembering the tube that morning, she breathed heavily on the glass and wrote her number in the condensation. The taxi revved up and drew away and she watched it go, still too much in shock to consider whether she had done the right thing. Only after a few moments did she realize that she was standing thigh-high in the sort of puddle that vexed Dr Foster.

'And then,' Mercy sobbed, tears unashamedly smudging her blusher, 'he left me.'

By this time Flirt was around the table with his arm about her jud-dering shoulders. She clutched onto one of his hands.

'Thank you, thank you. You're so gentle, Matthew.'

'He's not worth crying over. No man is.'

Treacherous even unto his own sex, thought Mercy. Is there no depth that a man won't sink to? Betray even his own brother. They dis-gust me. They'll always disgust me.

But Mercy's routine hadn't been perfected over five years for noth-ing. She knew that tomorrow there'd be flowers delivered to the

Second Floor. Later, there'd be the clinch and later still the admission that he loved her. And then. Well, it was just a matter of how high she wanted to take him, which all depended on how big a mess she wanted to make of him at the end. She looked into his big, open, caring eyes. A bloody massive one, a really vast one, she thought, as she clasped his hand, a really huge devastating mess. Love is such a formula. It's crazy that people are still falling for it.

As the evening wore on, Peersnide could not draw himself away from looking at Flirt. Barry had proved quite useless for any other pertinent information. In fact he was getting a little too chummy for Peersnide's liking. At every moment he seemed intent on demonstrating his complete lack of culture with an almost indecipherable use of the vernacular. Yet even that little unconscious scratch at his behind had a childish, ignorant, endearing quality.

'We're not a United Kingdom no more, we're a divided country now. The Welsh and the Scots, they're pissing off, and the problem with England, the problem with England is that it's got no identity. That's why we're not world leaders no more, we haven't got no empire. Look at the eye-ties and the frogs and the dagos and the krauts and even the yanks and the pakis. What've they got that we haven't? Shall I tell you?' Peersnide was not remotely interested but Barry was going to tell him anyway. 'Takeaways. They've all got takeaways in every civilized corner of the world. Those are your embassies nowadays. Forget your diplomats, we make our minds up about other countries over the counter of a fast food restaurant. You see they've all got national dishes. They've got pizzas and frankfurters and burgers and curries. There's even those snails and paellas. The Scots have their haggis and the Irish their spuds. So, what we need, you see, is a little bit of England in all these other countries. And what's wrong with the humble fish and chips I hear you ask?' Of course Barry didn't hear this because Peersnide was successfully ignoring him and gazing at Flirt. 'They're not English, they're British. No, what we need is a dish of pride, that says Eng-er-land, says football and lager, says Charge of the Light Brigade, says Two World Wars and a World Cup too, doo dah doo dah. We need a noble nosh you won't get nowhere else. What we need is the jellied eel.'

Peersnide stared at Flirt and flipped through his mental filofax of faces. He began to undress Flirt with his eyes, his bandage, that is. In Peersnide's head he unwrapped that turban and it slowly began to dawn on him where he had seen Flirt before. The taxi. This morning.

The last bandage fell away, Flirt appeared completely unwrapped, just as he had at the taxi window when he had snatched the book from Peersnide's grasp. It was him. The one who had caused all this trouble. A rage built in Peersnide's head, a tempest between his temples, a storm of indignation, and suddenly all his cool intellectualism, all his mind before meat, all the fear that induced him to always pacify those more physically able than himself, departed him. He stood up and pointed at Flirt, and shouted as if the very word were a bullet of ire, 'You.'

As this shout was somewhat unspecific, it was no surprise that the whole pub looked round. And when they found that 'you', this time, did not mean them but someone else, they settled themselves comfortably to watch a little drama, a moment of catharsis, a scene which each was inwardly grateful did not involve them. There might even be a fight.

'How dare you,' Peersnide marched through the motley flotilla of tables and stools. Anger blindly gripped him. His face was red and the veins mapping his forehead pulsed vividly. 'Where's the book?'

Flirt had looked behind him, expecting, as everybody else had, that the 'you' was not going to be him. It was.

'That's the loony from the tube,' Flirt whispered to Mercy with only the slightest hint of fear in his voice and stood up. Peersnide looked him in the eye. 'Where's the book?' he repeated as menacingly as he could.

'You're fucking crazy,' Flirt shook his head.

'Give it back.'

'Go away.'

'Give it back.'

'I don't have it.'

'Now.'

'I do not have it,' Flirt repeated.

'Where is it then?'

'The girl, I gave it back to her, all right? Now go away.' Flirt turned round so he could find his chair to sit down again. There was a distinct sigh of disappointment from everyone watching in the pub who had, at the very least, expected some argy-bargy if not a full-on fight.

Peersnide looked at Flirt's back and saw in it an indignant challenge to his authority, a snub which must be answered. Peevishly he lunged out and pushing Flirt in the small of the back caused him to trip over his seat and fall sprawling to the floor. Peersnide could hardly believe his strength. He held his hand out before him and looked at it in disbelief that such a thing could belong to him.

'You div, you fucking div.' Mercy's voice reached Peersnide only slightly before her slap. She had stood up and had given him such a mighty crack to his jaw that a globule of saliva was briefly left suspended in the air where his mouth had been only a moment before his face had been forced violently to the side. 'You assault Miranda on the tube,' Mercy shouted as she slapped him again, spinning his head the other way and sending pain ripping through his cheek. 'You nick her book.' Peersnide stumbled backward with the third slap, which caught him on the nose causing blood to burst from it. Mercy pursued him. 'Then you come in here and attack this . . .' Mercy swung her arm out to gesture towards Flirt who had sensibly decided to pretend to be too stunned to stand up again. Peersnide watched the arc of Mercy's hand and cowered from the next, inevitable, swing, putting his hands to his face to protect him. 'Now piss off, just piss off,' Mercy concluded. No slap or punch followed and Peersnide cautiously straightened up to face her. The frenzy in her eyes had gone and she seemed to have calmed down. This was the second assault he had suffered at the hands of a woman that evening. Who the fuck did they think they were? He began to straighten his tie and dust down his waxed jacket. The stream of blood from his nose dripped into his mouth, making it taste sour. Calmly, in the quiet of the enraptured pub, Mercy said to Peersnide, 'Do you fancy being a landowner?'

Peersnide looked confused.

'Here's a couple of achers.' Mercy took hold of Peersnide's shoulders and smartly brought her knee up into his groin. If eyes actually did have stalks, Peersnide's would have been out on them. As it was, tears quickly welled and poured down his swelling cheeks. He involuntarily expelled a rush of wind from both mouth and arse and grabbed his damaged testes. In his agony he faintly realized that the whole pub had begun to cheer Mercy.

Eventually Peersnide managed to clear the water from his eyes and stand straight again. This was too much. They'd gone too far. He reached into the deep inner pheasant pockets of his waxed jacket and pulled out the two Beaumont-Adams duelling pistols which he had 'borrowed' from the auction house the moment he had secured his job as a real-life spy. Pulling back the hammers with a loud click, he held one in each hand, his arms outstretched like a highwayman, the barrels pointing in Mercy's face. The power was his.

'Don't,' he panted. 'Ever,' he said, catching his breath. 'Hit me,' he exhaled heavily. 'Again,' he wheezed.

Now there are some pubs where you can pull out a gun and not an eyelid will bat, indeed it is a required accessory in most hostelries in the vicinity of the Mile End Road. In other pubs, such an action would cause the entire clientele to dive to earth, cowering. However, there are some pubs, and the Bushwhacker was one of them, in which pulling a gun is a very unwise thing to do as there is bound to be someone there who has a bigger one and wants to show you. Indeed, a burly man standing just behind Mercy, and a little to the right, promptly pulled out a lightweight Sten hand gun and levelled it at Peersnide.

'Who the fuck do you think you're pointing those at?'

Before Peersnide could think of a sensible answer, a willowy man standing behind him whipped a .45 from inside his jacket and pointed it rather erratically at Peersnide and the burly man. 'Yeah?' he said, shaking the weapon. 'Yeah?'

'Put them away,' the voice of the landlady rang out, 'put them away.' Everybody looked towards her, standing behind the bar, holding a glinting 1970s Beretta double-barrelled shotgun.

At this, there was a chorus of clicking as practically everyone in the pub felt compelled to pull out their own shooters. Forty-seven guns of various shapes and sizes suddenly appeared, all of them pointing at Peersnide in the centre. With his own pistols shaking slightly but still levelled at Mercy, Peersnide slowly and nervously peered around, surveying the wall of gun barrels that pointed at him. This was the moment when, in the cartoons, a large gulp would sound. Of course in the cartoons the victim could be riddled with bullet holes and would remain standing but simply resemble a Gruyère cheese. In the cartoons the victim would take a drink and water would spray out of each bullet hole. Funny the things you think about when you're suddenly faced with a painful death. Each tiny, dark void that he stared at yelled 'the end'. A universe of little black holes and every one loaded.

Every one loaded, that is, except for the two duelling pistols in Peersnide's own hands, for which suitable ammunition had not actually been manufactured since 1874. Suddenly Peersnide realized what true impotence felt like. He found himself wishing that his guns contained little flags which, when fired, would unravel from a stick to reveal the word 'Bang' printed on them. Something as harmless as a little flatulence which he could simply let off and laugh off.

Now I am older, and have learnt all those explanations, and believe that I know better, I do not fear others, or those more powerful than me, for I know that they are human and face the same mortality as I. Dreams still steal their sleep, years still clutch their flesh, and a dose of the runs still stings like billy-oh. I can take comfort in knowing these things and knowing the world, although now it has lost the enchantment of its mystery and magic. That is the pay-off I suppose.

So I am old now. I have aged — but only because I could find no other method for not dying. We all grow up and as we do, it all seems like a progression, an advance towards understanding and towards a realization of our life goals. But are those goals ever really tangible? The spiritual ones are unreachable in our corporeal state, and the materialistic ones are only short term, there is always something more, or something else, to get.

Perhaps then, any progression we do make in life is simply a by-product of our true journey through it; we are not going towards anything, we are, in fact, only travelling away from something. Life is not a voyage to somewhere, it is a flight away from something that we do not like and, in growing, we are trying to put as much distance as we can between us and it. That 'it', that 'something', I believe, is fear. The things which scared us most when we were small.

As we get older we learn and are no longer afeared. Growing up is just our attempt to escape the fear of the innocent mind, a retreat from the terrors of childhood.

As Shakespeare poetically described, in the excerpt from *Cymbeline*, it is only in death that we are relieved of our life of fear. As so many tombstones attest: only when we die do we truly get to 'Rest In Peace', nothing to worry or frighten us any longer. And, when we look at the corpse of a brilliant loved one, as all of us must do at some point, and we think how all their learning through life, all their understanding, brought them to nothing in the end, just to earth and ashes again, we may feel that life really is without worth. But their achievement, all that learning, all that interest and study, is a mark of their success, an indication of just how far they got from fear, from the vulnerable frightened baby to the civilized and knowing less-fearful sage.

Ever afraid of the unknown, we only want to know because we fear not knowing. We spend our lives discovering and finding out, not because we have clear goals to achieve, but because we are running like frightened rabbits from the terrible diverging headlights of an infinitely more powerful world.

Fear may seem a rather negative motivation for our lives. Our instinct is to resist believing such a thing. We are always loath to believe that we are any less important than we think we are. We would rather be the hunter than the hunted, yet, as I will show, 'negative motivation' is one of the central flaws of the human condition.

Perhaps conquering fear is a goal in itself, something we head for, yet if fear is still the prime cause, the runner's starting block, the attempt to vanquish it is not a positive action but a reaction. Yet fear is never conquered, it is only forced further into retreat; witness the millionaires who are driven by a fear of poverty long after they have reached a comfortable income, or the politicians who are driven by a fear of impotence long after they are controlling nations and have fathered uncountable bastards.

However, it is a mark of love's power and virulence that losing it has become humanity's greatest fear. Today we have our own armillary globes far more expansive than those in the Scone College Library: these astrolabes are today's media, and they describe for us the paths of our new stellar system, through the golden circles of society, our true icons of fear, our modern stars, our superstars. Those gods who beg us to love them through film and music, television and print. It is they who are driven by, and we all recognize it within them, the fear of admitting that we are in the end alone, the horror of loneliness, the terror of the unloved.

It was John Donne who wrote,

> 'No man is an island, entire of itself,'

yet there is far more evidence that,

> 'No man is a continent, a mutual commonwealth.'

We are all, in fact, just growing away from being that scared child whose mummy has gone and has left us alone in a world which is full of powers and energies far vaster than anything we could ever really master. We survive merely at the whim of a planet's temperature. We exist within the tiny margins of wobble in the earth's orbital path, within a narrow stretch of wavelengths.

15

It Was All a Little Too Spooky

MORE THAN HALF THE PEOPLE WHO HAVE EVER LIVED ARE ALIVE today.

i don't know who worked that out, or how, but it's quite a thought.

It's one of those statistics which the inexorably dull will drop into a conversation prefaced by the words, 'Did you know', a phrase used to excuse the fact that they cannot find a creative way of engaging a thought. And in this way many great thoughts have been lost. As most things that follow the words 'Did you know' are usually something you did know but had studiously forgotten or something you never wanted to know in the first place, the words themselves become an unconscious trigger for listeners to block out what follows, safe in the knowledge that they are missing nothing. i remember, in the library, P. T. Jenks the celebrated crime writer prefaced all her clues with the words, 'Did you know', and nobody ever guessed whodunnit.

However, there are also certain thoughts which are probably worth obscuring with an idiot's idiom because once you think about them they really can drive you mad. This one, i believe, is one of them. i mean, if you think about how many people must be dead already, over all time, then think how many people must then be alive. Think how impossible walking down the street is without bumping into someone who hasn't had the decency to die yet.

Thoughts like that, the overwhelming population growth, were considered so scary in the first half of the twentieth century, a madness did, in fact, ensue. Pursuant thoughts such as 'eugenics' and 'genocide' became palatable, even fashionable. Many people, enough to fight a war anyway, believed that a mass of humanity could, should, rightfully die: 'just not me, because I'm an individual.' So, let me start again.

Did you know that there are more people living today than have ever died.

And so it is no surprise that there are ever-increasing numbers of old people tying up hospital beds, ambulances and catheter tubes. And with beauty treatments, holistic medicines, skin creams and cosmetic science being what it is today, it is ever harder to qualify as a rattling, wrinkly, 'bony'-fide old person. For even in this modern and secular time, life is marked by rites of passage. A boy may not be considered a man until he can drink sufficiently to burble incoherently, crawl, vomit and soil himself; a girl is not a woman until she can convincingly use a headache as an excuse not to have sex; and an ageing person is not officially old until he or she has broken a hip.

This last one is like receiving your card of official oldness. It is a licence to give up all responsibility for oneself and leave all the fretting about your bed-sores and urinary infections to the younger generations, of which there seem to be so many. So it was not by complete coincidence that Mavis Bacon, 82, a great beauty in her day – 3 July 1948 – broke her hip and saved Peter Peersnide's life at some considerable discomfort to herself.

For at the same time that Peersnide had imprudently pulled out his pistols, barely a few streets away, Mavis had woken up lying awkwardly at the bottom of her stairs. Realizing that her last memory had been somewhere half way up the stairs and that moving caused sharp pains in her back, she gleefully reached for her pendant panic button and pressed it with all the gusto of someone who had been dying to do it for years, just to see what would happen. The bright yellow pendant with its temptingly large red button was not normally found hanging around her neck, but Mavis had been visited that day by young Francis, who had bought it for her years ago, and she always made a point of showing him that she wore the ugly plastic thing and didn't really leave it hanging in the airing cupboard.

With that, Mavis lay back on the carpet and thought about whether the batteries would still be functioning, how long she should give it before trying the more traditional method of dragging herself to the hallway telephone, and how Francis was now bound to get her one of those nifty little stair-lifts that they advertise in the *Radio Times*. She kept herself jolly and blitz-spirited with thoughts of how she could now get a stick to thrash whippersnappers and of the lines of hunky young doctors queuing to examine parts of her which had gone unseen since that night Albert, God rest his soul, had got into bed, lifted the sheet and said, 'Oh God, I just can't keep on pretending.' With that he trooped off to sleep on the sofa, which remained his bed for the next twelve years until a sympathetic bus ran him down and put him out of his, and consequently Mavis's, misery.

Little did Mavis know that, apart from the endless tea and sympathy she could look forward to from the Greens-voting family on the top floor, who were barely capable of concealing their eagerness for her to move to a home or higher place so that they could buy her flat, she was also saving a life, if not preventing an entire massacre.

Neither did the ambulance crew speeding out of Charing Cross hospital have an inkling of what was going on, nor the part that they would play in saving numerous lives. They could not know, as they turned into the Goldhawk Road and found, as usual, a disorganized traffic jam, what effect the switching on of their siren would have.

Nor did Miranda have a clue as the ambulance weaved towards her, lights flashing, horn hooting, siren blaring, what part this would have in her story. With all the practised city dweller's blasé indifference to other people's tragedies, she barely noticed it. She marched towards the Bushwhacker clutching the note Mercy had left on the door. 'Dear Randa, sorry about today. PMT probably. Got a surprise. Come to the BW. Love Mercy.' PMT? Miranda knew that was a poor excuse. It's the one you give men for being a woman to stop an argument. Hardly Mercy's style. Miranda stopped as she crossed the road and the ambulance swept past, narrowly missing the old man standing foursquare to the traffic armed with nothing but his Zimmer frame, singing, 'Relax, dondoit, when you wanna . . .' Another blast from the siren.

Had all gone well, at this point, Peter Peersnide would have been watching Miranda approach and then lost himself in the pub crowd to observe her. Once he had established that she would be settled for a while he would then ring Burnt. As it was, he was staring down the black abysses of a barrage of gun barrels and sweating more profusely than at sports day on a fat farm.

It was at this point that Mavis's hip came to the rescue for suddenly, like a divine intervening light from heaven, the ambulance's glint of flashing blue came blazing through the Bushwhacker's frosted windows and was sent splaying by their glaze, splashing across every face there and the various artillery on show. At the sound of the siren there was an answering chorus of 'Coppers,' 'Bill,' 'Filth,' 'Rozzers,' 'Sweeny,' 'Knickers,' and a flamenco rattle of clicks as every weapon in the pub suddenly disappeared. The silence that was so unbearable only a moment before seemed never to have happened. Everybody was laughing and talking, albeit a mite too heartily, and apart from Peersnide, Mercy and Flirt who stood looking about them in bewilderment, the pub appeared as any other pub might, a genial hostelry of comfort, cheer and fellowship in alcohol, or might to any passing plod.

With a total disregard for timing, it was barely a minute before Miranda pushed open the door of the pub. Expecting the worst, every head turned to look at her and the silence momentarily returned. This was followed by a number of sighs of relief that she looked nothing like an officer of the law.

It is disconcerting to walk into any place in which you consider yourself a stranger and have everybody look at you, let alone if you're a woman and the place where everyone is looking at you is a pub. Miranda smiled feebly and her obvious sense of unease inspired the man who had been brandishing a service revolver barely a minute before to say in a loud and friendly voice, 'Come in, come in, what'll you have?' Then he laughed a big false laugh. At that point most of the pub joined in laughing just as falsely. If Miranda sensed that she had just walked into a Broadmoor day out party she barely showed it and laughed along. It sounded like they were recording the laughter track for *Last of the Summer Wine*. Only more genuine.

Suddenly Miranda was everybody's friend. She was jostled by the crowd to the bar and an inebriation of different coloured drinks appeared in front of her. As they crowded round her, Peersnide watched open-mouthed, and would have stood there dumbfounded a while longer had it not been for the firm hand of the landlady, a woman built more for shot putting than shotguns, on his shoulder and the sudden jarring of her fist in the small of his back. In this manner she accompanied Peersnide to the door, opened it and pushed him so forcibly he couldn't stop himself tripping at the curb and landing with his cheek on the road in a substance which did not smell, or feel entirely unlike canine faeces. A moment later Barry came hurtling out in the same manner with an 'And that goes for your boyfriend too.' An indignity Barry would have felt more keenly had he any concept of what dignity meant. As it was, being thrown out of a pub, even if it was for something someone else did, was rather exciting.

'Yeah and fuck you,' Barry shouted wittily back at the door. He turned to Peersnide and helped him up. 'You all right, mate?'

'Thank you, yes,' said Peersnide, taking off his glasses and with his handkerchief trying to clear the excrescence which obscured them.

'Bunch of wankers in there anyway,' Barry said as chummily as possible. He had never known someone who had real guns before, even if they did look a bit knackered, but he'd seen enough British gangland films to think he'd do rather well in that world. 'Fancy a kebab?'

Little would have appealed to Peter Peersnide less at that moment but he needed to find a telephone and suddenly didn't feel as brave as he had. The idea of this youth providing cannon fodder in the line of fire seemed a very good one.

'Shish or doner?' he found himself saying as he laid a gentle hand on Barry's back and ushered him hence.

Because most of the pub were still standing when Miranda made her entrance, Mercy, being somewhat shorter than it says in her passport, was unaware of her friend's presence. It was not until Miranda was ushered to the bar that Mercy caught a glimpse of her. Mercy shouted and tried to wave but all she managed to do was knock Flirt in the nose. As he recoiled, he placed a foot sideways to try and steady himself which Mercy proceeded to step on, driving her stiletto heel not only through the canvas of the shoe but also the cotton, flesh and bone inside. Flirt fainted to the floor and Mercy turned to him to see what was the matter. She knelt down to cradle Flirt's bandaged head, still unaware that her heel was embedded and then feeling her foot caught, ripped through the webbing between two of Flirt's toes. Flirt was spared this last agony by remaining unconscious. A habit he seemed to be mastering.

Meanwhile, Miranda tried to look beyond her wall of burly men and began to bounce up and down from her stool to see if she could spot Mercy. She bobbed up a couple of times before she caught site of Mercy's blonde bombshell coif. She bounced up again in order to wave and shout at her but then froze. There, in Mercy's arms. Flirt. Bandaged, but definitely Flirt. It looked like they were snogging. 'A surprise,' her note had said. Well, that was a bloody surprise. The moment Miranda meets a nice man, Mercy has to get her grubby paws on him. Mercy just couldn't bear a little competition.

Anger has a way of dismissing all rational thoughts, such as: how had Mercy found Flirt? Such as: why was she bothering to get upset, she had just had dinner with the man of her dreams, and not just her dreams, any girl's dreams. Such as: there might be a perfectly innocent explanation. But there are times when one doesn't want innocent explanations. There are times when you've been keeping yourself controlled, restrained and reined in all evening and you just want to explode. There are times when you've been denying your basic urges of lust for hours and stopped yourself ripping your dream object's clothes off. There are times when you've controlled yourself to the point that you have been left watching a taxi disappear into the sunset. At these times, you don't actually want reasonable explanations. At these times you simply want a fight.

Miranda slipped off her stool, pushed through the scrum of new admirers and stormed up behind Mercy.

'And this is your surprise? This is you being a friend?'

Mercy dropped the still unconscious Flirt and turned to look at her.

'You little cow,' Miranda added, somewhat gratuitously.

'What are you on about?' Mercy had just been through one public scene and was sure it was not quite right to have two in such close proximity.

'I tell you about the one decent bloke in this city and in seconds you're sucking face with him.'

'Oh come on, look at him.'

'Yeah, I just have to look at a bloke and you're on him like a leech, you little tart.'

'Shut your face,' Mercy spat back, now riled. 'I came all the fucking way over here to apologize and . . .'

'What "Oh sorry, I'm only fucking that bloke you were banging on about all day."'

'I'm not doing anything. He's fainted.'

'I don't want to hear it. I don't want to hear any of your crap. I'm sick to death of you. I really . . .' A lump bubbled up in her throat and stopped her saying any more. Her nose began to feel pinched and tears stung her eyes. She rushed out again and breathed in the cool air of the street.

'She's just come out again. Yes, I can see her. She's just down the road.'

'Chilli sauce, my friend?'

'Go home? Now?'

'I say, you want chilli sauce?'

Peersnide looked at the sweaty man who held his pitta bread like a castanet. He pointed at the pay phone he was talking into, to indicate that he was busy.

'You just nod, my friend. Chilli sauce?'

'Yes, yes,' Peersnide nodded, 'I can be there tomorrow morning.'

'Just say when, my friend.'

'Uh-huh.' Peersnide nodded excitedly. 'There's a load to tell you.'

Barry slammed the nudge key on the fruit machine opposite the counter. A clatter of coins hit the tray.

'Absolutely,' Peersnide nodded, 'getting time off will be no problem.' He watched out the window as Miranda crossed the street. He strained to see at an angle through the glass. She was heading back to her place. 'Yes,' Peersnide kept nodding, 'and her friends. I think this is really big.' He eyed the greasy kebab man, who was looking at him a bit suspiciously. 'What time?' The line had begun to break up. 'When?' he said and then louder, 'WHEN?'

By the time Peersnide had put the receiver back, the kebab man was wrapping his kebab. Barry slapped his winnings down on the counter and they both picked up their packages. Walking out onto the street, Peersnide could just see Miranda reaching her door. He looked at Barry, who was grinning inanely at him, unwrapped his kebab and took a deep bite.

Miranda opened the familiar front door and stomped up the familiar stairs. She passed Tony Fromnextdoor's familiar smell and put her key in her familiar jiggly lock. The door swung open with the familiar squeak and she did the familiar 'I'm home, honey. Oh. Thank God, I'm not married' joke before she flipped on the familiar light switch and looked at a completely unfamiliar room. Miranda looked at her door. It was the right number. She looked back at the room. It was her room, it looked a bit like her room, but it had lost something. It wasn't that it had changed obviously. Just its familiarity. It was like some other dimension Miranda, an ur-Miranda, a Miranda who was a bit more efficient than she was, was living there. Miranda suddenly felt a chill. The room was ... well, it was eerily tidy. Pictures which had hung a little lopsided were now straight. A chair which she had never seen aligned with the make-up table was tucked in straight under it. Her bed was made. The sawdust in Cally's cage was flat and even, free of little gerbil droppings. Cally, instead of rabidly jumping at the cage bars when she came in, reminding her that she had forgotten to feed him that morning yet again, was lying contentedly asleep. It was all a little too spooky. Miranda didn't want to touch anything. This had been a bit of a weird day and she wasn't keen on any more weirdness. Usually in these circumstances, as if these circumstances could be called usual, she would have called up Mercy and gone to stay with her. As it was, she had burnt that particular cantilevered bridge.

Of course the MI5 'sweepers' are usually meticulous, but they are more used to searching neat offices and embassies, not tatty bedsits, so you can't blame them for tidying up a bit while they were there. They were searching for me, of course. But i had been tucked up snugly in her bag.

Miranda edged into the room like a guest in a strange place, unsure of the etiquette of the location. Maybe it was how she had left it. Maybe it was just a weird day altogether: from Barry to Ferdinand in twenty-four hours, taking in Flirt on the way. Or not as it turned out. Maybe if enough different things happen in a day it can alter your perspective. Exhaustion swept through her as she began to think of everything that had happened. Dropping the bag, and me, by the bedside, she crumpled onto the crisply made bed. She stared at the one part of her room left completely familiar. The ceiling. She imagined Ferdinand going back to his sterile flat, cursing himself that he didn't at least kiss her. The image didn't really fit. He was probably in some nightclub sitting with a couple of bimbos at that very moment. She thought about Mercy and Flirt but couldn't really understand why she felt so betrayed. She was lying on her bed in what had become a strange place and she felt just so uncomfortable. She should have kissed him, she should have. She imagined what a kiss from Ferdinand might have been like. That firm chin locked cradling her own, the warmth of his mouth. Being possessed, being held safe in his arms. She sighed. The only perfect thing in her life was hindsight. What was the point? She was probably just an excursion for him, a little aside into 'other-half' life. A momentary skim above the waves for a high-flyer. He'll never call. Don't think about him. Don't.

Looking over her strange room, Miranda took herself somewhere familiar. She skied down Alpen mountains to the Silvikrin mountain meadow. She drove round endless mountain roads in the latest car. She roller skated with the tight white-trousered, tanned Californians of Tampon USA. But the Milk Tray Man was gone, the man from Marlboro country was nowhere to be seen. Where was the Ferrero

Ambassador? Anybody? Even the bloody man from del Monte would do. None of them would come to her. Only the lost cause of Ferdinand. She must think of him as lost. She couldn't let herself think anything else. It's so easy to make an expectation. And so difficult to have one shattered.

She looked around the room yet again. She looked at her Fuzzy-Fur® sausage dog draught excluder. It was facing the other way. She stared at it. It definitely used to look at the wall, not into the room. It never looked into the room. Never.

Flirt woke up with a glass of Pernod splashed in his face. Rubbing the stinging alcohol from his eyes, he stared up at the spinning fan on the Bushwhacker's ceiling. It was, he supposed, intended to disperse the pub's choking cigarette smoke. All it actually did was deal the stuff out evenly to every lung in the place.

Mercy's face appeared upside down and peered at him.

'You all right?' She offered him a hand and tried to help him up. This worked, until he put weight on his right foot and collapsed again on the floor. Mercy looked down at his foot and said, 'Christ, your foot's covered in blood.'

Flirt looked at his glistening red shoe.

'I think we need to get you to hospital.' Mercy disappeared from view for a minute and then came back with two of the burlier gun-slingers. With a little pulling and pushing they got him upright. Flirt leant heavily on Mercy's shoulder as he hobbled to the door. Even through the pain the temptation for his hand to slip onto her breasts was immense. Somehow he denied himself.

Outside, they limped down the step and Mercy nearly deafened him calling, 'Taxi.' A dozen minicabs immediately pulled up and a dozen other vehicles braked because Mercy just stopped traffic naturally.

She bundled him into the nearest car and said, 'Hospital.'

Tony Fromnextdoor opened the door a fraction and peered out. He saw who was standing there and opened it wider with a huge smile. 'Hi.'

'Do you know if anybody has been up here? You know. In my room?' said Miranda.

As a matter of fact Tony did know someone who had been in her room just that morning. Him. He didn't do much. Look at her underwear. Put on a couple of her dresses. Masturbate. That sort of thing. Harmless stuff. Did it most mornings. He had taken a bra of hers some time back. It was a stiff grey thing now hidden in his desk drawer. Occasionally he would just hold it, stroke the cups. 'Er, no. No.'

'Maybe the landlord or a cleaner?'

'Is there something wrong?'

'I just think someone's been in my room.'

'Really?'

'Been through my stuff.'

'Is it your bra?' Tony said, his voice rising slightly.

Miranda unconsciously felt for her strap. 'I think you're supposed to ask if there's anything missing. Something like that.'

'Is there anything missing?'

'No, no, it's all, sort of, better.'

'Right.' Tony had that faraway look. Miranda shifted from foot to foot.

'Look, could you do me a favour? Could I kip here tonight. On your sofa or something.'

Tony was obviously shocked by this prospect. He was lost for words and stumbled a little backward into the room. Miranda took that for an invitation and followed him.

Tony's room was much like hers, but dark. The only light was a large computer monitor with what looked like a lot of static on it. What illumination there was revealed a comfortable mess. Clothes on the floor, piles of used Kleenex around the bed. On each wall there were stacks of old polystyrene burger boxes piled to the ceiling. Miranda stared at them long enough to make Tony sufficiently uncomfortable to explain.

'I eat quite a lot of junk. But you know they don't biodegrade, and there's no, like, recycling bins for them. So I keep them. They keep the room warm and sort of soundproof. If there was anyone in your room today I probably wouldn't have heard them.'

Miranda nodded. 'Didn't know I was a noisy neighbour.'

'No, no, you're not, it's the . . .' Tony found it hard to finish the sentence. 'It's the noises I make.' One of those noises being a high-pitched 'Miranda'. So he didn't. He left the 'the . . .' hanging in the air with a palpable three dots after it.

Miranda pointed at the sofa. 'I won't disturb you . . .' She didn't want to add, 'whatever it is that you're doing,' because she really didn't want him to tell her, and left three dots of her own. Sometimes, she realized, when she was talking to someone, she would adopt their mannerisms despite herself. The way everyone in a Woody Allen film has to stutter like the director.

'No, no. Please. Take the bed, it's . . .'

'That's really sweet but I can't, I . . .'

'I insist. Please. Then you could . . .'

Miranda stared at the *Star Wars* duvet. 'The sofa will be fine. You can . . .'

'The bed. Please. Use the bed.' There was something a little shocking about Tony being so forceful that he finished his sentence. Miranda duly obeyed.

There, still wrapped in Ferdinand's jacket, she lay down and watched Tony turn back to the static on his screen. He didn't type anything. He just stared at it. His head blocked out much of the light. Miranda felt her eyes close.

'Well,' said Doctor Scudder. 'We've cleaned it up and bandaged it so you'll lose no more blood. We'll take a proper look at it tomorrow.' Flirt, lying on a trolley in Charing Cross Accident and Emergency, nodded a thanks. 'I'm afraid we've a bit of a backlog at the hospital at the moment and we've run out of beds. So unless someone pops off in the night, I think you're going to have to sleep here tonight.' Flirt looked about from his trolley. A few drunks with bloody noses, moaning. A boy with a superglue tube stuck to his nose, a man lying very still with a vacuum cleaner tube hanging out of the side of his sheet and an old lady propped up and munching her way through a bar of Fruit and Nut.

Dr Scudder patted him on the leg, smiled and walked away. Flirt could still feel a huge throbbing pain in his foot. He felt a shadow of disappointment fall over him. His life had been all right, it was going OK, until he picked up that book for Mercy's friend. Now he had been to hospital twice, been beaten up and nearly shot to death. But now there was Mercy. Wondrous, beautiful, mind-fucking Mercy.

'Care for a bit?' said a voice next to him. He turned to see the old lady in the next bed proffering her chocolate bar.

'Don't mind if I do.' Flirt nodded.

'Looks like you've done something nasty to your foot.'

'Got a stiletto heel through it.'

'Oh, that is wonderful. I wish I'd thought of that one. Girls today, they're so . . . It was a girl, wasn't it?'

Flirt nodded.

'Well, you can never tell nowadays. But that's such an inventive wound. I'd love to have done that. To my husband, God rest his soul. Was it revenge?'

'No, an accident. I think.'

'I suppose it must have been. You're not in the Revenge and Retribution ward are you.'

Flirt smiled. 'Was yours bad?'

'My what?'

'Your accident.'

'Oh no. No, it's wonderful, it's like being a debutante,' said Mavis. 'I've just come of old-age.'

We live on a knife edge between gas and liquid, earth and air, our fragile consciousness and unfeasibly complex physiologies manage to live somewhere between the unliving and the dead. The precariousness of our existence is too frail to calculate and all known life has only existed for the merest blink of the universe's time. All the telescopes and listening devices we use to scan the universe of stars draw a blank. From squinting astronomers to wide-eyed ufologists we just cannot bear to contemplate that our fragile existence is simply a flaw in the universe, an impossibly repeatable accident, and that we are, in fact, alone.

But in our home-grown pop-stars, film-stars, our universe of celebrity, we see a universe we can grasp, a space we can understand, a reflection of all our own infernal, eternal, internal conflicts. They are driven to succeed, to demand attention, long after they are adored by millions, because fear is the nature of love. Love can never be possessed absolutely, it is a spiritual, a nominal goal, so there can never be enough of it. Like tomorrow and heaven, the happiness love promises is always just out of reach. This is one of the most important things to comprehend if we are to understand exactly why we are so fascinated by, grasping for and, in the words of the haremed crooner Mr Robert Palmer, 'Addicted to love'.

CHAPTER VI.

LAYING DOWN THE LAWS OF LOVE

Laws are like cobwebs, which may catch small flies, but let wasps and hornets break through.

Jonathan Swift (1667–1745)
A Critical Essay upon the Faculties of the Mind

AS I HAVE SHOWN, WHEN YOU ARE YOUNG, FEAR IS EVERYWHERE. You are small in a world of big people and inexplicable things. Likewise, when our current civilization was young, fear was everywhere too, the minds and imaginations of the people of the Middle Ages were like those of children. The world was full of powerful warlords, and the secrets of the unforgiving, inexplicable Nature would not bear elucidation for several centuries. Death, darkness, hellfire, damnation, starvation, drought, flood, plague, pox, pariahs, ghosts, witches, robbers, tortures, wars, infidels, demons, all the Seven Circles, God, Popes, Kings, Lords, Masters, and no doubt the knock of the Jehovah's Witnesseth at the door, they were all to be feared.

For the medieval European, fear was more than a way of life, it was life. And it was feudalism which bore and perpetuated the rule of fear. All and everyone understood it or suffered the consequences. They feared the powers and the punishments of their lord and, even more, the Lord. The expression was, after all, 'God-fearing' not 'God-loving'. He was an angry, wrathful, vengeful God.

What kept the serfs in line was not some airy, aspirational longing of theirs to be rewarded by riches in the hereafter, it was not some life-long desire to eventually find rest beyond the pearly gates on the fluffy clouds of Heaven. No, what kept them on the old straight and narrow was purely the total and utter terror of hell and the eternal tortures therein; instilled by the brimstone clergy of the time.

In some ways it could be said that they believed in, and thought about, Satan far more than they did about God.

16

Don't Mind If I Do

IT WAS CHRISTMAS. IT WAS CHRISTMAS, NEW YEAR AND TONY'S birthday all at the same time. It was the day he saw a UFO, the aliens had landed and the Grandmasters of the Illuminati came clean. Imagine. You're in love with the girl next door. You've never dared tell her. Then she just appears at your door and asks to stay the night. Tony willed himself not to turn round, to watch her. But why now? Why had she come round now? Had the Grandmasters got to her? Had they ordered her to get inside? Was she going to be their spy? The polystyrene was fine for stopping directional mikes and microwaves but she'd see it all. Ever since he had designed 'Everything 1.1' and left Digital Corp he knew they were going to come after him. After all, he was still hacking into their Kray super-computers. And he was too dangerous to just be left to carry on.

He tapped a command and brought up the archive directories. He scrolled down to the 'Miranda' folder and her face beamed from the screen. Every couple of seconds a new picture flashed up. She really was beautiful. Tony sat and watched and thought for most of the night. Going over the possibilities.

What about someone being in her room? If they had been, then she was probably clean. They were probably installing listening devices, transceivers. Anything. Tony let himself quietly out of his room and into Miranda's. He switched on the light. She was right; it was clean in a way he'd never seen it. He supposed for a moment that she could have cleaned it up just to back up her story but doubted that she would really go to the lengths that whoever did, did. Them. And if they were this close he knew he was going to have to move. Soonest. Set up somewhere else. And Miranda would no longer be there. Tony felt a heaviness thump into his stomach. But his quest was bigger than he was. He had to keep going. He had to get to the end of 'Everything 1.1'.

Maybe. Maybe she would come with him. If he told her everything. Maybe she would come and . . .

Tony's computer wailed as he opened his door again. He had forgotten to do the security doorknob sequence. He rushed to his computer to turn the sound off but Miranda had sat bolt upright in the bed. She was staring at the screen. She was staring at herself.

With rattling persistence, the late trains at Clapham Junction shook Mercy's window. The sash banged loosely against the frame. Mercy found the one thing in the world not eager to come to bed with her: sleep. She lay awake and listened to the trains. Occasionally a flash of electric sparks would light up her room. None of this usually kept her awake. It wasn't Randa. Mercy had cleared her conscience of that by schlepping all the way over to Goldhawk Road. Randa was obviously just in a shitty frame of mind and would probably come out of it tomorrow. It wasn't her conscience. It wasn't facing a loony with a gun, or a raft of them in the pub. It wasn't the sickening smell of the hospital. It wasn't Flirt. It wasn't the old wound, the bastard. It wasn't her roots, though they would need to be done. It wasn't. Hang on. It was Flirt.

Now that Mercy thought about it, she realized that she had acted completely contrary to her nature. Or what she thought was her nature. She helped Flirt, a man, she got him to hospital, she played bleeding Florence Nightingale and let her friend, a woman, storm off in an hysterical fit of temper. That wasn't her. But he needed help and no one else was offering. What happened to Mercy the man-eater? Maybe it was because he was so pathetic. Maybe it was that honesty in showing he was the weaker sex. Maybe because he was quite cute. It'd been a long time. A long time.

Barry was also finding it difficult to sleep. He'd had to creep in because his mum was sleeping on the settee again and the mix of alcohol and kebab was dancing in his stomach keeping his brain buzzing. Such a lot had happened and, never the quickest of minds, he had to take the time to piece it all together.

He was getting in with some of the big boys now. Men who carry guns and aren't afraid to wield them. Not only wield them but wield them at women. And not just any woman but that bitch Mercy. Barry sincerely believed that nothing would have given him greater pleasure at that moment than watching her head being blown off. Well, maybe having sex with her would. In the video game that was Barry's curiously monochromatic mind the sex and violence of these two thoughts co-existed quite merrily.

As these thoughts of Mercy danced brightly in his head he decided that he wasn't going to get any sleep until he had fetched the Andrex. Thus once more Barry selflessly saved the world from his progeny.

Going to sleep in the bed of an obsessive who regularly dresses up in your clothes is perhaps not the most sensible thing a girl can do. But then, politicians' wives seem to be able to live with it. See it from Miranda's perspective. She knew Tony was odd, but odd can be endearing in a just-don't-get-too-close sort of way. Tony Fromnextdoor was not exactly dangerous, he was too clumsy to be dangerous, and too socially inept.

But now Miranda was watching herself as she had never seen herself. As she had never been. It looked like her, but it wasn't her. It was, perhaps, that other Miranda who was so conscientious in her cleaning habits. Miranda could barely believe she was seeing pictures of someone who looked almost exactly like her but was not her. Some were naked, but with breasts she didn't have or legs or thighs. Some were clothed in clothes she didn't have. Some looked more like her, some less. But it was her. Maybe she had been drugged and forced to perform these things. Tony had attempted to switch the computer off when he'd returned but she had knocked his hand away from the keyboard. Now she watched as image after image flashed up. She couldn't remember being in any of these poses. She wondered what had happened, how long had she slept, was she still in Shepherd's Bush? She looked at the Styrofoam walls. It certainly seemed to be Tony's little room.

At last she spoke. 'Is that me?'

Tony bit his lip as if weighing up what he should tell her. Finally he said, 'No. It's not you, it's just images which look a lot like you.'

'Images. Like you make them up? Like from photographs or something?'

'No, no, I don't make them. The computer calculates them.'

Miranda pointed at his computer. 'That thing?'

'Oh no,' said Tony. 'No, a super-computer at Digital Corp.'

'Those were the people you used to work for.'

'Yes.'

'Why is their computer making, er, calculating pictures of me? They're not all that accurate, you know.'

'It's not just you. It's everything. I just saved some of the ones I thought looked like you.'

Miranda was not really grasping what was going on. Tony obviously did have a bit of a thing about her, but she'd never imagined it had come to this. She checked to make sure she was still fully clothed. It was Ferdinand's jacket still around her but nothing seemed to have been disturbed.

'I think that this might be the reason they were in your room.'

'Who was in my room?'

'Well, it could have been people from Digital, or Secret Services, or some agents for the Grandmasters. I couldn't tell you.'

This was all a little too weird. A Miranda playing the piano flashed up. 'The Grandmasters? Are they like a rap group or something?'

'No, they're the two hundred and fifty, the ones who really run this country, the world. It's all a conspiracy. I know because I read it. There.' He pointed at the screen which now showed Miranda bending backwards. 'I've read so many of the secrets they want to keep from us.'

Miranda nodded and tried to look serious. 'Conspiracy,' she said slowly and then, 'ah.' As if she had managed to place him nicely in the definite harmless loon category.

'Can you keep a secret?'

'Oh, I think so,' Miranda said as unpatronizingly as possible. Her one concern was to get out of there before Tony started telling her about how Masons are really aliens.

'These pictures, how they're made, it's, like, why I left Digital.'

Miranda nodded and smiled, knowing that whatever it was Tony was about to explain, she wasn't going to understand a word of it.

'It's a program I wrote when I was there.' Suddenly on his home ground, Tony became unhesitating and articulate. 'I called it "Everything". It was just a tiny thing which started at one and counted and kept counting in binary. And for each 1 in sequence it put a black pixel on the screen and for each zero it put a white one. So gradually it would go through every permutation from a completely white screen to a completely black one. You see what that means.'

Miranda stared a consciously blank stare.

'It means that anything that can be pictured in black and white, in two dimensions, will be shown somewhere between all white and all black. Everything that could ever be on a screen would be there at one point or other. Everything.'

'Which is why you called it "Everything",' Miranda ventured, kind of getting it.

'Well, yes. Think of anything. The surface of planets, nude celebrities, every page ever written and not yet written.'

'Like the monkeys and the typewriters.'

'Exactly, only this is not infinite. It will write every page of *Hamlet* and *Hamlet II The Sequel* and every play Shakespeare forgot to write. But though the number is not infinite, it is very very big. All the numbers between 1 and the number to make the whole screen black are . . . well, if you wrote it down the zeros would stretch to the moon and back.'

Miranda was getting a bit lost again.

'The problem was sorting through all these images; most of the time there would be just screen snow, static, so I then wrote "Everything 1.1" which only saved images if there was more or less than 10 per cent covered and there was a tolerance of contiguous pixels.'

'Tolerance of contiguous pixels,' Miranda repeated.

'Recognizable shapes, large enough to be objects.'

'And I'm one of the objects?'

'Everything is. I just sorted out some of the ones that looked like you. You see I have an awful lot of images to sort through every day. You can see why I couldn't leave it alone. I might miss something. I was spending all my time sorting through the stuff it churned out. That's how I know about Grandmasters. I read it there.' They both looked at the screen as the calculated Miranda did something curious with what looked like a goldfish. Tony carried on, 'Then they sacked me for not getting on with my job, but "Everything" was bigger than me. I had to keep it going.'

'It's not finished?'

'Oh, no. Nowhere near. It really is a huge number. You see, when it's got through everything I will know the truth. Every fact, every image. I will have seen it all. That's why I needed the Digital Corp super-computers to run it.'

'But they sacked you.'

'I'm hacking in on the chairman's account. I'm tying up 20 per cent of their computing power and they don't know a thing. But after tonight I'm not quite so sure. Maybe they've cottoned on.'

'They. The ones who tidied my room?'

'Yes. And if they're on to me, I'm going to have to move somewhere else.'

'Right.'

Miranda wondered why these pictures didn't particularly offend her. Maybe it was because if they were just part of 'Everything' it was somehow indiscriminate, maybe because they weren't actually her, maybe because she looked pretty good in them. Far better than the real thing, which must be on there somewhere too but Tony probably didn't recognize it. Even with this program the truth was what you wanted to see.

Miranda looked at a pneumatic version of herself and thought that it looked like a cross between her and Mercy. She then looked at the door and wondered about her room. If there really were Secret Service men or whatnot going through her stuff, the sooner weird Tony moved the better.

'Miranda, could I ask something which might come as a bit of a shock.'

Miranda didn't have time to say no.

'It's just I really like you and I. Well, I'm going to have to go. Move. And. Will you . . .'

Miranda willed the three dots to be 'look after my goldfish', 'forward my post', anything but 'come with me'. Please not 'come with me'.

'Er,' hesitated Tony, 'come with me?'

Oh, God.

'We could go anywhere. I've got an untraced account at Citibank that I've filled to the brim.'

'Look, Tony,' said Miranda, 'you're very sweet but . . .'

Dawn was gently nudging away the shadow of night when Miranda left Tony's room. She might, she thought, get a few hours in her own bed; a place which seemed far less strange after Tony's polystyrene fortress. The sun also rose in Vauxhall, skimming the satellite dishes and high-tech paraphernalia of the giant, flash, post-modern MI6 offices. Only after it had cleared the sandstone building and set it alight in blazing gold did it attempt to penetrate the dull grey dusty windows of the more pedestrian Victorian MI5 buildings.

It is now necessary to return to those offices and one in particular, which might, or indeed might not, be on the fifth floor of that building. There an early morning meeting was to take place which would have a devastating effect on Miranda's life, and our life together.

Let us start with who was there. It is perhaps reassuring for patriots to know that there are many highly qualified people working for the nation's Secret Service. Indeed most of them have endless strings of letters after their names. However, in espionage circles, the post-appellatory letters most coveted and treasured are AKA. They mean you really are involved with some shifty business and aren't just some lowly database maintainer, form-sifter or such like. The meeting in question was awash with AKAs, albeit ones that i have found it prudent to give them. Attendant were: Burnt Umber AKA Ferdinand AKA Whoji Whoopsi; Peter Peersnide AKA Vermilion Lake AKA Leon Trotsky and Rose Madder AKA The Administrator AKA Snuffles (but only by the memsahib). They gathered to once again discuss the growing problem of Operation Love Nuts and the destiny of a certain Miranda Brown AKA The Love Interest AKA my first love.

Unfortunately i find that i must again obscure my description of the office to comply with official secrets and offer you no knowledge which might put you, my dearest, in jeopardy. The jungle office was, perhaps, a little misleading, though hoped it gave a certain amount of the true essence of the place. In order to give you the flavour now, i think a Whitehall farce might be more appropriate. Thus the receptionist who showed Peersnide onto the stage drawing room could only be described as a dolly bird. She ushered him through the door and smiled sweetly as it slammed shut behind her, artfully catching her skirt. Peersnide sauntered towards the armchair, causing her to suddenly rush forward to prevent him from sitting on her pussy which just hissed at him. With that, her entire skirt ripped off, leaving her displaying her long legs clad in stockings and suspenders. The audience laughed loudly as she pouted at them, knocked her knees together and tried to cover some of the more essential parts with her hands. She edged over to Rose Madder, who sat on the sofa, a brandy glass on a silver salver resting on its arm. She whipped the tray out from under the glass to try and cover her crotch just as Madder, with immaculate timing, picked up the glass for a swig and unconsciously stopped it from spilling. More laughter issued from the fourth wall which remained obscured by the bright lights. The receptionist then started edging to the door. Almost there, she halted at the sound of a man shouting off-stage, 'Brandi? Brandi?'

'Oh, heavens,' the receptionist gasped, 'my boyfriend. Sir, he can't see me like this. Don't tell him where I am.' With that she ran to the door on the opposite side of the stage.

'Glad you could make it, Lake,' said Madder as he tried to put his glass back on the salver and then looked confounded at its disappearance. A couple of giggles from the audience. 'Not too early for you?'

Peersnide shook his head as he sank into the armchair. It made a loud and completely uncoverable farting sound. Someone tittered but it didn't get the laugh the set designers had hoped for.

Madder gave him the appropriate withering look which he meted out to all his finks.

Ferdinand, clad in tennis whites, then walked in through the French windows bearing a tennis racket and in shorts so tight they not only displayed his religion, they threatened to change it.

'Anyone seen my balls?' he called out in a hearty fashion and to thunderous laughter.

'Sit down, Burnt,' said Madder, indicating the sofa next to him. Burnt athletically leapt over the sofa, landing next to a tea biscuit which bounced up and landed in his mouth. Applause.

'Now I'd like to hear you first, Lake.' Madder was keen to get the obscure and probably totally tangential brief out of the way first before he got the proper one from Burnt.

'Yef fir. Well I wov in fe pub an . . .'

'Look, I'm sorry to stop you there,' said Madder, 'but I can't actually understand a word you're saying.' He looked at Ferdinand. 'Can you work it out?'

Ferdinand shook his head.

'Forry,' said Peersnide. 'Ah burnt ma tun aft nye.'

'What?' said Madder, getting a little redder.

'Ah – burnt – ma – tun – aft – nye.'

Burnt leant forward. 'Sir, I think I know the dialect.' He looked at Peersnide and said earnestly, 'Ah yer al ight? Sit yer tun?'

Peersnide looked towards the gantry with despair and nodded.

'He burnt his tongue last night, sir,' Ferdinand said smugly. Peersnide really hated him.

'Aw a keba.'

'Right. Sorry to hear it, Lake. Hope it gets better.'

A man in a blazer, cream trousers and sailing shoes entered through the reception door. 'Brandi?'

Madder held up his glass. 'Don't mind if I do.'

'No, Brandi, sir. My girlfriend. Your receptionist. Have you seen her?'

'Er no. No, haven't. Sorry.'

'Sherri,' called the young man.

'Don't mind if I do,' said Ferdinand, reaching for a glass of his own.

'Sherri,' the man shouted a bit louder, 'we're safe here.' A tall redhead entered looking around. The man grabbed her and began to kiss her passionately.

'Well,' said Madder, turning to Ferdinand, 'what about you, Burnt? Debrief.'

'Sim Salabim, sir. Contact made yesterday at the Love Interest's place of work. Used standard issue City character.'

'Name?'

'Well, the bods at ID came up with Ferdinand.'

'What, like the bull?'

'Er. No, sir. Like the Shakespeare character. *The Tempest*. They reasoned that if she had a Shakespearian name she probably knew the play and an appealing member of the opposite sex might have the corresponding lover's name.'

'Don't patronize me, Burnt.'

'No, sir. Lake helped me re-establish contact on the underground after she finished work and we went to dinner.'

'The three of you?'

'No, just she and I. I had Lake cover her home in case I lost contact with her.'

'Ah waf in de pub.'

'Sorry to hear that, Lake.'

The redhead managed to disentangle herself from the young blazered man and took a huge breath. 'But what about Brandi?'

'Don't mind if I do,' said Madder and Ferdinand in unison. Laughter rippled from the stalls.

'She'll never know,' said the man, trying to kiss her again.

'But you must tell her. I'm not going to be your bit on the side. You're like a sailor with a girl in every port.'

'Don't mind if I do,' said Ferdinand and Madder again. This time the audience chanted with them.

'All right. All right. I'll tell her as soon as I see her.' At that he took the redhead in his arms and resumed his kiss.

Madder looked at his watch. 'Let's keep this brief, I've got an Intelligence Agencies five-a-side friendly later and a lot of work. What's the upshot, Burnt?'

'She seems to have read the book, sir,' replied Ferdinand. 'But my impression is that, though she is nice enough, she lacks inspiration to do much. She's not a world-changer. She does have an interest in love.

I couldn't really establish whether it was personal or anthropological. Emotional or conceptional. I asked her whether she believed in love at first sight and she said something about "love at first night". A line I recognized came directly from the book. I have to imagine why she might have picked out that book in the first place. It's not that she wants to be in love, maybe she's just curious why others are. That in itself is nothing alarming. I did try elementary level one seduction.'

'Coffee, her place,' said Madder, smiling and remembering.

'She proved resistant.'

'I fun a ma who ha slet wif her.'

The two men turned to Peersnide. 'I think he said that he found a man who had slept with her.'

'Go on.'

'She was very col, no wanning to ge infolfed. No inrested in a relayfinhip.'

Madder was beginning to understand the charred tongue. Burnt looked surprised. For the first time there was a waver in his voice. 'Even so. I took her to be uninspired to spread this any further. I think she is looking for other things in her life. This really isn't worth wasting any more resources on in my opinion. I don't think the book will make an impression. We should just steal the book and forget her.'

'You know we had sweepers in her place looking for the book?'

'She carried it with her.'

'But you think it is of little importance to her.'

'Even if it had any significance to her, I don't think she has many friends to tell about it. It'll be contained by her own personality. She is simply a lonely and shy young girl. She has gamma leadership qualities.'

Peersnide nearly jumped out of his seat.

'Na. Na. Yer wron.'

'What?'

'Laf nye in de pub. Neely a hunar peple dere. She wal in, an de whole pub greet her. Dey al say hello, an boar her dinks.'

Madder furrowed his impressively hairy eyebrows. 'Are you sure?'

Peersnide nodded his head vigorously then sat down. He was in a farce and he could feel his trouser buttons popping, eager to fall down. Madder looked at Ferdinand.

'Doesn't sound very consistent.'

'Sir, I can only tell you the impression I got. She really isn't worth all this.'

'Can't risk it. Let's eliminate her before this spreads. If we'd cleaned up properly after getting rid of Pennyfeather we would never have had this problem. Kill her, Burnt.'

'With respect, sir,' Ferdinand replied quickly, aware that the faster you challenge a decision the more likely your chance of changing it is, 'if Lake is right, if she has all these friends, it'll take a few days to cook up a convincing accident and by then she could have started a whole coven of whispers needing containment.'

'All right. We can't do her in. Not here anyway. But we need to isolate her quickly. You'll have to be a honey trap I'm afraid, Burnt. And get her out of her social by this afternoon. All right? Far away.'

At that moment Brandi walked in again, a towel around her waist. 'Sir, I thought I'd better remind you, you have an 8.30.' The young man quickly pushed Sherri behind the sofa and turned to face Brandi plastered in lipstick.

'Brandi!' he said in mock surprise.

'Don't mind if I do,' came back the mantra.

Brandi looked at him. 'You've been kissing someone.'

'No, I haven't.'

Brandi pointed at the lipstick.

'Ah. I cut myself shaving.'

'Who is it?' she screamed. 'Tell me. Is it Margarita?'

'Don't mind if I do,' everyone shouted back. Even Peersnide joined in.

The young man shook his head.

'Don't tell me it's that Bloody Mary?'

'Don't mind if I do.' And at that Sherri stood up.

'Who's this Margarita?' demanded Sherri.

'Don't mind if . . .'

'Sherri,' said Brandi in disbelief.

'Don't mind . . .'

'Brandi,' said Sherri.

'Don't mind if I do.'

Both women walked up to the young man and slapped him hard. He recoiled and fell over. The women smiled at each other and walked off. Madder waved his glass at the man as he stood up. 'I know you, aren't you that Jack Daniels?' Big laugh.

'No, sir. My name is Glen.'

'Oh,' said Madder, looking glumly back at his glass.

'Glen Livet, sir.'

Hoots and whistles accompanied the roar of 'Don't mind if I do.'

Madder nodded and stood up. He turned to Ferdinand. 'I just want this stopped. Do you understand? Use your initiative.' He looked at his watch. 'Whatever happens, you need to conclude before the new tax year.'

'Te thicks o apewill?' Peersnide asked.

'No, first of the month. New annual department funding starts.'

'But sir,' said Ferdinand, 'that's the day after tomorrow.'

Madder nodded. 'That's all. Good luck. Burnt. Lake.'

'Sim Salabim, sir,' nodded Burnt and taking Peersnide by the shoulder conducted him off-stage.

Madder turned to Glen Livet. 'I dare say after all that Sherri and Brandi you'll need a strong coffee.'

'Oh, I've seen him, sir,' Glen replied. 'He's not so tough.'

Curtain.

It was, after all, in the Middle Ages, in that southern part of
France, dominion of some of those Courts of Love, that the cult
of the Cathari emerged, a medieval community who believed in
Manichaean dualism; that Satan and God, good and evil, were a
Yin and Yang affair, of equal power and draw. Equal.

For the Church, desperate to hold on to their power through
God, this was a heresy too far. The Pope launched yet another
Crusade to destroy the heretics. It is said that, before the massacre of the Cathar city of Narbonne, one holy general asked
the Pontiff how they were to tell the heretics apart from the
true Christians. The Pope's answer was simple, 'Kill them all
and let God sort them out.'

What this demonstrates is just how brutal the Church was willing to be to hold on to its power to put the fear of God in people.

Simply put then, in those times, one did not live a goodly life
to better oneself and one's society, one lived a God-fearing life
in order to avoid slipping down into the burning lakes of hell.
Indeed, fear proved an ideal way to define oneself. It is easier
to explain who one is through describing one's fears and mis-
eries than outlining one's confidences and joys. This is why I
see the feudal system, where might was right, as being one of
the major instigators of, or if it is in our genetic nature, one
of the major creations of, 'negative motivation'.

So it was, out of this fiery world, fuelled by fear, that love
arose, phoenix-like, from the ashes of their despair.

Why, we must ask? Why did the noble idea of a high romantic love grip these people who lived in terror? On the face of it,
it would seem a far too happy prospect for those who held onto
fear to place themselves. Yet in much the same way that Heaven
was an ethereal destination always beyond their grasp whilst
alive, the perfect loving relationship was a similar spiritual goal.

Even today, love seems an easy enough state to achieve and
yet if we are honest a truly stable love is a dream, it is impossible because our hearts are fallible. Love is a shape-shifter, an
ever-mutating thing, which, for those in pursuit of it, will
always be just out of reach. Love changes more swiftly than an
Alaskan stripper, for it is impossible to know another's heart
completely, and what stands true of love today may be lying
tomorrow. This is why love defies definition; forget the scud
missile, love is the ultimate moving target.

So right from the outset all the medieval notions of love, like
Tristan and Isolde, Lancelot and Guinevere, were tragic; just as
Heaven was unattainable, stable love was unobtainable.

Fig 1. Rules from *De Arte Honesti Amandi*

1. The state of marriage does not properly excuse anyone from loving.
2. He who does not feel jealousy is not capable of loving.
3. No one can love two people at the same time.
4. Love is always either growing or declining.
5. Whatever a lover takes against his lover's will has no savour.
6. A male does not fall in love until he has reached full manhood.
7. The mourning period for a deceased lover is two years.
8. No one should be prevented from loving except by death.
9. No one can love unless compelled by the eloquence of love.
10. Love is an exile from the house of avarice.
11. It is unseemly to love someone you would be ashamed to marry.
12. A true lover does not desire the passionate embraces of anyone but his beloved.
13. Love that is made public rarely lasts.
14. Love easily obtained is of little value; difficulty in obtaining it makes it precious.
15. Every lover regularly turns pale in the presence of his beloved.
16. On suddenly catching sight of his beloved, the lover's heart begins to palpitate.
17. A new love drives out the old.
18. A good character alone makes someone worthy of love.
19. If love lessens, it soon fails and rarely recovers.
20. A man in love is always fearful.
21. The feeling of love is always increased by true jealousy.
22. When a lover feels suspicious, jealousy and the sensation of love increase.
23. A man tormented by the thought of love eats and sleeps little.
24. Everything a lover does ends in the thoughts of his beloved.
25. A true lover considers nothing good but what he thinks will please his beloved.
26. Love can deny nothing to love.
27. A lover cannot have too much of his beloved's consolations.
28. A small supposition compels a lover to suspect his lover of doing wrong.
29. A man who is troubled by excessive lust does not usually love.
30. A lover is continually, without interruption, obsessed by the image of his beloved.
31. Nothing forbids one woman being loved by two men, or one man by two women.

17

Do You Actually Understand What We at Y Branch Do?

MIRANDA OPENED HER EYES AND STARED AT THE CLOCK. 8.15. SHE WAS late. Willing every muscle to life, she threw off her duvet, pushed herself up and stumbled to the chest of drawers. She pulled out a faded pair of pale blue knickers and what was once a lacy black bra but now was so frayed it more closely resembled a tassel fringed belly dancer's *büstenhalter*. Once, a long time ago, she had bought it to cheer herself up, but function had long since replaced both fancy and form and now she strapped and fastened it to herself as unconsciously and efficiently as a car seat belt. Sitting down again on the bed, she rolled her tights up her legs and began to hunt around for her workskirt. She looked under the chair, felt beneath the bed. Threw up the duvet. It was nowhere. And then she remembered leaving it on the tube. 'Bollocks,' she said, 'fucking bollocks.'

She reached for her 1 dress and dropped it over her head. Pulling her widest belt out of the drawer she put it round her waist and then slipped into her blouse. She carefully rolled the blouse at the bottom and tucked it all under the belt, so it looked, to all but the closest inspection, like the shirt was tucked into a skirt. Fine, she thought, as she looked at the mirror. Fine.

She sat down in front of her reflection and stared at the wreck before her. She stared at this washed-up thing and wondered what could be salvaged. The make-up from last night had wandered about her face and now, now she looked like the Miranda she had come to know and loathe. There was something nice about seeing this familiar Miranda, after Tony's fantasy girl last night. She dragged some baby nappy-wipes over her face. That was a Mercy tip; the cheapest cleanser on the shelf. With a little early morning shake she managed to get a swathe of mascara and a smear of lipstick on. Grabbing the bag, and me, she shot out of her door, past Tony's, down the stairs and out of the front door. She was half way to the station before she realized that she hadn't thrown up that morning. She'd had a big dinner last night and it had all stayed down. As she smiled to herself she heard the distinctive rumble of a train approaching the Goldhawk Road railway bridge. She sprinted to the station, slammed her single button, ran up the steps and at the very top she tripped. Trying to correct her balance she leant backwards. With that she then started toppling the other way, she started to fall, falling down the steps. Careless, careless, she thought to herself as she fell. The ground loomed closer to her head.

Miranda opened her eyes and stared at the clock. 8.30. She was late. Willing every muscle to life, she threw off her duvet and started the whole process again.

The lovers' time is a paradox: without each other it extends and slows until days feel like years; but with each other time races and hours feel like seconds. It seems the only way that lovers could spend more time together than apart would be to fall out of love. Maybe that's why we do, eventually. But i was in the throes of wildest love, despite all the evidence that was slapping me in the cover. So there was Flirt and Ferdinand and candlelit dinner. So what? In lovers' time it had seemed an age since she last held me but as she sat down on the tube, almost as a reflex action, she pulled me out of her bag and we resumed our connection. i tried to pick up the tatters of our relationship, i tried to tell her about the futility of human to human love, i tried to talk her out of it. You can rely on inanimate objects. You can rely on me. Love me.

You can tell when a reader's not paying attention. A glaze comes over the eyes, the pupils diverge and lose their focus. You do it sometimes. i've seen you. i understand enough to know it's just human. It's not personal. It doesn't mean you think less of me. But at the time it really annoyed me. i was trying to speak to her and she was elsewhere. A fog of memories from the night before. A smile for Ferdinand though he'd never see it. She briefly came out of her reverie at Latimer Road, half expecting to see Trotsky appear again. He didn't. Paddington pulled up outside but no book-snatching, no rescues. Back to everyday. The day before had been extraordinary and she would just have to leave it as a weird and wonderful memory. Life's not like that.

'Maybe I didn't make myself clear yesterday. You are a vital component in the infrastructure here.' Mr Scrufstayn paced up and down behind his desk, recalling the vocabulary list from *Managing for Dummies*. He linked his arms together, grabbing the wrist on each arm. 'Like all of us, like the chairman, like me, you are a link in the chain of strength that makes this operation work. If you are a weak link then the whole chain is weakened. You threaten the smooth running of the entire process. Do I make myself clear?' Miranda began to think that getting sacked might be preferable to having to listen to Scruffy's management analogies. But he'd never actually sacked anybody. 'I believe that I have given you ample warning and yet. And yet you insist on flouting the rules. Rules that have made the Second Floor one of the greatest departments in the store. Is it, perhaps, because you don't believe that we are good enough for you?'

People like to say yes, said *The Idiot's Guide to Management*, ask questions that invite positive answers. Mr Scrufstayn floundered as he remembered this. He looked at Ms Brown but it didn't look like she was going to answer him. Seeing her there, trying her best to look contrite, he wished for a moment that they could change places. Wished it was he being disciplined by this young woman. Perhaps she would taunt him with cruel put-downs and jibes. He imagined her telling him how naughty he had been. He imagined her saying she was going to have to spank him now and she was going to get very sweaty thrashing him within an inch of his life. She would strip down to her bra and panties and make him strip naked. Then she would take out the thorny rose stem he kept in his desk and she would whip his bare bottom until the welts bled.

Miranda began to feel a little uncomfortable. She wasn't sure whether she should answer or not. She couldn't believe he wanted her to answer that question truthfully but Scruffy had stood there saying nothing, breathing hard and looking at her, for an awfully long time.

Mr Scrufstayn closed his eyes and his shoulders shook. A cloud of dandruff flew up and glittered in the sunlight. He pursed his lips and silently drew a deep breath. He opened them again. Miranda was looking rather concerned. Mr Scrufstayn jerked the bottom of his blazer down and cleared his throat. 'I think I've said enough. We'll have no

215

more tardiness. Do I make myself clear?' He nodded and Miranda got up. She was nearly at the door when he spoke again. 'Ms Brown, I want you to whip,' the word brought up magical visions for him, he coughed to cover himself, 'I want you to whip up some enthusiasm for what can be very rewarding work.' Mr Scrufstayn smiled to himself for implementing another golden management paradigm. 'Try to use "carrot" words like "reward".' That particular gem he had found in the number one bestseller, *Patronizing Management Clichés for the Completely Clueless Arsehole*.

In an underground car park opposite Lambeth Palace, Peersnide and Ferdinand stood looking at a low, sleek, dark green Bentley Continental GT. An engineer leant into the engine bay and was making a whirring noise.

'Might as well go with something pokey,' smirked Ferdinand, 'if the department is going to pay for it.'

Peersnide looked at the vehicle with that curious mixture of distrust and disinterest which only non-drivers can display. He had been sitting with Ferdinand in Engineering for a couple of hours while they sorted out a car. He had spent most of the time swilling cold coffee around his mouth and his tongue had begun to recover. Hoping that they would not have to start talking about cars, a subject he knew nothing about so had always pretended it bored him, 'I haven't really understood what this honey trap is?' he said.

'I think that was Madder having a joke. It was a term used by the Russians in the cold war. It was a branch of the KGB made up entirely of beautiful young women. Their sole purpose was to seduce diplomats, embassy staff, businessmen and the like. Unfortunately, young and beautiful did not necessarily mean bright and cunning, and most of the Natashas were so obvious it would have taken quite some effort, and an awful lot of vodka, to reveal any secret by accident. So in the wonderful days of the cold war, the more sexually active diplomats would head out to Moscow just for the free totty. They would put it all down on expenses as a disinformation dissemination mission. Get it? De-semenating. Well, it was an awfully good joke back then.'

'So now you're going to be a honey trap. You're going to seduce Miranda, The Love Interest.'

'Romance her,' said Ferdinand, looking at him seriously. 'It's not sex she is in danger of disbelieving. It's love.'

'But this is the bit I don't understand. So what?'

'You've read the book. Love is a near perfect method used to subjugate and suppress the idealistic and the revolutionary. And the only way it can fail is if people begin to realize that it is controlled by others, not this rough poetic idea of a heart. Keep them trying to fuck each other and no one's going to have the time or energy to fuck with the State.

'Yes, but it looks just like any other conspiracy theory, it's marginal. There will never be enough people to believe it to turn over the conventional thinking that love exists. If you honour the idea by over-reacting to it aren't you in danger of exposing it as the truth?' Peersnide had never been struck by love or the idea of it, he felt no loss at acknowledging a more cynical agenda behind it.

'Listen, Peersnide,' said Ferdinand fiercely, 'do you actually understand what we at Y branch do?'

'Spy?' said Peersnide hopefully.

'Oh, you really are in the wrong place, aren't you,' said Ferdinand sympathetically. 'We don't gather information. We spread it. We make up stories. We gossip. We rumour monger. We are the ultimate purveyors of disinformation. So, you see, we know an awful lot about conspiracy theories. We should. We start most of them.'

Peersnide nodded and felt a shudder of cowardice shiver through him. In his spy books, when an agent starts telling someone what's really going on it is only because he is confident that it won't go any further and that is because he is going to kill him within five pages. In real life, Peersnide had supposed, they would shoot first and not bother with the details, but then the reader would feel cheated that no one actually did explain what was happening. With a deepening fear, Peersnide now wanted Ferdinand to stop. What he didn't know couldn't hurt him.

Ferdinand continued. 'Conspiracy theories are very useful to any controlling power because they strengthen people's fear of the State. We use paranoia to keep the public in fear of authority. The fact is that governments and the like couldn't do half the things they're rumoured to do, but it is the rumours which make them seem far more powerful and over-reaching than they are. That's why we are the branch of Military Intelligence never written about or exposed or even rumoured about. We know too much about those things and who does them best. We are dedicated to false intelligence and misleading the public so the people are kept in fear. And that,' Ferdinand said emphatically, raising an eyebrow, 'is why a gossiping book dealer like you is so useful to the branch and it is also why it falls to us to deal with the problem of this book.'

Peersnide nodded, praying that Ferdinand was not going to draw out a weapon at that point and say, 'And now I have to kill you.'

'But this theory is different,' Ferdinand said. 'That's why Pennyfeather and his book couldn't be tolerated. For one thing, it wasn't a conspiracy theory that we had started, secondly he was right, and thirdly it's one particular control methodology which only works if no one knows about it.'

Peersnide couldn't quite see how this all boiled down to one book and one girl. 'But what if one person doesn't believe in love?' he said. 'So what? Anybody who's had a broken heart has probably felt the same.'

'Yes, but they don't have a clear and reasoned argument to back it up. The broken-hearted are a negative class of word spreader. Any theory they might expound would just be put down to the individual cynicism of bad experience, not a unified theory of oppression. They are also not community leaders and you're the bloody one who made Madder think that she was a social guru holding sway over a school of acolytes. So you see the danger that The Love Interest poses is not that she won't believe in love but that she will disseminate a clear and overbearing argument against it and jeopardize this form of control. We would really need to nip this in the bud.'

'So you're going to seduce her.'

'My job will be to romance her, use her natural impulses to induce a feeling of love.'

'Then what?'

'Well, then I dump her, I break her heart and no amount of clever chat will convince anybody that she has a case apart from the bitter lover.'

'Seems a little callous.'

'It's the business.'

'And if you can't? If she's already gone too far? If she cannot love?'

'Then I will kill her,' said Ferdinand with just the right matter-of-factness to leave Peersnide in no doubt that any treachery from him would result in the same conclusion.

The engineer slammed the bonnet of the Bentley down and threw the keys to Ferdinand. 'There you go, mate. You'll get 200 out of her easy.'

Ferdinand thanked him, walked to the car and eased himself into the driver's seat. He beckoned Peersnide to get into the passenger seat.

'There's a few things I need to explain about this vehicle. This is not your average Continental GT, this car has been developed by the MOD as a class one weapon. It has more tricks up its sleeve than David Copperfield but you don't need to know any of them. It drives like any normal supercharged car. The only thing I have to warn you about is the key.' He held the key in front of Peersnide's nose. 'Never ever press the alarm button on the key more than twice consecutively.' He pressed the button once and there was a loud tweek noise. He pressed it again and the same noise filled the car. 'Because this is what happens.' He pressed the button one more time and Peersnide realized that the wheels had started screeching, the hand brake flipped down and the car shot off across the car park. Peersnide felt his lips opening to a sneer with the G-force of the acceleration pushing him back into his seat. And then with another tweek the car stopped, Peersnide slid forward and was only held from going through the window by Ferdinand's steel-like arm. 'It's an evasive tactic built into the car, if you should press the alarm three times without a minute's pause, the car will high-tail it away. And will only stop when you press the button a fourth time. Clear?' Peersnide nodded, although he was not quite sure if it was just because his entire body was still shaking.

Ferdinand placed the key in the ignition, turned it and the engine issued a dull throb. He held down the clutch, slipped into first gear, turned away from the wall that they had nearly hit and began to lift his foot. The wall at the far end of the garage leapt forward in front of them. He smiled as Peersnide clung to the seat. Peersnide hated cars. They brought back memories of being taken on summer holidays. Sitting in the back while his father steered the 2CV with such erratic driving skills that Peersnide would spend most of the journey hanging on to the door handle to save himself from being thrown from one side to the other or knocking himself out on the seatback every time they slowed. He also remembered being regularly beaten for staining the car seat with sick.

Ferdinand spun the car around the garage a few times and then headed for the exit. He eased into the traffic and seemed to take great care in telling Peersnide all the features of the car and what each knob did. Peersnide, who understood none of it, forgot almost immediately. 'You understand I'm going to have to take The Love Interest away, but I'll need you there as back-up.' Peersnide smiled and tried to look confident whilst feeling nauseous. This was all getting a long way from his books and his cosy office of spite.

As they drove over Lambeth Bridge Ferdinand talked about routes and Peersnide listened without hearing. At Victoria Station, Ferdinand pulled up. He turned to Peersnide and said, 'Now I expect you to be there by 2.30pm on 31 March, that's the day after tomorrow. Do you understand?' Peersnide nodded and was about to ask how he was supposed to get there when Ferdinand held up the car keys and dangled them before him. 'I'll see you there,' Ferdinand said, 'promptly.' The keys landed in Peersnide's hand.

'But . . .' Peersnide began but then thought, what sort of spy doesn't know how to drive? 'Oh, nothing.'

Ferdinand leaned over so close to Peersnide's face, Peersnide could hear the stickiness of his saliva as he opened his mouth. 'This car,' Ferdinand whispered menacingly, 'has over a million pounds' worth of surveillance equipment, stealth radar masking, and counter-attack implementation, it is the state of the art in armoured vehicles and it goes at 220 miles an hour. If there is a scratch, a single scratch, on it when I see it again, I will get demoted and I will personally see to it that your digits are removed one by one and your family dismembered alive like lab rats.' Although the last part, about his family, sounded rather good to Peersnide, he could only shiver at Ferdinand's sincerity. And then, as if he had said nothing, especially nothing about disembowelling and dissecting his colleague, Ferdinand smiled, patted Peersnide on the leg, got out and walked towards the station while Peersnide beat his head against the dashboard.

To say that a frost gripped the Second Floor that morning might be considered a slight understatement. Staff virtually had to don furs to chip away at the malicicles of hate that instantly froze again in the sub-zero air between Miranda's demonstration counter and Mercy's 'Clinically Clean' soaps and smells range. Even those shoppers unaware of the climatic power of these two personalities could sense that temperatures noticeably dipped in the region of Personal Hygiene. No one could walk between the two without being stabbed by the icy daggers they were looking at each other and it was a couple of hours before one foolish shopper, an ageing lady in a comfortable cardigan, stopped to ask Mercy about a bath oil.

'Do you think a man might like it?' asked the lady.

'If you want to know what men like, you better ask my colleague over there, Madam.' She pointed to Miranda as a queen might indicate the next to be beheaded.

The poor lady looked in Miranda's direction. For lack of anything better to hand Miranda held up a tampon as if it were a finger and to suggest that Mercy swivel on it.

'Oh, my word,' said the lady.

Miranda raised her voice pointedly. 'I may like them, but at least I don't steal them.'

'Steal them? No. She's too busy prostrating herself before them. She claims she's your friend until there's a man about and then wham bam, you can fuck off, mam.'

'Oh, my goodness,' tried the old lady.

'That's because I know what a friend is. And a friend doesn't steal a bloke.'

'Yeah, and a friend doesn't jump to conclusions either.'

'Or jump on a man you're interested in.'

'Oh, grow up, Miranda, I wasn't jumping on him.'

'You were all over him.'

'I was reviving him if you must know.'

'What? In a swoon after one of your kisses, was he?'

'He injured his foot.'

'So he needed the kiss of life?'

'He fell down. I bent down to see how he was.'

'Yeah?' said Miranda, unable to think of anything to challenge that.

'Yeah.'

'Well. Well, I wasn't interested in him anyway. So you know where you can stick him, which knowing you, you probably have already.'

That was too much for Mercy. She pushed the bottle of oil into the old lady's chest. 'You've been asking for this for some time.'

Miranda saw Mercy's compact bulk heading for her, her breasts crashing into each other, unable to establish a rhythm in the pace. As most people suddenly and unexpectedly threatened with violence do, Miranda suffered a moment of doubt. She froze. She didn't think it would get physical and felt completely unprepared.

Everyone on the Second Floor was watching but nobody moved to stop them. Even Mr Scrufstayn, who had popped over to check on Lingerie, as he so often did, stopped to watch and rather hoped that there would be a fight. In fact there was not a man on the floor who did not ache to see Mercy getting bodily with another woman and wasn't willing it to happen.

By the time Mercy had crossed to Miranda, she too was having doubts. Miranda seemed bigger close up, and she wasn't backing away. Mercy began to think she really shouldn't be doing this. She stopped and the two girls looked at each other for a good long time. A pool had already started in Ladies' Separates giving odds of 5 to 2 on Mercy beating the crap out of Miranda. Though shorter by a good few inches,

Mercy had the bulk in her frame. They all remembered what she had left of Adrian in Accessories, and all he had done was stoop to tie a shoelace when she was passing in one of her short skirts.

Mercy felt the weight of her reputation egging her on. She saw Miranda's bucket of blue dye. She could soak Miranda. She could chuck it over the counter and make her point in vivid blue. It was as if the entire Second Floor were shouting, 'Fight. Fight. Fight.' Having now lost her momentum Mercy took the time to survey the pack of spectators. The men had seen the bucket too and she could almost smell their testosterone, eager to see two girls in blue-drenched see-through blouses wrestling on the shop floor. Every breath was held. Mercy felt herself cresting on a wave of revulsion for what they were silently spurring her on to. Looking back at Miranda she reached into her skirt pocket and repeated, 'You've been asking for this for some time.' She held out a pound coin.

Miranda unconsciously put out her hand to accept the coin and smiled. She looked over Mercy's shoulder and spoke to the old lady, 'I can confidently tell you that men go wild for bath oils. Guaranteed to put him in the mood. One bath with that stuff and you'll be fighting off the best-smelling, hungry love machine in London.'

'Oh,' said the lady again, demonstrating that she really had exhausted her reactive vocabulary. 'But it's for my son.'

Disappointed, the rest of the Second Floor turned back to their counters, voices rose again and the shop was once more filled with noise. Mr Scrufstayn put down the suspender belt that he was holding – after all, the one he was wearing was still perfectly good – and hurried back to his office to see if *Lobotomized Management* had any advice about this particular event.

Miranda gave Mercy a big hug and felt some tears swelling. Mercy winked at her. 'Lunch-time, OK,' and she headed back to her counter. Miranda let some of the tears fall before mopping them with a spare pad. She looked directly at her friend. Flirt was a small price to pay to keep her friend in bitterness; after all he and she had barely spoken. The day before had all been a little much. Today they would resume the friendship and Mercy would tell her the plans for ripping out Flirt's heart. Miranda felt aglow with empowerment. Even if it was just for one night, one evening, she had got her tall dark handsome stranger and she had waved goodbye to him. She could do it. Though he was gone, she had, at least, done it once. And if she had done it once, she could do it again. She could.

*

Barry had missed the potential grand slam between the women he hated. At that moment he was sitting in Dispatch studying the latest piece of debris to have been excavated from his backside. He had been keeping himself to himself all morning. Far away from the witches. The phone began to ring. He had been trying to kick this sour feeling of pissed-offness with the world but it just wasn't going. He tried to think that it was better to be pissed off than pissed on, but that didn't cheer him up. The phone continued to ring. Probably more orders. Barry ignored it. He shouldn't be taking orders, he should be giving them. The phone remained insistent and Barry could little suspect that if he answered it, it would change his life for ever. Even unwittingly, Barry resisted change. He bit into the hairy nodule on his finger. The phone kept ringing. It was probably a woman. Fuck 'em. She could wait. The phone continued to cry until Dispatch Dave came in. He sneered at Barry and reached for it. 'Hello? Barry? Yeah, he's just here. Right by the phone. Wait a minute, I might have to explain to him how to use it.' He passed the receiver to Barry and whispered as he did, 'Just remember to wipe after use.' Quite justifiably, Dave, like everyone on the Second Floor, dreaded Barry's finger-itching sanitary habits and hated sharing a phone with him.

Barry pointedly rubbed his finger in the mouthpiece before putting the receiver to his ear and saying, 'Hello?'

*

Between then and lunch-time Miranda managed to refer all her customers to soaps and smells and Mercy had directed all her customers to the wonderful sanitary towel demonstration. By the time the clock had reached one, Miranda had gone over the Ferdinand story enough times to tell it as a wonderful anecdote and to come out as the victor over the sorry man who didn't even get coffee. Mercy was dying to tell Miranda about the disaster area that was Flirt.

As Miranda packed the last of her demonstration equipment away, a small gum-chewing woman staggered out of the lift trying to manoeuvre a vast bouquet of roses. The flowers cleared Hair Care and were headed straight for them. Typical, Mercy was always getting whole gardens of blooms. Another doomed admirer. Miranda knew it would be Flirt. The roses sidled past Manicures and Mercy began wearily to clear space on her counter for them. But they reached Mercy and carried on. Stopping in front of Miranda the flowerlady dumped the bouquet on her counter and said, 'Miranda Brown, Sanitary Towels, Second Floor?' Not the most glamorous of addresses but Miranda had to admit that it was her. 'Sign here,' said the flowerlady, chewing loudly and handing her a dispatch form. Miranda signed and she snatched the form and marched back to the lifts. Miranda could hardly believe that Flirt would still be interested in her. Mercy too, obviously a touch concerned about such an eventuality but trying hard not to show it, rushed over. Miranda opened the little flowered envelope.

> Dearest Miranda, thank you so much for a wonderful evening. I am having to go away for a while, but I will go crazy if I do not see you before I go. I'm at Victoria Station. There's a cab outside waiting to bring you. Don't let my world fall apart. You hold my life in your hands. Sim Salabim. F.

The shock was made somewhat more intense by the overpowering smell of the flowers. She handed the note to Mercy, who read it quickly and looked up at her. 'F?' she said. 'Flirt?'

'No, no,' said Miranda, 'Ferdinand. I wanted to tell you about him last night but . . . Do I? Should I?'

Mercy smiled at her. Hopeless fucking romantic. 'Lunch is off,' she said. Miranda didn't move. 'Go on,' urged Mercy, pushing her. 'Go.'

Miranda started to rush for the lifts. She turned back to Mercy for an instant. 'Thanks. For everything. I'll see you at two, yeah?'

O no we won't, i thought.

For example, one of those troubadourial inventors of romantic love, as we know it today, was the poet Andreas Capellanus.
It was he who wrote *De Arte Honesti Amandi* (1186), *The Art
of Honourable Love*, a book of rules for loving, commissioned
by the Countess Marie de Champagne.

Let me draw your attention to Figure 1, the list of the 31
qualities of true love outlined by Capellanus. The ladies of
court enjoyed working through this list to see if their ideas of
love were up to scratch. I believe it is still current in women's
magazines today to publish similar lists, with which the reader
is requested to agree or disagree in order that they may discover whether their love-life is 'Fab or Flab'. Certainly I believe
that over eight hundred years later many of us could reply 'Yes,
how true' to almost all the items.

However, let us note the number of references to the pain,
agonies and anguish inherent in this incarnation of 'love'.

> 16. On suddenly catching sight of his beloved, the
>   heart of the lover begins to palpitate.
> 20. A man in love is always fearful.
> 23. A man tormented by the thought of love eats
>   and sleeps very little.

No wonder, then, that love was something to be feared.
From the very outset, Capellanus is in no doubt that this 'love'
is a torture in many ways. He writes that, 'Love is a certain
unborn suffering.'

These are not too far from Ambrose Bierce's twentieth-
century definition of love as 'a disease curable by marriage'. But
why were so many ideas of discomfort sewn into the fabric of
love at this, its outset? Why, I must keep asking, were fear and
love bound together in such a way?

Remember that these lusty, pretty, cocksure young men and
these lovely, repressed, frustrated young ladies were talking,
writing and singing of all the rituals and rules they had set up
around that basic genetic need to mate: lust. Yet they were all
in the thrall and fear of the punishment of their genetically
jealous feudal overlord and therefore felt unable to consummate their needs.

By setting up a culture of behaviour around the desire to
have sex, and yet not fulfilling their genetic destinies, these
inventive young people separated lust from the act of sexual
intercourse. Like separating tiredness from sleeping, hunger
from eating, they severed the desire from the deed just as

Plato, over a millennium before, had severed lust from divine delight. The nature, to take what one wanted, to obey one's genes, was curtailed by the culture that the troubadours and queens created and maintained to keep themselves alive and not end their days on the point of the lord's sword.

The lover's heart palpitated, he ate or slept little, because he feared the consummation, which was likely to be punished with death, and yet his loins burnt. The French, even today, maintain the ecstasy of sex is 'la petite mort'. The little death.

Thus we can finally answer our question. That divorcing of carnality from the passions it inspires was done through fear and, for ever more, fear would be integral to love.

This is why I place the invention of love at this moment. It was the single step from which all our romantic ideas of love today are descended. Think what a vast culture has grown around this joke, this game they played called love. It has been eight hundred years since one could just indulge in the sex that one's genes demanded, without having to dress it up in any fancy words or notions. In those days before the genesis of love, when you felt those urges, you knew exactly what they were. They were not confusing, heart-racing, soul-questioning feelings, they were not surrounded by a million messages complicating the issue, calling it love, demanding that you act in a way which is culturally imposed rather than what your natural feelings desire. When you wanted sex you knew you wanted sex.

Now, after eight hundred years of cultural pressure, we all believe in the politeness and behaviour of loving and yet somewhere beneath we all still feel those primal urges. Is it any wonder that our hearts, our heads, our very souls are sorely tried by this severance, this split, this dichotomy?

The definition, then, that those naked dwarfs in that cartoon were searching for, I believe, is that 'Love is ... lust confused by society.'

We have been repressed by this invention 'love' for too long. I would be the last person to suggest that we should just go out and have sex with whomever we feel like, however, I do believe that, if we were able to re-evaluate the usefulness of 'love', we might be able to cope and deal with it more rationally and no longer labour under its oppression as if it were still some feudal overlord.

Why, we must ask, and how has this imposition been maintained for so long?

That, I am coming to.

18

The Big Book of Romantic Clichés

THE TAXI DRIVER LOOKED AT HIS WATCH, 'YOU'VE GOT ABOUT FIVE minutes before it leaves. Just over there.' He had parked at the side of the station and was pointing at a side arch into the station. Miranda could see some carriages at the platform. She once again smoothed down her 1 dress. She had lost the shirt on the way over, shoving it in her bag with me, thanking God for the accident which meant she was wearing her one decent article of clothing that day.

'How much is that?' she asked, fondling me as she searched for her purse.

'It's all covered.'

Miranda got out into the grey, exhaust-dioxided air of Victoria and hurried into the station. As she got closer to the train she could see Ferdinand further up the platform and smiled. He was standing there, like our man in Havana, in a crisp, light, impossibly uncreased linen jacket, talking to a porter who had a number of Vuitton suitcases. Now even porters travel in style.

Ferdinand turned as if almost sensing she was there and burst into a big grin, rushing towards her. 'Miranda. I am so happy you came.' Like there was a chance in hell that she wouldn't have. 'This is really embarrassing, look, I, I don't have much time but I just wanted to say that, well, I haven't stopped thinking about you since last night.' A bit thick, i thought, but consummately performed.

Miranda was expecting a little more thrust and parry. She smiled and shrugged. She could say something ironic but it seemed she had proved herself adequately in that field. She had proved herself a match for him and now, she supposed, was the reward for such diligent work. He was showing that now they could be a little more honest and open.

Some of the hydraulic couplings next to them hissed as they were checked and primed; the first panic sign for any lovers who have had to part at a train station.

'Look,' said Ferdinand staring seriously at her, 'as you can see I have to go to Venice on business.' He waved at the train.

For the first time Miranda took in the train. The gold-trimmed Pullman coaches, the porter dressed in white, the ancient signs on the windows, the wording along the top of the carriage: 'Venice–Simplon–Orient Express'. If you were looking for romantic ways to say goodbye you could have picked it straight out of the big book of romantic clichés. Which was pretty much what Ferdinand had done. In this day and age of jet travel, why on earth someone might be going to a business meeting on travel's equivalent of a sloth in Chanel clothing didn't really occur to Miranda.

'Will you be gone long?'

'No, no, but there was something I had to ask before I left.' Miranda's mind boggled. What question couldn't wait a few days. 'I wanted to ask you.' Ferdinand bit his lip, a terrible mutilation of something so lovely. 'Ask you to come with me.'

Miranda quickly looked at the train and back to him. 'You've got to be joking.'

'No. No. Never been more serious. Come with me.'

'My lunch break's only an hour.'

'It's the most romantic place on earth, Miranda, and I want you to be there with me.'

'You're mad,' Miranda laughed, 'what about my job?'

'Don't worry about it, just drop everything and come.' Further up the train a few doors were slammed shut, which just served to heighten the tension.

'That's all right for you to say, but I can't just walk out of my job.'

'Don't worry about that, my company own a big chunk of the store. I'll talk to them. You'll be back before you know it. Come on.'

'This is crazy, I haven't got anything, I haven't packed.'

'I packed a case for you,' Ferdinand said, waving at the pile of Vuitton now being loaded onto the train. 'Just a few essentials.'

'I haven't got my passport.'

'No problem.' Ferdinand whipped a little red passport out of his jacket and flashed the last page at her. There was a picture of a woman who looked like her, only nicer, a lot nicer than she looked in her own passport photo. 'Cynthia, in Accounts,' Ferdinand breathlessly explained, 'looks a little like you, lent me hers.'

'She lent you her passport?' Miranda was astonished.

'It's only for a couple of days.'

'I can't just . . .'

'Don't think of reasons not to come. Think of the reasons you should.'

Miranda faltered. This wasn't quite what she was expecting. She always thought she was spontaneous but now that it came to it . . . A whistle blew and a guard walked down the platform slamming doors. Ferdinand looked at her imploringly and grabbed her hand.

'I know this is a surprise but you have to take opportunities, Miranda. Sometimes they just come and slap you in the face and you have to be able to grab them because they're the things which change your life and any change is good because if you can't change you're dead. You have to seize life, grasp adventures or you're not living.' The guard reached them and looked at her. He held the door, eager to slam it and carry on down the train.

Miranda felt a well of panic. She yanked her hand from Ferdinand. 'Don't you dare tell me what I have to do. Don't tell me I'm not living. Don't presume about what I do with my life. What do you know?' Now she was shouting at him. 'You know nothing. I don't have to do anything. Opportunities are . . . you don't just grab every one that comes along. I pick. I choose. I take the ones that are right for me. It's not about grabbing, it's about discriminating, between bad and good.' She was crying now and the guard cleared his throat so loudly Ferdinand turned to him. He stepped into the carriage and the guard closed the door, continuing down the train. Slam. Slam.

Ferdinand pulled down the window and leaned out. Miranda moved to the door and looked up into his green eyes.

'Sorry,' he said, shaking his head. 'Sorry. Silly idea. I just. I just really wanted you to come.' Slam.

'I can't just drop my life the moment someone has to go on a business trip and wants me to go with them,' she said, putting her hand on his, resting on the window sill. Slam.

'But what have you got here?' he tried. 'What are you staying for?' Slam.

'Just, just my life,' Miranda said, now unabashed about her tears.

'I can only live one and maybe it's not a great one but right now it's all I've got and I'm proud of it and proud that I'm the one who decides what happens with it.' Slam.

Ferdinand nodded, looking down the platform, trying to avoid her eye as if fighting back a tear. 'I understand. I do.' It was time to up the stakes. 'Maybe I'm too used to business, think I can convince people to do things which they're not ready for.'

'What do you mean?'

'Just, I'm sorry, I shouldn't have put you under all this pressure.'

A whistle blew and the train jerked as the brakes were released.

'Maybe I'll see you when I get back,' said Ferdinand.

On the surface, this last statement sounded like the decision would be Miranda's, but it was said with just enough ambiguity to suggest that he might mean it would be his. This suddenly sounded quite worrying. Maybe this was it. Maybe she was pushing away the last chance to be with him. Another whistle blew and Ferdinand leaned out of the window and kissed her. The sweetest, warmest, most beautiful-smelling, gentle kiss that had ever laid on Miranda's lips. She tingled and closed her eyes as the lips were torn from her and the window began to move. Ferdinand turned quickly away and disappeared into the oak-lined carriage.

Yes, i smirked within her bag. Yes, see the sap off. Wave goodbye. It's you and i kid, all the way. You don't say no when a book transports you off to the world of romance.

Barry, completely uncoincidentally, was also in Victoria, or more accurately, he was in heaven. At the moment Ferdinand was turning from Miranda, he was outside the station running his hands lovingly over the powerful lines of the racing green Bentley, the uncontested ultimate object of desire. There were more pictures of this car on the walls of Dispatch than naked women, and there were a lot of naked women.

'And you want me to drive this?'

'Well, I can't, I'm afraid,' said Peersnide.

'Across Europe, to Venice.'

'Yes. I will pay you.'

It was like God had dropped from the clouds, shaken his hand and said, 'Really, Barry, you are the man, you know what I mean, the man.'

Peersnide already had a multitude of reservations about going anywhere, let alone on a long car journey, with this rather odious, uncouth boy, but he had gone through every possibility, calling him only when he realized he knew no one else who drove.

Barry was becoming just a little too excited. 'I'll be ready to leave straight after work then,' he said. He had to go back. He just had to show Dave and the rest of the smug gits what a real smug git can look like, one who parks a Bentley Continental GT in the loading bay.

Peersnide gave Barry the keys. 'Do you think you could give me a lift to Bond Street?'

Burnt Umber looked around his compartment. Somewhat cramped, but luxurious considering he was on a train. It was panelled in a rich dark wood, each panel dully reflecting the light at a slightly different angle and so giving a slightly different hue. Clever Edwardian labour- and space-saving devices sat snugly in each corner. His luggage was neatly stacked and a bottle of champagne sat rattling in an ice bucket. He went over to the bottle and pulled it out. A few drops fell back into the bucket but the ice was still fresh and white with frost. The label barely glistened with the few drops that had melted: Château de Rhône Que C'est Ce Q'onc 1978. A little brutal, but he was impressed. He sighed with satisfaction, money no object, no deadly assassins, no hairy commies, just a pretty enough girl and a pile of romance; he really was going to enjoy this mission. As he began to strip the foil from the bottle he silently thanked Peersnide for inadvertently building this into a nice big-budget case. The cork popped satisfyingly with a fountain of sticky white bubbles streaming from the bottle's lips. Gently and slowly he began to pour two glasses.

'How did you know, you arrogant bastard?' Miranda's voice came from behind him.

He didn't turn, just smiled a confident smile. He knew she had been behind him for well over two minutes. You need a lot of stealth train-ing to sneak up on an operative like him. Indeed, he had noted hearing the carriage door slam fifteen seconds after he had turned towards his room. 'I didn't,' he said, lifting the glasses and turning to her, 'just hoped.'

Miranda smiled as the train jerked and rocked. She shrugged her shoulders. 'Well, I just happened to be standing on Platform One with not much to do with the rest of my lunch hour so I thought: well, Venice, on the Orient Express, why not? It's either that or a baked potato and cottage cheese again.'

'You really are quite lovely,' Ferdinand said.

'Are you aware if there was anything on the item which caused the wound?'

'It was a shoe.'

'Yes. You said. A very sharp shoe.'

'Yes, the very sharp heel of a very sharp shoe.'

'So do you think that that shoe might have stepped in something before it inflicted the wound?'

'Well, yes. I suppose that it might well have done.'

'Maybe a faeces of some sort. Maybe canine?'

'It is entirely possible. I'm sorry but I'm getting rather agitated at this abstruse line of questioning.'

'It's just that the wound appears to have become infected and, I'm afraid, it appears quite virulent.'

'But the thing was treated with antiseptic last night.'

'Indeed. However, it does not seem to have penetrated deep enough into the wound.'

'Do you think you could give all this to me a little straighter. What are you getting at?'

'Gangrene.'

'Gangrene? But it only happened last night.'

'Which makes the whole thing quite interesting.'

'With all due respect, doctor, bollocks to your interesting, that's my foot, what can be done about it?'

'Well, we could give you intravenous antibiotics but if they don't get to the infection fast enough we could be looking at removing your leg.'

'Sorry. I came over a bit woozy there. Could you say that again?'

'There is a risk in prescribing antibiotics because they might not work fast enough to save your leg.'

'You, you are having a little medical joke with me. Aren't you?'

'I'm afraid not. The only other choice is to operate immediately so we'll remove as little as possible.'

'And. And. And. Just how little is possible?'

'A toe.'

'A toe?'

'Or two.'

'Or, or.'

'Nurse, 10mls of adrenaline, patient's fainted, needs to be awake for the anaesthetist.'

*

i feel i need barely waste your time in describing the antiquated luxury and splendour of the Orient Express as it clattered through the Home Counties. Such a set fixture of the romantic register is it, i think we can both accept that it is firmly established in the popular psyche as a very good place indeed if you want to impress a date. Which of course is exactly why Burnt selected it. Though, why something that is most famous for a particularly bloody murder being set on it is considered romantic, is far beyond me. Perhaps now i have distinguished the Hammersmith and City line by featuring at least two chapters set on it, it will become the line of choice for metropolitan lovers to moon and court.

And perhaps not.

Still, surely i need do no more than refer you to the host of other works which have featured the train, if you feel that you are not up to speed on the subject; books that shared my dusty shelves in Shepherd's Bush Library. Between Christie, Greene and the *I-Spy Book of Trains* you will, i believe, get all the 'colour' you could desire. i, on the other hand, love you and would not cheat on you like they do with endless descriptions, i have the story to tell and things are just starting to get rather exciting.

The champagne had bubbled its way into some very excitable synapses in Miranda's mind and she found herself eyeing the Vuitton cases. She was burning with curiosity to find out just what Ferdinand had thought to 'pack' for her. They had barely cleared Sevenoaks when the sonorous, understarved maître d' came to take their orders for lunch and furnished Miranda with a perfect excuse.

'Well, if we're going to eat, I should freshen up.'

'Good idea.'

'And maybe slip into something more. More.'

'Comfortable?'

'Well, I don't really know, do I?'

Ferdinand laughed generously. 'You want to see if my taste is as poor as my timing. I'll see you in the restaurant,' he said, getting up and going to the door, still open from the maître d's struggle to get out again. 'That is, if you are not too embarrassed to show yourself in those,' pointing at a case.

He closed the door and Miranda almost ripped the calfskin straps to get the case open. What greeted her was an unprepossessing neatly folded stack of clothes, their labels facing up. A pile of labels that looked as likely to have come from Rodeo Drive as a rodeo. Not a recognizable tag there, not a designer or international couturier amongst them. First round to Ferdinand, he had judged her spot on. Miranda was unashamed as a shopgirl. She had never got into designer clothes, metaphorically or literally. She was still young enough to believe that they were for a different world, for the women on the other side of the counter. As she and Mercy concurred, women desperately unhappy for having sold themselves to the richest husband and then only able to find brief respite in the dubious pleasures of 'retail therapy'. For Miranda, a thorough training in charity shop wardrobe selection had been enough to teach her how to recognize shape and quality and know what was tat. It was only those people who were unable to recognize quality who longed for labels. Some guarantee.

But in no charity shop had she ever found something like the black dress she picked out first. She held it up. It was seamless and so black it could swallow suns and time. Miranda excitedly tore her 1 dress off to get it on and it fell about her like a liquid shower of cotton and silk with, she conceded, a touch of lycra. And there it was, in the mirror. Almost as a second thought she realized that she was there too. If there was a perfect little black dress, which would show your good points and hide your defects, this was it. Miranda, who excelled at involuntarily resisting perfection and had always cursed that she was not a perfect size anything, looked at herself in the cupboard mirror. It fitted, perfectly, and for maybe the first time in her life she thought she looked, well, perfect.

Even she was aware of the peculiarity of such a thought. What was happening to the Miranda of guaranteed low self-esteem? Surely this 'retail therapy' of a single dress couldn't really cure the self-doubt that constantly bedevilled her? Puzzled but too excited to dwell, she checked her make-up and headed to the bar. But i knew the answer, i'd been through it, was in it at the time, i even thought my own cover was beautiful when she looked at it. You start to believe how a lover might see you. Miranda was falling, at break-neck speed, in love and there was nothing i could do. All my words just fell on blind eyes. Love was, after all, for her, the thing which made the world turn, life's purpose.

Ferdinand jumped up when she walked into the 3674 Salon Bar. 'Princess,' he said, 'I'm waiting for a dowdy little salesgirl to get changed at the moment, but I would be honoured if you would sit with me while I wait.'

Miranda wanted to kick him. She also wanted to kiss him.

'What do you fancy to wet your lips on?' he smiled, pointing at the bar. Snaking her bare arms around his head Miranda pressed her lips to him and kissed him hard. Ferdinand staggered back; he'd gone a little, charmingly, red.

'I meant what do you want to drink.'

'I know what you meant,' Miranda replied. She raised an eyebrow but her cool was cut short by the booming nasal American tones of a large man standing at the bar and somewhat more over-dressed than a five thousand island salad. In his bright white tuxedo and bow-tie, he was performing the duty of all Americans in Europe: to banish all noise from the earth save the sound of their own voices. Conversely, it is the duty of every European who talks to a loud American to employ a high level of irony. Despite a straining cummerbund and a dignified head of white hair, the man was struggling to find the appropriate vocabulary for the situation.

'Don't tell me that, you cocksucker,' he shouted, loud enough to wake the sleepers rattling beneath the train's wheels.

The guard looked at him with a sorry face. 'I'm afraid, sir, there is nothing I can do to rectify the situation.'

'I said don't tell me that. God damn this country. You're stuck in some fucking ice-age. It's not like I asked for a bath, I just want a god-damn shower, you little piece of shit.'

Perhaps sensing that in dressing down the guard in such a manner the American was transgressing Noblesse Oblige, or at least *Argent* Oblige, Ferdinand interceded, 'This train was designed over eighty years ago and they didn't have the ability to include such fittings.'

The man turned on Ferdinand, 'Did I ask you, ass-wipe? You and your goddamn history. How come no one understands that there are basic sanitary needs and bathing is one of them? I ain't gonna sit on this pile of shit for two whole days without washing myself.'

'Then maybe you should alight when we get to Folkestone.'

'The hell I will. I paid two thousand dollars for this railroad trip and I expect basic sanitary equipment. And don't tell me they didn't have the space. If they had made these goddamn coaches in America they'd have fitted showers made for rockets by NASA.'

'With respect,' said Ferdinand, employing the full force of obliga-tory irony, 'these carriages were made in America.'

The bow-tie strained a little as the man swallowed and was forced to think for a moment. 'Well. How long ago? We're not afraid to modernize. You fucking whoresons only have your history and you cling onto it like it's your mother's tit. In America we use airplanes. No one travels on trains to get anywhere. And our trains run on proper wide track not this little narrow gauge shit. And we have proper safe metal interiors not all this creaky wood and . . .'

Admirably, Ferdinand spoke loudly enough to interrupt him. 'If you felt like that, sir,' he spat, 'why on earth did you book to go on the Orient Express?'

The man turned to a string-thin woman at the bar, so riddled with plastic surgery she looked like an enormous stretch mark in a ball gown, now on her fifth Martini. He shrugged.

'I thought someone might murder my wife.'

Lunch was served and spent looking at Kent and each other. If there were sweet nothings that might have been exchanged at this meal they were postponed, as all Ferdinand and Miranda could hear was a string of invective on every subject under, and also including, the sun, of which there was not enough on this goddamn continent, at a decibel level that threatened to shatter ear drums. The trouble with any public transport, however exclusive, is the public; you cannot choose your company.

And thus any thoughts or doubts Miranda may have had were drowned before they had a chance to live. It was not until they had got to Folkestone, been ushered onto the giant, and definitely not period, catamaran Sea Cat and she was looking at the vast expanse of grey water surrounding her country, that the first memory pang of her 'real' world started to re-surface in her mind. Mercy. She was probably worried sick that Miranda hadn't come back, probably thought that she had been kidnapped and taken off for the white slave trade. Miranda looked at Ferdinand with some concern when that thought popped into her head and then: 'Oh my God, Caliban, who's going to feed Caliban?' Miranda imagined him climbing the cage with hunger and then, finally, rolling over with exhaustion, his sharp little talons waving slowly at the ceiling and curling up for ever.

'Do you think there's a phone?' she asked Ferdinand.

Burnt was certainly not going to let her talk to anybody without having a good listen. He fished into his jacket pocket and passed her his mobile phone. As they crashed through the waves she asked Sasha Rowland, the Second Floor's unofficial receptionist, whose Safety Rollers demonstration counter was next to the pay-phone, to get Mercy.

'Miwanda,' Sasha said, 'where are you? Thcwuffy'th gone thcwewy looking for you.'

'I'm on a ship at sea. Could you please get Mercy,' said Miranda a little cruelly.

'Thip at the?' wondered Sasha. 'I'll get Mer-thee, thtwaight away.' Sasha loved showing that she had no shame about her speech difference. It wasn't a defect. There were, after all, a blather of cheeky cockney presenters on TV who had more problems with their delivery than a postal strike. So she saw no reason to avoid her Ss or her Rs. Indeed some men loved her Rs and had said it was well rounded and very pretty.

You will be happy to know that all proceeds from that gag go to the Jim Davison old jokes retirement home. A resting place for decrepit one-liners where they might live out their last laughs and be prevented from becoming a burden to the thrusting young humour of today.

Mercy came to the phone. 'Miranda who?'

'Stop it, Mercy. '

'Oh Miranda. My mate who dumps me for a lunch date, pops off for an hour and never comes back again.'

'Sorry. I said sorry. I just thought you might be worried.'

'Worried? Me? What made you think that? I'd be in a pretty sorry state if I allowed myself to worry about someone who hides everything from me and won't tell me anything that's going on in her life. First it's the Finger and then some flower boy called Fred.'

'Ferdinand.'

'Whatever.'

'I was going to tell you. I was. But things just all went a little fast.'

'I'll say. How long you been seeing Fred then?'

'He was a customer, he only came in yesterday evening, just before closing.'

'A customer?' shouted Mercy with exasperation at her friend's naivety. 'A bloke comes in to buy a packet of muff absorbers. You don't think that's a bit strange? And then you run off with him? Wherever you are, Miranda, just get out of there now.'

'I can't. Listen, I'm going to be away for a couple of days. Will you feed Caliban for me?'

'Where the hell are you?'

'At sea.'

'I meant actually, not mentally.'

'Somewhere in the middle of the English Channel on a bloody great boat.' That shut Mercy up. There was a long pause as Miranda waited to hear what Mercy would say to that. The pause continued and

Miranda imagined that she had seriously gob-smacked her. After a little too long Miranda cautiously said, 'Mercy? Mercy?'

'We're probably out of range,' Ferdinand said, comfortably noting that she hadn't even had the chance to say where they were going. Madder had said 'isolated' and he was going to make sure that, from now on, any telephone she came into contact with did not work.

CHAPTER VII.

TYRANNY

All thoughts, all passions, all delights,
Whatever stirs this mortal frame,
All are but ministers of Love,
And feed his sacred flame.
          Samuel T. Coleridge (1772–1834) from *Love*

LOVE IS A PERVERSION.

Or, at the very least, completely unnatural. It is a man-made creation which we have been persuaded to experience when we misinterpret and try to repress the feelings brought on by the natural stimuli of lust. Persuaded by centuries of cultural conditioning.

Before I explore the implications of this assertion, let me briefly review the chain of reasoning which has led to this remarkable conclusion.

First, the only part of love that we have anything approaching 'evidence' of natural existence for, within *homo sapiens*, is the desire to mate, to procreate, to have sex and continue our genetic march towards world domination. This, let us call 'lust'.

Because of socially indoctrinated misinterpretations of early 'love' writings, we actually have no real evidence of love, as we know it today, existing before the twelfth century. Therefore, we can assume that it was lust which ruled in what was, essentially, a man's world. As long as one gender was completely subjugated to the will and the sexual urges of the other, there was no need for love which, as we observed, is only a behavioural pattern that surrounds and ultimately delays the realization of lust in the act of sexual intercourse.

Then, an extraordinary social upheaval occurred in that period in history, which resulted in a significant reversal in the sexual power balance, in favour of an educated gender of nobility who were unused to being empowered and lacked the language, or customs, to express their own sexual urges and genetic procreative needs. They longed to declare their needs and yet feared consummating them, for they faced almost certain death if they did. Caught in this paradox, they identified, and dilated, the difference between the desire for sex — lust — and the act of sex — intercourse itself. In this gap, they created a game, a play of meaning, a madness; they called it love.

It was they who began this culture of severing the need from the realization, the hunger from the feeding, which lasts to this very day. A culture which attempts to endlessly defer and delay the moment of consummation, the moment of sex, the orgasm, the ecstasy.

What they invented we now call 'courting', a direct reference, and homage, to those 'courts of love' which originally outlined the 'correct' patterns of behaviour whose dance steps we still follow.

So, continuing the argument laid out in the previous chapters, we are drawn to the conclusion that love is, indeed, unnatural, artificial, synthetic, a plastic emotion, created by man or, indeed, woman.

We have seen the reasons that necessitated love's making, and how it was in the interest of these early proto-states to perpetuate it, but just how do the state of love and our modern state today relate?

If I were to tell you of a regime which compelled its citizens to starve themselves; which robbed them of sleep, sanity, reason, rights and riches; which imprisoned its people in a strict and incomprehensible social order; which tempted them with illusions of happiness yet punished those who failed to achieve it with tortures, even driving those less able to cope to take their own lives; which was administered by 'thought police' who allowed no liberty, no choices and forced the masses to spend their waking hours worrying for their own security, pulling their nerves to exhaustion; which made its subjects perform the most humiliating actions as publicly as possible, and then encouraged derision for them; which demanded that its populace confess their souls, their everything, in long, harrowing, spirit-shearing letters drawn through tears of pain; which then took these intimate disclosures, laughed at them, revealed them, revelled in them and ripped them to shreds; if I told you these things about this regime, this dictatorship, this fascist state, you would be in no doubt. That, you would say, is a tyranny.

No, I would reply, that is love.

19

The De Rigueur *Thing to Wear for Saints*

WHAT IS IT? IS SOMETHING BOTHERING YOU? SOMETIMES I CAN'T TELL. You're always so silent. i know i've been going on about me and her but i'm not ignoring you. i'm there, in the story, but i'm here too, here for you. i know i was rejected and that really should be the end of the story, i mean, we're here now, you and i, no harm done. All the world before us. But it's just the whole inevitability of Miranda's route, it was just, well, so compelling.

Miranda was so obviously entranced by the most transparent of lies and her own desire to fulfil a fantasy destiny. But what would you have done? Say you loved someone and you could see them walking into the jaws of the lion but were completely incapable of wielding the tamer's chair and whip? You see the lion hadn't bitten, there was still hope. And whilst there was still some uncertainty to Miranda's destiny i kept alight a tiny flame of hope. Maybe i was wrong to. Maybe that will be the fatal flaw to get between us but at least you will know that i can still kindle hope when all others have extinguished theirs and gone home. i'll try to be quiet now, tell the story, let you judge for yourself. i need to get over this bad habit, this controlling thing i have, the urge to shape your opinion. i have to trust that you will see the truth and not hate me for it. i trust you.

'That's it, I really have had enough,' Mercy said angrily. Having only heard Miranda say the word 'somewhere' before the Sea Cat had burst through a wave and skimmed into a continental cell reception area, Mercy had assumed it was just her friend's new and annoying habit of being secretive.

'Fine, if you want to be elusive and mysterious that's great, but don't waste my time with it, I don't buy it. It'll be one of your stupid magazines; you've read somewhere that men like a woman with a bit of mystery. Well, fuck it, I'm your friend and if you can't tell me things I think you're going to have to find another one. I thought it was like a little blip, that we were going to be friends again. Randa, unless you can find the decency to tell me straight what's going on and treat me like a friend I'll never speak to you again.'

Mercy slammed the receiver down so hard a ten pence piece dropped nervously into the coin return hole. She waited by the phone for Miranda to call back and say sorry. Sasha, who had heard everything, tried to console her.

'Of courth thee'th your fwend. Weally. A gweat gweat fwend.' Mercy felt she could really do without her thympathy. Why wasn't the phone ringing? What had happened to Miranda? Surely she couldn't just leave it like this.

'The watthed phone never wings,' said Sasha philothophically.

The phone rang and Sasha turned back to her counter with a look of defeat. Mercy grabbed the receiver. 'Very funny. I knew you couldn't just go away like that. You know I love you.'

'This is all so sudden,' said Flirt.

'You again. Make it quick, I'm expecting a call from Miranda.'

'I'm still in hospital.'

'Yeah. So?' Mercy felt she had gone above and beyond the call of duty, not that she owed one to any man, by getting him there in the first place. She thought she was fobbing him off when he asked for her number by giving this one. He was the reason she'd rowed with Miranda and she really wasn't interested in anything he had to say. 'What do you expect? A ward visit?'

'Hold on. I thought you just said that you loved me.'

'Dream on.'

'Well, I'm calling because the doctors want to know if there was anything on the weapon you stabbed my foot with.'

'What are you talking about? I didn't stab your foot with any weapon.'

'Well, that's what I keep trying to tell them but they reckon anything which can do this much damage has to be classed as a weapon. I just call it a shoe.'

242

'I did that, did I?'

'They just want to know if you might have stepped in any dog shit before you stepped on me.'

'I suppose I might have done.'

'They're quite interested in getting a sample if there was any left on your shoe.'

'Why?' Mercy quietly asked.

'Why?' said Flirt, his voice now getting a little angry. 'Only because it's one of the most infectious substances they've ever seen. It's only given me gangrene in less than twelve hours and they're about to cut off half my foot. That's why.' And then added more quietly, 'Since you ask.'

'I did that?'

'Not intentionally.'

Mercy hung the phone up and stood, completely stunned, looking around the now swaying Second Floor. Had this happened as the end to some sort of relationship it would be different. She'd be feeling rather proud that she had wreaked such a wonderful revenge. But she hardly knew Matthew Flirt. She tried to feel happy about it but she couldn't convince herself that he was really doing any momentous wrong in misleading Miranda. Not that merited gangrene anyway. Mercy was starting to feel the most extraordinary and unpleasant sensation which, being neither Catholic, Jewish nor ever having known social exclusion, she found unrecognizable. It was guilt.

Mercy didn't like the feeling at all and it seemed that she wasn't going to get rid of it until she could comfortably justify Flirt's wound. There was only one thing for it: cause and effect. Or in this case, effect and cause. She was going to have to start some sort of relationship to justify the hurt she had already done him.

The sweeping yellow and green hills of the French *pays* beyond Boulogne were already chugging past Miranda and Ferdinand by the time Peersnide was standing outside his house, ready to go, and waiting for Barry to turn up. He had neatly packed a small bag and was dressed in a bright blue suit with a red and gold tie; the clothes he believed would help him be inconspicuous in Venice, blend in with the Venetians. Having never actually been to Venice, or met a Venetian, his knowledge of the place, and the people, was limited. It had been informed only by endless monographs on Venetian artists with colour plates. And in almost every one the *de rigueur* thing to wear for saints, patrons, Madonnas and the like, was a combination of blue, red and gold. He reasoned that though cut might have changed through the years, traditional tastes in colour probably hadn't. So he stood on the kerb looking like he was about to entertain a nightclub with filthy jokes, and he wondered where Barry was.

Peersnide knew it was important to have available transport on a 'mission' and he was excited that this was his first one, but did he really have to drive there in a car? He considered the next twenty-four hours spent in close proximity to that vile boy who was unable to communicate in words of more than two syllables, and had questionable sanitary habits. Peersnide experienced the sort of dread which only those who feel recently elevated to the middle classes, and therefore do not know how very difficult it is to escape once within it, have of rubbing shoulders with the working classes. But the combination of Barry and car seemed unspeakably horrific. He remembered how much he hated cars. Those childhood memories of misery being bumped around in a noisy, airless, confined space flooded back. So vivid and ghastly were these thoughts, Peersnide was about to turn back to his house, finally admitting to himself that this had all been a dreadful mistake, he hadn't the constitution to be a real spy, when there came the throbbing sound of distant drumbeats. The sound got closer and closer and Peersnide looked to either end of the road. In a cloud of smoke the Bentley appeared at one end screeching through a handbrake turn. The car then tore down Peersnide's street, coming to a halt in front of his house leaving marginally more rubber on the road than might be found at a bondage convention. The throb of the music was almost deafening now. Then the passenger side window lowered and the blast of sound nearly knocked Peersnide over.

Barry looked out of the window. 'Come on then, thought you were in a hurry.' He felt certain he had scored a job driving for the mob and speed was of the essence. They were going to Italy and so this was going to be like *The Italian Job*. This Peersnide was like that posh ponce in prison, he reasoned, so he'd get to do a lot of driving through sewers and over buildings.

'Could you turn that down a minute,' shouted Peersnide. Barry dutifully did so and Peersnide managed to collect enough of his thoughts to remember to put his bag in the boot. He then climbed into the passenger seat with the delicacy and adroitness of one of those pensioners who have nothing better to do than wind up bus drivers all day. 'What was that?' Peersnide said after he had managed to sit, settle and do the seat belt up.

'What?'

'That noise.'

Barry pressed a button on the dashboard and a little shining disc emerged with the label, 'Raving Acidic Trance-portation'.

Peersnide shivered. He felt that he would have to quickly draw the lines of who was in charge. 'Now, I want you to drive carefully and considerately,' said Peersnide. 'I feel I need to warn you that I am not a good car passenger. I am extremely prone to car sickness and I would appreciate it if you would drive with a caution and sensitivity to my condition.'

'Course I will,' said Barry, slamming the CD back into the player, spinning the wheels until they squealed and releasing the handbrake with such suddenness that the car lurched forward with a force which nearly made Peersnide swallow his dentures.

Through the dark from Paris, curving along its track, the Orient Express visibly expressed its orientation. A chain of yellow lights flying slowly eastward through the night. Beside the track the grass and trees would light with a flickering spray of amber only to be once more swallowed by the darkness when the train had passed. It rattled over the sleepers as rhythmically and assuredly as a heartbeat and in the 4141 *Lalique* restaurant car, surrounded by the writhing silvery grey inlaid women who graced every panel, Miranda and Ferdinand list- lessly looked at their dinners but made only token attempts to eat. Occasionally they would look out of the window but it was so dark beyond the glass all they could see was a reflection of themselves.

'It's very off-putting,' Miranda said, pushing a potato to the side of her plate, 'eating next to a mirror.'

Ferdinand smiled, 'It's true. It's difficult enough to watch other peo- ple eat. It's such an imperfect necessity. No one can do it right. But then watching yourself do it no better is really depressing. That's probably why there are more etiquette rules for eating than anything else.'

'I suppose that's why there are so many mirrors in McDonald's. Get them in, then get them out again quick.'

Ferdinand nodded, 'And just to make things worse, all the bright lights,' inadvertently revealing a terrible inconsistency in his chosen character.

Miranda just laughed. 'So you have been there, you fraud. "What's a happy meal?"' she said sarcastically – but we lack a typeface for the ironic so the best i can do is quotation marks.

Ferdinand laughed too, a little nervously, that he could make such a mistake. But it was good they were laughing. A little vulnerability could go a long way. A few mistakes. But they had better be deliberate from now on.

'I guess we're not showing off any more,' she said. Ferdinand shook his head and pushed his food a little more with his fork. He had expected to be hungry but probably the excitement of trying to keep in character was affecting his appetite. Loss of it was famously a sign of falling in love and he would exploit it to the full. Now was the time, if there ever was one, for some honesty, or at least a damn good impression of it.

'You know. When I first saw you. In the shop. Spinning one of your things above your head, you looked so . . .' He paused.

Miranda could only think to fit in 'ridiculous', 'idiotic' or 'insane', so what he said came as something of a surprise.

'Beautiful.' Miranda began to blush. 'I really didn't know how to tell you. I just. I just knew I had to see you again. It was like staring down a tunnel and seeing the distant light that I was reaching for. Like suddenly seeing my future and knowing it was all right. God that sounds so presumptuous.'

Miranda shook her head.

'If someone had told me I'd feel anything like that an hour before I'd have thought they were mad. I've never believed in love at first sight or anything like that.'

'Love,' Miranda gulped, feeding on what Ferdinand was saying as if it was her dinner.

'But when I saw you it just. Hit me. Like a damn great truck. I didn't know what to say. I just. Wanted so much to be with you.' He glanced at her a few times and then quickly turned to the window to study her reflection.

He was saying all the things she couldn't find the words to say. She put her hands on his and he turned to her.

In books somewhat older than myself, what Ferdinand was doing would traditionally be called 'making love'. Any time a man opened himself, or appeared to, to a woman and spoke of love with her he was 'making love to her'. Of course it was soon adopted as an ironic synonym for what might be its successful conclusion, and became so over-used it at last transformed into the polite term for sex. However, we still sense the sham in the misappropriation. Ask anybody over the age of twenty and they would admit that there are huge differences between sex and making love. But what Ferdinand was doing was indeed making love. Unlike Miranda, he knew it wasn't something

246

that you just slip and fall into; that it is, to the empowered, something one chooses to be in or not.

What made him think that? Because he had read me, that's what. Or at least one of my destroyed, what shall i call them, brothers, may they rest in peace. Which was more than Miranda had. With the conviction of self-belief that only the arrogant can have, Ferdinand attempted to construct 'love' as one might a house of cards, delicately laying all the right components on top of each other. First he was boastful, then vulnerable, then petitioning, then persuading, then fixing, then euphoric, then adoring, then securing, then prospecting. Part of a list i think he cribbed from me, bastard. Using my doctrines to get himself in cosy with my love. But a house of cards is a delicate thing, and all too likely to come crashing down around your ears the higher you take it. And love is a dangerous weapon to wield, if i may shamelessly mix my metaphors, as it has a good chance of backfiring. Still, Ferdinand believed in himself so firmly, it seemed a slight thing to convince Miranda to do so as well. If only he had bothered to observe Miranda instead of desperately constructing some emotion, he might have seen that he had already won her heart and all he was doing was sending it into palpitations.

By the time they walked down the corridor to their adjoining rooms, which they had made sure were at the opposite end of the train from the swearing American, Miranda was feeling hopelessly besotted. Hers was the first room and he stopped at her door. Ferdinand started stuttering again, which is a sure sign that an Englishman is trying to make love. 'If it's all a bit fast, I understand. If you're a bit wary . . .' Then –

'Oh, bloody hell,' said Ferdinand with a surprising ferocity, and he kissed her. And this was new again, it was long and warm and calm and safe and the juddering of the train mingled with their pulses until it felt like they were all one throbbing machine. With her eyes shut Miranda let herself plummet into abandon. And then he had disappeared. Which he seemed quite good at doing. Miranda slid open her door and, without turning on the lights, lay down on her bed and listened to the dark.

Surprisingly, Barry behaved himself impeccably as French customs picked their car out for intimate inspection. Not once did he reach for his buttocks or act suspiciously as the uniformed men sniffed the ashtrays and took more than an interest in the singular lack of luggage. Peersnide watched them with a degree of nervousness, which just prolonged the search as each time they looked at him he grew more pale. He had had enough of guns the night before and had not packed the pistols but was sure he had probably overlooked something which would reveal the true purpose of his mission.

'What is the purpose of your visit here, monsieur? Business or pleasure?' Now that was a bit of an awkward question. Peersnide didn't want to say it was business because they might ask what business, and he was sure that espionage was one not welcomed in their country, but from what he had experienced of the vomit-inducing white-knuckle journey so far, it certainly wasn't pleasure either.

'Pleasure,' Peersnide lied.

It was, in the end, the very thing which had singled them out for inspection, Peersnide's bright blue suit, which settled the matter for the little customs man. The trip was one for pleasure indeed, this man was obviously *en anglais* 'theatrical'. He stroked his neat mandatory moustache and looked at brutish Barry. There was only one reason for such an odd coupling, he concluded, the boy was a little bit of *le commerce rugueux* for monsieur. Still it was his duty to prevent crime when he could. 'May I have a word wis you,' he said, taking Peersnide aside. 'Ours is a tolerant country,' he whispered, 'you will find no prejudices here against the *passion anglaise*, but I must warn you that your friend, he looks, well, monsieur, I have seen such brutes make the meat of mince out of respectable men like you, and all for a single night of love.'

Peersnide only got his meaning in this last reference and replied in a loud voice, 'Sir, I resent what you are implying.' The customs man shrugged his shoulders and walked away. He had seen it all too often.

Peersnide was actually glad to be on the road again. He was glad as well that night had fallen during the shuttle journey; now he had less the sensation that he was driving at a dangerous speed down a motorway of death but in some video game of flashing, whizzing lights. Every now and again he had to wind down his window and pay at a motorway tollbooth but Barry had grown bored with his CD and seemed to be concentrating on the road.

'So what are the roads like?' Barry asked, trying to sound professional.

'The roads?' said Peersnide. 'Where?'

'In Venice.'

'In Venice?' Peersnide repeated. 'There are no roads in Venice.'

'What do you mean?'

'There are no roads. No cars.'

'So how do they get about?'

'By boat. It is full of water.'

Barry had never heard of anything so monstrous. 'What, no cars at all?'

'Not one.'

Barry sat and thought about it for a while. 'So why do you need a driver if you can't get a bloody car in there?'

By now Peersnide was feeling indignant, especially after his near-brush with the customs man. 'I didn't ask you to ask questions. I asked you to drive. We've got to get to Venice and that's all I need tell you.'

Barry accelerated into the fast lane to vent his frustration. Only after a stream of flashing lights and horn hooting did he realize that he was in the slow lane because they all drove on the wrong side of the road. He stopped flashing his lights and hooting his horn at the Renault 4 he had supposed was blocking the fast lane and pulled out into the middle again

'And please slow down a little,' said Peersnide a touch nervously.

'I thought we were mates,' Barry said. 'I thought we were in this together.'

'Have you any idea what "this" is?' said Peersnide. 'Have you any comprehension of what is going on?'

Barry shook his head.

'And that is the way it will stay,' Peersnide said in a superior tone. 'I don't know what made you think we were "mates".' The last word was said with such exaggeration of Barry's accent that even Barry noticed. He was getting rather tired of driving and he was getting even more tired of being bossed about. Forgetting that Peersnide was a dangerous man who was tooled up, he veered suddenly onto the verge and braked violently. Peersnide was winded by the seat belt and sat breathing heavily, clutching his chest.

'You taking the piss?' Barry said as threateningly as he could.

Peersnide was gasping for breath.

'I said are you taking the piss?'

Peersnide nodded his head unintentionally as he gasped.

'Oh,' said Barry, who had never had any answer to that question but denial. This man really was hard. 'Well. I'm sick of you being so bloody bossy. If you don't want me as part of this you can bloody well drive yourself.' He got out and slammed the door, marching off up the emergency lane.

Peersnide looked at the steering wheel in horror. He quickly got out of his side, totally unaware that the emergency lane of a motorway is one of the most hostile environments on earth. He ran after Barry and was completely unprepared for the force of the lorries as they blew past, creating a turbulence of hurricane proportions that buffeted him like a paper bag. 'Barry, Barry,' he screamed into the wind before he was blown over and started rolling towards the lanes. Barry turned round and saw Peersnide being tossed into the path of the bright diverging lights of a juggernaut. He ran back, and grabbing Peersnide's legs, pulled him from the certain path of at least sixteen of the lorry's thirty-two wheels.

'I'm sorry, I'm sorry,' Peersnide whimpered as Barry sat on the road cradling his head. Suddenly Barry felt protective towards this little man. He was bloody awkward and thought he was dead hard but he was like your criminal mastermind type who had really no understanding of how to cope in the real world. He needed looking after. And in feeling protective Barry felt empowered and started to feel good about himself, and from that moment on would associate feeling good with being with Peersnide and knew, somewhere in that primal heart, they had a long way to travel together.

Now here is a curious thing. Barry's strange new feelings were not a million miles away from Miranda's. Both had left their jobs suddenly to pursue their heart's desire. Both were in unfamiliar places, beyond the restrictions of their daily lives and the rules they normally unconsciously followed. For Miranda it meant sleeplessly watching the lights that occasionally shot in and across her little panelled room and thinking deeply about where she was, who she was and what she was doing; for Barry it meant slowing down to ninety at junctions. An overwhelming feeling that she had run away to join the circus possessed Miranda. She had somehow deserted all her codes and preconceptions to become a part of a carnival of chaos and uncertainty. The moment she had stepped on the train she had simply abandoned herself. One small step for her, one giant leap for her heart. It was as if she had finally allowed herself to step into the unknown, to let go, make the leap of faith and that she would be all right, that she would remain safe. She had always thought she would gradually give herself, in bits, until she woke up one day and she was in love and loved, but now she could see all she had to do was give herself completely, step into the air, he would be there to catch her.

Getting up and creeping to the adjoining door, Miranda had her hand on the handle when she felt giddy as if she were in a dream, her head spinning. This was everything that she had dreamed about. A handsome stranger on a night train to Romance Central. The epitome of all she had imagined all those years with her novels and heaving bosoms and cold distant heroes. She tried the handle. It turned and she tiptoed into the shadows of Ferdinand's compartment. He was asleep, breathing heavily with the rhythm of the train. She looked at the dark form and she could smell him. She longed to climb in and just be close to him. But what happens when a dream becomes reality, a fantasy becomes flesh? Doesn't the romance, the mystery, the perfection of it all go? Doesn't 'he' become a dull mortal. Miranda began to feel dizzy as the train shook over sleepers. Maybe she should just stay away from him, keep the dream. Suddenly feeling sick with anxiety and indecision Miranda clutched onto a cabinet beside the door. Her brain felt as if it were filled with helium, floating away from her, pulling at her neck. It felt that if she took another step she would be losing everything that she had, herself. Miranda felt the familiar churned emptiness in her stomach and knew she was about to throw up. She dashed back to her room and managed to find the sink before she splattered it with the Orient Express's undigested *haute cuisine*. She pulled herself up again only to be hit by another retch. Tiredness grappled with her muscles and weakened them to a wobble. She decided to lie down for a moment before she had to throw up again. And there on the floor beside her sink, closing her eyes, the rhythmic jolting of the train rocked her to sleep.

Having woken the moment he had heard her turning the door handle, Burnt's every muscle had tensed imperceptibly. Were this a different mission, a different target, he would be calculating the time it would take to get to the gun under his pillow and what trajectory would be most effective. But this was no agent, this was an ordinary girl and all she needed to do was fall in love with him. He smiled to himself. Cushy, he thought.

He had been half expecting her. He had watched her through a veil of his eyelashes and when she dashed into her room again to start making wet slapping noises he had crept to the door. By the time he peeked around the open door she was fast asleep on the floor, a fragment of new potato glistening on her chin. He took a blanket, covered her and picked her up. She was cold and involuntarily, instinctively, she snuggled into him. Easy, job's as good as done, he thought to himself as he laid her on his bed. He lay down beside her and drifted back to that half-sleep peculiar to spies and the parents of newborns.

*

251

Peersnide was also surrendering himself to sleep despite the terror of the road. The dull monotony of the oncoming lights was hypnotically lulling him towards slumber, his eyes were beginning to shut. Unfortunately, so were Barry's. After a few minutes the two of them had their eyes tight shut, their heads were lolling, and they were ripping down the motorway at a hundred miles an hour.

If love were natural and we were tortured and abused thus by the very essence of our existence, then it would just have to be put down as an unfortunate side-effect of life, to be tolerated and accepted, rather like the pug-dog who must accept that, due to its rather unnatural inbreeding, it now suffers from a natural never-ending mucous discharge and will for ever make such unpleasant noises that it cannot be discerned from which end they issue.

If love were natural we would have accepted and adapted to its tyranny, no doubt developing drugs to combat it, or isolating the gene which creates it, for the relief of the habitually love-sick and those unable to cope with all those unpleasant effects.

If love were natural then this tyranny would have to be accepted.

All tyrants need to engender acceptance, as if there were no alternative, and Nature is the ultimate element that none can argue with. If something is natural it is the state of play and cannot be overturned. So love, like all tyrants, pretends that its despotism is the natural order, for if it is natural it is right. Nature is always right, even when it makes something as ridiculous as the duck-billed platypus and something as inedible as the cabbage. Nature will always win over nurture, biology over psychology. That is why Hitler claimed the natural superiority of an Aryan race, Ghengis Khan of the Mongols, Ozymandias of, well, I suppose, the people of Oz, and why, I am afraid, our civilization today claims the natural superiority of the lover. 'All the world loves a lover'? No, all the world loves a sucker, at least all the world's powers do, and who is a bigger sucker than a lover? Who are more easily ruled than the foolish and who in love does not play the fool?

But what of the joys, the ecstasies of love, the happinesses, the very reasons why such so-called tyranny may be ushered in? Is it not worth enduring the tyranny in order to suffer its pleasures? Does love not take the heart higher, wider, deeper, and to better places than it could reach if it did not believe in love? The delights, the raptures, the very bliss of love must make all pain worth it.

Does it? Philosophers like Nietzsche believed that one cannot really know joy unless one first knows pain, that emotions are relative and comparative. By that argument, a world of half measures is a world of the mediocre and the grey, so striving for extremes brings life purpose. Maybe. It also means that the extremes of love are merely an illusion brought on by an over awareness of fear, loneliness and suffering.

In that vision, the happiness of love is the joy of the prisoner who glimpses the sky, the taste of water to the tortured, the drop of rain on the parched land; it is only comparative and only great because of the greatness of the pain it briefly relieves. It is the Italian who mourns Mussolini because he made the trains run on time, the Spaniard who misses Franco because the streets were clear of hooligans, the German who grieves Hitler because you can no longer get a decent Sachertorte in Berlin. The evil that men do lives after them, but the good is sometimes not interred thoroughly enough with their bones, however little that good was. The joy of the pleasures is in no way comparable to the pain that was suffered to achieve them. Thus is love.

Love is nothing more than a tyrant and we are all within its power and control, for who does not believe in love? It is a roller-coaster ride between the depths of pain and the heights of pleasure, and, as long as the coaster keeps moving, none dares to look over the side.

But what if they did? It is, after all, just a ride, an illusion. If lovers dared to look they would see that they have barely left the ground, it is safe to step out. Yet, as long as lovers fear falling off, out of, love; as long as they refuse to see the possible happy safety of being outside it; as long as they do not dare to take that leap of faith into the unknown, into the world of those who are beyond love, they will be caught in its grip, its clasp, and they are puppets to its whims.

The tyrant love only remains in power because it claims to be natural, yet I have shown that it is far from natural. Why, I must therefore ask, have we never noticed that love is a tyranny?

20

The Luminous Dips and Rises of an Exotic Dancer

'IT'S TRUE. WHEN WE WERE MONKEYS WE NEEDED THEM. BUT SINCE then they've been getting smaller and smaller and for the last few million years have been next to useless. Could you ever move them separately? Did you ever actually do anything useful with them individually? They're a genetic anomaly, a hangover, a throwback, they're like nipples on men. We should have got rid of them a thousand generations ago, by now we should all have just one big one for balance. So look at it this way, you're a trailblazer, a trend-setter, you're taking mankind into an advanced period, you're first in a genetic trend that may take millions of years to evolve. You are the Galileo of future pedestrians, ahead of your time.'

'But they were my toes. I liked them.' Flirt looked at his bandaged foot forlornly and felt a little sick. He wasn't sure whether it was the horror of losing the toes or the after-effects of the general anaesthetic.

Dr Scudder put the sheet back over his legs. 'It's after midnight now, we only operated a few hours ago and you're bound to feel a little groggy. A little disorientated. Try not to think about it and get some sleep.'

'Try not to think about it? With half my foot gone? What am I supposed to do? Count sheep?'

'You only lost three toes.'

'I didn't lose them. You took them. I want them back.'

'Think positively. We've stemmed the gangrene. Probably.'

255

'Probably? What do you mean, probably?'

'Probably. I mean probably. We can't guarantee that that has happened, but there is a really high chance that we have cut it all out.'

'A high chance? You took three of my toes for a high chance?'

'Medicine isn't an exact art, it's all about probabilities and trying to lengthen or shorten them. By cutting your toes off –'

'Shortening my leg.'

'By shortening your leg, then, we have lengthened the odds of the rest of your leg surviving.'

'But if it's all about odds, what's the difference between going to hospital and going to the horses?'

'I don't know. The horses are probably more fun.'

Flirt turned over, away from Dr Scudder, and clutched his pillow. He didn't want her to see him cry. His table light cast dark shadows in the folds of the curtain that surrounded his bed. And beyond he could hear the chorus of geriatric wheezes that kept the night nurse informed that nobody had died yet. At least Dr Scudder had displayed enough sensitivity not to do the 'How many fingers am I holding up?' test when he had woken.

'Try to get some sleep,' she said, picking up her stethoscope and disappearing through the curtains with a magician's swish. Flirt studied the pattern as the curtains returned to their corrugated stillness. He stared until he slept and he slept until he dreamed. And he dreamed. What a dream. He dreamt the curtain began to twitch as if someone was trying to find their way in. Then a hand with long, deep red fingernails appeared at the curtain's breach. It slowly pulled the stiff cloth back, to reveal the soft dappled shadows of a bare shoulder and collarbone and then further to expose Mercy. Dressed to kill. Or revive, depending on your viewpoint. The white rising twin curvature of her breasts burst from the top of a tight black corset, itself a fountain of lace, and above, her neck rose like a tower of blinding light to a mouth blackberry stained and glistening. Flirt swallowed hard as his eyes dropped to her waist, her black skirt, tightly binding the curves and turns of her hips and legs as if they were being swallowed whole in the snakeskin of a constrictor. And in the black a slit, a single shocking lightning bolt of white leg spurring upwards towards her waist, too impossibly high for any underwear to be present. He thought for a minute that a thousand saxophones blew mellow strip-tease music through a fug of smoke. The wolf in Flirt clapped his paws together like a seal trying to whistle as his eyeballs popped out and did a dance on the bedside table. He tried to think of something to say, but the only thing that came to mind was some very deep breathing and the phrase 'Va va voom'.

She crossed to him, swaying as she had never done before, her eyes half closed, and silently sighing as if each bump and bend of her body was intensely erogenous and each movement of each part was bringing her to an ecstasy unknown outside the drug dependency ward on the fifth floor. Her hand ran up his leg, a sharp nail biting a path towards his crotch. It stopped and came to a gentle rest, an agonizing hair's breadth from his genitals. She looked him in the eye, sucking him into her deep black lashes.

'Just thought I'd come,' she said, pausing and closing her eyes slightly, 'to see how you were doing.'

This was crazy. It was a dream but he could feel it all so vividly and he could feel his throat lumpily swallowing his words.

'I'm OK. You know,' he shrugged.

'Bearing up?' Mercy raised an eyebrow and lowered herself on top of him. Everything felt so tangible, so real, and yet to know that he was dreaming filled him with a sense of both potency and futility. He was in a dream but feeling completely conscious, so he was like God in this world, he could direct it as he willed, he could do what he wanted without any fear of reprimand. Nothing that he did, however exploitative or degrading, meant anything. His primal instinct, his unfettered id, could have its wicked way and nothing mattered. But, then, nothing mattered. And if nothing mattered, why bother? He would go through all the motions, expend all that energy, and God knows what else, and for what? Achieve nothing, change nothing, go nowhere. He'd wake up again and have done nothing, got nowhere, the world would be the same place and he would be the same sad pobble with no toes that he was when he went to sleep. If not a little sadder for having such an outrageously fantastical dream. Her breasts were bearing firmly down on him and he found himself caught between his cock and a hard place.

Then. Fuck it, he thought. Why not? It's not every day you get to do what you like to a fantasy woman. It was his dream after all. He laid his hands on dream Mercy's shoulders and gently guided her down his body. Oh yes. If only every dream could be like this. You could row row row your boat and never go back to reality. Flirt suspected for a minute that the general anaesthetic drugs were probably having this effect on him and he wondered why he had fought shy of drugs all his life. It just felt so good. Her dream hands working over him, she gradually picked up speed.

'Oh God,' he groaned. He never talked or made noises during sex, but he had always wanted to. Self-consciousness and the need to keep it quiet from his mum during the habit-forming early years of his sexual career inhibited his vocal passion. But now this was his dream, his fantasy, his party and he could damn well cry, shout and scream if he wanted to. By now the pace was working towards frenzied and Flirt found he could think no longer. Mercy had risen to her knees and seemed to be everywhere, her mouth, her fingers, her thighs, her breasts. He abandoned himself to the inevitable, unfightable, longed-for rush which he could feel swelling inside him and which every muscle was straining to withhold, to keep the pleasure going as long as possible. But it could not would not be stopped, 'Oh God!' he yelled. 'Yes Yes!' he shouted. 'No no no no no!' he shouted. 'Oh Oh Oh Oh!' He thrust his hips back and forth, up and down, harder and deeper until he had stretched every muscle in his body to breaking point and there he froze for an agonizing moment of climactic ecstasy and then he let go and let go and let go and fell and as he fell, 'YES!' he screeched at the gods, closing his eyes and gushing, releasing his flood, his ocean, his loving teaspoonful.

Limp and wasted, Flirt opened his eyes. His bedside light was on. As the tears cleared he began to make out the disapproving face of the nurse who was standing in front of the curtain. A rude awakening if he had ever had one. 'Whoops,' thought Flirt, realizing, with a sinking disappointment, that the dream was gone. He had probably shouted out in his sleep. A surge of embarrassment overwhelmed him and he smiled sheepishly. Then, in an attempt to cover any tell-tale wet patches, Flirt quickly pulled his knees up and was a little taken aback to find that there was someone under the sheet between them.

Of course, dreams do come true every now and again. Just going by whatever laws averages adhere to. However, considering that most don't, it seems a little odd why anybody bothers to wake up. Look at all the futuristic dreams and idealistic predictions of the 1950s sci-fi comics and satirists. But we have reached into the third millennium and humans still don't have biological rocket propulsion, 200-year life spans, or conscious cars which can decide which way to go, how fast, and what movie you want to watch on the Heads Up Display.

Despite this, in a twenty-first century two million pound car, it would not be too whimsical to expect a few safety features beyond seat belts, air bags and hot drink 'tipple preventers'. Indeed the standard Bentley Continental GT has 550 brake horsepower, ventilated disk brakes, Bosch anti-locking 'Brake Assist' traction control and with emergency brake force distribution can decelerate from 100 miles an hour to standstill in a little over 210 yards. That is, if the driver is actually awake to press the brake pedal. It can stop in a much shorter distance if he isn't.

The Secret Service Continental is not equipped to deal with anything as mundane as a driver falling asleep at the wheel, an unlikely scenario for an institution which trains its agents to stay awake and alert for up to a week at a time. It does, however, have a pressure-sensitive steering wheel which monitors the driver and is aware of a prolonged absence of hand pressure. The car assumes that the driver has lost consciousness and this is, in turn, assumed to be due to enemy activity within the vehicle. In such an event the car automatically adopts evasive action. First it brakes in a little under 210 yards, throwing any potential back-seat assassin pell-mell at the bullet-proof windscreen. At standstill, the car's doors burst open, letting loose an ear-piercing siren and flashing a confusing array of dazzling lights.

Four bloodshot eyes tore open widely, wildly, in alarm. Lights flashed into them and two brains tried to orient themselves, work out who they were, where they were, and why their bodies were being pulled towards the windscreen with a force that was leaving strange seat belt-mark bruises on their bodies. Eventually the car stopped altogether and their limp bodies were suddenly subjected to normal gravitational forces petulantly flinging them back into their seats. The doors burst open and the siren continued. Barry was first to come to his senses, only because he had less of them to come to.

'Shut up,' he yelled uselessly at the dashboard, 'shut the fuck up!'

Peersnide put his hands over his ears and looked out of the back window. They were in the middle lane of the motorway and could see the rapidly approaching lights of oncoming vehicles. 'Put some lights on, close the doors!' he screamed.

In fact, from the outside, the car was lit up like a Christmas tree. The approaching gravy train of European parliamentary limousines which ply between Strasbourg and Brussels was already slowing to rubber-neck and tut tut about road-safety regulations.

Barry only just heard Peersnide over the sirens and he yanked at his door. Peersnide did the same and now the noise became totally deafening. They pushed every button, pulled every lever, they rattled every part of the dashboard, but still the sirens pierced them. Then, unable to think of anything else to do and already feeling the frustration of an unrealized adrenaline rush, Barry lashed out in the only way that he couldn't think how. He leaned forward violently and nutted the steering wheel. Barry blessed the steering wheel with a Glasgow kiss, an aggressive and pointless gesture towards a technology as far beyond his grasp as GCSE woodwork was. It was also, coincidentally, absolutely the right action to close down the system. And just as suddenly as the alarms had begun, they ceased. All they were left with was the purring of the engine and the ringing in their ears. Barry jammed his foot on the accelerator and the car tore away again.

'So what,' gasped Barry, 'the fuck was that?'

'I don't know. I was asleep.'

'You don't know? It's your bleeding car.' Barry then remembered the sort of company that he was keeping now. Peersnide was part of the major league criminal fraternity, so he added cautiously, 'Isn't it?'

'No. Why would I have a car? I can't even drive.'

For the first time Barry realized that the car must have been stolen. That was why they were going to the city with no cars. Who would think to look for it there? And then it was going to be shipped somewhere. A knowing grin crept onto his face.

'Oh, I get it,' he said. 'Now I know what it's all about. I'm driving for the mob, aren't I.' Peersnide, whose ears were just clearing, didn't quite catch what he said.

'Driving for the what?'

'The M.O.B.' Barry spelt it out. Peersnide, who was in the process of carefully dealing with the resounding tinnitus echo in his ears by jamming his forefingers into his earholes and squeakily twisting them, removed his fingers and stared at Barry. He was sure that he had heard Barry spell out the initials of the Ministry of Defence. He had underestimated the perceptiveness of this crude young man. Barry had well-hidden, innate intelligence. He obviously had a talent for putting his finger on the deepest pulse of an issue and extracting the gritty essential matter.

'Not a word,' Peersnide breathed menacingly at Barry, 'of this to anybody. This mission is of the utmost secrecy. If this gets out, you realize that I must kill you.' He needn't have tried to be so menacing, Barry's imagination had already done the work for him.

The car sped into a blur of mist, streetlights dribbled along the windscreen, as they crossed the floodlit bridge over the seething, troubled Rhine.

'I propose,' said Peersnide, 'that we keep each other awake by telling stories, like Chaucer's pilgrims.'

'Is that another gang?' asked Barry.

'Do you know any stories?' persisted Peersnide.

'I know one about a dyslexic nun, a German schnauzer and half a gallon of sump oil.'

'Does it, by any chance, involve a punch line in which she realizes she has mixed up the words god and dog and has let the wrong one enter her?'

'You've heard it,' said Barry, a little disappointed.

'Just a lucky guess.'

For three minutes the jiggering jolting juddering stopped. Too early for the window blinds to shed anything more than a pale colourless unshadowing light about the compartment. Miranda opened her eyes in the sudden stillness and stared into Ferdinand's. He was smiling.

'Sim Salabim,' he whispered.

Dearest. Beware this moment, beware the dawn. There is many a slip between nod and kip. In the yawning morning. There is a dangerous time in the half sleep of waking where truth lurks to ambush you. It is a time most like being drunk, when thoughts you think you are just thinking you are in fact saying. Had Burnt just woken too, even he might have dropped his guard for a moment in the welcoming warmth of Miranda's body. But he had woken twenty miles before Zurich, anticipating Miranda's stirring.

Miranda tumbled into those eyes and murmured, 'I love you.' She dreamily closed her eyes again and slept for a minute. Then suddenly she opened them and stared with a bewildered horror at Ferdinand. 'Did,' she stammered, 'did you hear that?'

Ferdinand shook his head and then said, 'It's just some people on the platform, we're in Zurich.'

Miranda closed her eyes with a peaceful smile and pushed her body closer into his.

Oswald Scrufstayn had woken suddenly. He lay in bed and stared at the immaculately ruffed, shiny, nylon peach curtains. He smiled. It was not yet dawn but the clicking of the carriage clock and the courage of his dreams had startled him awake. Today was the day, he could feel it in his bones. Today was the day he would sack someone and join the pantheon of super-managers.

Miranda Brown had gone too far. First she kept on being late despite warnings and then she had disappeared at lunch-time and had not bothered to turn up for the afternoon shift. Now he could legitimately, justifiably, bravely sack her and everyone on the Second Floor would watch with awe and respect. They would know that his was the hand of God. You don't mess with Oswald Scrufstayn. And word would pass up to the deities in upper management and they would make a note to invite him to the boardroom for lunch. Here was a man with a future, a man who knew how to manage, a man ruthless in his pursuit of a smooth-running profit-making organization. A man who might, one day, helm the business. And it would all start here. Today.

Scrufstayn had enacted and re-enacted the moment in his dreaming head, worked out each possible response and emerged each time the victor. With all the courage of a reverie, with none of the repercussions of an actuality, Scrufstayn had convinced himself that he could do it, that he would do it, that to all intents and purposes he had done it already. She might cry a little when he broke the news, he thought, but girls like her always did. They didn't make them like Mrs Scrufstayn any more, barely a wince at the crack of a whip. He would stand tall, brandishing her P45 in his hand as a sword of vengeance. A man of power, of influence, a man who let nothing get in his way. He would smile proudly and say, 'Miss Brown, your cards, I presume.' No, no, 'This, Miss Brown, hurts me more than it hurts you.' No, no, 'Miss Brown, you seem fond of prolonged absences, but I have decided to give you another . . .' here she would think the word chance was coming, so a dramatic pause would be crucial '. . . another absence, and I will prolong this one . . .' another pause for the sake of weight and solemnity '. . . indefinitely.' Oh yes. Rather witty. Rather cruel. Rather good. I must write that down. The words of the all-powerful. The god of the Second Floor. 'My name is Oswald Scrufstayn, manager of managers. Look on my works, ye mighty, and weep.' A god unchained by the conventionality and mercy of mortals.

The god started to rise to get a pen but, as he tried to sit up, a loud clang and a sharp pain in his wrists stopped him. 'Dear?' he said quietly. 'Dear, are you awake?' The dark form of his sleeping wife bundled under the night's snatched covers shuffled a little. 'Darling?' he tried again. 'Have you got the keys to the handcuffs?'

Miranda was a very long way from being shown her cards or, indeed, anybody else's. Ferdinand was still keeping his frustratingly close to his chest, and she found herself wishing he would just put them on the table, show his hand, tell her what was going on. If this was just going to be a dirty weekend for a shopgirl and a wealthy executive, why weren't they shagging their arses off right now? Or, if it really was the romantic prelude to a lifetime of bliss, why wasn't he more open? Was he shy? A white slave trader? Or could he possibly be some deluded form of 'real gentleman'? And when you ache to see the big picture, you resent having to talk about the little one and it becomes quite a chore.

'Tea?' said Ferdinand. They were sitting up in dazzling white sheets, still crisp from the night's stillness.

Though they had woken embracing in the brightness of the rattling morning they had not made love, they had hesitated. They had withdrawn from the front as if that was another battle they would wait for, could wait for, as if to assure each other that there would be time, it was all right to pace things, they really had a lifetime ahead of them. By going only so far, Burnt believed he would do enough to encourage Miranda to think it was not going to be a simple case of *vacances sexuelles* but a romance that could break her heart, that could cleave her voice from her throat and rip her stomach in two, an affair to dismember.

The flashing golden light of a shiny new day surfed along waves of muscle in his arm as it held out the little glittering silver teapot. Their breakfast sat on a sparkling silver tray beside the bed and Miranda realized that everything around her seemed sharp, more than real, and the only thing that lacked clarity was Ferdinand himself. There was something about him that was blurred in a world of focused intensity.

'Yes. Thanks,' she said absently, feeling a twinge of naustalgia for the morning vomit session that she had come to know and loathe. But somehow it didn't seem right in this world where people had breakfast on silver trays. Just having breakfast was novel enough to suppress a habit.

Ferdinand poured a winding stream of translucent bronze into her cup and smiled a hazy grin. 'Milk?'

'No, thank you,' Miranda said with a tiny wave of her free hand above her cup.

'Did you sleep well?'

'Yes, yes I did. Very. You?'

'Like a log.'

'Oh good.' Miranda couldn't really think of anything else to say, that was that and they might as well just look out the window for the rest of the day. There seemed so little to speak of, not even an embarrassment of small talk, though screeching deep beneath her an iron chronicle of war and wounds, events so big they shaped nations, thundered by in showers of sparks.

To travel by train across the Continent is to course the very veins of the twentieth century. These tiny tracklines pulse with the blood of concentrated European history. That sleeper was the very same that saw Charles I of Austria, last Hapsburg Emperor, realize that he was never going back, that he had lost everything his ancestors had so violently accomplished over a thousand years.

'Looks like a lovely day,' said Ferdinand, where a thousand shell-shocked Austrian soldiers rolled, returning in resigned defeat, dead though not yet finished living, in the last days of the Great War.

'Yes. It does. Seems a bit of a pity we're going to be stuck inside.' There, where an endless awe of open-mouthed toothbraced new-world teenagers, naivety stuffed into their brightly coloured backpacks, stared out of the window at the same trees, clutching their inter-rail cards, and watched their own pale reflections and virginity slip away.

'Yes, shame.' Not an inch to the north, not a millimetre to the south, slow descending coaches laden with swastika-stamped gold bars lumbered towards Geneva with the dreams of a Third Reich, a new world order and an early retirement from the filthy masses.

'Right.' Packed, standing with their own shit running down their legs, human cattle transported to a distant shower of gas.

'What the fuck are you doing?'

'Sorry?'

'Look. I didn't leave my job, get on a train with a total stranger and travel across a continent to talk about the weather and feel as awkward as a second tongue.'

Ferdinand realized that he was losing the plot and the battle for her heart. He couldn't just ride it and let the train take the strain; he'd have to do a little work himself. He awoke his self-possession and brought his face close to hers. 'What's so awkward,' he asked as he kissed her, 'about a second tongue?' insinuating his into her mouth.

Miranda spat him out again. 'You can't talk properly with two.'

'We're not talking properly? What makes you feel that?'

'You are always making me talk. Asking questions and never saying anything about you. Quite frankly, I don't know if I've run off with the world's shyest man or its most secretive.'

'What do you want me to say?'

'No, what do you want to tell me?'

'I don't know.' Ferdinand shrugged.

Miranda got up and ran to the door of her room. She started searching the Vuittons for some more immaculately chosen clothes. 'I think I'd have a more interesting time if I got off at the next stop.'

'It's on top of a mountain.'

'Then there'll be a nice view,' Miranda said, picking out a figure-hugging sky-blue dress.

'What? What do you want me to say?'

'I don't want you to say anything,' Miranda called from her room. 'Well, nothing you don't want to say. It would just have been nice to know, I don't know, a little about who you are, how you got here, how you got to be someone who invites girls he doesn't know away on romantic weekends.'

Burnt began reciting the MI5 'Ferdinand' biography as he listened to her dressing. It felt dry in his mouth, as if it was an obituary. And then he did something strange: he embellished. He added. Something harmless enough in itself. Nothing that would threaten his secret identity, but something true from his own past. A true story. And so he departed for a brief moment, for the first time since puberty, from the tangled web he had so carefully woven all his adult life.

'You know, my big sister, she really hated me.' Ferdinand looked into a middle distance reserved for those who want to look like they're saying something so emotionally important they can't bear to look at anything else. 'I was the baby. I was the golden boy who got all the attention and she hated that. She used to punch me really hard and, before I could even think to cry, she'd scream to our nanny saying I had smacked her and I would be punished. She would steal things and then put them under my pillow. There was this one day, she must have been about thirteen, I was eight; holidays, and she announced at breakfast that she was going to "South Ken" that morning. Now I had heard a lot about "South Ken", it was where Mum got cakes from and I knew there were shops and places to buy treats, it was an exciting place for an eight-year-old and I really really wanted to go. So I asked if I could go too and of course she said no. And I pleaded and begged and finally Mum said that she should take me. Then Mum went off shopping herself. My sister was fuming and she said that she couldn't possibly take me then as it was her turn to do the dishes and she wasn't allowed out until they had been done and she had just painted her nails so she wouldn't be able to get round to the dishes for hours. So you know what?'

'What?' said Miranda, now standing at the door in a dress that swooned all over her body and fell about her curves like a fainting mist.

'I stood on a chair and I washed the dishes. I scraped and polished,

I dried and I stacked and I made a pile of gleaming crockery and pans. I showed it to her and said, "Can we go now, can we go to South Ken?" My sister went back to reading her magazine and she looked over at me and said that we couldn't go because Mum had said she had to clean her room before she went out and she didn't feel like doing it right then. So you know what I did?'

'You cleaned her room too?'

'I cleaned it, I tidied it, I folded her clothes, I dusted, I even dragged the vacuum cleaner over it. It looked like a new room when I'd finished it. And I showed her her room and she did all that running her hand under the bed to find dust and looked really frustrated because I'd done such a good job. And I kept banging on at her, "Can we go to South Ken now? Can we?"'

'Did you?'

'No, because she then said she wasn't going anywhere with me looking so scruffy so she said I had to put on my Sunday suit, which I hated. It had a tie and a scratchy collar and I looked like a complete dork in it. But I put it on and I let her comb my hair down in a nerdy central parting so it stuck to my head like two wet flannels. And looking like a total idiot I kept saying, "Please, let's go, let's go to South Ken."'

'Tell me you went.'

'Well, finally she put her coat on and we went downstairs together to the front door, and we were standing outside the house, just on the front steps and she said, "Bye. This is as far as you go." And I was brought up short and said, "What do you mean?" You know, tears already welling in my eyes. She just looked at me and said, "I'm off. Leaving you here." So I started crying, "I wanted to go to South Ken. You promised. You promised to take me to South Ken." She just went off down the street leaving me in floods of tears. Half way along the block she stopped and turned to look at me, then she shouted, "You live in South Ken, you little arsehole." Then she ran off round the corner.'

In the hush of 500 tons of steel scraping across tensile iron girders at sixty miles an hour, Miranda cocked her head at Ferdinand. 'Is that true?' Even though whatever sensors a woman has to call her intuition had already told her that it was. There was enough bitterness in the way he hissed the word 'sister' to tell her that.

'No. Not a word of it. I love my sister, she loves me, and we have always lived happily ever after.'

'You poor thing.' Miranda came into the room smiling and sat down beside Ferdinand. She kissed him and he kissed her and found that, in a way, he actually meant it. There had been something weirdly liberating about telling something true. He thought about the truth setting people free and knew that that was the sort of rubbish used to get people to talk and reveal secrets. But a little bit of truth couldn't hurt. It wasn't as if she was an enemy spy, an agent of the Comintern who would exploit him.

No, Burnt, she was something far more dangerous: an innocent.

There is a blue-grey haze which sleeps late on Lac Léman and will not rise before the sun has reached over the mountain peak of Les Diablerets and damned with faint rays the lake's most eastern shore. Then, magically, church spires, woods, cliffs and side-slung sailing boats appear just woken to the day, materialized in perfect composition as if ready to be set in paint. Peersnide could only gasp at the beauty as the sweep of the motorway above Lausanne provided an uninterrupted panorama of the dissolving mist and emerging silver lake. A sight that would have touched the soul of the most base of creatures and made a poet of the least couth man. Barry scratched his arse, hawked some weighty phlegm, rolled down the window and spat it into the vista. Some malignant Swiss clean air turbulence sent the expectoration right back whence it came and a web of green snot stuck fast to Barry's face. 'Morning,' said Barry jovially, turning to Peersnide and using his sleeve to wipe away the sticky mess. 'You're awake then?'

'Where are we?'

Barry looked down at the map and managed to veer across three lanes before Peersnide's squeal made him look up again. 'We're just coming up to somewhere called Montreeyucks.'

'Montreux, the flower of Lake Geneva. We're in Switzerland?'

'Yeah, the border was a breeze. You slept right through it.'

'And you've been driving all night.'

'No, I stopped for a kip about seventy miles back. We're not behind time, are we?'

Peersnide grabbed the map and looked at it then looked at his watch. They were doing much better than he had expected. They might even get there ahead of time. He smiled at Barry and realized that the young man's eyes were crazed with red threadlines, his pupils like pinpricks.

'I think we deserve a coffee,' he said. 'Take the exit for Montreux.'

Barry dutifully soared the purring Bentley to the right and they descended into the waking town.

*

Like a dark feather boa snaking around the luminous dips and rises of an exotic dancer, running along dark wet tunnels and bursting out into the spotlight of the sun, the Orient Express ran through, over, around the bumps and curves of the Austrian Alps. It hugged the walls of the rock as it rose tantalizingly towards the southern sun. It plunged into dark crevices and slinked through shadowy forests glistening with frost. Panting its rhythmic clatter, it climbed ever higher into the bright clear air, teasingly it pulled over flat-bellied meadows, freckled with flowers and the wrinkles of streams. Then, at last, caressing the firm, elevated, round mountain peaks, standing proud in the cold of the altitude, the train let out a loud steaming whistle that echoed against the bare rock.

And inside, in love, in transit, in the confines of the compartment, in touch, entwined, intimate, in and out of darkness, Miranda and Ferdinand tumbled madly. And they talked, O how they talked. Small and big alike. It was as if, with his true story, Ferdinand had managed to pull the plug of deception from the dam of credibility and the conversation just flowed. Hopes or fears, inanity or insanity, politics or poetics, inny or outy bellybuttons? They were, for the first time, both conscious and comfortable with each other. Ferdinand felt oddly pleased not reciting the practised lines and Miranda was happy that the iceman melteth. There is much to be said for the light and fluffy, the humdrum. Too many a relationship founded on the depth of philosophical agreement has foundered on the quality of the prattle, because lovers cannot become truly snug without making the banter connection. And for Ferdinand and Miranda the small talk came as tiny and naturally as the springs that flowed alongside the track.

Even the silences were comfortable. They had risen finally at the sound of lunch, the clanking of trays and the smell of smoked food, and afterwards, as the grey rocks grazed the side of the coaches and streams ran beside the track spreading about boulder-strewn river beds, Miranda turned from the silent window and caught Ferdinand's eye.

'What are you thinking?'

'Nothing.'

'You can't think nothing. What you mean is, "Mind your own business you nosy woman."'

'No, no I don't.'

'So what are you thinking?'

'You.'

'Me? That's not an answer.'

'About you then.'

'What about me?'

'I. Well. Aren't thoughts supposed to be private in the quiet of the mind, otherwise we would just speak them. And the world would be full of noise and chatter.'

'Sometimes thoughts just don't know that they are allowed to come out, that it's safe.'

'So what are you thinking?'

'I asked first.'

'I'm thinking, "What are you thinking?"'

'You know what I think about people who can't share their thoughts?'

'No. I can't read minds.'

'People who cannot share their thoughts are thoughtless. And they are pompous twats.'

'And people who continuously speak their minds are in constant danger of demonstrating that they don't possess one.'

'But you do have one.'

'You think so?'

'Those pompous, thoughtless twats, Ferdinand, value themselves over everybody else, they think that their thoughts are so bloody wonderful, so great, that other people are not worth sharing them with.'

'Isn't it the people who have to tell you every notion in their mind who believe their thoughts are so amazing that others will want to listen to them?'

'No, they're offering their thoughts up for criticism, bringing them out for anybody to judge, they have no fear, they are welcoming contributing thoughts from others. Imagine if Einstein had had a great thought about relativity and never shared it. Or Isaac Newton had decided to keep the apple to himself. Where would we be if Max Factor had hidden his thoughts under a blusher? The pompous twats who don't know how to share a thought, they're left with poor, lonely, undernourished, underdeveloped thoughts. They are pompous, they are superior and their thoughts are poverty-stricken so they're stupid as well.'

'You thought all that up on your own?'

She smiled a smile so tiny it was barely a smillimetre. Edelweiss idled in sun-filled pastures. Glaciers dripped and chocolate boxes melted.

'All I was thinking just then was how lovely you are,' Ferdinand said finally, 'and that I'm lucky. Lucky you came, that I was in that shop, on that tube. I was thinking that I really don't know anything about you but somehow, somehow I know you. I can look in your eyes and see it all, you don't need to tell me your thoughts, your eyes speak them. When I look in them you do not lower them, or guard or deflect, you open your eyes and honesty floods out.'

Miranda laughed. 'Well, for all that truth and honesty, I haven't the foggiest why I'm here. I think I'm just following my heart. But I don't know what you see in me. Maybe, maybe if I spent less time thinking I wouldn't wonder why so much. I'd just enjoy it. Live it.'

'So the only problem between you and me is thinking.'

They both smiled and the train rattled through a chorus of cowbells. They both smiled because they knew that the other believed they had got the upper hand. And that they had touched a common nerve, the one that was struck when they first met. And if they had a common nerve, they were similar, they were not such worlds apart; they did have a chance.

Smoothly, along the level flood plain of the river Po, past Verona and Vicenza, Barry played tag with the Italian drivers on the autostrada.

'Unbe-fucking-lievable,' said Barry as yet another Alfa Romeo attempted to chicane him.

'What?' said Peersnide, opening his eyes expecting to see a juggernaut hurtling towards them.

'It's like everybody on this road thinks they're driving an AstraVan.'

'An AstraVan?'

'Yeah, tool of the trade, delivery van, like what I drive.'

'And?' said Peersnide impatiently.

'And when you're behind the wheel you have to obey the unwritten laws of the speed god Astra. You know, spin the wheels at traffic lights, give the finger to anyone who tries to pass, switch lanes for no apparent reason. They do it all here, but they're not driving AstraVans, they're in nice cars.'

'Ferkle shereekly flackshaner turgidal flertlyfile,' would be a rough approximation of what Peersnide heard coming out of Barry's lips. He knew nothing about cars, he didn't want to know anything about cars. Still, he thought that if he just kept his eyes closed and repeated the mantra, I'm still alive, I'm still alive, it might still be true when they got somewhere.

'Whaddya fucking mean that wasn't the Simplon Pass, shit-fer-lips. I paid to go on the goddamn Venice–Simplon–Orient Express, you don't go nowhere near the Orient, you don't go to Simplon, you're not express, for christsake are you sure you're gonna go to Venice?'

'We use the Brenner Pass because the train visits Innsbruck,' replied the steward with a practised tone of patronization carefully honed to be detectable only to those he is not addressing.

'Then why the fuck don't you call it the goddamn Venice–Brenner slow train, you ass-wipe?'

The loud American, whom Miranda and Ferdinand had managed to avoid up until now, had finally joined them in the bar. He sneered at the view and then muttered some more obscenities into his drink and in the direction of his walnut wife.

Having conquered the Austrian Alps, the train was descending gracefully into Italy. Every now and then, as it cornered past another pillar of rock, they could glimpse the distant, green, flat plain of the Veneto, even as far as the sea. The high air was clear and the sky was as blue, still and cloudless as if seen from an aeroplane. But far away, on the horizon, above the city of Venice itself, vast white, baroque cumulus clouds towered, billowing. In enormous dazzling columns full seven leagues high, enough water to drown the Serenissima a hundred times was suspended, poised in a delicate balance of temperature and air pressure as soaring cushions of twisted alabaster, ready to plunge at the very first thunderburst.

'Looks like rain,' said Ferdinand, nodding towards the gathering storm.

CHAPTER VIII.

I LOVE THEREFORE I AM

A man goes to his doctor and says, 'Doc, you've got to help me, I'm having an identity crisis.'
So the doctor asks, 'Why didn't you come to see me yourself?'

OUR IDENTITY, AND HOW WE DEFINE OURSELVES, ALWAYS DOES, BY its very nature, feel incredibly personal – for all of us. Yet, all of us use, pretty much, the same standards and criteria to delineate our individuality: the way we look; the things we wear; the way we think; and, of course, what and how we love. In considering our uniqueness we, in fact, act *en masse*. Therefore, we are caught in another loop of paradoxes. The very decisions we suppose are individual and personal, are actually group decisions. We all do it, and we all do it, mostly, in the same way.

What does this have to do with the tyranny of love? It is that love has never seemed a tyranny because we have all laboured under the belief that it is 'personal', special to us. The tyrant's spectacular success – especially in this modern, post-humanist culture, which placed the individual at the centre again – is due to its insistence, its pretence, its feigning that it individuates, that it is only picking on one person, and that one person is you.

You the lover.

The lover thinks: it is I alone, and only I, who suffers, who truly feels. Everybody else who believes they love, gets it easier and incurs less damage than me. Love has picked me to be its martyr. I am special.

But why do we all feel that? As far as our feelings go, we want to be apart from, not a part of, the mass. Your feelings must be yours alone. After all, what and how you love is one of your defining constituents, core of your very sense of identity. But you are not alone. We all feel as you do. We are all lovers. It is, perhaps, a sad truth, that we are more alike than we are different.

41

What makes the anguish of each individual so important to study, consider, deliberate then liberate, is that if we are all lovers then we are behaving not as individuals but as a mass in our reactions to the despot's domination. We are not alone as lovers, and we are not alone in being abused by the system, the decrees, the authority of love. If it only subjected one slave to its confusion of sexual, whiplashing vexations, love would be a dominatrix. Yet love is a tyranny because it imposes itself not on one but on us all, however much we may believe that we are responding as individuals and that its reign is a personal torment. Love is the most subtle and insidious assault on free will known to man. And yet think how much of it remains unknown. Think how it veils itself, its origins, its true meaning. Think of all those millions of definitions, none right but none wrong.

We must face the truth, that whether we toil or laze, we are under its power; if we suffer or enjoy it, in pain or in ecstasy, we are all, all of us, lovers, a controlled, controllable, influenceable mass. To misquote Jean Jacques Rousseau, 'Man was born free and everywhere he is in love.'

Think of all the appeals in television adverts for us to enter our sense of love into the market of barter and commerce. They ask us to buy gifts for our loved ones because, it seems, it is those gifts alone which have the power to show that you love them. They imply that love will end if the gifts are not bought, that you sit on a time-bomb which will explode and hurt you if you do not conform to their rules of 'love display'. These advertisements reach millions of lovers. Are each of us so arrogant as to believe that we are the only ones they speak to, the only ones to really love? The only ones who hurt? The only ones to whom love is real, not some pale words of mutual affection? The only ones who know the depths, the heights, the pain and pleasure? Are we so selfish that we cannot admit that we all feel?

Is love innately selfish or does it just make us selfish? Is there, in fact, any more selfish an act than demanding fulfilment, the complete attention and adoration of another human soul?

We must awaken to the fact that we have all been played the joker, the fool, the sucker, the dupe. We must take a strong inhalation of the aroma of the coffee and admit that for a few brief moments of happiness, and a misplaced feeling of individuality, we have sold our souls. We have signed our names in the blood of our hearts, to a Mephistophelian contract of love.

21

Striking Thoughts

A THOUGHT STRUCK MIRANDA.

Mind you, that was just because of where she was. i don't mean emotionally; i mean where she physically was. Of course there are some thoughts that happen spontaneously, but most of them are just lazy and lurk around places waiting to pop into people's minds. Thoughts prefer to loiter, like cerebral muggers, ready to hit any who pass their way. Haven't you noticed that? That, for instance, a whole headache of thoughts gather outside the house, hanging about to strike you when you are no more than three yards from the front door; the 'Have I got my keys?' thought, the 'Oh, it is raining after all,' and 'I did remember to put my trousers on. Didn't I?' thoughts are well known for mooching around there.

At certain key areas of the world legions of thoughts jostle for head space: outside the Taj Mahal nearly everyone finds the 'It's not like the postcard', 'Isn't that the bench Princess Di sat on?', 'Christ, it's hot', 'How many more legless beggars can I stand?' thoughts, and a mindful of others all noisily scrounging for attention.

Other locations are the home of more metaphysical thoughts waiting to cross your mind. Who has gone to St Paul's whispering gallery and not encountered the 'Go on say it, say "fuck", it's not as if there's a God to hear you, or is there?' thought? There is a spot just twenty feet above the ground surrounding most tall buildings where 'What if there is a hell?' elbows for room with 'The acceleration of a falling body is ten metres per second per second', and 'On the other hand . . .'

There are still other places which are dangerous no-go areas for thoughts, places devoid of contemplation. Television game show studios are such places where no thoughts dare linger, as are civil service offices, tables for two and the White House.

However, many thoughts do not travel well and like to make their home and presence felt in one place in particular. Take, for example, the thought 'Opposites attract'. You know, one of those tedious paradoxical laws that physicists love to spout. They only love it, of course, because of the desperate hope it brings them. What nerdy, acne-infested, grant-reliant, socially inept, lonely physicist with four-inch-thick glasses wouldn't want it to be true? Wouldn't want to believe he or she could attract an opposite? It's either that or have some mad scheme to take over the world. i don't know but wouldn't magnets collapse into themselves if both ends were really so attracted to each other? Aren't opposites actually poles apart?

i suppose if you are in a budding relationship and can't figure out what the other person sees in you, it is a happy idea to fool yourself with. i mean, Miranda and Ferdinand were quite opposite but they were attracting each other. Even if one of them was under orders to do so and the other was so soaked in romantic fervour she wouldn't recognize an impossibility if it slapped her in the face with a wet desert. What i have to admit though is, however opposite they may have seemed to each other, they still had far more in common than Miranda and i did. For a start they shared 99 per cent of their biological material, and even more before the end of the next chapter; they both nourished their digestive systems and evacuated their bowels similarly; they both even enjoyed the Eurovision Song Contest, but i don't think that they ever found that out about each other.

Opposites retract from each other though, that's what makes them opposites. my physical opposite is fire and i'm about as attracted to that as a nun to fun. But you and i, we're sharing our time, my story is becoming yours, we're the same here in the world of your mind and i love you, i think i really do. That's really embarrassing, isn't it? But you've read my story so far and we are alike because i am becoming a part of you, your consciousness. The trouble with Miranda was that although she picked me up and looked at me often, it always seemed as if her mind was elsewhere, she never read me, like you do. There was none of this sustained intimacy that we have. Quick fumbled glances really was all i got. But if you've never known anything else, it feels an awful lot like love. So maybe it was unfair to say that i had another reader before you, just that i could have had another type of reader before you. Maybe she would have been a bit more like you if it hadn't been for Ferdinand.

Opposites only attract as curiosity leads them. You might want to sleep with someone very different, but you'd want to live with someone similar. Yet the myth of attractive opposites persists, however untrue it is, because it is a neat platitude that can be trotted out whenever opposites enter close enough proximity to curiously sniff each other out; which brings me, Miranda, Ferdinand, Peersnide, Barry and a host of romantics to the place where the 'opposites attract' paradox has become supreme resident. It is neither a laboratory nor the Quasimodo Dating Agency for the Genetically Condemned as one might expect, no, nowhere is this maxim more repeated than on the lagoon shores of the town of Mestre in north-eastern Italy.

Mestre. Say the word without hissing the conurbated villain, and pitying its citizens.

As quickly as they can, two million tourists pass through, or by, Mestre each year, and each one will be struck by the same thought as they wonder at the aesthetic opposition that it represents. Mestre is an ugly town but ugly only in the same way that Michael Jackson might be described as eccentric or a Tabasco Vindaloo flambéed in rocket fuel might be described as warm. Mestre is almost excremental in its hideousness: a fetid, fly-blown, festering, industrial urbanization, scarred with varicose motorways, flyovers, rusting railway sidings and the rubbish of a billion holidaymakers gradually burning, spewing thick black clouds into the Mediterranean sky. A town with apparently no centre, a utilitarian ever-expandable wasteland adapted to house the displaced poor, the shorebound, outpriced, domicile-deprived exiles from its neighbouring city. For, just beyond the condom- and polystyrene-washed, black-stained, mud shores of Marghera, Mestre's very own oil refinery, less than a mile away across the waters of the lagoon, in full sight of its own dispossessed citizens, is the Jewel of the Adriatic. Close enough for all to feel the magnetism, there stands the most beautiful icon of Renaissance glory and, like so much that can attract tourism, a place too lovely to be left in the hands of its natives, the Serenissima itself, Venice.

Between the two cities there is one slender bridge. It sweeps out over the water, bracing a skitter of tiny stone arches, hopping over marshland and lapping water. And there, the railway and the road converge, running side-by-side straight to Venice's huddled islets, the city of romance. As the Orient Express burst from the fetid smog which pervades Mestre and struck out across the bridge, Miranda and Ferdinand both watched the choppy waters of the lagoon with that sense of relief that every passenger experiences, sheer irrational gratitude that the train had not terminated in Mestre. They sipped their champagne and watched the first hard spatters of rain ricochet off the glass as a shuddering thunderclap announced the arrival of a traditional Mediterranean tempest, which was pretty much how St Mark found Venice in the first place.

A thought struck Miranda. 'Opposites attract,' she mused, looking out of the carriage window. For a while she just swivelled her head between the urban and the urbane, the picturesque and the grotesque as the rain splashed against the window.

'Opposites attract,' thought every other traveller bound for Venice.

'Opposites attract,' thought Ferdinand as he watched the parallel road along the bridge and noted with a smile the Bentley powering across it; the pinnacle of automotive engineering being propelled towards a city that has no roads to drive. But then, the car was just a back-up, a precaution, a plan B; however unlikely, if he had to neutralize Miranda and escape the city fast, it had to be there. Still, it was good timing, Peersnide might not be as cack-handed as he suspected. He looked at Miranda, the girl whose heart he would either break or stop before the next day dawned. She seemed intent on trying to look at where she was going and where she was coming from all at the same time. It started to make him dizzy so he turned back to the tail lights of the Bentley blurring in the rain, unable to see that the car had more than one occupant.

'Opposites attract,' thought Peersnide absent-mindedly as he watched Barry and his powerful Neanderthal brow concentrating on the road ahead.

'Opposite side of the road,' thought Barry. 'Opposite side of the road, opposite side of the road,' as he had to continually remind himself. He switched on the windscreen wipers as the rain began to pelt and the glass momentarily became a mosaic of shifting shapes. The sudden cloudburst thundered on the car roof and the wipers threw water from the screen in waves. As even the Italian cars were slowing down in the face of the downpour, Ferdinand lost sight of the Bentley surging forward in a mist of tyre spray.

'And it could have been so perfect,' he said as Miranda looked at him. ' Still, it's kind of romantic, isn't it?'

'Anyone,' said Miranda, 'who believes rain is romantic has

obviously never lived on the Goldhawk Road, under a roof which needs more Tupperware on the floor than a party for bored house-wives.'

'Oh,' said Ferdinand, trying to look a little hurt.

Miranda could hear the words coming from her and she knew that they weren't hers; it was Mercy talking, saying those things. Something about the reality of actually living out her fantasy was making her put up all sorts of walls just for some stability. And though they were paper-thin, stage-prop walls which would fall down in the slightest breeze, she felt obligated as her own romantic heroine to maintain at least a veneer of self-possession. If he was going to come over all romantic, well, she would just have to prove what a self-sufficient, self-reliant girl she was. No pushover, a woman who sticks to her standards. Until she was absolutely sure this man felt for her a tenth of what she felt for him, she would have to keep quiet the truth about dancing in the rain on tropical islands with Bounty Bar men.

Behind the curtains of rain, large blue signs declaring 'Venezia' swam past. Letters of blue and white slowing until, with a chorus of tiny squeals, all motion stopped. Doors began to clunk open and only then did Miranda feel she was somewhere foreign, unknown, really away. The realization flooded in with the gloriously unfamiliar sounds. Rain clattering on each platform glass canopy, shouting of lyrical alien names, bells chiming distantly, hissing water pipes, mur-muring voices finding each other, children wailing 'MaMaaa', gurgling nasal tannoy, the tremor of drumming engines, and somewhere Romance calling out, bobbing about, peering at each disembarking passenger holding a felt-tipped sign marked 'LOVERS?'

She was helped down from the narrow door by the sinuous tanned hand of a thin, black-eyed porter. Once on the platform Ferdinand ushered her away, palming her elbow and guiding her along the car-riages, dodging families, trolleys laden with crisps, piles of luggage and smoking porters. Out onto the steps of the station and there Miranda had to stop just to gasp. There it was: Venice as she imagined it, Venice like the paintings, like the postcards, the Grand Canal, a domed church, motor launches with drivers in white caps, a man in a stripy T-shirt beneath two large umbrellas selling straw hats and another sell-ing ice-cream, and yes, he really had them, Cornettos. The Campo Ferrovia resembled a glass lawn as a million shiny blades of bouncing raindrops splashed off its glittering surface.

'Come on,' laughed Ferdinand, pulling her into the deluge.

They ran across the empty square. Miranda's thin clothes becoming heavy, flesh-slapping, nipple-hardening, completely sodden, before they were half way to the canal's edge. At the white stone shore Ferdinand jumped without breaking pace and landed squarely on the wooden deck of a taxi launch. He turned to look up at Miranda and grasped her by the waist. She leant forward as he lowered her into the launch. Slowly she descended as if falling into his eyes, pu-pools start-ling in their clarity, cleaned by the streaming rain that pounded at his face. His eye-lashes were coronets of shining droplets and his cheek-bones rivulets of pouring water. As soon as her feet touched the floor, they scrambled into the boat's auburn veneered cabin and Ferdinand nodded to the man who sat there in his white shoes, shirt, socks, shorts and sailor's cap. 'Taxi?' he asked.

'Sì,' nodded the man.

Then 'Il Palazzo Gritti, per favore, faccia presto, non vede che la Signora è bagnata!' Ferdinand said in such fluent Italian Miranda half expected him to break into 'Nessun dorma', and start pinching her bottom for good measure. Not that she thought her bottom was a good measure for anything but hot-air balloons.

'Ci giurerei,' replied the man in white as he left the cabin. They sat on the highly polished leather cushions and from the stern a deep throaty throttling noise belched into the canal as the launch swept out into the centre of the waterway. As the prow hit each little storm-tossed wave a spray of fishy canal rained through the open doors of the launch. 'What about the luggage?'

'They'll be taking care of it now. It'll probably be there before us.'

'I don't think I could get used to this sort of travel,' sighed Miranda. 'If you give up responsibility for everything, what's there to do on a holiday? If you can't worry about your luggage going to Murmansk how are you supposed to occupy your time?'

The boat smacked into a cross wave, and then an even angrier one, suddenly sliding Miranda into Ferdinand's arms. He steadied her as he pushed her upright again.

'You're right, there may be a risk of relaxing,' said Ferdinand as the boat swerved to miss the prow of a gondola that had broken moorings and swung out into the canal. Ferdinand was now flung at Miranda, his head butting hers fiercely. 'Oww,' she added, holding her nose. The boat plummeted over the crest of a wave made tidal by the narrowness of the canal and Ferdinand slid into Miranda pressing her face against the launch window, squashing it into a wobbly flat white pancake against the glass. 'Nearly there,' he said cheerfully as he pushed him-self away from her.

With a loud slurping sound, Miranda peeled her cheek from the cold glass. 'Great,' she said.

'Left, no left, no left. Left, for God's sake. That way. That way's your . . . was your left. Wonderful, now we've missed it.' Peersnide looked hopelessly over his shoulder.

'It's all this driving on the wrong side of the road,' moaned Barry.

'Well, we'll just have to turn round and go back to the Parking sign, God knows where this will take us.'

'Can't right now.' Barry pointed ahead. They had reached a traffic queue and a man in a raincoat and sunglasses was tramping towards them. Peersnide wound down his window and was slapped in the face by a hail of raindrops. The man leant into the car to get some respite. 'Due per il Lido, sì?' he said.

'Parking, we're trying to find somewhere to park.'

'Sì. Plenty parking at Lido, signori. Plenty parking. Cinque euro per favore.'

'Right.' Peersnide grabbed some money from the glove compartment and gave it to the man. Then in very slow English, 'Where is the Parking?'

'Sì. At Lido,' repeated the man, handing them a ticket. 'You go on that.' The ticket seller pointed through the rain and Barry and Peersnide realized that the queue of cars led to the lowered steel door of a car ferry. Just as the cars in front started to move onto the boat, a superhumanly patient Italian driver behind them hooted his horn. Conditioned like Pavlov's dogs, Barry automatically swore and lifted his finger at the sound of the horn. The ticket seller disappeared behind them and Barry followed the other cars onto the ferry. Having lined the sides of the deck with cars, more men in raincoats and sunglasses ushered Barry to the front of the boat so he faced the exit ramp at the far end. Rain streaked down onto the deck here and they could see and feel the water churning around them.

'I feel a bit sick,' said Peersnide, rushing out of the car and immediately slipping on some oil on the deck. Though still tethered, the boat tipped to such a degree, Peersnide skated to the edge of the deck and, caught in the stomach by the bar, bent double over it and sent his vomit into the brine.

Sliding into a narrow canal, the taxi engine throttled down and began to glide, trailing a yard-high wash skating along the ancient brick walls. As the water slooshed beneath tiny marble bridges, Miranda held Ferdinand's hand tightly. Shadows echoed over their faces and through their eyes, as they swayed with each little lunge of the boat. They shared a smile and a sigh and watched the walls go by. The cry, 'Oè!' ricocheted at every corner as the boat approached each turn, and between was the quiet of the rain pelting on the roof and the muffled city beyond. Suddenly the engine roared and the boat swung to the right. Miranda looked out, it was the big canal again, on the other side there was a huge domed church enrobed with statues, saints clinging to it like ornamental leeches. Curlicues and windywhotsits coiled about its columns and masonry, it was the most amazing building she had ever seen. For an architectural aesthetic educated on a council estate and at the finishing school of Shepherd's Bush, it was breathtaking.

Ferdinand watched Miranda's open-mouthed wonder. 'The Salute. It's beautiful, baroque, like a wedding cake,' he said, evoking the cliché and hoping that the word 'wedding' might resonate a little in the romantic atmosphere he was building.

'No,' said Miranda, still gawping at it, 'it's like, it's like seeing a really fit bottom, hard as you like, tanned to perfection and then stuck in some totally frilly knickers. It's great.'

'Well, you better get used to it,' said Ferdinand, 'it's our view.' As he was speaking, the engine growled into reverse and the boat slowed. Beside them, on the near side of the canal, as they pitched and yawed, was a calm and stately red-carpeted landing stage covered by a white canvas roof. Behind that, some flower-decked restaurant tables were lined up along the waterside and above them towered the Renaissance splendour of the Gritti Palace. Its name was depicted in large gold lettering on the dappled pink brick wall. White marble windows punctuated the façade as if they were an harmonic notation on a music manuscript. Miranda tried to guess which one was theirs.

The driver threw a rope to another man on the landing, also dressed in immaculate white. He offered Miranda a hand to climb out of the boat. Ushered and flattered and greeted and grovelled to, Miranda and Ferdinand made their way from landing to reception to lift to room and only then, with the door closed and the uniforms left behind, did they feel alone with each other. It was like being suddenly released from the world into their own shared passions. He grasped her in his manly hands as she stared into his steel eyes. Then as his face neared hers, his lips neared hers, their wet clothes steaming in the embrace, Miranda began to squirm. 'Sorry, I can't do this,' she said, peeling herself away from him and catching his quizzical expression. 'I'm bursting for a pee, all that water and rain and, do you know where it is?'

Like glowing instead of sweating, there are certain things which, despite women's suffrage, a girl still feels she ought not be perceived doing: drinking pints, scratching her crotch and belching like a foghorn are among them. Many, like Miranda, feel that growing underarm hair, having a body odour that doesn't come out of a French bottle, or eating anything that doesn't have the proviso virtually fat-free, in public, are also no-nos exclusive of her sex. Urinating is, of course, one of those things that a true lady does absolutely silently. Unfortunately, Miranda was a hoverer not a sitter. Had she sat down, the vacuum of thigh, buttock and seat would have been more than adequate insulation. However, as she hovered above the Siena marble toilet, the stream of a pee echoed deafeningly like an indoor Niagara. If ever there was a mood-killer, the loud gush that resonated from under her qualified as a totally proficient assassin.

But it was a very different kind of killing that was on Ferdinand's mind. Whilst Miranda hovered, paralysed with embarrassment, trying to listen for any sign of his movements and the general acoustic qualities of the walls, Ferdinand crept about stealthily, vetting the room for a place to hide his Silver Hawk 2:2 calibre semi-automatic gun. He didn't want to take it with him. Nothing could be worse than finding yourself in a hurried cuddle and taking a girl's eye out with the butt. According to the 'Booker' – the MI5 handbook, which is cunningly hidden beneath the dustjacket of the latest Booker winner on the basis that although almost anyone could be excused for owning one, no one would bother to try and read it if they found it lying about – the best place to hide illegal items was always in someone else's luggage. Unfortunately Miranda didn't have any, so Ferdinand decided to place the gun at the bottom of the case that he had given her.

Miranda silently wiped herself and stood up. Quietly, quietly, she pulled up her knickers and held her breath as she listened. How could she go back in and resume the embrace? How could the romance continue after a force five storm had come booming out of her bladder? She could hear nothing, save the pounding of blood in her ears. Did he hear or didn't he? It was unbearable. Suddenly, all Miranda wanted to do was leave the hotel room, get on with the next chapter. Peeling off her wet clothes, she opened the door just enough to stick her bare arm through and said as huskily as possible, 'Could you pass me something dry to put on? Something appropriate, if we're eating in the hotel, or are we eating out?'

'Out, I thought,' replied Ferdinand, as with one hand he extracted a long velvet dress with some strappy high-heeled shoes, and with the other placed his weapon at the bottom of her case. He draped the dress over Miranda's extended arm, hung the shoe straps on her fingers, and watched them snap back into the bathroom.

Only when the dress and shoes were on did Miranda take a look at herself in the full-length mirror. And then she had to check that the woman who stood there was indeed her. The dress clung and tapered about her legs as if she were a sleek black pen balancing on a stiletto nib. O, what that pen could have written. She was transformed: a dress, a foreign city, a leap of faith, a dream come real, a goal nearly realized; somewhere along the way the shopgirl swinging sanitary napkins had become, well, a woman. A woman who pees like a hydrant at the wrong time, but someone she had only ever imagined being some-where about page 284 of her romantic novels. Miranda was determined not to let the gushing embarrassment ruin the evening. She flung open the bathroom door to reveal the diva that she had become . . .

'Well, let's catch a drink before dinner, shall we?' she said, swiftly launching herself towards the suite's door.

They stepped out of the hotel and into the rain. She huddled close to Ferdinand, both of them under his raincoat, and they ran.

The rain came down so hard it hissed against the paving stones. It spat as it bounced from the rippling surfaces of the narrow canals and in the wide channel between the Zattere and Giudecca Island it drew white claw marks on the agitated inky waves. There, the car ferry *San Marco* plied stately, slowly, through the foaming lagoon waters, its lights glinting in the burgeoning darkness. It rounded in a gentle arc about the city as, under the sodden sky, twilight quickly dimmed. So, apart from the dull ginger haze that illuminates any city under an evening cloud, the dusk had fully surrendered to the night by the time the ferry passed the Piazzetta. This gap in the waterfront buildings between the Ducal Palace and library was where travellers for centuries caught their first glimpse of St Mark's Square, its soaring bell tower, its automaton clock tower and the delicate eastern domes of its cathedral. Despite the downpour, most of the ferry passengers gathered on the port side to gape at the wonder, its composition uncluttered with people, abandoned because of rain. This made it even more spectacu-lar as out of the darkness, painted with orange streetlights, it appeared like a stage set waiting for its players. Act One, the stones glistened in gentle peaches and yellows, light played with the dark where columns and windows were dusted with blue grey shadows. Even Peersnide, drenched by the rain, looked up between vomit retches and was stunned into involuntary swallowing as he saw the apparition, the subject of so many paintings. With his somewhat paternalistic view of the Renaissance, this sudden bright vision, rising out from the seething black waters, seemed to Peersnide alight, burning with a gem-like flame. Only Barry barely glanced at the glorious architectural fireworks, the city's pride. He stood alone, above the car deck, gazing lovingly at the Bentley below. This was the first time he had got the chance to really look at the car, admire its bullish lines which still managed to understate its power, revel in being in possession of the key. He knew certain clubs in Essex where the key alone could ensure a good shagging every night of the week. He pressed the key button and with a loud tweak he armed the car alarm. The unexpected noise and flashing indicators made many on the bridge turn, momentarily, to see who would disturb their reverie of light. Barry smiled smugly and disarmed the car's alarm, again pointing the key dramatically at the vehicle. Two of the best tanned, most gorgeous Italian girls Barry had ever imagined came over to him, giggling.

'This is your car, no?' said the taller one, eyelashes widely drawn.

'Oh yes, well, just one of my runarounds.' The girls smiled, they knew a chauffeur when they saw one.

'Oh, you are a big man, you must have a big cock, no?' They turned to walk away and burst out laughing.

'It is mine,' whined Barry, 'look.' He armed the alarm once more.

Peersnide listened to this third consecutive tweek and remembered Ferdinand's lecture on the car. He dragged his head round from the boat's edge to register the roar of the Bentley 6-litre W12 engine bursting into life, the wheels beginning to spin on the rainsoaked deck, before taking grip. He looked up to the passenger deck where Barry stood next to two girls; his arm outstretched pointing the key, his eyes terror-wide.

'Press it again,' Peersnide screeched up to the passenger deck but Barry was fearfrozen. Peersnide watched helplessly as the two million pound car, a grade one weapon, accelerated to fifty in the three meters between standstill and the front ramp of the moving boat. By this time everyone, even the ferry captain, was watching as the car sped up the ramp at over seventy miles an hour and reached a hundred as it achieved the ramp's zenith. Then, continuing into the air, it launched itself towards the storm clouds. Against the backdrop of the island church of San Giorgio Maggiore the Bentley gracefully arced above the water, as if circumnavigating its dome. With the engine still howling, its wheels spinning uselessly, the car reached an almost suspended apex, a majestic pause as it slowly tipped downwards and began its dive back towards the tar-black water. Then, with barely a splash, the most sophisticated land vehicle yet produced by the Ministry of Defence plunged beneath the clasping waves in front of the oncoming ferry and slowly sank, the tail lights dimming in the dark stirring waters. All eyes turned to Barry who, with his mouth still open, appeared paralysed. His hand was still held out, pointing at the empty place on the car deck where once the most beautiful beast on four wheels had stood. After a moment he fainted, opening his hand and letting the key fall clattering to the deck below. Peersnide felt another, deeper retch welling up in his throat and turned quickly back to the boat's side.

I am sorry. I realize that no one likes to think that they have made a mistake, but how else are we to learn? Mistakes are useful. How many trillions of mistakes do you think Nature went through, how many species and ridiculous animal lines do you think were born, developed and died before it got to us? Of what future ideal race are we the mistaken, less than perfect, ancestors?

Let us admit that we have made a mistake, that love is something we do not have to languish under but is, in fact, a matter of choice.

We can choose to suffer those extremes it offers or we can turn our backs on it and not feel any less human, any less a woman, any less a man. We were not born of some fall, some original sin that we all must pay for ever after, that is the legacy of a Judeo-Christian guilt culture which aimed to enslave believers in shame. We do not have to martyr ourselves to the pain and torments of love and life. There are alternatives and, though it may be wonderful for some, we will not be stigmatized for turning our backs on it.

We live as what the chanteuse Ms Grace Jones called 'Slaves to love'. These 'slaves' will shake their heads and pretend to pity you who have thrown off the shackles of love. They will not understand that you know you can choose to love or not, that you greet it on your terms, that love is subjugated to you and not the other way round. We must beat the tyrant who only holds us by our imaginations and fetters our spirits.

Do we really have a choice? No, most would tell me, we do not. Love 'hits' us − look at the very violence of the language − and we are lost to its power. The heart leaps and begins its rattling ride on the big dipper. There is no choice, it just happens. Biologists will tell us of the endorphin release and story-tellers will speak of Cupid's arrow that pierces the heart in an instant.

I listen to these arguments but what I hear is the caged bird singing, whilst there it sits, as is its habit, remaining on its perch even when its door has been opened. I hear the slave who has grown accustomed to his master and cannot imagine anything else, any other life, freedom. I hear the serf, the vassal, the proletariat who labour under the tyrant's rule and repeat on their broken lips the mantra, the propaganda, 'There is no alternative. There is no choice. I love, My Lord. I love, Big Brother. I love.'

So in the world of the lover there is no choice. You can fall in love in a second. One minute you're quite happily minding your own business, the next you're devoting all your time to your personal hygiene and worrying whether your clothes are attractive or your hair's brushed in the right way. Love at first sight? Be honest. Isn't it, more often, love at first night?

The lover looks back and seems to remember the moment eyes met and the sting of the arrow, but we shape our memories to fit the culture, the custom, the way it is 'supposed' to be. For each occasion that the lover remembers as that piercing moment of undeniable love, there are hundreds where events and circumstances prevented furtherance and further action. She didn't look back, he never noticed, they went their separate ways, mislaid a phone number, were already engaged somewhere else. These moments are conveniently lost and forgotten because they did not succeed and in love we only want to remember our successes. The painful truth is that, in love, success is rare and only ever fleeting.

This selective memory only shows that you do have a choice. The lover chooses, the lovers agree, to be in love. That is the lover's choice though he thinks that he has none. You have a choice, you can choose fear, pain, insecurity, or choose to live.

If love were natural then there might be no choice, we might be slaves to our genetic destinies. But it isn't and we are not. The true individual, the person who knows who and where he is, knows that he has a choice.

22

Oov

SOMETIMES YOU'VE JUST GOT TO LET GO OF THE PARANOIA AND ADMIT that only a god could be responsible for a certain situation. Sometimes things are just too big, or too shit, to blame anybody, not even ourselves. It is exactly for those moments that we have our deities, and it is why they have survived rationalism, science and trendy priests speaking in dated tongues. It's their job to be accountable when all others fail. We'll always want the buck to stop, a god to blame for writing our fates so inexplicably.

Of course, it is precisely for these situations that insurance companies employ hordes of theologians to contemplate and interpret what exactly is an act of God and what could be put down to coincidence, bad luck or sheer cack-handedness and therefore not covered.

Yet not all these moments are disasters. Once in a while, maybe only once in each lifetime, less common than a blue moon and nowhere near as frequent as a month of Sundays, there might be a moment when absolutely everything that occurs is perfect. The entire world seems to be conspiring to make everything right for you. You are doing exactly the right thing, at the right time, in the right place. Everything is infinitely right. $\infty\sqrt{}$.

$\infty\sqrt{}$, oov.

And what makes oov so ultimately perfect and perfectly satisfying is that you are absolutely conscious of how right everything is as it happens because it includes, as a free gift, a cognisance of the whole event. You are absolutely aware of how fantastically the world is finally working for you. Oov is endowed with an almost extra consciousness that just makes you want to shake your head and say, 'Goddamn'; fairly inappropriately. An ecstasy where you almost leave your body to observe how completely a part of everything right you have become. But oov is no simple instance of synchronicity, for though it shows you your oneness with the universe it is not just a moment, it could be an hour, a day or, in Miranda's case, an evening. Oov. An obscure word for an obscure thing and yet that night in Venice it was exactly what happened to Miranda.

No combination of international powers, secret services or union of global conglomerates could have made it rain when it did and stop when it stopped, no mortal authority could have predicted that every tourist in Venice would look at the rain and give up the evening as a lost cause, getting an early night. Neither MI5, MI6 or William Gates could have predicted or calculated when the thunder would roll, the lightning strike, or where the moth would rest. No, it was all perfect, it was Miranda's night, it was oov.

They ran slipping and sliding through glassy squares and dark-filled deserted streets, their shoes splashing through colours swimming in puddles and echoing. Ferdinand guided Miranda through a narrow maze of weathered, crumbling walls, dashing over bridges and sheltering under awnings. They scampered under gushing water spilling from broken drainpipes and filling the close-walled alleys with torrential water sheets. They grazed endless mocha brown walls, deeply scarred as if the brickwork had been described with chisels and knives. Past sinister rape-dark doorways, where only tiny yellow lion's eyes glinted brassily. Past luminous white church façades, streaked with pigeon shit. And then out into a big deserted campo, a statue of a man leaning on a bronze pile of books in the centre. In a corner, outside an empty café window, chairs were stacked on chairs as a cascade of raindrops filtered through them. A larger bridge loomed, arching in a tangle of wooden struts, away into the rain. They pelted up its wide steps, pausing momentarily at the top to peer down at the black Grand Canal. An empty vaporetto plied towards them, its interior lights ablaze as it was tossed from side to side. Ferdinand's arm was at Miranda's waist as he gently urged her to move again, down the other side of the bridge. Into another wet alley. Quickly along an abrasive graffitied wall, awash with waves of ivy curling down from the top and scratching to the rhythm of the wind. Along and left again and into a tiny passage, out of the rain. And here in the dark, dry passageway, barely wide enough for single file, Ferdinand took Miranda's hand and led her swiftly to the further end. Possibly he was calculating that the confusion and sinister route would make Miranda cling even more closely to him. Miranda, however, was too engrossed in noting how alleys even in Romance Central still smelt of wee. They turned a corner at the end and at last Ferdinand stopped. He pulled the raincoat off their heads and peered at a dark doorway before crying out, 'Bugger.'

The rain now streaked down their faces. 'What?' said Miranda. 'Bugger what?'

'The restaurant, it's closed.'

Miranda looked at the anonymous doorway dubiously.

'It's lovely inside,' Ferdinand tried to reassure her, 'a secret vine-covered garden and seafood to die for.'

'Well, the weather's good for the fishes. Not sure about the garden.'

Ferdinand looked sheepish. 'It's like the whole city's taken a rain check.'

'Come on, there's got to be another one.' Miranda took Ferdinand's hand and started running again.

'Another one?' he protested. 'Did you see anything open all the way here?' But this was Miranda's night and she just knew that it was going to work. It was going to be perfect.

'You know, there's something wonderful about getting lost in an unknown city. You look much harder for the clues. Space and places. You check each building to make sure you're not going in circles. You get as many senses going as you can to retain some sort of control and yet the whole thing swallows you.'

'It's like seeing snow for the first time.' Miranda paused to look around her. 'Have you got a clue where the fuck we are?'

Ferdinand shook his head and looked down at his menu. 'But I know it says food here, so at least we won't die of starvation.' The smoke-laden, lace-curtained café they sat in was a long way from Quicklinose. The misty yellow light in the restaurant was all-pervasive as the dust of weeks old cigarette smoke hung in the air like the foggy algae of a fish tank. Ferdinand was genuinely confused about exactly where he was; of course, he could have referred to his standard issue global position-ing system receiver in his watch, but at that moment he was sulking. He didn't like it when he went to all the bother of making a plan and then found that he had to improvise. As every trueborn Englishman must, he took a moment to curse the weather.

Miranda had led them a dizzying series of twists and turns, but somehow never met a blind alley; it was as if she had been guided by the gods themselves. And then there it was in front of them, the one, solitary, open trattoria in Venice. A little red lantern darkly illuminating a small, shuttered shopping calle beckoned through the pouring rain. Maximum romantic. Real red and white oilcloths on the tables, a real surly waiter, and the only other diner a real dour priest. Ferdinand looked embarrassed, but for Miranda it was perfect.

Later.

'We've come a long way.' Ferdinand smiled.

'Looks like the rain's stopping,' Miranda said, still staring vacantly through the lace curtains.

'"Small showers last long, but sudden storms are short,"' replied Ferdinand, gazing at her as she turned to consider her untouched tiramisù. 'Pick me up, pick me up,' he then cried in a tiny squeaky voice.

'What?'

'Tiramisù, it means pick me up. Like a tonic. Lift your spirits, lighten your load.'

'Increase my weight.'

'That too.' Ferdinand nodded, letting a silence descend like a theatrical fire curtain. 'Miranda. I feel. I feel as if my whole life is changing.'

She turned to him. 'From what exactly?'

'Scusi.' Ferdinand waved curtly to the waiter who was resting his stomach on the counter.

'I've heard about your childhood,' Miranda continued, shaking her spoon as if she could dig a little truth from him. 'I've heard about your uni days. But any which way I ask it, I seem to draw a blank about you now. These last years of your life. The important bits which brought you here now.' The waiter had set his body into motion and slowly approached them. For the first time Ferdinand found himself beginning to wish that this was a normal job. This was getting awfully fiddly. In a normal job the biography was just a back-up. Generally you just supplied consistent snippets to verify authenticity, not the entire blow-by-blow life. Your average foreign agent didn't want to know how many girlfriends you had, what you felt about growing up, when you first snogged and if there's been someone 'significant'. Put that way, infiltrating the KGB was a doddle to infiltrating a lover's knickers. 'Coffee?'

'A little truth?'

'Black, isn't it?'

'Sì?' said the waiter.

'I'm coming to suspect that that's probably the case,' Miranda said sourly.

'Your coffee, I mean.'

Miranda nodded.

'Uno macchiato e uno liscio, per favore.'

'Va bene,' grunted the waiter and shuffled away.

'I want you to tell me one thing about you that happened in the last year.'

'I fell in love.'

'Oh,' said Miranda and then, a little hesitantly, 'and what happened?'

'I brought her to Venice and now she's asking stupid questions.'

'They're not stupid. I'm like an open book to you. I tell you everything. You always make it look like you're being open and honest but something, I don't know what, something in the way you do it sounds like you're just making it up as you go along.'

'I love you,' Ferdinand tried hopefully. 'I can't get more genuine than that.'

'So how do you know?'

'I just do. You hurt. Here.' He pointed to his stomach.

'Maybe it's indigestion.'

'Why do you have such a problem hearing that? You do believe in love, don't you?'

'I don't . . .'

'I'm kind of sick of telling you how I feel and you just button up when I ask you.'

'Of course, I mean, I feel I love you.'

'In love?'

'I don't know.'

'So it's a little one-sided, isn't it.'

Miranda looked down at her plate; she felt as if she might cry.

'I don't know. I wasn't expecting this. It all seems right but it's like it's not happening in the right way. Something is wrong.'

'Wrong? Why wrong? We're alone, in Venice, with no one to tell us what to do or take us away from each other and somehow you think, or want maybe, for it all to go wrong.'

'It has to go wrong, I just know it will. It has to because I don't understand you and you've got to lose something before you realize what you had. I'll only understand when I've lost you and I'm just wondering how I'm going to fuck it all up.'

'What sort of bloody logic is that?' Ferdinand took a moment so that she could perhaps think about what she had just said. 'So it's got to be boy gets girl, boy loses girl, boy gets girl, has it? Now where have I read that before? Oh yes. Just about every hackneyed romantic novel ever. Just let it happen, Miranda.'

Ferdinand looked at his watch. In a few hours' time he had to have her declaring undying love or there would be another kind of dying to do. He really really didn't want to resort to that. A hit should have some sense of justice somehow. He was anxious to finish this the right way. If it was the gain, lose, gain romantic template that she wanted, she would get it. In an inspired piece of theatre Ferdinand stood suddenly, waving his arms, knocking the waiter with his precarious caffeine cargo to the floor, and began shouting.

'You want to know how this is going to go wrong. Let me show you, you fucking loony bitch.' Ferdinand threw some euros at the scalded, screaming waiter and stormed out into the street.

Miranda sat for a moment and then stood too, apologizing to the cursing waiter. She ran out into the street, looked both ways but couldn't see Ferdinand. Perfect, she thought, just perfect.

The rain had indeed stopped and now the paving stones glistened like a solid silver walkway. Fuck him, thought Miranda, wanker, and she set out not to find him. She decided to go one way, started out in the other direction, changed her mind and turned to go the other way, took a step and finally set off in the opposite direction. Lost is lost after all. The streets were empty, there was no one to ask the way. She was pissed off and a little tipsy and she didn't really want to bother to think about orienteering. It was an adventure and somehow she knew that she hadn't seen the last of Ferdinand, somehow it was all going to be fine.

As soon as she had turned her first corner, Ferdinand stepped out of the shadows of a doorway and followed her. He'd wait until a little panic set in before he revealed himself. Let her get a bit scared, a bit relieved to see him come to rescue her from the labyrinth. Miranda, however, was in no mood to be scared. The sleeping city was too exciting and the darkness nothing but intriguing. Had she not been so angry, had she not been cushioned by both her ire and her excitement about being in love and loved, she might have started conjuring up the usual monsters that lurk in the dark, those that prey on vulnerable lone girls in tight dresses who tap tap tap as they walk unfamiliar streets.

After a few hundred turns, countless bridges and, Ferdinand calculated, at least five times in a complete circle, Miranda thought that she recognized a place she had been before. The path that took her beside a canal ended abruptly in a dark door and went off to the right. The door was very distinctive in that it looked as if it had been ripped off a medieval castle and placed there with absolutely no regard to culture, history or place. Hinged black riveted steel bands crossed thick wood. A shuttered spyhole the size of a letterbox was cut into the door at head height and a small sign below it declared, 'El Suk', and in smaller writing beneath, 'Discoteca'. No lights shone enticingly, no 'Ladies' Night Special' posters hung nearby. Just this dark door. Miranda knocked. There was absolutely no point in being all dressed up and nowhere to go.

The spyhole slid open and two eyes glared at her. 'Sì?' they said.

'Hi,' smiled Miranda, 'I'm a little lost and . . .'

'Inglese?' interrupted the eyes.

'I'm English.'

'We full up.'

'Please, maybe I could just ask directions . . .' The spyhole slammed shut. She knocked harder. It opened again.

'Sì?' The eyes didn't seem to recognize her.

Miranda just smiled. Another voice from within said, 'Chi è?'

'Una donna. Sola,' said the eyes and turned away.

'Sola?'

'Sì.'

'È carina?' The eyes returned and considered her for a moment. 'È vestita bene,' they said.

'Falla passare allora.'

The heavy door creaked open and a large man in a fez beckoned to her to come in. Another one dressed completely in Arabic garb sat behind him with a hookah bubbling beside him. 'Welcome,' he said, emphasizing the two syllables so distinctly it sounded as if he were pronouncing the result of shellfish sex.

'I have no money,' Miranda said apologetically.

'Ladies, they are free tonight,' he said, bowing slightly and pointing towards the stairs going down to the music. Plastic bubbles emanated orange light from the side of the stairway and as she approached the cellar she could see that amorphous, primary-colour shiny plastic shapes served as tables, chairs and the bar. Miranda suddenly thought that it might be a seventies night and then, with mounting horror, taking in the worn carpeted walls of orange velveteen, a décor effect last seen in the Feltham Odeon in 1982, she realized that every night was probably seventies night and had been since the seventies.

Another slightly disturbing realization was that the entire club was empty save for a bar tender and a middle-aged man in a stripy shirt with a bright red handkerchief around his neck. When he saw her descend he beckoned her over and Miranda, having been in for so many pennies and pounds in the last two days, found herself fearlessly approaching him. If he was a white slave trader, he certainly was a comical one. Balding, paunchy and with a thin scarlet nose, he was very very drunk.

'Ah,' he said as she came close enough to hear him over the music, 'una bella donna.'

'Where?' said Miranda, swivelling her head.

'You.'

She smiled indulgently.

'I am Guido.'

'Miranda.'

'I am a gondoliere.' And before she knew it Miranda was in the midst of a seduction that put Ferdinand's flowers and expensive clothes and trains and luxury hotels to shame. Within five minutes she felt she had the measure of Guido and that he genuinely valued her opinion, that she was important to him. He poured out his heart with ingenious genuineness. He had enough experience of life to place Miranda as a certain type, a type that felt obliged once they thought that they were involved. Tell them about your terrible life and they have the ego-maniacal self-centred arrogance to believe that they can somehow sort it out. So Guido related the painful life of a gondolier, the endless aria-singing, the repetitive strain injuries from rowing, the insecurity of never knowing where your next fare may come from and, worst of all, having to go home to Mestre. All, of course, complete lies. Miranda began to feel very very sorry for him, and was amazed that she could find more in common with this middle-aged drunken Italian, than with Ferdinand. Well, fuck Ferdinand. Stuck up, anally retentive, pandered public school boy. If he couldn't share why should she care?

Ferdinand was, at that moment, upstairs and meeting stiff resistance from the doorman claiming that he couldn't let him in on his own because it would upset the delicate numbers of males and females in the club. Ferdinand wheedled and pleaded and eventually bribed but to no good effect. He decided to swim in through the canal doors around the side. This was becoming less and less cushy by the minute. He turned away from the spyhole and nonchalantly said, 'Well, Sim

296

Salabim, then.' At that, the door magically opened. 'Avresti dovuto dire prima la parola d'ordine,' said the bouncer. Call it luck if you will but it was, in fact, the true world conspiracy. Of course, Ferdinand had to stay dry and get in to see Miranda or everything wouldn't have been infinitely right for her, her oov would have been postponed, or worse, cancelled.

By the time he descended the stairs, Miranda had convinced Guido to row her back to the Gritti Palace, and Guido was feeling pretty confident that there would be an invite for coffee at the jetty. But then there is a certain stage of drunkenness which does a lot for optimism.

'Miranda,' came Ferdinand smilingly, 'I've been looking all over for you.'

Miranda was not at all surprised to see him.

'Who is this man?' Guido's optimism was beginning to wane. 'He bothers you, no?' He stepped between Ferdinand and Miranda.

'He's fine, Guido, a bit confused.'

'I not let him through.'

'Look here,' Ferdinand said, 'I'm trying to talk to this girl.'

'Woman. She is a woman,' Guido pronounced with gusto.

'Miranda?' Ferdinand pleaded.

'Guido, it's my boyfriend.' There, she said it, 'boyfriend', it slipped out of her mouth before she could consider the significance. 'Boyfriend', and she watched Ferdinand as she said it. But he didn't flinch or pause or pale or faint, just stood peering around Guido's shoulders. Boyfriend. It was like there was this sudden bond, a strange unutterable pact. Once he became a 'boyfriend' an argument was just a tiff, something that could be worked out later. With a boyfriend there is always a 'later'.

Guido lost his grip on decorum and the bar at the same time. He put his fists up to offer a fight, realizing too late that the bar was the only thing keeping him upright. He fell to the floor where he continued to challenge anybody to a fight if they were up for it.

'Come on,' said Ferdinand as he took Miranda's hand and led her over the flailing Guido and up the stairs. 'Friends?'

'Friends,' replied Miranda.

'Lovers?' Ferdinand tried.

'That depends, doesn't it?' Miranda laughed coyly and, she hoped, somewhat coquettishly, skipping off in front of him. With no fear of the unknown or the dark or the lapping canal waters, Miranda sped off again. She felt like these alien empty shiny streets were her playground. Everything seemed hers and safe. And so it will for ever remain a chicken or egg question; whether being in love is a product of naivety or naivety a product of being in love. Watching him run after her, at each corner she realized that, perfect though he seemed, he had as many flaws as her in his own way. Maybe he was just an uptight, City type trying to escape his demons. Perhaps he really believed that he was in love and just lacked the vocabulary to express it. Perhaps she really did have something to give to him, even if it was some mixed-up philosophy blended from too much romance and a too cynical best friend. Everything was just perfect.

Miranda was still ahead of Ferdinand, running and laughing, when she got to a bridge on the waterfront. She took the first two steps in a single bound and then stopped. Looking at the next grey step, she realized that it was moving or, more accurately, fluttering. Focusing on the step, she recognized the shape of a creature, with grey wings outstretched, resting on it. A moth, a moth with giant outspread wings, the size of a bird. Its vast, grey wings hovered minutely above the grey step, delicately trembling. An almost incredible creature, otherwordly; fantastically, delicately beautiful at the same time as being frighteningly big, with enormous insect legs and probing antennae.

Ferdinand caught up with Miranda and spotted the moth. 'It's beautiful,' she whispered.

Ferdinand studied it. 'It's a freak of nature,' he hissed.

'Who said it was natural?' said Miranda. 'It's probably the escaped genetically modified result of a lab experiment. But it's still beautiful.'

'Even if it's artificial?'

'If you believe in something, you make it real.'

The vast wings flapped and Miranda felt the currents they produced in the still night air. When they rested again, Miranda studied the patterns of embroidered point work symmetrically reflected on each wing. On each the pattern swirled like a cyclone in great spirals. And as Miranda stared into them she felt herself falling down and down into the eyes of those storms.

They walked silently, hand in hand at the edge of the strand, the waves of the lagoon lapping rhythmically in pace with them. The moth seemed to have touched them. There was really no need for words, they seemed beyond them, as Miranda approached the eye of the vortex, the centrifuge of oov. She could sense that it was coming, the moment that would define the night, that would stay with her for the rest of her life. The wall they were walking beside ended abruptly to make way for a monolithic white stone porch. And, a little further on, the pavement itself ended in a point jutting out into the black water. Here the waves of the lagoon rolled and crashed into those of the Grand Canal, and on the next bank, gloriously luminescent, was Venice's perfect panorama, the empty Piazzetta, the Doge's palace lit up with the waterfront of Venice stretching into the distance, an undulating stream of streetlights flowing to the black horizon. Miranda drew breath and held it just to silence herself, as if it were possible, if she was quiet enough, to hear the beauty of the scene. It was here she knew, she could feel, she could sense, that everything right converged, colluded and connected.

Close to the water, at the tip of the point, a solitary lamp-post illuminated itself in a soft circle of light and it was beneath it that they stopped and kissed. Miranda found herself completely immersed in her senses, as if they were all a part of the view, as endless as the water and the stones; as if she possessed the place both beyond and within her, the watery sounds, the smell of their hot damp bodies, the touch of warm flesh and the taste of Ferdinand's mouth. Here in this time and space, the very centre of Miranda's oov, she felt herself absorb and be absorbed, a part of everything and everything just right. Here, in the breathtaking beauty of the moment. Here, in the movie, the camera would swirl around the lovers as they dizzyingly fell into each other's eyes.

Yes, they had had to run through the rain and get lost and find a seedy café and have a silly argument and meet a drunken gondolier and see a fabulous moth, because that made it perfect, they were all vital parts of the time, the place, the way of everything being infinitely right. Oov. And now Miranda could see herself, yet still feel herself, giddily drinking it all in. As she kissed Ferdinand so passionately, she realized how totally totally in love she was and even if it was a storm of emotions, a moment, an evening, a night, she would remember it for the rest of her life. Everything that she had lived through was just a prelude to this place, her whole life had been an express train to this very moment. A time for loving, a place for loving, a man she loved, a feeling she loved, a sensation she loved, even herself, at that moment, she loved.

On the whole, one person's oov is rarely anybody else's, yet the feeling and the force of the moment were not without effect on Ferdinand. As Miranda kissed and nibbled and rubbed, he found his own feelings being aroused to a level that was strictly less than professional, even if his profession meant he was a whore of sorts. He found himself instinctively rather than consciously mirroring her rhythm, his breath becoming shorter. She was, he realized, or maybe had always known but had forbidden himself to admit, very very sexy. His neck began to sweat and he could feel an urgency filling up inside him like an insatiable hunger, the more they kissed. He found himself desperately wanting to make love there and then. He searched for the professional justification, excuse, for immediately having sex, but he found he could only think with the wrong organ, the dominant one, reasoning solidly from below the belt. What better way to achieve a declaration of undying love than to make love? He only had a few hours to get it after all, or kill her, so it would all be for the best.

Miranda, who could feel Ferdinand's growing interest grinding against her stomach, was surprised when he pulled his face away. He panted sharply, recovering his breath as she looked up at him. A few drops of rain splashed onto her face and a low roll of thunder predicted more storms to come. She felt wet.

'Our hotel, I think,' said Ferdinand, pointing across the Grand Canal, 'and quickly.' Miranda grinned a broad grin. Perfect, she thought, perfect.

There is no way to put what followed delicately, because it wasn't, so i won't. Personally, or bookly in my case, i would have preferred to recall the next scene as humans tend to, hazily. The before and after somehow more memorable than the during, which is usually a small collection of caught images and half-remembered sensations. i'm not hesitant because i was jealous, i wasn't. Look at me, i was never built to get physical with Miranda. It's just that people change when sex is involved, and so do books, styles, goals. People are more willing to suspend their disbelief about their own lives and think themselves into other, more glamorous, dirtier, or just more basic roles. The experience is such an extraordinary shift from daily life, it is so abnormal to be naked and uninhibited and to be allowed to admit that you are driven by pure passions and adulterating pleasures, that you change. You become an other, you release a part which is dormant until summoned, a more perfect you, a more honest you, a you that understands the truth about giving and receiving without the baggage of social etiquette. For those few brief moments, the only time in your life when all five senses are evoked and stimulated simultaneously, you become a character of your own fantasies, unfettered by reality.

Miranda had hitherto always imagined that making love with her knight and white charger was going to be something so far beyond the

300

human experience as to be inexpressible, a collection of those three little dots ... which were employed by so many of my more timid romantic colleagues in the library. Or, even worse, it would be a varied collection of veiled metaphors from his 'growing manhood' and her 'quaint modesty' through to his 'passion missile' seeking her 'tunnel of love'. But for you to get any idea of the impact of what followed i must use Miranda's everyday words: it was his 'cock' that was aroused and her 'pussy' getting wet. Fundamental maybe, but then, what's wrong with admitting and relishing the down dirty, basic, joyful experience of sharing flesh and fluids?

Maybe, had she replayed it later, she would have given it a more elevated name, called it 'making love'. Or, for him, perhaps it was just having sex. Either way, at the time it happened they were just two sides to the same coin which, either way you flip it, still buys the same amount of mint humbugs. What happened for Miranda had no name; it was an ecstatic physical expression of feelings she was unable to contain in words and gestures any longer.

And how i saw it, from my bedside sideline? Well, if you watch it, it's pornography really. She was the star and he was the stud. But then i would think like that, wouldn't i? That's how i work. At least with pornography, like a fetish, even something as, supposedly, soulless and inanimate as a book can cause a stir. So.

By the time Miranda and Ferdinand returned to the bedroom, the wind was shaking the window whilst the rain beat dreamily against it. As Ferdinand closed the door behind them, neither he nor she made a move for the light switch. The room was dappled with restless soft lights. It was alive with diffuse streetlights, reflected and echoing from waves down below, moving silently about the walls and ceiling, over the bed and flashing in the mirror. Magically the glowing beams streamed across his face and poured onto hers, projected from the prismatic raindrops which streaked down the panes. The lights softly caressed the two of them as they looked at each other and kissed silently, urgently.

As Ferdinand's hands slipped gently round to her bum he stopped. For a panicked moment Miranda thought he had only just realized the full horrific magnitude of her gluteus multi-maximus. Then he put his lips to her ear and whispered, 'Get 'em off.'

Miranda felt no impulse to resist. She calmly took a step back from him, bent forwards, ran her thumbs up the sides of her thighs under her tight dress and inched her pants down until they dropped around her ankles and rested on her shoes. As she looked up again, Ferdinand held her shoulders gently, supporting her as she deftly stepped out of the elasticized manacles. Suddenly, without them, as the air coolly made contact with her pussy, she realized just how wet she had become.

Passionately, Ferdinand's lips warmly enveloped Miranda's mouth again as he guided her steadily backwards into the room until she sat down at the end of the bed. Then, his mouth left hers as he trailed kisses down her chin and neck, down to what cleavage she had managed to persuade out of her dress. Kneeling at her feet, he slowly, carefully, began to roll up the tight black dress, revealing, gradually, her legs, looking long and luminously white in the monochromatic lights. Following the dress hem's agonizingly, blissfully slow progress, and helping to nudge it up her legs ever higher, Ferdinand's tongue softly flicked and wetly lingered along a path which led upwards and inwards. Miranda lay back on the bed, closed her eyes and concentrated on his journey. From her own sharp ankles along her shins, up over her knees and across the expanse of her thighs. First one leg, then the other, the hot wet point of his tongue leaping between them. Miranda lay helplessly, feeling that slow, trickling, tantalizing advance, willing it to its inevitable destination and spreading her legs inch by inch as they continued to escape the restricting constraints of the dress.

For once, Miranda lost all of her usual self-defeating self-consciousness. She didn't worry if her legs were too hairy or that she might be smelly, she just melted into the terrible anticipation, opening her legs, welcoming him closer and closer. Eventually, finally, she felt the cloth roll back over her pussy and, without pausing his tongue, he pushed her legs wider than ever until her shoes found the edge of the bed and dug into the covers. Now surely. But, frustrating her desire to at last feel him pressing hard against her soaking pussy, he began kissing those little parts of flesh on the inside of each thigh, an inch below her vulva, that always touched when she stood. Now she could feel his hard chin, slightly scratchy as it worked nearer and nearer. Miranda felt her clitoris swelling, aching, dying for him to touch it. Surely it must be soon.

Then, just when she could not imagine opening her legs, her lips, any wider, with his arms beneath her thighs, his hands at her sides, his chin pressing, she felt it. His stiff pulsating tongue touched her clitoris and Miranda groaned. It worked its way around and up and over and beneath, turning about her swollen clitoris, massaging it, enticing it, persuading it, first slowly and then quicker. Occasionally his lips would surround it and she would feel his hot mouth sucking it until she imagined it huge and engorged. And all this time his hands worked the dress ever upwards, up over her stomach, over her breasts, until it was a tiny loop under her arms. His almost effervescent tongue grew faster and faster as it turned her clitoris around and around, lapping at the sides of her vulva, and she yearned to have him inside her and could feel the throbbing build-up of a climax. His hands rode over her stomach to her bra, pushed under it and rolled it up to her dress. Miranda crossed her arms over the dress and bra and yanked them over her head. She was naked, her breasts taut, gripped in his hands, her nipples hard and erect and being pushed and rubbed in time with her clitoris. Her pussy was now so wet she felt it dribbling down the crack between her buttocks. She pushed herself back and forward against his mouth in rhythm with his tongue. In and out, faster and faster. She opened her eyes to see the coruscating lights swirling about her like the moth's wings, she felt dizzy and lost, out of control, with nothing but the pleasure of coming in front of her. Faster, harder, more, more, it was coming, it was inevitable, it was . . . And then, in an instant, like a sudden burst of butterflies, erupting from her pussy, flying through her stomach and shooting out to every nerve ending in her body, she felt herself coming, she felt the tension of a high wire snapping inside her, letting every part of her cave in, fall back, deep down, as if into a well of cushions, and rest gently at the bottom in a disconnected jumble.

Miranda found herself breathing deeply and heavily, taking some time to recover, to orientate herself from the dizziness and to clamber up again from her imaginary cushion pit. She raised her head and propped herself up on her elbows as she blinked, looking down over her pale naked body and legs. She seemed unable to contact her legs, as if they belonged to someone else. They were still spread out widely and she noticed that the heels of her shoes had ripped deep welts into the covers of the bed. As her eyes got used to the dark she looked up between her legs and saw Ferdinand, now totally naked, towering in front of her. He placed his hands on her raised knees and she realized that they were still her own legs. She brought them in slightly, more to support him than to be unwelcoming. His body was much darker than hers, his flesh-sea of rippling shadows. Muscles gently undulated under his skin along down his glistening arms. His chest seemed wider naked, a paragon of symmetry, as the lines of his torso united as arrows pointing downwards, down to his navel and down along a thin line of dark hair to his cock. Startling, massive, stiff, an almost shocking imbalance in proportion with the rest of his body. It almost levitated between them in a thick long knot of sinews. Miranda found herself unable to stop staring at it and its smooth dark head shining. She could feel the skin on her thigh nearest to it, prickling. Suddenly she realized that her own body was starting to get excited again. This time, after the previous tension-breaker, it swelled inside her much faster. She wanted that cock, him, inside her, she was somehow incomplete without him filling her, being a part of her, captivated by her. A little daunted by the size of his cock, she reached out to touch it. The heat almost seared her hand, and as she drew it back, a long elastic train of pre-cum stretched and bent, pulling her fingers to it again.

Ferdinand reached to the side of the bed. Miranda looked over and saw him probe his trousers. From a pocket he recovered a small silver sachet. 'Shall I?' he said, holding it up.

Miranda felt like screaming: no, I want your babies, I want you, you, now. She nodded meekly.

Ferdinand ripped the packet, throwing it over his shoulder, and then placing his thumbs inside the condom he swiftly drew it over his cock and rolled it down along the shaft. As his fingers finished the job, they instantly travelled to her pussy. He gently rolled her sensitive clitoris and Miranda grabbed his shoulders violently. Pushing with her legs, she pulled him down on top of her and up the bed. She fumbled between her legs and grabbed hold of the hot, hard cock.

'I want you inside me. Come inside me.' She bit on his ear as he drew his teeth along her neck. With her fingers she forced her lips apart and guided the massive head in as it stretched every part of her, tightly filling her with a moment of ecstatic pain. Bloated with his cock, her whole body hardened for a moment of blissful paralysis. And then the motion started. He moaned slightly and he kissed her, her eyes, her mouth, her neck, her cheeks and her lips, everywhere he could reach he kissed. In a frenzy of tongues and lips, he wildly caressed her with his mouth, completely disorientating her, leaving her feeling like she was floating in an orgy of kisses. The only thing she could be sure of was his body developing a rhythm back and forth, sliding up and down her, and each time it felt a little deeper and her clitoris pulled back and forth with heavenly aching, and his balls slapping against her buttocks and she gripped hold of him tightly as if he were the only thing in the world that could stop her floating away. Swept by the tide of her mounting orgasm into an endless lost whirlpool of her own emotions. They rocked and thrust until the tension grew too much, her pelvic floor muscles gave way to an uncontrollable series of contractions, tightening against his cock and forcing his hot cum to shoot inside her. He yelled with pleasure and, as if the sound was a trigger for her own pleasure, Miranda cried out as her entire body was released from the tension into the longed-for relief, the moment when every part of her trembled with satisfaction, before falling deep deep asleep.

After a minute, could have been an hour, Ferdinand felt able to move again. A little cramp had set in in his knee and he rolled off beside Miranda's spent body. She sighed sleepily. Ferdinand looked at his watch. Ten to midnight. Phase one of the mission ended in ten minutes. Did she love him? Could he break her heart? Would phase two be an emotional destruction or a physical one? Would she really feel enough, after such a short time, to be devastated by him? Ferdinand felt rather uncomfortable; he was a creature of command and obey, he didn't like questions and, worst of all, questions that had no absolute answers. He sat up and watched her breathing. One breast pushed at the sheet, the other fell haphazardly out, rising and falling peacefully.

'Do you love me?' he asked the sleeping form.

'I love you,' Miranda almost whistled in her breathed somnambulistic reply.

Well, there you are, she loved him, he could just dump her in the morning, break her heart and piss off back to London in the Bentley. Job done. Ferdinand continued to look at her as the rain began to beat more heavily at the windows. She was very beautiful, very innocent; she would never know what happened.

Ferdinand was thinking hard but the reason you want to sleep after sex is because your mind is on its own then and knows instinctively that there is no more dangerous a moment for thinking than in the cold light of afterwards. The post-coital thought is insanely rational, unemotional and self-analytical. Ferdinand started to think, as he so rarely did, about what he was doing here now, in his life. Questions multiplied and thick and fast they came at last, more and more and more, all jumping through the frothy waves and leaping to the shore of his consciousness. What had he done? Who could say if it was love, in love, whatever? Everything was on a sliding scale, no surety, completion, closure. It was all variable. The whole mission had been a fool's errand, there was no absolute marker to say this is being in love and this isn't. Love wasn't something that you could quantify and qualify, switch on or off. How could he go back and definitely say that she had been in love, it was such an indefinable feeling. The effects of being jilted could last for the rest of her life or she could brush them off in the morning. He got up off the bed as lightning flashed into the room. A few seconds later there was a thunder crash that shook the bed and he noticed that her delicate breasts shivered slightly.

Ferdinand paced the room one way, then the other. Questions, questions, no answers, this was not how an agent should act, think, feel. Lightning white shocked the room and in that illuminating brightness he stopped. He realized in that split second that there was only one end to the mission, one fileable, definite, quantifiable result. As another roll of thunder followed him through the room, he quietly crept over to Miranda's bag and retrieved his gun. The heavy metal butt felt friendly and sure. Something secure to hang on to. Finding the silencer, he screwed it onto the cool barrel and tip-toed back to Miranda. Her mouth was open now and she had begun to snore. Nimbly he climbed onto the bed and sat astride her. With all the composure of an accomplished killer he quietly unfastened the safety catch and with steel steadiness placed the barrel in her mouth. He stared at her: lovely, lonely, more vulnerable and open than she would have ever been in her life. He looked and, as he was trained, imagined her already dead. Somewhere beyond the pelting rain he heard the distant chime from a lonely church bell. Slowly but surely he began to pull the trigger, and something clicked.

Chapter IX.

Imagine

Je suis allé au marché aux oiseaux
Et j'ai acheté des oiseaux
Pour toi mon amour.
Je suis allé au marché aux fleurs
Et j'ai acheté des fleurs
Pour toi mon amour.
Je suis allé au marché à la ferraille
Et j'ai acheté des chaînes
De lourdes chaînes
Pour toi mon amour
Et puis je suis allé au marché aux esclaves
Et je t'ai cherchée
Mais je ne t'ai pas trouvée
Mon amour.

Jacques Prévert (1900–1977)
Pour Toi Mon Amour

PERHAPS YOU FEEL THAT I HAVE BEEN TOO HARSH ON LOVE. MAYBE you think I am merely concentrating on the negative aspects and ignoring its glories. Conceivably, you feel that love is too broad a term, too wide a subject, too mysterious a phenomenon, to be treated in this analytical and defining manner. Indeed, why shouldn't you? For centuries we have believed that one can as much nail down the multifarious manifestations of love as one can batten down the wind, capture the moon in a puddle or pull down the stars in the cast of a fisherman's net.

And even if it were possible, who would do such a thing? Are these natural things not all the more beautiful for where they are, for their very inaccessibility? Is not part of their charm, their distance, their unharnessable power, their very mystery?

Yes, it is exactly this, their connection to our imaginations, which makes them so compulsive, so fascinating, so beautiful. Love seems to dwell in the domain of the imagination because it seems beyond the material, empirical world, beyond quantifying, beyond analysis or definition, it connects to our imaginations and fetters us in our minds far more effectively than the whips and chains of a physical despot. We can break the manacles of steel, but who would damage the wonderful castles in the air of the imagination?

What I must ask then, is: what makes the imagination so sacrosanct? I believe that the imagination may just be the way humans cope with failure. It is an admission of our inadequacies. As I discussed before, the only thing we can know about our 'nature' is that we have a desire to dominate, with our genetic progeny, all that we survey, to rule the world, to absolutely control our environment, make it safe for our super-race. Isn't it possible, then, that the imagination is merely our manner of controlling mentally what we have failed to do physically? That it is our desires realizing in fancy what our bodies cannot do in fact? What we cannot control we give over to the domain of the imagination, for it is there that we can move mountains, hold back the tide, take command of the winds, direct the thunder and conduct the lightning.

Think of the dreams, all the fictions, the stories, the colours of the artists, are they not all a reconstruction of Nature according to our fantasies, a depiction of how Nature would be, were it in our control? Do we not repaint the world, with our imaginations, as the despots we long to be, where all the powers of Nature are harnessed to our will?

If art is a conduit of the imagination, through it we can see how we reshape and reorganize and reconstitute the world to suit our designs, so we may laugh at it and say that it is ours even before it is, if ever it could be. If this is so, we must also admit that the imagination, art itself, is a basic recognition of failure. It is an acknowledgement of our actual inability to bridle the world around us, a planet, a universe which remains ever more powerful than ourselves.

In art, we can write a hundred beautiful women, we can paint a thousand, sculpt a million, yet not one will live. You can sing a song, write a poem, draw your muse but it is just a semblance, a thing which is not the thing it wants to be; it is a pale allusion, controlled, codified, symbolized, mortified, petrified. Dead. Art is just an obituary for reality.

All the most beautiful fantasies about the moon, its green cheese and the faces within it, were created before we stood on it, measured it, confirmed it. In art we can pickle a sheep, cut a cow and calf in half, we can suspend a shark as if caught in a single moment of life, forever dead, and we can wheel it from room to room and say look, we are the master, Nature is ours.

23

You Sure That Was a Gun in His Pocket?

AT THIS POINT, I SUPPOSE, YOU MAY HAVE SOME QUESTIONS. WHAT clicked? What happened to Miranda? What are the following 165 pages about if she did bite the bullet? The last thing you probably want to know about is what happened to Mercy and Flirt. So. Going back a little; after their undercover encounter of two nights before, Flirt and Mercy had begun a friendship that appeared to develop as rapidly as Flirt disassembled. So rapidly, in fact, that by the time the storm began raging again outside Miranda's bedroom, Mercy was thunderously wheeling Flirt down the wooden access ramp and out of the hospital.

'You should have stayed,' she shouted over the traffic as she pushed hurriedly.

'Bollocks.'

'You should have, just until they gave you the all-clear.'

'Bollocks.'

'No, no. They know what they're doing.'

'Bollocks.'

'Stop saying bollocks.'

'I'm just thanking the lord that I've still got them. I swear they'd have been the next to go. Mind the bump, mind the, shit.'

'Shit, what shit?'

'No. "Shit" as in "oww" not shit as in excreta.'

'Sorry.'

'Five times they gave me the bloody all-clear, five times they came

309

back and said it was still spreading. Round there, come on, before they catch on I've escaped.' Mercy put one foot on the back crossbar of the wheelchair and started pushing with her other as if it were a scooter. With increasing speed she weaved in and out of the drunks on the Fulham Palace Road and had rolled Flirt onto the platform of the Hammersmith and City Line terminus long before Nurse Goebbels had even glanced at his bed. And then, all she did was sigh and tut at their pathetic attempt at subterfuge, a collection of pillows stuffed under his sheet that indicated that someone akin to the shape of the Elephant Man was sleeping there.

Just one stop on the train and Mercy bounced the chair down the steps at Goldhawk Road station.

'Where are we going?'

'Miranda's place, she's been gone for almost two days and no one's fed Caliban.'

'Caliban?'

Mercy raised her eyebrows mysteriously. 'The beast that lives with her, we're going to feed what's left of you to him.' Flirt laughed but not very convincingly.

At Miranda's doorsteps, Flirt felt a sudden *déjà vu* and then realized that he actually had seen it all before, in fact he had fallen asleep there just after the whole nightmare began. He began to reason that maybe that was what it had all been and he was about to wake up at any moment. Just as he began to pinch himself, Mercy yanked him from his wheelchair and hopped him up the steps. Leaning him against the railing, Mercy got Miranda's spare keys out of her bag and opened the door. Turning back to Flirt she smiled at him and touched his stump. He laughed. 'Stop it.'

'Sorry, does that hurt?'

'No, it feels like you're tickling my foot.'

Mercy could not stop herself from looking down to where his foot should have been. Flirt followed her eyes and sighed. It might have been all right if it was just the foot that wasn't there. But to take in the yawning gap between his hip and the floor was at once fascinatingly novel and sickeningly unnerving, just as standing on the edge of a rock face and staring down at the crashing waves beneath quickly reminds you that your own means of stability are precarious at best and down-right pathetic in the bigger scheme of things. Realizing that he would suffer this form of vertigo every time he looked down at his one good leg, Flirt, instead, looked upward.

'Which floor's she on?'

'Top.' Mercy pointed up and Flirt's eyes followed to those unhoppable heights.

'Bollocks.'

Click. It's kind of mechanical. Apart from the sound fingers can make when asking a waiter to gob in one's food, it's usually the sort of noise equipment generates. Light switches, camera shutters and certain bra straps designed for the newly post-pubescent all have distinctive and satisfying clicks. A gun's safety catch will click, but then so will a piece into a jigsaw. Things click when they fit together. But the something that clicked in Venice, in the Gritti Palace, in the suite, on the bed, was inaudible. As Miranda snored into the barrel of his gun, something clicked in Ferdinand's mind. Something that he had never even suspected he was trying to put together. But after his uncharacteristic deliberations before mounting his victim, he had his first ever doubt. And like lies, doubts have the nasty habit of leading to more questions and more doubts in a logical process of vacillation towards the goal of completely debilitating uncertainty.

Perhaps Ferdinand should have been celebrating. Questioning, like excess ear hair, is a sign of maturing; though more pleasant. The world might be a better place if we aimed education at the people who actually had questions. After all, when you're a child you have no questions, you know it all but are force-fed answers anyway. As you get older you start to question and get fewer answers until, on your deathbed, you have nothing but questions no one can answer.

Still, when you pride yourself on being an efficient killing machine and you are sitting on top of your imminently dead victim with a gun in her mouth, doubts seem a bit of a distraction.

Was this right?

Ferdinand had never doubted anything before; he had performed his duty automatically. He had killed a dozen spies and annihilated whole platoons in war zones. He had murdered great intellectuals and mindless henchmen. But they were different; they had all been playing the game. They knew the risks that came with the territory. But Miranda, she would be his first innocent. Of course people had been caught in his crossfire and it was not as if she were without sin, but this was cold-blooded and, what's more, she would never realize what had hit her. Maybe that was what was bothering him. Perhaps it was because she would never have even seen it coming, it seemed unsporting. Should he wake her and explain. Of course it was only pride that made one want one's victims to understand what was happening to them, but pride is precious to those who suspect that they might be inherently shallow. Yet as Ferdinand thought how he might explain it all, it became dreadfully unjustifiable and sending a bullet through her cerebrum seemed, more and more, the best option.

He quietly pulled back the gun's safety catch again and although the above internal dialogue had taken less than a couple of seconds, he had committed the cardinal sin of 'security' work. He had hesitated. A single second before and he might have pulled the trigger and very neatly disposed of his unanswerable questions. But the world can change in a second. Or, more accurately, an electrostatic charge, building eighteen hundred feet above one, can reach an intolerable level and discharge in far less than a second. Lightning flashed into the room with the white intensity of a blizzard, momentarily obliterating everything in light.

That's the trouble with epiphanies; they usually come with flashes of light, and bright light is one of those things that temporarily blind the pupils and are equally difficult to sleep through. So when the ensuing thunder roared and Miranda opened her eyes, she saw Ferdinand raised above her screwing his eyes tight shut. She was aware of a metallic taste in her mouth and focused quickly on the gun barrel. Panic gripped her and she kicked out, throwing Ferdinand off her whilst fortuitously landing a knee in a soft spot which quite recently had provided her with so much gratification.

Confused, naked, dazed and just awoken: not the most comfortable condition to find oneself in, although, arguably, somewhat better than being dead. Miranda hysterically stumbled from the bed as Ferdinand lay moaning on the floor clutching his bedding tackle. Pulling the sheet with her, she ran to the door and opened it, fleeing along the corridor and then down the emergency stairs, dragging a train of flowing white silk behind her, tears blurring her vision, her chest too tight, her breath too short even to scream. At the bottom of the stairs she entered the low-lit lobby, listening to the thunder of her heart and the roar of her own tiny breaths. There she saw the concierge writing behind his desk. Safety. All she had to do was go to him and explain that her 'husband' had tried to shoot her and was now lying upstairs massaging his testicles. Then she would be safe. She took a step towards the bright light of the desk. But then Miranda became possessed by the very same impulse that takes hold of young girls in horror movies whose boyfriends have just been ripped to shreds by evil personified, which impels them to visit the cellar instead of legging it out of the front door. He'll think I'm mad, they'll lock me up. What's he going to do if

Ferdinand comes down with his gun? What sort of protection could a couple of gold epaulettes and a condescending smile be against real bullets? She must keep running. Keep safe. Maybe if she simply walked out of the front door, swanned right past him? But not out into the rain, wrapped in their best silk sheets.

Miranda heard someone entering the stairs above her and turned away from the concierge. Swathed in her ghostly white silk, she stole the other way through the shadows of the empty lobby and slid through the canal doors. Out on the jetty, the rainy wind caught the sheet like a ship's canvas, tugging at it and filling it, until it billowed out behind her as she sailed along the sodden red carpet. To one side she caught sight of a gondola tied up, the rain beating down on the plastic sheeting that covered it. She slipped down onto the boat, crawling under the plastic, pulling it over her as she went, to lie on the dry wooden deck. She held her breath, listening to the clatter of the rain against the plastic. Footsteps on the jetty disturbed the rhythm of the rain. They tapped and creaked closer and closer, slowing as they approached her hiding place until they stopped. The wind, hissing and whistling through the pitching metal prow of her gondola, suddenly tore open a piece of the sheeting which flapped and banged against the boat's side. Then the footsteps started again and receded into the pattering rain.

Miranda shifted, trying to get comfortable, and came upon a rolled up carpet. She tried to crawl into it. The carpet moved and kicked back growling, 'Vafanculo!'

Four landings, and twenty crash landings, later Mercy propped Flirt against the banister. Just for caution she knocked at Miranda's door before opening it. Instantly Tony fromnextdoor opened his door, recognized Mercy and beckoned to her.

'She's not there,' he whispered, looking from side to side.

'No, I know, she's away.'

'Taken.'

'Sorry?'

'They've taken her.'

Flirt now moved and said, 'Who have?'

'Who's that?'

'A friend.'

'Not mine.' Tony slithered back into his room and slammed the door.

Mercy banged on his door. 'Tony, Tony, he's all right, he knows Miranda.'

Tony peered out of his door again.

'How come I've never seen him, then.'

'Why should you have?' asked Mercy.

'Who took her?' Flirt urged.

Tony tapped the side of his nose.

'That's not very helpful, Tony,' Mercy said with a sigh.

Tony tapped the side of his nose again and hissed, 'Intelligence.'

'Would that be Nasal Intelligence?' asked Flirt, getting a little frustrated.

Tony smiled at him indulgently. 'No, I'm just trying to stop idiots like you from getting up my nose.'

'Girls, girls,' Mercy boomed. They both looked at her somewhat gobsmacked. 'Now, Tony, tell me right now what the fuck you are talking about.'

Tony ushered them into his room which was now full of large cardboard boxes.

'Going somewhere?' asked Mercy. Tony started speaking in a falsetto voice that would have been the envy of the castrati. 'I've been under surveillance for some time,' he squeaked.

'Too right,' said Flirt, turning to Mercy as if the obvious mental condition suddenly allowed him to talk as if Tony wasn't there. 'How come they haven't locked him up, he's barking?'

'Why are you talking like Pinky and Perky, Tony?'

'The bugs,' chirped Tony, 'have background noise reducers, they don't pick up sounds above six kilohertz.'

'The bugs? Like cockroaches?'

'Mikes.'

'The cockroaches have names?'

'Microphones. Electronic ears. Spies.'

Mercy and Flirt nodded indulgently and started back towards the door.

'They know about Everything.'

'Everything, really?' Flirt smiled, jiggling the doorknob behind his back.

'I'll show you,' said Tony, adding under his breath, 'patronizing wanker.' He pulled open a cardboard box and pulled out a tiny black box. Flipping it open he revealed a little LCD screen and miniature digital video recorder; he pressed play. Flirt and Mercy could see Miranda lying on her bed reading. Tony quickly stopped it and pressed fast forward. 'After Miranda said that she thought someone had been in her room, I set up a camera on her curtain rail.' He pressed play again and now the room was empty. Then, as they watched, her door opened. Two men in grey suits and surgical gloves entered with balletic synchronized movements. In just a few seconds they seemed to have opened every drawer and cupboard in her room and sorted through every book. The taller of the two motioned to the other to look in the gerbil cage. After putting his hand through the cage door, suddenly the shorter man reeled back with a brief scream, quickly muffled by his colleague's hand. When he had calmed down, he lashed out at the cage with a kick, sending it to the floor. In the next instant the two were gone. Tony clicked the screen shut with a satisfied, 'There.'

Mercy stood with her mouth open. 'What? Why would they want her? Who?'

'Secret Service. And they want her to get to me,' said Tony with a new superiority to his falsetto. 'They know that I spoke to her about my project. It's this . . .'

'Shut up, shut up,' cried Mercy. 'If it's true and you tell us then they'll be after us too.'

Flirt peered at him. 'Why go for her, why not just get you?'

'Because it's not finished yet. When Everything 1.1 finishes, they'll want all the data, the secrets. But I'm not taking any risks. I'm getting out of here.' Then, dropping his voice to a normal tone and a little more loudly, he finished, 'Taking a plane to America tonight.' Tony put his finger to the side of his nose. 'Don't worry,' he said in falsetto, 'I'll find her.'

Miranda held back a shriek as the carpet unravelled and a large body rolled out next to her. Out of the darkness, a man's face leered at her with menacing anger. He let loose a torrent of Italian invective, the effect all the more frightening for being lost in their terrible sound. No one can swear like the Italians, after all, nothing denotes a language in maturity more than the amount of curses available.

'Sorry, scusi,' Miranda yelped.

The man stopped and his face came so close she could smell the fumes of embittered wine on his breath. 'Signorina Miranda?'

'Guido?' said Miranda.

'Oh, you come, you hear my serenade and you come. I row here to get you. You are my love of my life. Sì? You cannot resist your Guido.'

'What are you doing here?'

'Sì. I will fight the man who take you from me. I come here to make fight with him but . . .' Guido scratched his head, apparently lost, and looked round at his darkened boat for the first time. 'Am I sleep?' His

315

eyes had grown used to the dark and he could see that Miranda was in nothing but a silk sheet. 'Sì, sì, yes. You come to me. Like dream.' Guido grabbed Miranda's sheet and pulled. She spun round onto her back and was left lying naked on the boards. 'Good dream, yes?'

Miranda pulled her right arm around her and landed a loud, and hugely satisfying, smack against Guido's cheek. He stood up in shock and pain, his head ripping through the boat's rain covers. Now the cold storm beat down on them, the wind whipping around the naked woman and the fat gondolier. Miranda yanked her sheet back, managing to topple Guido, who was standing on it, and sent him banging down onto the deck.

'Listen, Guido.' Miranda sat up proudly and spoke in her most strained, calmest, quietest voice, the school-mistress voice which always seemed to take hold of her throat when she was under stress and pretending not to be. 'This is not a dream.' Sounding not unlike Miss Jean Brodie, constipated but squeezing out her morning side. 'That man I was with, Ferdinand. He is trying to kill me. He was here a minute ago and he will probably be back. Can you move this thing?' Miranda indicated the gondola they were sitting in. Guido looked dumbfounded at Miranda, her neck a rope of sinews, her face a streaming, blotchy pink and white mask bombarded by raindrops. With torrents streaming down her face, mingling with her tears, she watched Guido scratch his head and teetered over the brim of her patience. Shouting at the top of her voice, with every last bit of breath in her lungs, 'Now!'

Forceful women had a peculiar effect on Guido. Lashed by the rain, and confused as he was, he rolled back the rain sheet from the bow of his gondola and cast off the ropes like a rock against the elements. The thin craft pitched violently in the waves as it was swept from the jetty. Though still suffering from the effects of alcohol, he stood foursquare on the stern cover grasping his oar and expertly lunged forward, catching the very rhythm of the waves. The almost instinctual action possessed him and he pushed again. In a few strokes they had crossed the stygian Grand Canal and were coursing along beside the wall of a facing palazzo. Miranda sat back confidently and glanced over her shoulder at the hotel. There she saw Ferdinand, dressed all in black, rush out to the jetty. Their eyes met for an instant across the water. Ferdinand leapt to the end of the jetty and, without hesitating, dived into the waves. Miranda's confidence suddenly crashed. 'Guido,' she screamed, pointing back, 'can't you go any faster?'

Miranda watched the surface of the canal as Guido increased his

316

pace. But Ferdinand never appeared. She cast about but could see nothing. The wind had dropped and the rain was stopping. The black water was still choppy but no head appeared. This only served to unnerve Miranda all the more. Afraid of what he might do when he surfaced, afraid of what she would feel if he didn't. Emotions are slow and cumbersome things, not the best at adapting to new situations, and barely an hour before she had finally admitted to herself that she had fallen deeply, completely, in love with this man. Now he was the stalker from hell. She stared into the water. Any moment he could reappear. From where she was sitting she couldn't see the prow of the gondola, nor the hand that rose suddenly out of the water to grasp it.

In Miranda's bedsitting room, everything was left just as Mercy and Flirt had seen it on Tony's camera. Flirt set Caliban's cage back on the chest of drawers. The creature lay on its back, its little paws pointing stiffly to the ceiling. Flirt could not see any breathing and opened the cage. About to pick Caliban up, he was surprised to feel a tiny wet tongue licking his finger. Caliban lazily opened his mouth and calmly bit into the fleshy meat. God, it tasted good, the blood sated his thirst, the flesh that he stripped from the bone was succulent and delicious. Then dinner tried to get away with an almighty scream.

Caliban's jaws locked around the digit. He had a taste, a craven craving, for human flesh and nothing would make him let go of this one. He had gone without food for longer than he cared to think, his last meal had got away and had tasted a bit rubbery, but now, this scrumptious pink morsel was manna or, more specifically, man. Blood coursed through his whiskers and matted his fur but still he hung on. He was waved about in the air and finally knocked against a wall. The knock banged his jaws shut around the fingertip, severing it from its owner. There was no time to swallow it, however, as he fell to the floor and coughed the fingertip out again. The screaming man had also fallen to the floor and was scrabbling around manically. Miranda's female friend pointed to the uncooked joint lying in front of him and shouted.

For a moment, man and gerbil eyes met. Between them lay the blood-soaked fingertip, the hard, glazed nail glinting in the bulblight. Then both made a dash for the meat. Flirt lunged and caught the tip first but the little thing eluded his grasp as the hand he was using was still in traumatic shock. Caliban wheeled about and chased after the food. He jumped and grabbed it as it bounced a second time. With his jaws firmly holding it, he scampered along the skirting board and into a mouse hole. An insulating gap led onto pipe that led down and under the ground into sewers. Only when he felt he was far from the scene of the crime did he stop and drop the meat.

Caliban began frenziedly to nibble, savouring the special taste of human flesh. But after barely half a dozen bites he became aware that he was not alone. Eyes watched him. Mean slits of shining light. He peered into the darkness only to be greeted by the sight of a hundred large and hungry rats advancing and hissing. Caliban meekly pushed Flirt's fingertip towards them in a futile offering and the eyes looked greedily at it and at him. Within a week the rumours would have spread through every drain and sewer in the city. Abandon ye corpses, cadavers and carcasses. Get your teeth into the red meat of living tissue. Human flesh is best, fresh.

Flirt was still moaning with agony as Mercy pressed wads of toilet paper around his bloodletting finger. 'See what happens if you don't feed those things,' she said.

'Oh, God, don't say you feel sorry for that little man-eating bastard.'

'No, it's just a salutary reminder that pets were once wild animals.'

'Well, see if you can find Tony's camera and we can send the tape to the *When Pets Turn* TV show.'

'I think we're going to have to go back to the hospital,' said Mercy, shaking her head at the crimson pile of toilet roll now spun around his hand.

'Bollocks,' Flirt's shoulders sank.

Outside the room, the phone rang and they heard Tony Fromnextdoor answering it.

'Hello. Yes. Oh hi. What? Don't shout. Yes? I have actually, I think she's still here. Have you had time to recon . . . Oh, right. Yes. All right, all right, I'll get her.'

Tony's head popped round the door and seemed glad to see the two of them sitting on the floor. 'Hi. Actually, Mercy, it's for you.'

Guido suddenly manoeuvred the gondola in a graceful arc around a vaporetto stop and began to tie up to the mooring posts of a door on the canal. 'Guido? We've got to get away. Don't stop now. He could be anywhere,' Miranda urged. They were moored to a small house next to the big wooden bridge she and Ferdinand had run across earlier, barely two hundred yards from where they had started.

'Beautiful signorina, Guido he like this life. You are big trouble for Guido. I bring you here.' He pointed to a small polished brass plaque affixed to the canal side door. 'British Consulate'. The window above the door was lit and voices and laughter could be heard, tumbling down from a dinner party. It seemed rather at odds with being shivering cold, terrified witless and stalked by a crazy killer.

Guido hammered on the big wooden door until a woman's voice with a brittle English accent started shouting, 'Sto arrivando per amor del cielo.' The door opened and light flooded out onto the water. A thin, dark-haired woman in a long black dress appeared. 'We are not open at this time of night.'

Guido pointed at Miranda and she took in the wrapped sheet and the shivering girl with arch disdain.

'Please,' Miranda said, 'I came here with a man who just tried to kill me.'

The woman pointed at the man. 'Him?'

'No. This one helped me escape. It's the man I came to Venice with, on the train, and just a while ago he put a gun to me.'

'And you're British, are you?'

'Yes. And so's he.' Miranda paused as a staggering realization stumbled into her head. Maybe he wasn't. She actually knew nothing concrete about Ferdinand at all. If he could stick a gun in her mouth after saying that he loved her, he could have told her anything at all, none of which might be true. Everything that she had been listening to over the last few days amounted to, well, nothing. She could remember where he lived, but apart from that he was a cipher, a spectre of a man, with nothing substantial that she could place. 'I think,' she added more quietly.

'Hotel?'

'Gritti,' said Guido and a smile finally came to the woman's lips as if to say, ah, money, despite appearances.

What she actually said was, 'Right. You'd better come in.'

Guido helped Miranda off the boat. As he did so, something very Italian stirred deep within him. As she stepped into the doorway his hands cradled her buttocks beneath the silk sheet and, despite representing thousands of years of evolution, he found he was but a slave to his instincts. He suddenly clenched as if grasping lumps of pizza dough. This practice is said to have maintained the gondola business for a century after it should have collapsed, because of its popularity with over-romanticized and undersexed young women craving gondola rides just for the disembarkation routine. Miranda retained her composure, but found her balance and the time to whip round and slap Guido for a second time before marching into the house.

Guido turned and cast off his gondola murmuring, 'So resistere a tutto, meno che alle tentazioni,' then with a lunge of his oar, 'e alle chiappe sode.' Surging through the choppy water, he didn't notice the extra drag of a body through the waves.

The thin woman led Miranda into a small, dark-green office. Small paintings, views of Venice, hung in gilded frames which, with their curlicues, matched the delicate, ornate furniture.

'Please try not to drip too much.' The woman gestured at the table and chairs, 'Louis Quinze. Would you like some clothes?'

Miranda nodded, looking down at her blue feet and pulling the sheet closer around her.

'Please do not touch anything. I will inform the Consul of your circumstances and he or an aide will see you shortly.'

The woman left the room and Miranda, alone once more, felt the tears well up. Looking at the desk she saw the phone and made a lunge for it. She picked up the receiver and then suddenly dropped it again as the door opened.

'Do you also need underwear?' asked the woman.

Miranda nodded and the woman nodded back.

'And remember not to touch anything,' she said as she closed the door.

Miranda looked at the phone, then she looked at the door. At the phone, then at the door. Phone, door, phone. She stroked the top of the phone gently, just in case the woman was looking through the keyhole. There was no reaction from the door so she quickly picked up the receiver and dialled Mercy. The phone rang. And rang. Miranda bit her lip and kept staring at the door. She hung up and dialled her own number. Tony Fromnextdoor answered.

'Tony. Listen, Tony, I'm in real trouble,' she whispered. 'I've got to ask you a favour. Have you seen Mercy? You have? She is? Well, get her, will you? No. Look I don't have time for this ... Just get her ... Put Mercy on the phone.'

Tony gave Mercy the phone. 'Hello?'

'Mercy, it's me.'

'Randa, where the fuck are you?'

'Venice. Mercy, I'm in Venice and in really big trouble.' Miranda was almost crying with relief.

'Fuck off.'

'No, I am. Ferdinand and I. We went on the Orient Express and, oh,

Mercy, it was the best and then, and then, he's got a gun. I woke up and he had put it in my mouth.'

Mercy laughed. 'You sure that was a gun in his pocket.'

'Mercy, I'm serious. It was a real gun, he was going to kill me.'

'No.'

'Yes. I escaped. Guido, he's a gondolier, he helped me. Mercy, I'm standing in the middle of the British Consulate stark bollock naked apart from a sheet. I'm wet, I'm cold, and Mercy, I'm so scared.'

'Tell me you're joking. Tell me you're in the pub.'

'No joke. Mercy, I . . .' and then finally the full sobbing came and Miranda found it almost impossible to speak. 'Mercy.' Then the click of the receiver being replaced.

Mercy put the phone back and returned to Miranda's room. Flirt had fainted. She slapped him around the face a few times until his eyes opened.

'Ever been to Venice?' Flirt shook his head. 'Fancy a romantic weekend away?' Flirt nodded. 'Got a credit card?' Flirt fainted again.

As Miranda sobbed, a cold hand came and took the receiver from her, placing it back on the phone cradle.

'I said touch nothing. If you cannot respect the rules you will have to leave and let the police deal with your problem. Dry yourself and get dressed. These should fit.'

'Thank you.'

The thin woman went to the wall socket for the phone and unplugged it. Taking the phone with her, she reached the door. 'The Consul will see you shortly.' She left and closed the door. Miranda swore she heard the door lock.

The clothes fitted as if they were tailor-made for an obese hunchback with a taste for quiet itchy martyrdom, but they were warm and they were dry and they were strangely English in this all too foreign place. Miranda sat down to wait. But almost as if she were being watched, the moment she sat down the door clicked and opened. In walked a short man with shiny slicked-back hair who bore more than a passing resemblance to Lord Snooty from the *Beano*.

'Tristan Andisault, Honorary Consul,' he said, offering her his hand in such a skewed manner, she wondered whether she should shake it or kiss it. 'I'm so sorry,' he effused with more camp than the ging gang goolie song, 'I was absolutely up to my eyeballs in work.'

'I heard a dinner party.'

'My dear, for a diplomat, that is work. Now, you poor girl, I hear that you have had a very nasty experience. Do do tell. I am all ears. Tea?'

Miranda nodded. 'Mrs Denvers?' he shouted and almost immediately the thin woman entered. 'Tea please. A pot if you don't mind.'

'Certainly,' she said and left again.

'Came with the post,' he said by way of explanation, 'a bit queer if you ask me.' Then he laughed and flopped his hands forward, 'But aren't we all, dear.'

Miranda was long past her tears but didn't really know how to answer that.

'Now,' he continued, 'tell Aunty Tristan, I want to know everything.'

And Miranda told him everything. Right from the sanitary towel demonstration to Guido knocking on his door. And when she had finished, the Consul demonstrated his best consolation.

'Oh, my dear, oh how terrible, awful. Really you just can't find a reliable tall dark and handsome stranger any more can you. What an ordeal, what a shock. You need to get back home, don't you?'

Miranda smiled and took some comfort in his words. Here at last was someone who understood, someone who could help.

'Now, as it happens,' Tristan continued, 'we have a man from London here who can organize everything. Your repatri . . . sorry, your return to blighty, a place to stay meanwhile and everything you'll need. You're in safe hands now. We are, after all, here to help.'

'Thank you. Oh God, thank you.' Miranda felt so relieved, so happy, so safe.

'Mrs Denvers,' Tristan shouted, 'could you get Mr Lake, if he is ready.'

Miranda smiled and picked up her teacup. Criticize it as much as you like but the British did civilized and comfortable so very well. She tipped her head back to drain the last dregs of her now cold tea.

'Ah, Mr Lake. Here she is,' she heard Tristan greeting. The cup empty, she straightened herself to look at her saviour over its rim. With the expectoration that left her lips at that very moment, she not only wet the Consul, she absolutely soaked the Louis Quinze.

'No!' she screamed at Trotsky as he marched towards her. 'No, he's one of the crazies, he . . .'

Tristan looked pityingly at her.

'Keep him away from me. He's fucking mad. He was stalking me. No.' Tristan shook his head as Peersnide put Miranda in a half nelson.

Peersnide looked at Tristan and put the finger of his free hand to his temple, making a couple of circles around his ear, and said, 'Just as I told you she would be.' Then he walked her out of the room.

'You know,' Tristan said to Mrs Denvers, 'they always seem so harmless, don't they?' He sipped his tea as he listened to Miranda's screams and then breathed deeply as he took in the silence which followed the sock stuffed in Miranda's mouth and the duct tape stuck over it.

This, it seems, might be an ideal place to stop for a chapter break. The heroine is in mortal danger again, there are no more heroes left and things couldn't look much worse. But of course they could and they do.

Miranda was bundled outside and fell heavily, slapping face first onto the narrow wet street. She felt her hands being tied behind her back and then she was lifted by Trotsky and another man, by her elbows, one at each side of her. She squirmed but it did no good. Her toes were scraped raw where her feet were being dragged along the ground. They hauled her through a dizzying series of streets and alleys, over bridges, round corners and ever deeper into darker, creepier and lonelier places. Places only the soul might recognize when it was having a particularly dark night. Suddenly they came to one totally isolated, black alley which ended, through a tunnel under a house, in the still waters of a canal.

'Here,' she heard Trotsky say. They dragged her to the end and dropped her at the water's edge, her face suddenly looking into a horrified, white reflection of herself. She looked dead already.

Miranda heard Trotsky tell the other man, 'You go back to the last junction and keep a look-out. I'll finish her off here.' She heard the footsteps leaving while she choked on the cloth in her mouth.

Trotsky bent down and pulled her shoulder round so she could see him.

'Really,' he said, 'this isn't personal. It's for the good of the country. Of the world. I know you understand. Of course your boyfriend was supposed to have done this, but he's slipping. They needed a professional.' He smiled a smile so faint, it barely moved a muscle in his face, but the menace was clear. Of course, realizing that he was about to actually, really, kill someone, Peersnide, who hitherto had been informed only by film and fiction, felt the need to orate a little gloatingly as was traditional before despatching someone to their death. 'You know, the wonderful thing about the Venetian canals,' he smiled, 'they are one of the world's most efficient waste disposal systems. Leonardo studied them before designing the sewers for Milan. These waters, you see, may seem calm, but for centuries the sea's tides have created subtle currents which wash out Venice's rubbish, its flotsam and jetsam, its,' he leered at Miranda, 'bodies.' He looked down into the water. 'By the time your corpse surfaces, my dear, you will be far out in the Adriatic.' Then Peersnide sneered at her and spat bitterly, 'You see, if you will fuck sharks, don't be surprised to find yourself sleeping with the fishes.'

Miranda's desperate bloodshot eyes squinted, cried and pleaded, she shook her head violently, she squirmed as if she might possibly stand up. But Peersnide calmly put his knee on her back and her shoulders snapped down again against the pavement. As she stared at the water, she could see his reflection above her. Miranda pitched about, trying her best to throw him. But he was unfazed, still smiling as he located in his jacket what looked like two small pieces of rounded wood, and between them a glinting wire. Miranda watched, frozen in slow-dawning terror. Her body became totally rigid as she envisioned herself garrotted. In the horror of that moment, all of Miranda's muscles gave way. Every orifice let loose and she felt a terrible blush as her new knickers filled with hot embarrassing substance. She was going to die in a piss-stinking alley in the backstreets of Venice, lying in her own shit, her body dumped into a canal. Why? And for what? No reason and for fuck all. No. No, it was for love. For a stupid dream. She had taken a risk, she had stepped into the unknown to pursue a fantasy. Fuck fuck fuck. Though she knew she was powerless, she writhed just one last time then felt the wire at her throat. It began to tear at her neck like a burning razor. Her lungs instantly tightened, her stomach muscles gripped, her chest felt like it might burst. In a few seconds, all she could think was, let it end, please let it end. Come, death.

What pitiful fools we are. Maybe we should be more circumspect perchance the earth should laugh at us and shake our frail bodies in the earthquake of its chuckles and drown us in the lava of its dribbled delight.

We give to the imagination what we do not believe we can control in life. We do not believe that we can control love, that it is completely natural, so off to the imagination it is consigned where it can draw down the moon and write roses in the snow. However, can we be sure that is where it is supposed to be? We cannot even decide what actually is within or beyond our imagination. We have five senses, a paltry five solitary ways of perceiving the entirety of Nature, the enormity of the universe. Is it any wonder then that we fail to fully comprehend, let alone control it?

Perhaps our senses just collude to please us. Perhaps we imagine them as much as anything else. Science has built us machines to translate the things that we cannot perceive into the signals our senses can understand, radio waves and light waves, for example, but how much is still out there, beyond us and our perceivable spectrum, that we have not the sense to sense? What poor creatures we are to have so few senses and only be able to use them in such a limited way. No wonder we are still so confused. No wonder our imaginations can rage and range so diversely.

If love were natural and, like most of Nature, uncontrollable, then it would be a fitting resident of the imagination. However, I propose that it is as much an artifice as art itself, a pale beautiful reflection of Nature and, like art, controllable. We all have the potential to be the artists and creators of our emotions, of love. We can control it, and not let it control us. We do not have to wonder at love if that wonder, that awe, creates fear, uncertainty and insecurity. The price is too heavy to pay.

In the kingdom of the blind, goes the ancient saying, the one-eyed man is king, and *Playboy* sales are poor. However, we have always found this world a confusion of Nature and the imagination, of the material and belief. Few can completely agree where exactly one stops and the other begins. If love dwells in the domain of the imagination because we believe we cannot control it, if it is love which blinds, then we must beware those who have one eye open. It is because of our confusion that those with clarity dominate and control.

You may think that I am destroying the beautiful, stepping on a dream, but isn't it better that we should all open that one eye? So that we will not be oppressed by those who already have the sight. The world is no more ugly when you can see it more clearly. Did life become less beautiful when, at last, we gazed upon the waltzing, entwining, loving double helix of DNA? In that infinite endless chain there is always a smaller mystery, an ever more intricate ever more beautiful detail, and I have been told, by people who believe such things, that God Himself is in the detail. Why are we so afraid of the new? Because it is the unknown? Because we may not be able to conquer it, control it, we don't know the extent of its powers? We are not doing so well staying where we are.

There is no destruction in seeing more clearly, just new, beautiful, distant mysteries. That is progress. To lose the beautiful and, let us not forget, frightening parts of love is only to open our eyes to new and perhaps more enchanting emotions. New is not necessarily bad. We cannot cower from the unknown or we will live our lives never progressing, never learning, never doing better than those before us.

We do not have to live a life tyrannized by love just because we enjoy our imagined control of it.

24

In a Priest's Hole

THEY'RE LIKE BUSES, AREN'T THEY; YOU WAIT AGES FOR A DECENT cliffhanger, then a whole precipice of them comes dangling at the same time. But then, life is led at different speeds at different points and generally the transition between them is a gradual one. A sedentary life can't help but take its time to gear up to one of death-defying action. But once there, nothing ever happens by halves again. Certainly, when Miranda stepped off the platform at Victoria and left her normal life behind, she was aware that she might be changing the pitch of her life somewhat, perhaps even setting off a roller coaster. She didn't imagine, however, that it would go quite so quickly.

Peersnide too had set in motion his own roller coaster and had accelerated from bookish wimp to conscienceless killer faster than 'The Fall of Death' at Margate Pleasure Palisades. All in blind pursuit of combining his ambitions and fantasies. He was not a killer by nature, nor by craft, like Ferdinand, but out of his environment, in his new role, it was the right thing to do.

Both Miranda and he accepted their new roles, victim and killer, without much question. Not that there is much time or space for questions in the heat of the murderer-victim dichotomy. Flirt, on the other hand, or indeed on the only hand he was about to have left, found the accelerating pace of his hospital visits rather aggravating. By the time Mercy burst into Accident and Emergency, wheeling him rather faster than he imagined safe, he was ranting and screaming, 'Just cut the fucking arm off, get rid of it, if my hand offends me, feed it to the gerbils. Munch, munch, gnaw, gnaw.'

Half an hour later, and back in the care of Nurse Goebbels, Flirt lay sedated and murmuring about desert rats. Mercy sat by his bed. She had found his mobile phone, plugged in his hands-free earpiece, and was calling the airlines.

'Tomorrow, yes, tomorrow. We can pick up the tickets at the airport. How much? You're joking, aren't you? Yes. Yes. Yes.'

Doctor Scudder approached her. 'Are you the patient's wife?'

'Yes,' continued Mercy.

'Can we talk?' said the doctor.

Mercy nodded then spoke to the phone, 'Could you hold on a sec.' She pulled the earpiece out and smiled.

'Analysing the blood samples,' said Doctor Scudder, examining her clipboard charts, 'I'm afraid I have to tell you that the rodent was a carrier of a severe form of meningitis. We can beat the bug but I'm afraid that his hand is most likely to gradually go black and then fall off.'

Mercy looked at the bandaged hand then nodded unsurely. 'Right.'

'Now we do have a choice, we could either give him a very long treatment to gradually block the blood flow and maybe save the arm. But he will be out of action for quite a while and there is no guarantee that the treatment will be successful. Or,' Dr Scudder hesitated and gave Mercy her understanding I-know-what-you're-going-through look, 'or, we could simply amputate the whole arm now and save a lot of time and heartache later.'

Mercy nodded thoughtfully whilst Flirt deliriously mumbled.

'Now I don't want to rush you into the wrong choice, it is a very serious decision.'

Mercy nodded some more. 'How long would this "long-term" treatment take?'

'He'd be in hospital for over two months. And maybe unable to move much for a lot longer.'

'And if you amputate, when would he be out?'

'Well, by a stroke of luck we actually have an opening in theatre in a couple of hours, and our vascular surgeon is in the hospital, so he'd be all bandaged up and ready to go by early afternoon tomorrow.'

'I see. And which would you recommend, doctor?'

'Well, it really is very difficult. The treatment route is very long and arduous but we could, maybe, just save the arm. On the other hand, I mean, I don't want to pressure you but what with the health service being in the state that it is, he'd be taking up a hospital bed and they're in terribly short supply . . .'

'But he could be out by tomorrow afternoon? With the amputation?'

Doctor Scudder nodded.

'If you make that midday, you've got a deal.'

Mercy plugged her earpiece back in. 'You still there? Right. Did you say four forty pm? Out of Heathrow? OK, I want two tickets please. First class.'

When she had finished her call, she and the doctor looked caringly at Flirt, who dribbled a little bit. Mercy squeezed his good hand, the one he could still use to sign for his credit card. 'It'll be fine,' she said, 'all over by tomorrow. And then we're going on holiday.'

The worst thing about Miranda's death was that she had to watch herself as it happened. She had never been fond of her own looks so having to watch herself die in the clear reflection of the dark canal seemed no less than an insult added to her injuring. She could see her face rolling forward in slower and slower circles, her hair draping into the water. Those were her eyeballs bulging out, those were her veins seething and popping around her neck like serpents, that was her tongue swelling out of her mouth. The sight was so ghastly and fascinating, the promised autobiography that was supposed to flash failed to appear. But there was Trotsky's face leering down at her, absorbed in the same reflection, fascinated by the process that he was administering. Eventually the view started to fade as the pain in Miranda's chest became so acute she could no longer believe it was hers. Black started to fog her sight, something in her was about to burst. She could see nothing. Suddenly it was all over, she felt her lungs fill, her breath return, her chest expand. That was it, Miranda realized, that was her soul being released. And all she could think was, thank God that's over. Wasn't there supposed to be a light at the end of this blackness? Then she heard voices. Both male, one of them very familiar. If it was God and the devil arguing over her she couldn't really be sure which was which.

'What the fuck do you think you're doing?'

'Well, she was yours but you fucked up. So she's mine now.'

'Fucked up? Fucked up? What makes you think I fucked up?'

'Because she turns up spinning some yarn about her boyfriend trying to kill her.'

'Well, maybe that's just part of the plan. Did you ask? Did you check with me?'

'Well, no. But it's pretty academic now, since she's going to have to go either way, she knows too much. If you want me to promise not to tell what a fuck-up you were that's fine but I've got a job to do so get out of my way.'

'Make me.'

Miranda's sight swam back. The next world seemed somewhat familiar. Venice again. Same walls, same canal, hands still tied behind her back, and those were no angels arguing over her soul. Trotsky was there and he was arguing with a tall man dressed in black. Of course, why hadn't she remembered; the Milk Tray Man would always come and save her. She lay there with a happy drooling smile as she half daydreamed that, after the Milk Tray Man had punched Trotsky's lights out, he'd give her a fantastic box of chocolates.

Trotsky whined, 'You had your chance, you should have killed her when you could. Now let the real man show you how it's done.'

'Lake, I am your superior. I order you to desist or I will have to deal with you. Apart from anything else, you're not licensed to kill.' No. Not the Milk Tray Man. It was Ferdinand, bloody trigger-happy Ferdinand. 'So, if anybody is going to kill her it will be me.' Oh great, he was in cahoots with Trotsky, well that figured, and now they were both arguing over who should kill her. Miranda felt she should be surprised but realized that she was suffering from shock fatigue and was all out of surprise. The best she could manage was a little cynical resignation. Whilst the men argued, she twisted herself to look at them. They were a few yards off and their argument was becoming heated. Trotsky stood with his back to her whilst Ferdinand was facing her prodding Trotsky. Though her hands were still tied, Miranda pushed herself onto her knees and then, leaning against the rough brick wall, pushed herself up to standing. She kept her eyes on the men, peering nervously through the gap in the curtain of wet hair-strands that clung to her face. Not sure if Ferdinand could see her or not, she edged along the wall as they argued, as far as the nearest corner, and then ran.

Tried to run, at least: as any near strangulation victim might, Miranda found her legs weak and unreliable, giving way beneath her. Without her arms to balance her, running was a series of short stumbles between falls. She reached a T-junction, now she would be able to lose herself. She turned the corner and bumped into a man pissing against a wall. She reeled back as he finished. She blinked a couple of times. Now she knew she was dreaming. Barry? Barry from Dispatch. Barry Crappyfinger. The faecal probe? In Venice?

'Barry,' she said, 'is that you?'

Barry nodded.

'God,' she sighed, 'I don't know what you're doing here but am I glad to see you. A friendly face.'

'You humiliated me,' Barry said quietly.

'What?' said Miranda.

'You think I'm a joke, you and Mercy, you're always laughing at me.'

'Barry. I've just escaped from a couple of dangerous lunatics trying to kill me, can we talk about this some other . . .'

'I'm like some hilarious idiot for you, aren't I? And you think you're so smart.'

'Barry, please,' said Miranda anxiously, looking behind her, 'just untie my hands.'

'Well, you've bitten off more than you can chew now,' Barry continued. 'You've crossed the mob and they want you dead.'

'The mob, as in the Mafia?'

Barry nodded. 'You're in Italy, aren't you?'

'Barry. Please just untie my hands. I don't know what you're talking about. And I am really really sorry if you ever thought that I was laughing at you but they'll realize that I'm gone in a second and they'll be after me.'

'Sorry, Miranda,' Barry almost spat. 'It's too late for the likes of you. I'm part of the family now.'

'The family? What family?'

'Cosa Nostra,' Barry said with conviction, rolling his Rs and emphasizing his vowels like Ál Pácínó.

'Barry. What are you on?'

'They made me an offer I couldn't refuse.'

'Look, Barry. Whatever is up, that's fine. Just please undo my hands and I'll go my way and you go yours.'

'Oh, no,' said Barry, grabbing her shoulders and bringing his face close to hers, 'that would be far too easy.' Then he started shouting, 'She's here. I've got her. She's here.'

Miranda could already hear footsteps running up the alley she had emerged from. She looked Barry in the eyes and hissed, 'Bedwetter.' Then brought her forehead down hard against his nose. His arms dropped to his side but he still stood there, stunned by her head butt. So she did it again, harder, and he fell to the floor. Then Miranda ran.

Mercy walked. She strolled. Having decided that it was too late to go back to her own place and that she would bed down at Miranda's, she perambulated up the dark tree-lined Hammersmith Grove, with apparent insouciance. Yet, deep beneath the elegantly teased blond hair, a mass of turbulent thoughts raced. Was Miranda all right? Had she been joking? Why couldn't she be there for her now? Was it Miranda who put the phone down? The fact that she had consigned yet another of Flirt's limbs to the hospital furnaces barely registered across a synapse. This may, perhaps, seem callous, but then what you don't let yourself think about is often the more worrying circumstance. Thoughts of her friend, far off and in desperate need, were just the right thing to obstruct the more disturbing ones she might have to consider about her relationship with Flirt. Concentrating on how she might locate Miranda once they got to Venice, she barely noticed that she had reached the Goldhawk Road and was crossing it. Suddenly a shout, 'Born to be wi-i-i-i-ld' followed by a terrible vocal rendition of a guitar solo, brought her to her senses, just in time to see a supermarket juggernaut bearing down on her. Close enough to be buffeted by the airflow around the lorry's cab, Mercy leapt backwards and into an old man with a few strands of white hair, a Zimmer frame and Walkman headphones standing at the curb. 'Born to be wi-i-i-i-ld,' he screamed again.

'Thank you,' Mercy said to him.

'De de daa de de daa,' the old man continued obliviously, nodding his head with furious enthusiasm.

Mercy gently lifted the headphones from his head to thank him audibly. Without his music, the man instantly seemed to turn white, looking about him as if suddenly lost.

'Thank you,' Mercy said once more. Then, with a concerned smile, 'Are you all right?'

The old man met her gaze and snapped, with a wave of his frail hand, 'Be collected. No more amazement.'

'I just took off your headphones.' She showed them to him, still playing. 'They're all right, I haven't broken them.'

'There's no harm done,' the man nodded.

What am I doing? thought Mercy. Here was yet another man that she found herself not only being nice to, but actually feeling concerned about as well. A man, a member of the species she had sworn to wipe out, or, at least, completely disappoint. And that was what was really bothering her about Flirt and ... But before Mercy would let the Flirt problem inhabit her head she searched for a diversion, something of the here and now, to preoccupy her mind. 'Fancy a drink?' she smiled at the old man.

With the blood from Barry's nose still dripping into her eyes, Miranda ran. Over a bridge, into an alley, round a corner. Sometimes staggering, catching her breath, looking over her shoulder. What was, only hours before, her very own movie-set, had turned *noir*. Now the emptiness of the streets only stressed her lone vulnerability. The oov was definitely over. The world's familiar conspiracy, purposefully shaping itself to fuck up her life, emerged. Now every other corner led to a dead-end, the same darkly glistening canal lapping at the steps. And each time that she was forced to retrace her steps, she hugged the cold walls and kept the shadows, because they, he, the killer who was probably just behind her, would now be in front of her.

Miranda found herself whimpering as she tried to stifle her loud breathing. Her canal-wet hair slapped in her face as she turned her head twitchily, trying to watch her back and her front. But they were there, they were close, she was sure. Every now and again she would hear footsteps, running, just a corner away. When she stopped, they stopped, but always just a little too late to be a convincing echo. As she reached the end of one long alley, looking behind her, she was sure she saw the shadows move.

Then, to the corner of a deserted square, weeds pushing through the gaps in the paving stones, presided over by a nightlooming, pock-marked church façade. From there the statues stared down at her with their dead marble eyes, writhing on their plinths, pulling against their marble chains with endless pain etched into their features. Water was spraying somewhere and it echoed, hissing across the statues' lips as snakes before the fatal lunge. She dared not run in the open, across the square, but keeping to the gloom of the church wall was an agonizing parade before the dead, the martyred, the tortured and the damned to stone eternity. And somewhere there was a face, not dead but death itself, watching her, coming to get her. A glint from a corner, a restless shadow. Miranda frantically tore past the church and made for the sanctuary of another alley. As she waited for her breath, she saw the silhouetted figure dash into the square.

Not waiting for her breath to catch up, Miranda ran down her alley past shuttered shopfronts. And now the footsteps behind her were closer. She switched direction again and again but the footfalls were constant. Another corner and they stopped. Miranda listened but heard nothing save the wheeze of her own breath. She tiptoed to the end of the alley and emerged onto the lagoon front, looking cautiously from side to side.

A fog had now possessed the lagoon and was gently rolling onto the waterfront. Its dusty haze was freezing and touched her skin like hands from beyond the grave. Its iciness caused her exhausted lungs to cough; a ruptured sound, sharp staccato, echoing with brittle mockery against the silent stone. Miranda could, in the awful silence which followed, hear the distant, lonely, solitary bell of a wave-washed fog buoy somewhere out there, tolling slowly, distantly, its terrible warning.

The footsteps started again. This time heavy, running. Miranda stumbled on again to the next alley, plunging into its safe shadows. Perhaps if the fog thickened she would be able to hide. She ran desperately, willing her legs to work faster and finding them unable to meet her expectations. She felt as if she were wading through a river slower and slower, her muscles aching, whilst her pursuer flew to her. The adrenaline response was wearing out. Now, travelling on the resources of her own muscles, she felt crippled.

Limping with exhaustion, Miranda crossed a bridge and stumbled across a square, past a single pale white column. Beyond she could see the cranes of a dockyard. She stumbled to the covered porch of a simple red-brick church which dominated the square. Turning her back to the doors, she wrenched at the iron handle and the lovingly oiled, dark wooden door yielded, swinging silently open.

Hobbling in as a latter day sanctuary-seeker, Miranda shuffled forward, head bowed, as she had always imagined was the proper way of entering a church. Then, looking up, she stopped in awe at the vision. She had seen the insides of a couple of churches in her life, a drunken gate-crashing of a Christmas carol service, the wedding of an imprudent school-friend; dull, red-brick, modern, Protestant, utilitarian places of worship. So nothing prepared her for the opulent glory and special effects of full-on Catholic interior design. The entire church, its dark heights and black distances, was a universe of tiny, glittering, starry candles. A galaxy of little flames which glimmered throughout the gloaming chancel. Red and white, they twinkled in eerie silence. Burnished, golden censers hung down from each archway and rafter, bursting with shiny points of light, reflections of the gleaming wax and camphor star system. Miranda walked reverently down the aisle, lost in the atmosphere, as if she had been suddenly transported from danger, as if this universe was hers, as if she had bucked the odds and recaptured her own miracle oov.

Miranda approached a bank of candles. Mesmerized for a moment by the array of fires, she turned her back and plunged her bound wrists into the flames. Hotter and hotter, her wrists burnt; the thin skin, already blistered by the rope, felt as if it were searing. The smell of burning hemp, or was it flesh, rose about her. She writhed her hands behind her until she believed she was on fire, unable to bear the agony a moment longer. Suddenly, with a snap, her arms sprang apart, throwing her forward as if to catch up with her own flying hands. The charred rope fell to the floor and Miranda burst into despairing tears.

Through the veil she found a pew and, removing her soiled knickers, she sat down, letting them drop to the floor. Aware of how useless the signs of pain and desperation are when there is no one to see them, she gradually recovered her composure. She looked up and about her, took in the rich fabrics, the dusty paintings, the candles, and sighed. There was nowhere to run any more, she would just have to sit here and wait. Maybe, just maybe, her pursuer had missed her entering the church. She looked at the crucifix above and thought about God, or at least her only experience of Him: endless school assemblies reciting the Lord's Prayer to meaninglessness. Then it occurred to her that if she had ever needed to be delivered from evil, it was now. She put her palms flatly together in front of her and closed her eyes. Her mind blanked. She knelt down with her clasped hands pointing heavenward. Nothing. Miranda opened her eyes again. She didn't even know how to pray. Where do you start? Damnation, as ever, was a hell of a lot easier than salvation.

As Miranda knelt there, staring vacantly, too tired, too disappointed, to think of anything to say to God now that she had knocked on His door, she noticed the massed candles flicker, watched them dance in a momentary breeze. Someone had opened the door. Someone had come in.

Without looking back to see who, Miranda ducked her head down and crawled along the pew floor towards the darkness of the nave's side. There she found a large, polished-oak confessional box. Two doorways faced her, hung with thick velvet burgundy curtains, like an antique photobooth, a perfect hideaway in a priest's hole. She slipped behind the curtains and sat down. What had made her think a church would be any respite from her pursuer? He wasn't a spirit member of the demon hordes, to be put off by a splash of holy water and a crucifix. He, whoever he was, was a nut, or more specifically, one of a group of nuts which bizarrely included the idiotic Barry. She wondered what the collective noun for nuts was: a lunacy? A bolt? A scrotum? And as she sat in her dark womb, she listened.

Soft footsteps proceeded up the aisle and paused. Miranda heard a man's voice gently recite, 'In nome del Padre, del Figlio, e dello Spirito

Santo.' Then the footsteps came closer, they came right up to the box. Miranda froze as the man entered the facing booth and sat. Through the grating that separated them, Miranda could make out his glistening eyes.

'Padre, perdonami perchè io ho peccato,' he said.

Miranda tried to pretend that she wasn't there.

'Padre? Sono venuto per farmi benedire. Ho peccato.'

It was no use, he knew she was there. Miranda coughed in a sort of manly way, just so he might carry on.

'Padre, devo confessare un fatto terribile. Ho privato una regazza della sua innocenza ed ho tramato per ucciderla.' He paused. 'Padre?' He leaned towards the grate and Miranda could see his nose and mouth. 'Padre? Sì è addormentato?'

Miranda could not carry her impersonation on any longer.

'I'm very sorry,' she said in very slow English, 'I'm not a priest and I don't know what you're talking about. I'm just hiding from someone.'

'Inglese. English davvero? Sì?'

'Sì. Yes.'

Then the man paused for a long, contemplative time. Quietly he started speaking English, his accent and pronunciation sounding almost exactly, if not totally conclusively, like Ferdinand's.

CHAPTER X.

THE RELIGION OF LOVE

> Love is my religion, I could die for that!
> John Keats (1795–1821)
> *Letter to Fanny Brawne* 13.10.1819

LOVE MAY ACT UPON US LIKE A TYRANNICAL STATE, IT MAY HAVE originated in the terror-fuelled feudal system, but a tyranny does not necessitate a tyrant. It does not necessarily mean that there is anyone, an evil mastermind or coven of plotters, who actually holds the world at their mercy wielding the weapon of love.

Love could just be an unlucky madness that, inspired by the state-controlling experiments of some twelfth-century queens, continues to this day because it appeals to a weaker part of the human imagination.

It would be nice if we could point to so-and-so or such-and-such as the Master of our Love Universe, demonically controlling our madness for his, or her, own ends. The film is always less scary when you've seen the monster, had a measure of the threat. However, even with everything we have explored so far, nothing emphatically indicates that, today, we really are enslaved by the insidious mind-control of a secret oppressor or despotic state system.

Or does it?

A clue may be found in the religious origin of this mad 'limerent' love.

Love was the bastard child of religion, an unplanned offspring, an unwanted birth, yet over time it proved itself, it came of age and, now, has inherited its father's realm. And, from the dawning of the Romantic period to the relative atheism of the modern world, we have been gradually coming to terms with the fact that love is our new religion, our new god, our guide, our guarantee of salvation, our bestower of worth and value in life.

As we have seen, at first, the child love mimicked its parent, the customs, forms, ethics, even religion's monopoly on morality. And, in the end, in the century when Nietzsche pronounced God dead, love acceded to religion's throne, taking its mantle, its position as the ultimate mysterious faith that we, as a society, hold sacred.

In this chapter I intend to look at how our concept of love has grown from the superstitions of religion; how it still maintains the mystery and how it has evolved and improved on its arcane prototype.

Love, like religion, centres on the worship of an other. Like a religion it requires the subjugation of our own egos in adoration and recognition of a higher power beyond. The difference is that where religions concentrate their attention on an invisible Immortal, love focuses on an all too tangible mortal – our human 'beloved', the locus of our lust.

Essentially this idea would seem an improvement on the classic religious 'reward when dead' scenario. Love promises a heaven achievable on earth, proceed directly to Nirvana, do not 'pass over', do not 'collect your chips'.

However, if you ever got to paradise why would you carry on? Achieve in love, we are told, and all our life's struggles are over. How effective would we be as a race, as a populace, as a workforce, if we could really find complete happiness in each other?

There is, of course, a catch. Something in the small print. You will never, ever, achieve perfect love, because what you're trying to love, your 'mortal' beloved, is and always will be essentially imperfect. Invisible God is smugly ideal, immutable and eternal but our worshipped 'beloved' is, in the grand scheme of things, fickle, limited and, no matter what, will die. As Jorge Luis Borges observed, 'To fall in love is to create a religion which has a fallible God.'

It is the very fallibility of the beloved which helps to ensure that there is no closure with love, it is eternally unsatisfactory, heaven is glimpsed but never reached. It's all right to promise heaven on earth if it is never actually obtainable.

Just as it is in religion, in love the first casualty is the ego. At the very beginning it may feel as if the ego is soaring, but one look up to see how precarious is the string that holds you and one look down to see how far away the ground has become and suddenly you will do anything to prevent yourself from falling, you will completely stifle the demands of your own ego to satisfy the one who you believe holds the string.

25

So Who Are You Then, Really?

AT ALI BABA'S ALL-NIGHT CAFÉ ON THE GOLDHAWK ROAD, THE COFFEE cups are white, washed to grey, veined with cracks just waiting to happen. The lights are a dim ochre and the smell of cooking oil burns like incense. A portrait of Atatürk, in apparent ataraxy, is framed by plastic flowers and hangs proudly beside the price-board: a series of blank spaces filled in with illegible marker-pen next to the repeated, printed, words '. . . and chips'. Never one to stray more than a foot from his till, Mustafa Baba lets the wife take care of the more mundane side of the business: the managing, the purchasing, the cooking, the cleaning, the serving and so on. For Mustafa has much higher things to think about, he has an armed struggle to run, a revolution to finance. When he was leaving Cyprus, over twenty years before, his brother Hassan was at the front line in Nicosia, throwing stones at the UN soldiers. Now, Hassan is a hero, an armed freedom fighter, calling Mustafa once a month to keep him updated on the glorious struggle to free Turkish Cyprus from the infidel imperialist Greeks. So for twenty years, whilst other caterers built chains and franchises, Mustafa proudly sent his profits to Hassan to procure arms and medicines and aid the war on the side of right. It was an arrangement that suited both Baba brothers: for Mustafa it gave him a cause and for Hassan, a brand new Range Rover and the biggest swimming pool in Kyrenia.

Mercy clashed the coffee cups in front of the old man and sat down opposite him. 'You don't mind if I just talk, do you?' The man shook

339

his head. 'You see, the problem with Flirt is, well, I'm not sure but I think he's set about destroying himself before I can. It's like he's second-guessing me. Every time I think I've got him, like he's devoted enough, you know, so that I can leave and devastate him, every time, he manages to lose another part of himself. And it's always in such a painful way that I kind of know that my exit would be like a nick, a scratch, in comparison. But the longer I see him, the more I realize that, by leaving him, I would just fulfil his self-destructive attitude. And it would make him really happy to be right.'

The old man brought a trembling, slooshing cup of coffee to his lips.

'I don't know how to piss off someone who is determined to piss himself off first. How am I supposed to get any satisfaction out of this relationship if he keeps on whipping the demolition job from under me?' Mercy paused to sip the hot water and milk, with a hint of coffee. 'And do you know the thing that pisses me off the most? The longer I stay with him, the more I care for his sorry self. He's actually so pathetic he's beyond ridicule, he truly has to be sympathized with.' Mercy paused again. 'I just didn't think that they made men like that.'

The old man's eyes wandered feverishly as a train of spittle descended from his mouth into the waiting cup beneath.

Mercy examined her perfect, sharpened nails. 'Maybe I'm not cut out to break hearts any more. But what am I going to do if I'm not going to take men apart? I'll never be able to take them seriously.' Mercy focused on the old man. 'I bet you've broken hearts in your time.'

The old man seemed actually to be considering her question, then with a quivering voice said, 'Do not infest your mind with beating on the strangeness of this business.'

'Yeah, but if I don't think about that, I'll think about Miranda and there's nothing I can do until tomorrow.'

The old man seemed surprised. 'Miranda? But how is it that this lives in your mind?'

Mercy hesitated; most weirdos live in a world of their own, it was a dangerous precedent to set by actually communicating with one. After all, you might find out that their world is better than your own. She worried for a moment that the state of her mind might have slipped. 'Miranda's a friend of mine,' she said cautiously. 'She's abroad and I think she's in trouble.'

'What seest thou else in the dark backward and abysm of time?'

Mercy smiled. He was as kooky as she had suspected, she was as sane as she remembered. Like every man she ever met, he was a perfect person for her to talk to herself.

'So what shall I do about Flirt? I can't really be falling in love with him, can I? I can't work out if it's that or just your everyday, common-or-garden, stress-related, time-of-the-month, three in the morning, boyfriend's dismembered, confusion.'

'Miranda. You know I've been looking for you all over town.'

Miranda eyed her velvet curtain, wondering whether it was worth making a dash.

'I'm sorry. I never meant it to happen like this.'

He would only catch her.

'Please, just listen to me. This is really, well, difficult, I have a strange relationship with the truth sometimes. I, it's my work. I. I'm not making much sense, am I?'

Miranda stared at the glints that marked where his eyes were; was she supposed to answer that?

'Bless me, Miranda, for I really have sinned, and I am so, so sorry.' His head bowed and Miranda could now see the outline of the mass of his thick hair. Wasn't he supposed to do the remorseful bit after the killing? 'I don't really know how to explain or where to go from here. Miranda,' he paused, 'I've never had to think about it, but, then, I suppose, I've never really met anyone like you.'

Why didn't he just kill her, shoot through the grate, what was stopping him?

'I know everything must seem very confusing and you're probably in shock. I wish, I wish I could just hold you, tell you that it's all right.' Then, more as a whisper, 'But I know, right now, I'm the last person in the world who could do that.'

Too right. After a long quiet, Miranda found a little voice from somewhere. 'Ferdinand, you put a gun in my mouth.'

'I know, I know. It was this, you see.' He pushed something beneath the grating, Miranda shrank back for a second, thinking it was the barrel of his gun. But it wasn't. It was something far more devastating. It was me. 'I realize now that you never knew that it was all about this.'

'My library book?' Miranda said with disbelief. i don't know why she found it so hard to believe that a book could be worth killing over. Miranda, to be honest, lover, was starting to pall on me a little.

'It's quite an important book.'

'Well, why didn't you say? I mean, you can have it. It's yours. Wasn't mine in the first place, I stole it.'

'I know.'

'Well, I'm glad that's sorted. You take the book and go your way and I'll go mine and we'll both live hap . . .'

'Miranda.' She wondered how she could still feel that goose-bumping shiver when he said her name in that deep, possessed way. 'The book was just a catalyst, a McGuffin, a reason.'

'No,' she said, suddenly very angry, 'no, I don't understand, this is bloody bullshit, there's no reasons, nothing, nothing makes sense.' She shook her head with exasperation. 'You want to kill me, Trotsky wants to kill me, even educated fleas like Barry from Dispatch want to kill me.'

'I can explain.'

'You tried, and what do you do, you show me a stupid book.' Charmed.

'Just listen, Miranda, that's all I ask.'

'Why the fuck should I? So you can shoot me with a clear conscience? "After all, I told her it was coming." '

'Miranda, I know you're angry with me, but please, just listen to me. If, if you don't believe what I'm saying, I promise you, you can just get up and leave, I won't stop you.'

'Or shoot me?'

'Or shoot you.'

'How can I believe you? You told me you,' Miranda felt the teary lump of a first sob well in her throat and swallowed hard, 'you told me you loved me.'

Ferdinand continued with quiet calm, 'I know. I know. All I ask you to do is just listen. But first of all I have to tell you that my telling you what I'm about to tell you endangers both my life and yours.'

That was telling. Still, Miranda reasoned, it was better that they were in the danger bit together as it probably meant that whoever killed her, it wouldn't be him.

'To begin with. My name. It's not Ferdinand. And I don't work in the City and I don't live in the flat we went to. I'm. Well. I'm a civil servant. I work for the military. I, Miranda, basically, I'm a spy.'

Whatever turned him on.

'That "stupid book" happens to be the only copy of a volume that we thought had been completely destroyed for national security reasons.' Miranda picked me up and looked at me with a new awe. One that I certainly had never witnessed when it was just the two of us.

'Books?' she exclaimed, unable to maintain her silence. 'Destroyed? That's barbaric.'

'Miranda, it used to happen all the time; what you read today is a very select diet. They've been destroying books since the Reformation. At least nowadays we don't burn the authors too.'

'And that's what you do, is it? Burn books.'

'No, no, there's very little need to do that now, not since the fifties, not since Conspiracy.'

'Conspiracy.'

'Well, getting rid of subversive books and silencing proto-revolutionary voices was always a financial burden for the developed countries, which educated their populaces to decent levels of literacy. And then, after the Russian Revolution and the First World War, they realized that the new danger would be mass electronic communication. Radio, TV and so on, you can't really burn that. So, first, they invented the soap, the sitcom and the thirty-minute drama to flood the airwaves with escapism and keep the populace from potentially subversive broadcasts. Radio licensing laws, waveband restrictions, and so on, kept most destabilizing ideas from reaching the public. Then, in the late forties, when even these strategies seemed to be threatened by the sophisticated propaganda machines set up in the Second World War – the machines we now call "the media" – a consortium of international government security services set up "Conspiracy".'

'Conspiracy? There's actually a conspiracy behind conspiracy itself? Is that what you're saying? Now I've heard everything, Ferdinand, or whatever your name is. I think you might be in need of a little help.'

'I know, I sound mad, that's exactly the point. "Conspiracy" is a system, a code, set up by the Secret Services, for spreading all sorts of rumours. Firstly the rumours make governments and states seem far more powerful than they are, for those who want to believe them. But, primarily, by making up theories so near the edge of the ridiculous, they neutralize and counter the power of any truly revolutionary ideas because, as soon as anyone mentions the word "conspiracy", theirs seems a paranoid notion ripe for the loony bin. So nobody believes anything and the status quo is maintained. All it took was a subtle, social redefining of the word "conspiracy", oh, and an academic practice of seeing "irony" in everything, so nothing could be certain ever again. Beautifully simple. If Rousseau tried to publish his *Social Contract* now he'd be laughed at all the way to David Icke's goalposts. Believe me, this plain piece of propaganda machinery completely slashed the costs of policing publishing and broadcasting. Subversive notions could be published and would be rubbished as "conspiracy theory". Laughed out of recognition, lumped in with all the silly ones we made up. That's why none of the "loonies" on the internet, with their endless and some- times totally valid theories, will ever be taken seriously.'

'And you? You make up these "silly" theories, do you? This smoke- screen?'

'No, no. I was just called in to work for the department that does. I'm trying to explain what happened with this particular book. You see, the author had limited resources and self-published. He only made a few hundred copies so, instead of organizing the usual machinery to ridicule the theory, it was decided that it would be cheaper just to destroy it.'

'So how come I got a copy from the library?'

'Well, obviously Pennyfeather was a bit smarter than they thought and managed to save a copy by hiding it there.'

'And what happened to him, then? He wasn't? Well, you know.'

'To be honest, Miranda, I don't know. That information wasn't rel- evant to this mission so they didn't tell me. Need to know basis, that sort of thing. I think they killed him.' There, that's where i heard it. my author. Dead. But you know, i felt nothing. i knew at that second, i had moved on. The moment that i left his hands i was no longer his, i was mine own, i was Miranda's, i'm yours.

'Mission?' Miranda repeated. 'This, this, was all a set-up?'

'Oh, yes.'

'With Trotsky as well? Like your henchman. Don't tell me he's your, what do you call it, spy-master. And this was all a mission to retrieve the book? But you could have done that back in London.'

'Yes, well, we also needed to assess how much you had read, taken in, and whether you believed it.'

'You were ordered to pick me up?' Miranda said with amazement. 'Did they . . . ? Oh my God, did they tell you to fuck me and all? Was that part of the plan or, or do you do that to all your, er, victims?' Suddenly the whole thing seemed horribly plausible. How come he met her on the tube when she was being pursued by Trotsky? Why was he giving Trotsky orders in the alley? And why would the British Consul hand her over to them? Unless. Maybe, just possibly, he was telling the truth. Miranda took deep breaths, suddenly hyper- ventilating; she felt like shouting. With me in one hand. she stormed out of the confessional, turned and screamed at the box. 'Or, or, or is that how you get your kicks? Do you shag them and then blow them away, is that your thrill? Am I just one of the hordes you've bedded then body-bagged?'

Have you ever shouted in church? Really, really, passionately shouted? No. No, of course not. An experience, on the whole, reserved for turbulent priests and altar-left brides. As you know, the acoustics are designed to carry a whisper around the entire auditorium in such a way as to give the sound no fixed location and listeners the willies. So, the roar of Miranda's shout served to deafen her by revisiting her several times at twice the volume. She fell silent to let her ears ring.

Ferdinand emerged from his side of the box, dressed in tight black, silhouetting his powerful frame, the very image of the Milk Tray Man. He watched her, bombarded by her own words, and put out his hands in a sign of contrition.

'No. No. Don't you see. I had to be in a relationship because, well, that's what the book is about.'

Miranda suddenly looked at me, read my title again, *Making Love*, thought about it then said, 'No, I don't understand.'

'You haven't actually read it, have you?'

'Of course I have,' she snapped, then tilting her head slightly to the side, 'well, most of it. Some of it. The important bits. I've read the . . . OK, no, no, I haven't read the book.'

My world plummeted around me. What? She hadn't really read me? She barely knew what i was about? But there it was. In black and white. All along. She had been faking it. i mean i had sometimes suspected it, especially when she held me upside down or turned pages backwards. But then i thought maybe she liked it like that, a little kinky, a little unusual, different. i'd never preach conventional reading, propped up in bed, pages wide open sort of thing. Whatever goes, goes, i say. But there, she admitted it, we had never really had text at all. Every time she had opened me and seemed to be reading me, i realized, she had just been gazing emptily, just playing with me, my words. When i thought that i was inspiring her, fulfilling her, satisfying her, her mind was elsewhere. Our whole relationship had been built on sham. She never really read me.

'And that's what makes this whole thing so ridiculous. The other agent, the one you called Trotsky, he maintained that you had read it, that you were an influential disseminator, that there was a danger that you would pass on the theory to a whole social stratum. I was ordered to either disabuse you of the theory or, if I failed . . .' Ferdinand stopped, his eyes pleading.

345

'Kill me.'

Ferdinand muttered, 'They like the term neutralize.'

'Kill me,' Miranda repeated more forcefully.

Now Ferdinand began to plead, 'It's my job, OK? That's what I do. It's a dirty job but someone's got to do it. But I didn't know what I would feel, I didn't know how you would be, I just didn't know. I've never . . . There are feelings there that . . .' Ferdinand thumped the side of a pew with frustration.

'You bastard. You complete and utter cunt.' Miranda flew at him, beating him with her fists. He did nothing to defend himself as her blows rained on him. Killer or deluded fool, she no longer cared, she was just so angry she cried out as she thrashed, 'It was all a fucking sham, you never felt those things, you were saying them because you were ordered to. You fucked me and you fucking lied and bastard, bastard, bastard.' Miranda ran out of names so just kept repeating herself until she fell to the floor with fatigue. Ferdinand sat down next to her and opened his mouth to speak. 'Bastard,' she muttered, cutting him off. This she repeated every time he began to utter a single syllable.

But something in Miranda still wanted it all to be true, for love to conquer, to believe that, perhaps, he might feel for her despite his 'mission'. She sat down at a pew and closed her eyes. 'So what's this book about, then?'

A liquid crystalline globule of spittle and mucus floated through the dark air before lightly splashing into the still surface of the canal, setting off the slightest of ripples, but then Barry had never had great expectorations. He was lost, tired, fed-up and staring down from a bridge somewhere in this God- and – which was worse – car-forsaken city. A life of crime wasn't supposed to be like this and definitely not if you've been hired as a driver. Peersnide was talking on his phone to someone important, Barry was trying hard not to listen. They had lost Miranda and had been wandering around this stupid maze of old buildings; in circles, he reckoned. It had seemed a bit weird Miranda turning up like that and it turning out that she was a key enemy player. He couldn't figure out if she worked for a rival gang, or maybe she was police. Peersnide wouldn't tell him and he wasn't going to push too hard. He knew he wasn't supposed to question. Maybe she had been working deep undercover at the Second Floor to keep an eye on him, because 'they' knew he was marked to become a driver. Still, the fact that she had turned up here, far from London, hobnobbing with the ambassador bloke, made it more than a coincidence. She was dangerous. He felt his nose and tried to make it out in the swaying reflection beneath. It had stopped bleeding but there was no way she could have done that to him unless she was a highly trained enemy agent of some sort, that was for sure.

'Yes, Burnt Umb . . .' said Peersnide more loudly. 'Yes, it's as I told you, he deliberately let her escape, just as I . . . yes, I know he's highly trained, yes, but this was a clear breach . . . yes . . . no, I don't know where they . . . by then it might be too late, yes, all right. Sir, I just thought it was my duty to . . . no, not at this time of night, not ever again. Right. Monitor. Yes.' Peersnide put the phone back in his pocket with a disgusted look. Barry watched him. 'What are you looking at? We have to find them. The only way we're going to get off the hook for losing the car is if we can get to him. Blackmail, persuade, whatever. Either that or kill him too. He's bloody fallen for her, I swear.' This delicate man getting all red-faced and fuming; he was kind of cuddly when he was angry.

Gradually, the shadowy chancel grew brighter as the glow of approaching dawn dully pushed at the windows and began to shake the darkness from the nave and apse. Miranda looked about her in the growing light as she listened to Ferdinand's hypnotic voice. It all seemed so logical, yet she desperately clung on to her doubt; she wanted to be unsure whether she could believe or not.

'It's not true,' she said, despite herself.

'If it weren't, do you really think that we would be here?'

Miranda knew the weight of their situation had probably tipped the scales beyond all hope of romantic recovery. 'Well, what's the point then?'

'The point?'

'Of anything? Without love?'

'There's every point, just because you know that laughing at people can hurt them, it doesn't stop you from ever laughing. All it is saying really is that romance is not something that controls us, it's something we make ourselves and we can choose it or not. You could look at it as empowerment rather than loss. It's just one more thing which we have been told to blame on an outside force rather than on our own desires, confusion and vanity.'

'But what's the point of loving if you know that you're just making it up? Fuck,' she said, 'either I'm the thickest shit that ever walked this earth or you're a liar.'

'I'm sorry.'

'You fucking should be. I fall in love, I find the man of my fucking dreams and it becomes a nightmare.'

Ferdinand looked at the marble tiles.

'So who are you, then? Really.'

'My name?'

'Yes, your name.'

'Ni . . .' he hesitated, 'Ni . . .'

'No. Stop. Stop. Leave me a little romance. The truth hurts. I prefer Ferdinand, if you don't mind.'

Ferdinand shook his head, 'So do I, frankly.'

'So.' Miranda looked straight at him. 'Am I the last to know this? Is this, like, something that everybody knows but never says?'

'No. No, of course not. Nobody knows, that's the whole point, that's what made you so dangerous.'

'Dangerous? Me?' Miranda even managed to laugh. 'Menace to society, Britain's most wanted.' She shook her head. 'And why, as they always say, are you telling me all this? Or do you need to break a girl's dreams as well as her heart before you kill her? Does that make it all cleaner?'

'Miranda, there really is no easy way to say this, mainly because of everything I've just told you, but I think I've fallen, well, no, some part of me that I just didn't know about, something in me, I.' He stopped. 'I love you.'

'What?' Miranda couldn't believe what she was hearing. 'You have spent the last hour explaining that love doesn't exist and how dumb a shmuck I am for believing it and now you have the fucking nerve to say that. Ferdinand, just put me out of my misery, put a bullet between these eyes because I really can't take any more.' She pointed at her forehead.

'Miranda, I don't want to kill you, I want to live with you. There just doesn't seem to be a better way to say it.'

Miranda's ire rose with her eyebrows. 'This is like some sort of game to you, isn't it? I give up, you win. Game, set, match, or in this case we're no match, nothing's set and it's a love game.'

Ferdinand had to smile at that; it was past five in the morning, she'd been up all night, and still she could deliver a *bon mot* that would drive Oscar wild. It was the very thing which made her so lovely. She couldn't help her own humour and, although he had never allowed himself to believe that he, hard man of the Secret Service, would ever lose control, would ever get involved in a relationship, he had at last admitted something he had known from the moment he put his jacket around her on the tube from Baker Street: she clicked into place in his life picture like the piece in the Ikea video rack which you didn't know you were missing until you saw it lying there, alone in the box, and which finally makes the whole thing stand up without a broomstick wedged against it. It must have been love. The very things which annoy and enrage developed relationships – backtalk and pessimism – seemed like the special bonus positive traits that indicate a worthy partner.

'All things being equal, then,' Ferdinand began, getting up and sitting next to her on the pew, 'I will try to explain it for the last time. When I told you I loved you at first, I was lying, it was work.' Miranda nodded but said nothing. 'Then, in the hotel I came to realize that no matter what you say about love, there is no guarantee of anything. So I did what any agent in my position would do. I decided on the more, um, permanent solution.'

'Bang.'

'Yes. But then, when I was ready to do it, I realized something that I had been too busy working to let myself know. I really was in love with you.'

'Only love doesn't exist.'

'No, the craziness, the doing insane things in the name of romance, the traditional overwhelming tricks are just conditioned lies. Brainwash. I realized that you are who I want to be with.' He half-laughed. 'Miranda, before that moment I didn't even know that I wanted to be with someone at all. But it all came clear; I was, well, I was trying to picture you dead, which is a standard pre-homicide psychological shock exercise, and all I could imagine was you and me together, alive.'

Of all the men in all the churches in all the world, this one, this killer, this loopy-lou, this insane, beautiful man had to be the one to say the things she had so longed to hear all her life. Only in her, one and lonely, fucked-up world could this happen. Most women get a few flowers and a trip to Bognor in the run-up to a relationship, but she, she gets a gun in her mouth and is nearly strangled in the back alleys of the world's dampest city. Only she could have come up with such a lover. 'So what are you suggesting? We go back to London now and live happily ever after as Mr and Mrs Spy, in a safe semi-detached, I polish your gun before you go off to work and ask you not to be late home because we've got Mossad coming round for dinner?'

Ferdinand laughed again. 'No, Miranda, I can't go back, not after this. You've opened my eyes. You can't have felt what I felt and try to play the game. I hesitated, I made a mistake. Your first is your last in my business. I'd be no good. I'd miss something and they'd get me.'

'So you're packing in the spy business.'

'No one packs it in. If you try to, you're a marked man, one day you'll get a knock on the door, someone will cross the street towards you, a shop assistant will offer to pack your shopping bags, and it will all be over. They won't let me go just like that. I have to run.'

'Run? Where?'

'Well, defect.'

'Defect? Like to Russia?'

'God no, no one does that any more, far too cold and unpleasant. America.'

'America? I thought they were on our side?'

'Miranda, the cold war's over, the intelligence agencies are at war with each other, trying to outsmart each other. Nowadays most self-respecting spies defect to California. And why not? One of the highest standards of living in the world and the CIA look after them in style for the rest of their natural lives. Half the Brits in Hollywood are MI defectors with too much spare time.' Ferdinand stopped and looked seriously at her. 'Miranda. Come with me.'

OK, now Miranda really had to take time out. She looked in his eyes and despite every lie they had perpetrated since she first met him, she could see a new depth, a new clarity, a new honesty. Maybe, just maybe, he was serious. And if he was? He had tried to kill her, but then he didn't actually do it; he had led her up the garden path, but then the course of true, well, whatever it was, ne'er ran smooth. She had nearly been strangled, and that had kind of made her realize how short some lives can be. 'If I said no. What would you do?'

'I'd go. I have to, I'm finished in this game, I've lost it and I know when to quit. Don't worry, I'd clear it with the Boss. All you would have to do is go back to London, mooch about saying what a bastard I was until your observation period was over, and then you'd be right back where you started.'

'You wouldn't shoot me, then?'

'If I was going to shoot you it would have been a long time ago and we both could have gotten some rest.'

'You're bloody morbid, you know that?'

'I know. It really does come with the job.'

Miranda imagined going back to where it all began, the same job, Scrufstayn, sanitary towel demonstrations, bedsit. But it would never be the same because this bastard had robbed her of her dreams. Somehow it was all bearable if she could imagine a way out. But back there, with no sunnier prospect? It all seemed pointless.

'How would we get to America? I don't suppose your spy-masters would let us just fly out of Venice Airport, would they.'

'You mean you'll come?'

'I didn't say that. I just asked how you propose to do it,' and, indeed, Miranda was far from agreement. Giving up everything, even her identity probably, to run away with James Bond Junior or the most deluded loony to get out of the wrong side of bedlam, was out of all proportion on her risk factor scale.

'Lake parked the car somewhere, we're going to take it to Bilbao; there's a container ship with a crew heading for North Carolina in two weeks. We're going to be on it.'

'You're going to be on it.'

'Miranda, please, I know it's difficult but let's keep going into the sunset, and be together and make everything that I screwed up better again.'

He was too convincing. Was this just another game? The church seemed to blaze now with the warm light of a new dawn. Ferdinand stood up and offered Miranda his hand. They stood hand in hand for a while in front of the altar, as if in a silent wedding. An echo of her oov swirled around her and all she could think was, I do, I do. He kissed her, with comforting force, like a seal to their agreement. Then, turning, he led her back down the aisle and Miranda could almost hear the organ.

Out in the grey canal-fronted square was Guido. Sitting beside his gondola.

'Guido,' Ferdinand called, 'we're ready.' As they crossed the square, in the new warm light of day, the reality began to sink in. With each step towards the boat, Miranda became more and more terrified of what she had, in the dark of the night church, decided. At the canal-side, she saw that their bags were neatly lined up in the boat, next to a rather angry-looking lobster snapping at the bars of its wicker pot. 'Half now, and half when I return the gondola,' Ferdinand was saying as he laid a wad of large notes into Guido's podgy hands.

Ferdinand jumped down into the boat as the sun began to soar over the square and into Miranda's eyes. He put his hand out to help her aboard. A chill breeze swooped along the canal and Miranda hugged herself. She looked at Guido counting his money and then at Ferdinand, his hand outstretched to her. 'No. No. I can't,' she said, 'it's too much, I want to go home. I'm going to go home. You. You just push off. Leave me here. I'll find my own way. Thanks but,' Miranda shook her head in the burgeoning sunlight, 'I can't, Ferdinand. I need to be stable, I need things to be secure. It's all too mad.'

Ferdinand looked at her. 'Please,' he said, almost plaintively.

'They'll be looking for you soon.' Her heart was breaking again. 'You get on. Good luck, heh? God speed, that sort of thing.'

Ferdinand shook his head.

'I don't want to go without you. You know that.'

Miranda nodded, 'I know. Yes, I know. You've told me the truth.' And looking at those eyes, for what would be the last time, she knew that was right. 'It's just not for me. I've had it with derring-do. Not looking for any more buckles to swash. Little semi back in Penge or something. I'll be fine.' She turned away from him as she felt her eyes fill with tears. Her head bowed, quietly she whispered, 'Please. Please go.'

As the vision of her feet swam with tears, she heard her little bag being pushed onto the quayside. 'Miranda,' he said, 'please just . . .'

'Go. Go. Why can't you go?' she cried.

'Sim Salabim, Miranda.'

She heard the slow swirl of water about the oar, and the clunk of wood on the rowlock. And splash by splash the sounds faded, until, by the time Miranda turned again, he was far away, beneath the bridge that led out to the lagoon, a dark figure pushing rhythmically at his oar, slowly vanishing into the rising morning mists.

Love is basically anti-egotistical, a self-destructive exercise. We who fall into its spell are willing to subjugate our own needs in favour of another; in religion God; in love our mortal beloved.

We can even witness a caste system developing from this ego-repressing emotion; a hierarchy of its victims and its victors. 'We', the proletariat, are the romantic masses, and 'they' are the winners and true powers, the movers and shakers of our society. 'They' are those who are above and beyond love, who have no need of it in its singular, one-on-one sense. 'They' have no time or inclination for love except to spin it and sell it.

The politicians, the captains of industry, the movie-stars, those icons of our world who smile 'Hello' so enchantingly from the colour pages of magazines, what do they all have in common? A lot of money or power, probably both, and an unerring belief in their own self-worth. Their egos are intact. They are not subjugated to another, they are reserved for their own onanistic self-admiration. Their egos, already the size of solar systems, are propped up by the hopes and aspirations of a million lovelorn dreamers. They take love without giving it and in every photograph of their manicured homes, their frozen embraces and icy smirks, these monsters of egotism are constantly peddling, in one way or another, the very system, the very soul-destroying, addictive, mind-bending, hallucinogenic drug that keeps us, the dreamers, comatose and paralysed, unable to tear these stars from our skies, the ultimate product: love.

In this love-dominated society, those who are egotistical flourish, find wealth, power and perhaps happiness whilst the majority of us, convinced that we will find a paradise in the love of another, are willing to do as we are told and subdue our own egos only to find ourselves crushed beneath the egotism of the love-liberated, petty-hearted and shallow-minded.

Financial and romantic successes appear implicitly incompatible. In the saying 'Lucky at cards, unlucky in love' the cards in question are Visa, Access and American Express.

And it is, maybe, the religious aspect of love which most clearly reveals the possibility of love's true hidden agenda.

Today, in these more enlightened times, we have distanced ourselves from religion and superstition and feel able to cast a more objective, critical eye over it. We are more open to Marx's suggestion that 'Religion ... is the opium of the people'. Many of us now see this as a cogent argument, that religion could be a tool of the State and the wealthy, used to subdue the poor, the uneducated and the gullible. Most religions are quite hazy about their rewards, offering them in places like the hereafter or threatening eternal torment there in order to elicit appropriate conduct. Obedience and servitude are demanded of their believers. Rather useful if you happen to want to command those believers. It is not too far-fetched to imagine then that religion could have been used by the more powerful and less credulous as a sedative, a drug, to pacify and subjugate the people.

Yet if we admit that love has inherited so much from religion, that it is in fact our modern religion, then neither is it too far-fetched to allow that love too could be like a drug administered by those who 'know', perhaps even the State, to us more gullible, romantic 'people'.

Love is the tranquillizer for the idealist in all of us, an addictive drug for those of us who, if we weren't so worried about our own appearance and how we appear to our beloved, might be tearing down the very walls of the State to create our new 'ideal' one.

The State, yours, mine, any of them, is by its nature, self-protecting, self-perpetuating and adept at obscuring the true nature of its power. Idealists, the young, the energetic and imaginative are a constant threat to the continuation of any self-preserving State.

Imagine that you are a State. If you play the dreamers the wrong way, they will be climbing your walls with their picks and power drills primed to dismantle you. Give them dreams, though, give them unachievable goals, give them false hopes and idle fantasies, give them love, ethereal or mortal, and the world remains your oyster, their blood, sweat and fears, your pearls.

If we can even imagine that religions had powerful and corrupt hidden agendas behind them, we must conclude that love could too.

If love is the advance from religion, if love is God all grown up, then let us briefly examine the advantages for the State, or those who wield such power and influence, of a love-obsessed rather than God-obsessed dominion.

26

Love Logic

COFFEE-CUP TIDDLYWINKS IS A MUG'S GAME, SO IS MAKING STUPID faces, and so is trying to trust a proven liar. Only, the first two aren't quite so likely to end in tears. How can you trust someone who has been nothing but an utter lie from the moment you met them? It isn't just sloppy plagiarists who are in danger of blotting their copybooks for ever; so does the exposed liar. If you can do it once you'll do it again, it stands to reason.

i mean, for instance, not far from where Miranda's very teardrops were exploding on the stones of Venice, a few centuries before, and of course a parallel world of fiction away, Desdemona betrayed her father by running off to marry Othello. Who could blame her for wanting Moor? Well, her father for one. He bitterly cursed Othello with a single seed of nagging distrust: 'Look to her, Moor,' he said, 'if thou hast eyes to see, she deceived her father, and may thee.' Of course, like love, the lies one has for one's parents are very different from the ones you might have for your lover but that was enough for the General's imagination. A little doubt led to distrust, led to madness, led to tragedy and, like most tragedies, it did end in tears, not to mention laceration, suffocation, suicide, multiple homicide and a sell-out season for the canny Willy.

Miranda had lied to me, she never read me. Ferdinand had lied to Miranda, shouldn't we just have called the whole thing off? What shred of trust or respect would any of us be able to save? But isn't there something attractive about lies? Something about the not knowing that urges us to see how far lies will go or if liars can make right their tangled webs? It is fair to believe that you can't trust liars, but then who has got into a relationship without lying, or at least glossing over the truth? In fact, aren't the early days of a relationship fraught with trying to lessen the lies that got you together in the first place? i'm the last one to act as an apologist for Ferdinand, the bastard who whipped my love's heart away from me, but fiction is part of my world and I know that liars aren't necessarily bad. Just creative. Admittedly, Ferdinand lied on a slightly more global scale than most, but then he also came clean, which is more than can be said for many relationships. There are any number of long-standing heterosexual relationships in which the man still believes that a hymen doesn't necessarily bleed when it's broken and in which the women still believe that four inches is positively massive.

If i'd had legs to walk away, perhaps i would have done, but then, Miranda was on her own now. Even if she and he were unable to bridge the chasm of deceit, it didn't mean that i'd have to be equally dramatic. We were going to be alone again and, well, perhaps she would put the lies behind her.

Weeping on the quayside, Miranda didn't think of me but wondered if she had done the right thing, knowing that she hadn't. Without even realizing the madness of it, she indulged in some love logic. Love logic? That totally irrational way of reasoning which involves following a logic based only on achieving a positive end result. It is usually employed as a means of justifying the most foolish things one does in life and though it all seems so right at the time, it is almost impossible to reproduce when the moment is past.

Miranda reasoned like this: Yes, Ferdinand was a liar. Yes, she had been deceived. But what is deception if not, to a degree, self-deception? She went along with Ferdinand's lie because that was what she wanted. She didn't let herself examine the possibility that it was a lie too deeply because she wanted the lie to be true: tall dark handsome strangers really could come into your life and sweep you off your feet. The real deceiver, the true liar, then, was herself. She had done this to herself, he was just the catalyst. So she was the liar, but what about him not telling the truth? But he did. She never 'found him out'. She didn't uncover him as a liar. He exposed himself, he came clean, he showed her the lies, and in doing so he had told her the truth, which is more than most men do. In fact it was more than any man she'd ever known had done. Which made him the most honest man she had ever met. So in conclusion she was a despicable liar who had just lost the most honest man ever to come into her life. And that is love logic. Stand that up in a court of law. 'Yer honour, when my friend said that he didn't steal the item he was not lying, he was just fulfilling our desire to think that he isn't a thief. We are at fault for believing him, not he for merely uttering our wishes.'

As thoughts swamped her, Miranda kept a steady eye on the tiny bright aperture, the little o which the distant bridge made with light and water, between its arc and reflection. The place where he had disappeared. She stared until she was sure that the image was burned upon her retina and etched upon her soul. Though she knew Guido was right behind her, she had never felt more abandoned, not during the last frightening night, not during the entirety of her life, so scarily dull in contrast with the last few short days with Ferdinand. Being with him was a tightrope between insecurity and wonder, but without him? She couldn't go back to her old life now. Even if she wanted to. Without him she was lost. Liar and lover, she loved him, deeply, passionately, never-endingly. And he was gone. 'No!' she shouted to the distance. 'Ferdinand!' she screamed.

'Shhh, you'll wake the neighbourhood,' scolded the voice behind her. Miranda whisked round to where she had imagined Guido to be standing. It was Ferdinand. He smiled. 'April Fool.'

Miranda looked to where she had seen the gondola disappear then back at Ferdinand, unable to believe the transformation.

'I'm not going anywhere without you. Not until they take me,' he said.

'Ferd . . .' Miranda could not even finish his name, so choked with tears and laughter and a bubbling broth of unnameable emotions. She leapt to him and kissed him and pulled herself into him as if she could somehow press herself inside him and never ever leave him again.

And only when her triceps ached and the kisses seemed not enough and words would come again did their lips part, but only by quiet millimetres. 'But,' she whispered, 'I saw you go.'

'Guido go,' he whispered back.

Miranda nodded.

'Look,' Ferdinand uttered. 'This thing won't get through to the brass in London until lunch-time. We've got at least a few hours before they come for me. We've got a hotel room at the Gritti with an empty bed. Spend my last morning with me, Miranda, please.'

'I want to go with you,' Miranda said urgently.

'I have no right, not after . . .'

'You. You said the book, me, it was all about being given the power to choose. Choose to love, choose to be passionate, choose to live at the extremes. I choose this, I choose you, Ferdinand. We'll do it together.'

Somewhere out in the broad, quiet, still Giudecca Canal, above the becalmed waters that followed the storm, 'O Sole Mio' began to chirp electronically. Holding his oar with just one hand, Guido recovered his phone. 'Sì, pronto? Ah, Signor Ferdinand. Of course, of course. Andiamo.' Then, digging his oar deep into the water, Guido revolved the delicate prow of his gondola and began to row back.

Morning in the Boddle's Club library, above the gathering traffic of St James's, is accompanied by the reassuring sound of snap, crackle and pop, not the lactating of cereal bowls, but a freshly lit fire licking the morning dew from the first log of the day. As a matter of routine, two elderly and somewhat tumescent gentlemen, of whom i cannot divulge any further description without compromising the Government Act which protects the official liars of the State, take their place in easy chairs before the flames each morning. These two, X and Y, let's say algebraically, in order to protect the guilty, indulge their morning snifter: whisky, cigars and an excess of hacking coughs clearing the passages for the day ahead.

'Awol?' choked X. 'Burnt Umber? No. He's consummate, a complete professional.'

'Exactly,' coughed Y phlegmatically, 'that's why we're treating three missed sign-ins as serious. Besides, the fink that went with him rang me up at some god-awful hour to report an altercation.'

'Well, you can't start listening to them. I thought you said that his mission was going to be harmless,' replied X, before a fit of coughing strangled him momentarily.

'It was ...' an overwhelming hacking cough interrupted, 'mostly harmless, a simple honey trap.'

'Oh God, you don't think he's gone the Profumo way, do you? I tell you, totty and this business really don't mix.'

Clearing his throat gratingly, Y said, 'Umber? Not a chance. I'm sure he gets all the crumpet he wants, far too collected.'

'Well, we lent him to you, you're just going to have to get him back.'

'Yes. But if he's jumped ship, he might not want to come back still ticking.'

'You don't think he's already dead?'

'No. We're getting life readings from his bio-chronometric transmitter.'

'Hey?'

'His watch, you know,' Y pointed at his own watch, 'like ours, standard issue to all operatives since last June. Reports pulse rate and other things, triangulates location.'

The first looked at his watch and coughed wheezily, 'Is that how my blasted secretary always knows where I am? I thought we were the bloody Secret Service, but you can't keep anything a secret nowadays.'

'Anyway, what do we do?'

'Leave the ruddy things at home, I say.'

'About Burnt Umber.'

'Well, he's one of our best. We can't afford to lose him.'

'We definitely can't let the other side get him.'

'No. Well, let's bring him in. Maybe he's got a bit disorientated. What was the mission detail again?'

'Just an appendix to Operation Love Nuts. Bit of cleaning we missed.'

'And where is he?'

'Italy, Venice.'

'Oh God. Does that mean we have to get those bastards at Six in on this?'

'Sorry. Bunch of tossers, I know. But they're the only ones who can mobilize out there. Send a retrieval force, KOC. Burnt will be back by tea-time. Tell you what, I'll pop over to the Perineum now and talk to someone from Six before they go to the office.'

'Isn't it the Athenaeum?' X asked, hacking convulsively.

'Probably,' said Y, draining his whisky, 'but every time I go there I find myself between an arsehole and a . . .'

'Country's not what it used to be,' snorted X.

The idea that any force, on a Kill or Collect mission, was in pursuit of them seemed almost impossible to Miranda. A remote fantasy, a distant harmless threat. She and Ferdinand were a world away from everything, silently gliding across the still, sun-burnished mirror of the lagoon in Guido's rented gondola. Alone in the vast, flat expanse of water. There's little like being all at sea, surrounded by the vista of a distant horizon, to remind you of just how small you are. They would be like pins in a haystack, if anyone came looking.

Before they had even passed the dark towers of the abandoned Stucky factory, at the far end of the Giudecca Island, Ferdinand had stripped himself of several items, including his mobile phone, and disposed of them into the deeps. Anything which might send a signal, give away their position. So there they were, all alone in the world. She sat and watched him as he rowed rhythmically, gracefully, gradually south. Through the golden water, bathed in light, softened in the last remnants of the dawn mist. Ferdinand thrusting forward with each stroke then gracefully letting the slipstream return the oar to him upright before thrusting again. Mesmeric. Occasionally they passed an apparently empty, walled island, trees overhanging the crumbling brick, promising secret gardens. Miranda had no idea where they were going. She could have asked but knew that any answer would be more disappointing than just enjoying the total trust in being taken. He would know the right thing, he would get them there, wherever it was. Questions like that now seemed pointless. As long as she was with him, as long as they were together, they could be going to the moon.

After an hour Miranda was sufficiently entranced by the regular beating of the oar to close her eyes, to pull Ferdinand's coat up over her, pull her knees to her chest and fall asleep.

Barry scratched his bottom cleft. He realized that he hadn't done it for quite a while and it felt rather comforting in these increasingly alien conditions. He was sitting on a wholly uncomfortable high-backed chair in a narrow white corridor at the top of the British Consulate. Behind the door that he was supposed to be guarding were Peersnide and several of the beefiest mobsters Barry had ever imagined. He wondered whether he was supposed to be stopping people getting in or out. He hoped that it was in, because he knew he didn't have much chance of keeping those men from doing whatever they pleased. Peersnide had told him it was some sort of briefing. He was glad to have, at last, caught sight of some of the other gang members but was a bit pissed off not to be in on the briefing. Was it a heist? The next step towards global domination? Or maybe they had plans to raise the Bentley? Peersnide still hadn't forgiven him for that. A piece of hardened skid dislodged under his fingernail.

'Look, as far as we're concerned you're a worthless piece of shit, but we're taking you along because we've only seen pictures of this guy and you can definitely ID him. You do anything else, you step out of line, you make a comment we don't want to hear and we will feed you to the fishes. Is that understood?'

Peersnide nodded. Disagreement really was not a conceivable response. He sat surrounded by bigger than life-size Action Men dressed in black, complete with eagle eyes, gripping hands, realistic moving parts and more ordnance hanging from each one of them than on an entire Colombian coca plantation. The tallest, who had just clarified Peersnide's intrinsic value to the mission, turned back to him with a vicious anger in his eyes. 'That, Lake, is "Yes, sir, Captain Remington-Wilkinson-Gillette, sir,"' he said with grizzly command in his voice, '"and thank you for not ripping my head off right now."'

Peersnide gulped and managed to clear the swallow from his throat before repeating, 'Yes, sir, Captain Remington-Wilkinson-Gillette, sir, and thank you for not ripping my head off right now.' The captain turned to the closest Action Man. 'So are we still getting a reading from the bio-chrone?'

'Yes, sir,' said the bruiser, examining a machine which beeped demurely and seemed to have fallen straight out of the Starship *Enterprise*. 'Pulse rate even. He's moving. Out south of here.'

'OK, now remember, crew, he's trained, he's good, but he's not that good, he's Five, after all.'

The group chuckled.

'I want no bodies, right? Except maybe this one,' he pointed at Peersnide, 'he's dispensable.'

Peersnide laughed indulgently, but none of the others did. He watched all their faces make a mental note, and wondered whether his terror was showing.

'Right, gear on and move out.'

Each man pulled on a fisherman's jacket and ran out of the door past Barry. Peersnide was pushed out by the captain. Barry stood up. 'Where you going?'

'This your monkey?' barked the captain.

Peersnide looked at Barry's frightened eyes, 'My friend, yes.'

'You keep out of our way,' Remington-Wilkinson-Gillette said, sneering at Barry. 'Stay here until we return, clear?'

Bright enough not to argue with a man wielding an Uzi, Barry nodded.

'That is, yes. Sir. Captain Remington-Wilkinson-Gillette. Sir.'

'Y-yes, sir, Captain um.' Barry looked at the ceiling as he tried to remember.

The captain fixed Peersnide with his eagle eye and tutted, 'You just can't get the staff nowadays, can you.'

Mercy could see the city from her window. Sitting in a silver blaze of sunlit water, shaped like a Stradivarius, crafted of red roofs and glinting canals: Venice. Flirt was next to her, still sulking. Even after the blow-job in the toilet! She had gone to all the effort of manoeuvring him in there, convincing the stewardess that she was his nurse and needed to assist him. There's no pleasing some people. So he'd lost an arm but hadn't she lost something as well? She had sworn to herself that she wasn't going down for any man, but then, in the situation, it was the only way to work creatively with the space and logistics of a cupboard bathroom and a one-armed, one-legged lover. It wasn't like it was her fault. He would have lost the bloody thing sooner or later. She had made the head concession because she thought it might cheer him up and now he just sat and moped. That was the last time she would bother to do anything like that.

The plane levelled again as it lined up for the final approach. All that was beneath them now was water and as the plane got closer to it they seemed to get faster not slower. Instinctively Mercy reached out for Flirt's hand. All she grasped was the sleeve of his jacket. Downwards, until skimming above the reeds and then, as if put there as a last-minute reprieve, a runway appeared below.

They quickly hobbled through customs and made their way to the airport boat that would take them to the city. Flirt had moaned about sea-sickness but it got lost in the general whine that he had emitted since waking up, that morning, unarmed. As they began to jet over the lagoon, somewhere out on the waters a shocking explosion echoed through them, and then another. Though distant, they were instantly identifiable, they were killing sounds. Mercy suddenly had a terrible premonition, a vision of Miranda lying somewhere, limp and unmoving. Her eyes searched the waters with an unfathomable sadness. Had she come too late?

Had Mercy possessed Action Man's eagle eyes, she might have spotted from the aeroplane a speed boat whisking away from the city with six men resembling the toy, replete with stubbled faces, obligatory scars and weaponry. With Peersnide, four of them held on to the sides as it bumped and plunged over the waves of the lagoon. One man studied a bleeping translocator and vaguely pointed whilst another steered. Somewhere between Fusina and the Lido, the navigator motioned for them to stop. The boat slowed, turned and then the engines cut as they sat quietly adrift.

'Why have we stopped?' growled the captain.

'The readings, they say he's here, sir.'

'Here?' said the captain, holding his shadowy square jaw and looking about them at the empty expanse of water. 'Where?'

'He's still moving, sir, but, erm, well,' the navigator pointed downwards, 'there.' They all looked over the side into the water, too deep to see the bottom.

'Scuba kit?'

'Probably, sir.'

'Oh, I see.'

'What, sir?'

'He's waiting for us. Of course, he knew we'd be coming. He's gone down there so we have to go and get him singly, not as a team. He thinks he can probably dispatch us one on one. He's good. Clever. No wonder they want him back.'

'Still, sir. He is only Five.'

'Exactly.'

'So what do we do, sir?'

'Well, we could wait for him to surface. He's probably got less than an hour. But,' chief Action Man spat into the water, 'we don't want to do that. Let's get the slippery eel up here. Do some charges, see what floats to the surface. Much cleaner. And we'll probably get some fish for tea.'

'Didn't they say they wanted him alive, sir?'

'Agents, Carter, good agents, never come back alive, right?'

'Yes, sir.'

'Get the charges.'

The one called Carter pulled Peersnide off his seat and opened it up. Peersnide was rather disturbed to see that he had been sitting on a large cache of grenades. Another man dropped a small orange buoy with a flag just above where they had located Ferdinand and the boat driver surged away from the buoy.

Once the boat had turned and settled again, facing the buoy about a hundred metres away, Captain Remington-Wilkinson-Gillette strode out onto the front deck, placing the grenade carefully on the canvas. 'Nine iron,' he barked and another Action Man opened a different seat, pulling out a golf bag. He took out a club and passed it up to the captain. 'Tee,' barked the captain. Another Action Man scrabbled to the grenade and pulled the pin out. Legs astride, the captain composed himself for the shot, whilst Peersnide stared at the armed grenade with heart-thumping anxiety. 'Straight drive,' said the captain to himself, licking his finger and holding it up in the windless air. Peersnide felt he might faint, numberless war movies had taught him that grenades tend to explode a few seconds after the pin is pulled out. Captain Remington-Wilkinson-Gillette squinted towards the buoy; he wiggled his bottom to get comfortable. He practised a few tentative swings with his club and, at last, made contact with the grenade. It flew through the air and dropped into the sea a few metres short of the buoy. There was a deathly silence as the whole crew put their hands above their eyes to shield them from the sun and work out how close the shot was. Then the sea swelled up, bursting open in a vast mountain of water. The wave shot towards them and rocked the boat so fiercely Peersnide imagined that he might be thrown out. Riding the breakers like a seasoned surfer, the captain stood foursquare on the foredeck, his club behind his shoulders, his eyes fixed on the buoy, which spun in the air and landed again.

'Bio-chrone reading?'

The navigator looked down to his monitor. 'Pulse racing now, sir. About three metres north of marker.'

'Tee,' ordered the captain. Another grenade primed and placed at his feet. He did his agonizing wiggle and practice swings, and then, with a crack, sent the grenade soaring. It plopped smoothly into the water beyond the buoy and then erupted like the previous one. As the boat rocked violently, the navigator's monitor let out a high-pitched continuous tone and then started beeping more slowly.

'Oh, good shot, sir.'

'Dead?' shouted the captain.

'As a doornail, sir,' replied the navigator.

'Hmm,' said the captain, with self-congratulatory smugness, 'that's a birdie, boys. Right, let's get over there and pick up the pieces.' Through a sea of dead fish the boat surged back to the buoy and passed it. They circled until the monitor beeped so quickly it screamed. They all looked overboard, but saw no body. Various exotic Mediterranean sea-kill floated passively around them. Until, 'There!' shouted one of the Action Men. 'Look.'

The entire crew rushed to where he pointed. There, on the surface of the water, extremely dead, a lobster bobbed, a state of the art Rolex firmly fastened around it.

Miranda rolled and smashed into the gondola's side. She opened her eyes to stare at the planks of the boat's floor and witness a trail of her own dribble running down towards her. Though as much as she could see seemed stable enough, her inner ear told her that she was far from steady, pitching and yawing to the extent that she felt the need to put her hands out to steady herself. Shifting onto her back and blinking out over Ferdinand's coat, she watched the great clear blue sky rotating. As she pulled herself up, she realized that Ferdinand was no longer there.

A little interrupted sleep confusion led to a mounting panic. Had they got him already? Where was she? Cast adrift? Did she know how to row? Had she really preferred Barbie to Sindy? Looking about her, as the gondola's rocking lessened, she realized that it was securely moored and merely skipping over the wash of some distant event in the lagoon beyond the horizon.

The rope at the gondola's bow end was fastened to a little hut, built on stilts in the middle of the water. Looking up, there he was. Ferdinand stood at the door of the hut.

'Rather thought that might wake you. Come on.' He jumped down onto the boat, which only set it rocking fiercely again, and he helped her up to standing. Still feeling far too delicate, she stood stubbornly still until the rocking had finished. Only when she felt confident that all her limbs were hers again and the world had stopped spinning, did she begin to move. Guided by Ferdinand, holding onto his hand tightly, she made her way to the little ladder and carefully climbed to the hut's door.

Miranda looked in and, though some vestige of sleep still blurred her eyes, she couldn't stop herself from laughing. It was the tree house you always dreamed of having as a kid. Only this one was not up a tree but stood high above mile upon mile of endless glittering lagoon water. It was just a perfect tiny hideaway. There was a bed in one corner, a Primus stove in another. Below one of the little windows with red and white curtains there were some bowls under a tap. In the middle two chairs were tucked under a little bright yellow table, which strained beneath the weight of a large vase exploding with wild flowers, colour and scent. Miranda could only laugh.

'What? What's wrong?' said Ferdinand, sounding a little disappointed.

'Nothing,' laughed Miranda, 'nothing, it's perfect.'

Ferdinand went over to the stove and shook a fish in a sizzling frying pan. 'I hope it's all right. I think it might be home for the next couple of days.'

'I love it,' cried Miranda.

The Albergo di Colleoni is a somewhat more modest hotel than the Gritti, situated as it is in the backwaters of Castello on the streets of San Zanipolo. It has a midnight locked-door policy and a curtain-twitching 'Signora' on the ground floor who lives to enforce it. A narrow corridor and steep winding staircase lead to another short corridor with four off-yellow doors which are so worn and pock-marked they seem battered, like a cod fillet. Had Flirt still been unconscious, he and his credit card might have checked into a more luxurious hotel; however, as it was, the spare little room that the dually cognizant couple booked into, with its window opening onto a narrow, stagnant canal, demonstrated a good compromise between her enthusiasm for extravagance and his recent anaesthesia. Mercy, after all, didn't hold all the cards, well, not the Visa one anyway.

'So is this romance or a manhunt?' said Flirt, lying on the bed and watching Mercy try to squeeze her wardrobe into the wardrobe.

'Both, lover.' Mercy placed a string of almost invisible knickers in a drawer.

'But how are we supposed to find her? This is a massive city. We don't even know where to start.'

'We know there's a bastard called Ferdinand and a gondolier called Guido out there somewhere.'

'Do you know how many gondoliers there are here? They're like taxi drivers.'

Mercy turned to him. 'I've noticed you've become pretty pessimistic recently, and there's no defeat like self-defeat.'

'Or in my case that would be defoot, singular, if you haven't noticed.'

'Oh, come on, get over it.'

'I was and lost my arm.'

'Well, I think it's sexy.'

Flirt looked for irony in Mercy's face but couldn't find it. 'Really?'

'Yes. It's unique, we can do things few people in the world can do.' She looked at his crotch and smiled and, as usual, Flirt's world melted. What a piece of work is animal lust.

Mercy finished the unpacking and retrieved what was perhaps the tiniest piece of clothing ever designed to cover a woman's immodesty. Flirt watched her stretch it about her.

'Right,' she said, throwing him a look so seductive he would have willingly cast off what limbs he had left just to kiss the hem of her micron-skirt, 'let's go get us some gondoliers.'

'He's taken us for a bunch of cocks, hasn't he, Carter?'

'Yes, yes, sir.'

'Which makes him a bit of a prime cunt, right, Carter?'

'Yes, sir.'

'And what, Carter, do cocks do to prime cunts?'

'Um, they have some sort of intercourse, sir?'

'They fuck 'em, Carter. They fuck 'em good and proper. They fuck 'em till they bleed. Don't they, Carter?'

'Well, we're supposed to treat, um, these issues with, er, delicacy, sir. Respect.'

'Course we are, Carter. In peace-time we don't fuck cunts till they bleed. We ask nicely and keep checking that it doesn't hurt and then say thank you afterwards, don't we, Carter?'

'I believe that that follows the guidelines that . . .'

'But Carter, this isn't peace-time, that cunt has declared war and the guidelines go out the fucking window when it's war.' True to his breed, the captain was spitting apoplectically as he screamed, 'So that cunt Umber is going to get fucking fucked until he fucking bleeds and I'm going to make fucking sure of that. Or my name's not,' Captain Remington-Wilkinson-Gillette paused for dramatic effect, 'or my name's not,' Captain Remington-Wilkinson-Gillette repeated for emphasis before looking around at his tenterhooked crew, 'or my name's not,' Captain Remington-Wilkinson-Gillette put his hands out to his men and smiled, 'Vic. Fucking right, men?'

The Action Men all cheered together, 'Fuck him,' witnessed only by a quivering Peersnide and five bemused seagulls which were celebrating what they imagined must be their joint birthdays as the sea around the boat had just offered up the biggest slap-up non-evasive fish-supper they had ever seen.

Peersnide was less comfortable with the idea of catching up with Ferdinand now. After all, it was Ferdinand who knew that it was he who was to look after the car. Edging up to the navigator, he asked quietly, 'Haven't we lost him, though? Umber?'

'Oh no,' said the Action Man, winking one of his eagle eyes, 'we've still got a lock on his car.'

'His car? The, the, Bentley?'

The navigator nodded, showing him his hand-held device. 'Look. We've got a precise location and it hasn't moved since we locked on. It's not like we'd let him disappear with two million quid's worth of armoured vehicle complete with warheads, is it.'

'Let's go get it, fuckers!' yelled the captain.

Peersnide suddenly felt seasick again; he managed to run to the back and retch over the side as the engines churned the water and the boat shot across the lagoon back towards Venice.

After the eating, after the sudden overwhelming desperate need for intimacy, after the abandoning of the clothes and any ideas of propriety, after the rousing of the senses, after the passions, after the breathing and pushing, after the ecstasies, after the drowsy reveries, after the silent swim of souls softly in each other's eyes, after all, Ferdinand and Miranda lay there in their Never-Never-Land Wendy House, finally feeling equals, finally feeling like the authors of their brave new world, finally in touch, finally there, finally fine. Miranda looked out of the bedside window. In the distance she could see a small strip of land, some houses.

'Where's that?' she said absently.

'The island of Pellestrina,' smiled Ferdinand, 'it's at the nether reaches of Venice's lagoon. Those houses? They're the fishing village San Pietro in Volta. I say fishing village but it's been a long time since fish was their business. Now most of them go to work in Venice, selling, feeding the hungry beast of tourism. That, or labour in one of the seven circles of Mestre. Most have abandoned their ways and their fishing huts. No one comes out here any more. There are lots like this one out here.'

'No, there's none like this.' Miranda snuggled up to Ferdinand. 'This is ours.'

Perhaps most obviously, love needs no expensive houses of worship, it doesn't even need a 'day of worship' for the proletariat to use as an excuse to skive off. It needs no bible, no guide, no messiah and, self-perpetuating in its own myths, it needs no formal organization.

Love is far sexier than any but the most arcane of eastern religions. And yet it still encourages marriage and biological perpetuation, all with a sense of total free-will. What could be a more effective neutralizer than sticking two incompatible and quite opposite genders together in deadlock. I'm sorry, I meant 'wedlock'. Marriage is many things but intrinsically it is a stalemate. A contract in which each participant agrees to absorb the energies of the other, both positive and hostile, and so defuse and dissipate each other's effectiveness, their subversive potential, in the context of the wider world. Loners do, couples argue.

Even in antiquity, the Romans realized that a triumvirate was the most effective form of partnership. Yet today we are still being persuaded to be in counteractive couples. Three may be a begrudged majority but two is an 'irreconcilable difference'.

And when life's injustices were too overwhelming, religion would need a get-out. Christians may wonder just why 'God moves in mysterious ways his wonders to perform...' But love has no come-back. If it goes wrong, as it inevitably does, the victims blame themselves, or each other, but never the State that they live in. Never the actual State that encouraged the madness under its auspices in the first place.

However, perhaps love's greatest improvement on the religious model is its infinite commoditizability. For this is a world of trade and capitalism where the only lasting organization relies on a promise of gold. The Church may have been profiting from merchandising for centuries, from the sale of medieval indulgences to twenty-first-century glow-in-the-dark votive Madonnas, but love can sell almost anything and, every time it does, it sells its own primacy too. When you see an advertiser using love you not only want the product because it promises to bring you love, but because love is shown to be the most fantastic thing imaginable. Love is beautiful in the commercials and don't those people who are in love seem to have the best kinds of products too?

Love sells and it does so by exploiting our most basic fear: loneliness. And there's the paradox, for love to work we must all feel lonely, we must share our loneliness on a global scale. All of us together in our loneliness. Yet love, or the cultures that manipulate our belief in it, forbids us to admit that terrible fear.

We never approach a potential mate with the one simple truth, 'I'm lonely.' No pick-up line ever worked without the manner of being infinitely loved behind it. It's a lie. Love starts with a lie, it ends when we can't bear the lies any more, so how on earth are we supposed ever to succeed in honest love? We can't. 'They' make sure of that.

27

Triangles

HER, HIM, ME. NOT THE MOST PROMISING COMBINATION FOR A LASTING relationship, though a classic formula as far as romances go. For the heroine, one of her amours is always the choice of heart, the other the choice of head. And mad, impetuous, as well as totally disaster-seeking as it is, the heart one always wins in the end. i knew that, and i knew which one i was likely to be. But i was still working things out with my own love logic and there's nothing like a desire to keep you hanging on to something way past its sell-by date, however sick you know it might make you in the end. Despite everything Miranda had revealed over the previous night, something inside me still wrote me that we had a chance. i was still fooling myself we had a future, that triangles could work, but then what sort of basis is that for a lasting relationship? It can't even be defined.

Ask a schoolboy what it is and there is no doubt that it's the booby instrument handed out to the tone-deaf kid who insists on being included in the school orchestra. He whose enthusiasm for music somewhat outstrips his ability. It has just one note, a clear bell sound, and because, apart from Liszt's 1849 Piano Concerto, there is almost no music written which includes it, it is usually seen added to the score in the music teacher's handwriting, requiring it to be struck not more than three times in any piece. To be given the triangle at school is akin to being the last picked for football teams, it is the kiss of social death and the shape may as well be worn as a patch on your clothes, defining you as a victim.

Ask a sociologist, if you must, and she will tell you of the fascination and symbolism of the shape. It is one filled with the mysteries of threes which haunt cultures and beliefs. The Father, Son and Holy Ghost, the three fates, three furies, three stooges, three repetitions to hit the joke's punch-line. The old one two three, shake, rattle and roll.

Ask a Bermudan and he will tell you it is a merchandising opportunity which makes ships disappear and sells T-shirts which claim 'I survived the Bermuda Triangle, next stop Tiananmen Square'.

Ask an architect and she will point to the pyramids and talk of the inherent stability of the shape. The solidity supplied by all the supporting sides which evenly distributes the structure's tensions.

Ask a mathematician and he may conjure up exotic names, the isosceles, Pythagorean, acute, obtuse, scalene, orthocentric, centroid, spherical, biquadrantal, before praising the Euclidian eternity described by the infinite recursiveness of the shape.

Ask me and i will tell you it is a complex love relationship between three people. A situation which is not musical, not mystical, and certainly not marketable. A love triangle is a structure which is both stable and eternal in the same way that the San Andreas Fault and the whole of West Coast America is, both tectonically and mentally. In short, it isn't. i can't say that i'm sure why they call it a love triangle. If it was remotely stable or eternal i wouldn't be here, right now, in your hands. From the moment that Ferdinand walked into Miranda's life, love became a three-way thing, which was as shaky and volatile as a Molotov cocktail. A triangle is a recipe for disaster and, i assure you, by the end of this chapter, one of us would go.

'I am Guido. Sì.'

'Have you seen this woman?' Mercy showed the old man a small picture of Miranda and her gurning at a photo-booth camera.

'Sì. This is you.'

'The other one.'

The old man studied the picture and scratched at his red and white stripy shirt but, quite frankly, Mercy's extravagant cleavage hovering just beyond the picture did little to aid his concentration.

'Maybe, I don't know, what did you say her name?'

'Miranda. Miranda Brown.'

The old man shrugged, 'It is possible, maybe in better light.' He leered at the photo and breasts. Flirt leaned towards him. 'Do you know any other gondoliers called Guido?'

'Who wants to know?'

Flirt pointed to Mercy, to an area somewhere below her neck and above her waist. 'She does.'

The old man nodded, 'Sì, I know many Guido, which one you want?'

'Which ones are there?'

'Guido, this is much popular name.' The old man started counting on his fingers, 'There is Guido the Short and Guido the Fat and Guido Four, how you say, Chins? Guido Big Muscles, Guido Who Hits Bridges, Guido Who Hits High Notes, Guido Who Hits Passengers That Don't Tip. Ugly Guido, Bad Guido and Guido Guido So Good They Name Him Twice, Guido the Virgin and Guido the Girl, she pretend to be a man to be gondolier. There is Guido Too Honest, Guido the Liar and Guido Take You for a Ride, but you already met him, he is me.'

'You'll take us to these other Guidos, yes?' said Mercy.

'Sì. Sì.'

'Come on,' she smiled at Flirt, 'we'll have found her by tea-time.'

The kettle shrieked as it boiled and, sitting in one of Ferdinand's big shirts cross-legged next to the Primus stove, Miranda reached for its black handle with a cloth. She poured the steamy water into two metal mugs and stirred with a plastic spoon.

They sat there sipping and looking out of the door at the calm, mesmerizing, sea.

'So,' Miranda said , 'where do we go from here?'

Ferdinand smiled. 'Away. Old Trotsky has parked our car somewhere.' Like so many of the things about Miranda, things she barely noticed, Ferdinand found himself envying her creativity. Lake did look like Trotsky, but he'd never thought to call him that. He could do lots of things, kill a man with a touch, survive in sub-zero temperatures, wiggle his ears, but actually make a joke, locate his funny bone, take the mickey out of life, it was a talent he just didn't have. 'Trotsky', absolutely, he loved using Miranda's terminology. 'It shouldn't be too difficult to locate. There's only so many places to park a car around here. When I find it, I've got a spare key, we'll take off for Spain. Around the Riviera, over the Pyrenees and through to Bilbao.'

Miranda's eyes had taken on an even further faraway look. 'And you and me, together.' She smiled. 'We're going to do this? I don't understand. It's too right. There's got to be a catch in it somewhere. I don't get it.'

'The catch is we're going to have half of the NATO Secret Services tracking us. The catch is we're going to have to spend two weeks getting to America. The catch is we're going to have to change identities, that's the catch.'

Miranda looked into the bottom of her mug and almost spoke to it. 'Ferdinand, you know why I'm doing this, I'm a romantic, I'm in love. But there's all that stuff you said about the book, love just being an invention, a way for the State to maintain the status quo. If you knew all that before you met me, why are you here?'

'Miranda, I know the stars are giant balls of gas, but it doesn't mean I don't want to reach out for them. I know that the world is owned by a consortium of high-powered conglomerates and secretive ultra-wealthy individuals, but I still want to give it to you. I know that romance is just a lie, something that we do to fool ourselves that the world is a better place than it is, but it doesn't stop me falling in love.'

'But if you understand something like that, and think it's true, isn't it just a matter of time before the glamour fades?'

Ferdinand silently looked at her and thought how naturally the doubts came to her. He would really have to think to come out with the same consistency of uncertainty. It wasn't always easy to think that deeply when you were used to simply not asking questions and keeping your head down. Ferdinand had so successfully repressed his faculty for scepticism, for so long, that the idea was both exotic and forbidding. 'Maybe,' he replied hesitantly, really trying to consider the matter, 'I don't know. I think the whole point of the future is that you have to wait and see. That is the sort of thing I could have answered for certain if you'd asked me before I met you. But Miranda,' he said, 'you've opened my eyes to real thinking. It's a pluralistic world. Infinite options and open ends. I could say that I knew how I would be in the future and then, when we got there, end up doing my damnedest to prove myself right rather than just admit that I had, back then, as much knowledge of the future as a goldfish with Alzheimer's. You see I could say that I knew, that I was sure it was the right thing, but then that would be ignoring the other possibilities. All my life it's been fix that, do that, job done. You start with a problem, you fix it, it works. Maybe it's because I'm a man, maybe that's why men like cars and football and things. There's a goal, get the car working, put the ball in the right place, and there is closure. But emotions, love, hate, so on, there are no absolutes. It's all the journey and no destination reached. You win one day to lose the next. You can never be sure, and yet there's always the hope that one day everything will be fixed and you will live in bliss for ever afterwards. But then what would be the point of that? It's like always having a goal you can never reach. I suppose that's why a man's reach should exceed his grasp or what's a heaven for?'

Miranda looked at him with an open mouth. Her strong, firm, dream man was starting to sound like all the other insecure geeks she had met on the way. 'You got all that,' she said gawping, 'from me?'

He nodded. 'I think so.'

'Don't tell me that I created those monsters of insecurity I've been dealing with all my life.'

'You know, my family was a military one, and you obeyed orders and didn't answer back and all that. So I didn't, but I think that I have wanted to all my life. You know you said you didn't know what I saw in you? Well, that's it, or at least one of the things.'

'What? My insecurity? My total inability to cope with life? That's what you see in me?'

'Yes. Look at what you just said. It all came out like questions. Good questions.'

'No, they're not. They were statements of such disbelief, they just sounded like questions.'

'You see, you can disbelieve. If you were me and had simply believed a hundred per cent in yourself like the smug git I've been, you'd know how enlightening this all is.'

'Oh great, that's all we need. Two bundles of neuroses and insecurities trying to survive while pursued by the forces of paranoia and military intelligence. Doubts just cause anxiety, Ferdinand, you're better off without them.'

'And there I was imagining that this whole thing would end up being all about striking a balance between the two extremes. That I'd try to be a little less arrogant.'

Now Miranda smiled, 'And I would be a little less unconfident. OK. I get it now.' She leaned over to him and gave him a big kiss. Ferdinand hadn't meant to come to a definitive conclusion like that, it just happened. He realized that uncertainty would need a lot more work. Miranda was nothing if not relieved. As their lips left each other, 'You really are a smug git, aren't you,' she whispered, assuredly, under her breath.

In the choppy waters of the Bacino di San Marco, motor boats, vaporetti, gondolas and cruise liners approximately the size of Preston but with more swimming pools, weave around each other to offer their passengers the best view of the famous Piazzetta. The passengers of one boat that circled in the Bacino, however, seemed more interested in an area of water some way off the celebrated sight. The boat bobbed over the waves as the Action Men aboard tried to peer into the depths.

'So could he have taken the transmitter out?'

'No, sir. The car self-destructs if the transmitter is tampered with, sir.'

'So it's definitely down there?'

Carter nodded. 'Sir.'

'The whole car?' The captain eyed the swelling waters. 'He sank the whole fucking car, the most lethal secret weapon to come out of Britain since the Millwall Supporter, in the busiest waterway in the whole fucking Mediterranean. He has a fucking nerve. Cunt. Carter? Scuba kit. Get into the vehicle and inflate the air bags. Get the winch attached and we'll drag this thing somewhere a little more fucking private.'

Now Peersnide could have easily kept his mouth shut. He could have just said nothing and watched the process and claimed to know nothing. However, the testosterone and the manly bonhomie of a true military mission had got to him and he was keen to participate. 'Sir,' he said, puffing his puny chest out and barking like a true play soldier. Captain Remington-Wilkinson-Gillette turned to the little man and glared.

'Yes.'

'Thought you might need these.' Peersnide held up the car keys he had confiscated from Barry. 'It's locked.'

The captain's eyes narrowed and Peersnide realized that he had perhaps said something wrong. 'Sir?' he tried, but the eyes stayed focused.

'And just how would you know that?' the captain's voice purred.

Peersnide had to think about it for a moment, and felt his world crumble beneath him. 'I guessed?' he almost asked.

The captain nodded as he approached Peersnide, to stand menacingly tall in front of him. 'And where would these have come from?' he asked gently, as he took the keys from Peersnide's hand.

'Spares?' Peersnide frantically attempted. 'Umber gave me the spares? You know, to look after?'

'Did he now? How very trusting. Perhaps he even told you what he was doing?'

Peersnide desperately shook his head.

Captain Remington-Wilkinson-Gillette placed his mouth an intimidating millimetre away from Peersnide's ear and whispered, 'So,

Lake, if we get down there and find that it is locked as you said, I think there will be a few questions that will need answering. And, Lake, I get my best answers when inflicting the most horrible,' he paused for a moment, looking down as if recollecting the grotesqueness, before placing his lips to Peersnide's ear again, 'horrible pain.' It was supposed to be threatening but Peersnide couldn't help but notice at the same time, how the hot wet feeling of the captain's breath in his ear sent shivers down his spine and sucked at his testicles.

'Mercy,' Miranda said suddenly, propping herself up on her elbows.

'Sorry, did I hurt you? Do you want me to stop?' Ferdinand's face appeared from under the sheet.

'No, Mercy, my friend from work.' The idea of a friend at work was a fairly alien one to someone in Ferdinand's line, but he had done enough background to know who Mercy was.

'What about her?'

'She'll be worried sick, I've got to call her, tell her I'm OK.'

'Why shouldn't you be? You've only been gone a couple of days.'

'Last night, at the consulate, I,' Miranda finished quietly, 'I rang her.'

'You what?'

'I, I was scared. Look, let's just call her, tell her everything's all right. I won't tell her where we are or anything.'

'Miranda, we can't. My phone is at the bottom of the lagoon, along with every other bit of electrical impulse equipment that I have. They can track it all.'

Miranda looked a little dumbstruck.

'Anything that bleeps or whistles or simply whirrs, is emitting or leaving a trace of something which can be followed. You don't think I rowed the gondola out here out of a sense of romance, do you?'

'No,' Miranda began to shake her head, 'well, a little.'

'Well, a little maybe. But outboard engines, diesel motors, leave a trail of invisible chemical changes in the water, the very balance of the hydrogen and oxygen minutely affected, but enough for the right equipment to lead them to our door. We're not phoning anyone, I'm afraid.'

'What about that town?' Miranda pointed to the distant San Pietro in Volta. 'Would they have a phone box?'

'Miranda, if I know who Mercy is, they sure as hell know, they'll be bugging her phone and will track it instantly. We just have to lie low. Do you think she'll come looking for you or something?'

377

Miranda thought about this and then settled back, lying down again and saying softly, 'No, no, of course not, I'll call her when we're safe.'

Dusk was softly settling on the city, like a mist, a purple reign of princely velvet. A silent darkening was breathing through the canals, before Mercy started to suspect that 'Guido' was perhaps generic rather than specific. A name used by all gondoliers, like the butler is Smithers or everyone who gets in the back of a taxi, Guv'nor. As the streetlights began to sparkle on the water, and little trattoria lanterns beckoned, the quest began to seem hopeless. There seemed no end to the Guidos and worst of all was the one who steered them round the labyrinthine canals. Flirt and Mercy were getting tired and hungry and what romance might have been found in the situation had long since waned.

'One more Guido and then it's Guido we go home,' sulked Flirt.

'Someone's got to know something,' Mercy sighed.

'A couple of suckers when they see them coming.'

'I can't give up on her.'

'We've still got tomorrow. Let's just head back to the hotel. We'll have a rethink. Anyway I think my dressings need changing.' Flirt poked gingerly at his bandages as if a putrefying pus might suddenly explode from them.

'Sì, sì,' said Guido. 'More tomorrow.'

'Not with you,' Mercy said with accomplished tartness, 'just take us back to our hotel.'

'Hotel? The name?'

'The bloody Guido Hotel, Guido Street, Los Guidos, Guidostria, what do you think?' Flirt exploded, and then more quietly, 'Albergo di Colleoni, San Zanipolo.'

Guido swung the boat's prow in a careful arc around the next corner and within minutes they disembarked at their hotel. Then, hop by hop, they made their tortuous way up the stairs.

In a windowless room somewhere in the Vicenza airbase, facing a surly group of Action Men drinking coffee, Peersnide's evening was also becoming quite tortuous. Naked, feet in a tub of water, tied to a metal chair, one crocodile clip attached to a fold in his scrotum, another to a roll of his foreskin and a variable direct current applied between them, Peersnide proved himself an admirable, if not somewhat hysterical, talker.

The five-watt mark on the transformer's dial, a power load barely perceptible to an earthworm and which might just about run a

378

Walkman, was enough to establish that Peersnide and Barry had sunk the Bentley and that Ferdinand had told them to do it, they were only following orders. The seven-watt mark, enough electricity to perhaps power a remote-control toy car, was sufficient to establish that Ferdinand had not ordered them to do it but they had fucked up all on their own and how very sorry he was. The ten-watt mark, with which you might just dimly illuminate a bicycle lamp, was adequate to ascertain that Peersnide didn't know anything else but would make up a lot of gibberish just to prevent the dial being turned. The five thousand-watt mark, at the far end of the transformer's scale, indicating enough power to burn out a fan heater and dim the lights, was only applied when one of the men jogged the dial accidentally, passing a cup of coffee, and it was generally agreed that the information garnered from that level should be disallowed, consisting as it did of one high-pitched, ear-splitting, blood-curdling, coffee-spilling scream.

Ferdinand slept as he hadn't done in years. Ferdinand slept like he meant it, like he had been meaning to for a long time. Ferdinand slept with both eyes closed. Had he been remotely conscious he would have appreciated that he could do this. That his instinct was right. Whatever had made him hesitate, at that fateful moment – the ability to see beyond the kill, think outside the mission, whatever it was – he had been right. That same intuition which had saved him from a hundred bomb triggers, the same sense that had warned him before turning that handle, that corner, that car key, moving from a sniper's sights, passing on that drink. Napoleon didn't want good generals, he wanted lucky ones, but you make your luck by listening to your instincts, your sensations, your ideas, believing the voices. He had been right, it was time to get out while he was still winning, before his psyche was too damaged by the paranoia, the suspicion, the consciencelessness, get out whilst he could still do this. As it was he slept.

Ferdinand slept and Miranda watched him. His slow breathing, the glint of his teeth in the darkness of his kiss-laden mouth, the twitch of his eyelids, the sweep of his dark hair against the white pillow. Beneath them, and all around, the waves of the lagoon lapped lullingly. Naked, save for the warm breeze that whispered through the timbers and fell about her body, Miranda crept from the bed and found me in her bag. She opened the door above the gently washing water and sat at the top of the ladder. The gondola tied beneath us groaned slightly as it rocked. A waxful moon, half bitten, a tooth-white smile, shone brightly in the clear night air, bathing us in romance, and i suddenly realized that this was it – my moment had come: me, Miranda and the moon-light.

She touched my cover softly, as if i really was precious to her. She opened me and we began to read and tell, look and show, become one, back and forth, a coursing passionate stream of consciousness, a river of conception, perception, reception. Both of us bared, uncovered, naked. And she was so gentle and slow at first, it was as if she knew it was my first time. Her eyes caressed me, slowly, cautiously, teasing and testing, before easing herself between my sheets and penetrating me. And that first joyful pain, my pages really parting, was such a sweet sorrow. And as her eyes focused on my words as they had never done before, i felt such an urgent natural flow of my narrative, prosaically closing about her mind, moving, swollen syntax, i felt that my words might burst from me, explode with hot, wet semantics. But gradually she went deeper and deeper into me, and i held on for the climax, the dénouement, the conclusion, our world becoming one, my thoughts her memory.

And for a while she had me, she had me, she had me fooled. For as she went on i watched her and realized she was reading me, but i was telling her nothing. She was simply going through the motions. She was treating me like an object. Something to satisfy nothing more than a simple curiosity. She wasn't there to be moved, or enlightened. It was a mechanical, passionless process. There was no build of tension, her disbelief had no suspension. She knew what i was going to say, that bastard Ferdinand had ruined it, he had told her everything about me and now it was simply the action of reading. She had no interest other than to understand why, how, i could be remotely important. A mere grubby clutch of paper. How i could have changed her life without her even knowing it.

And when she had finished me, did she place me on her breast in a lingering reverie of blissful thought? Bollocks she did. She thumped me down, turned her eyes to the moon and the stars and thought about Ferdinand, her future, her life with him. i had just been the passport, the piece of paper that had incidentally transported her. i felt used. Dirty. Betrayed. What sort of reader was that? A simple passionless read with no interest. i thought i was making love, but she was simply having text. i felt like a tuppenny paperback, a cheap novel, a penny dreadful. Worthless, spent, read, finished with, discarded. Lightly skimmed. Flicked through. She had had her way with me and now i lay on the floor, my covers bent, no longer a contender. He had won, i had no more to say to her, nothing to give her. For some it might be better to have been read and returned to the shelf than never to have been read at all, but the hurt, the knowing that i would mean nothing to her in the future, was unbearable. And until you, you came along and picked me up and held me as i had longed to be held by her, i never knew, or maybe i just forgot, that it was possible to be read like this, that someone might actually care what i said, might want to know what happens next. That we could communicate and be truly one connected world of imagination.

Mercy and Flirt lay on their bed.
    'Mercy?'
    'Yes?'
    'Are we here to find Miranda or are we really here to be romantic? Just tell me straight.'
    'Both.'
    'Which?'
    'Both.'
    'But how in God's name can you still look at me and think I'm desirable? If you're just using me that's fine, but I wish you'd drop the stupid pretence. I'm disgusting. And you disgust me by pretending to not care what I look like, no, worse, to actually find it attractive. You're just a fucking user and the worst kind, the least you could be is open about it. I am repulsive and you're a whore for fucking me just to get out here and yes, I'll sleep on the sofa.'
    Mercy watched him as he spouted his words at the ceiling. 'Have you finished?'
    'Not by any stretch of the imagination.'
    'Well, try to stretch your imagination for a moment, out of the tiny borders of your own perspective. Maybe you wouldn't shag me if I had only one arm and leg. But don't think that your pitiful standards apply to anybody else. You may be angry, but don't ever think you know what turns me on.'
    Flirt laughed.
    Mercy punched him. 'You arrogant bastard. Don't you dare laugh at me. You think I do this out of pity? You think I'm fucking Florence Nightingale? Think a-fucking-gain, buster. If I happen to fancy you like this, I fancy you like this. Just perhaps I have had it with men who have legs to kick with, arms to wave goodbye with. Maybe I'm sick of men who only have the damage to their egos to worry about. Maybe, just maybe, I think you are fucking sexy because you smell like a bull and you fuck like an animal. And even if I were a gift

horse, mate, you dare look me in the mouth and I'll fucking spit in your face.'

Flirt was nursing his bruised cheek but looked in amazement at the one-woman fury he had unleashed.

'You've had nearly three days with me. Three days, that's the longest I've been with one man since I was sixteen.'

'I'm honoured.'

'Shut your face. You really can be such an arsehole.'

'Seventy-two hours, that's thirty-six hours for each limb, what do you want me to do, hop for joy?'

Mercy stripped off her clothes and knelt beside him. 'That's thirty-six hours for each of these, don't tell me you don't think you've hit the jackpot.'

Of course, it is possible for any man to say that breasts are over-rated, that long legs are awkward, that soft skin, firm thighs, full lips are merely cosmetic and that the cheque is in the post, but faced with the glory, the overwhelming physical truth, of Mercy's perfectly toned body, the only possible thing a man could say which would hold any credence is exactly what Flirt articulated.

'Hubba,' he said.

And what followed was a kind of love, a paradox, where the union of bodies was only heightened by the discordance of their attitudes. So maybe love really is just a way for us to describe that no-man's-land, that place between the opposing poles of sense and desire, not a com-promise but a desperate fluctuation between the lucid and the libido. Flirt could veer from his self-hatred long enough to indulge in love and Mercy could swerve from her pride long enough to share her body with somebody else in a passionate heat of wet and sweaty bodies slipping over, under and about each other. Love. You make it what you will.

But three days? Was that all? So i had only known Miranda for four days, Ferdinand a day less, yet all our worlds had altered, mountains moved. Has it really taken all this to tell you what happened in such a little time? Time is a shifty thing at the best of it. Of course, there are times when life changes dramatically and has to be followed closely, and there are others when you let your concentration wander. You drive a car or read a book and wonder where the time has gone. You get involved with something, become absorbed, you look up and sud-denly you're ten years older; you're married, greying and think: shit, I swore I was going to stay awake for this.

And love? What sort of love can be the eternal, never-ending kind, in such a short time? Could Ferdinand and Miranda really have loved each other so deeply so quickly? If love is a gradual growing dependency built on trust, respect and knowledge of the lover, then no. But, but if it is really at 'first sight', a miracle of the heart, then yes, their love was no less than any other. Eternity can never be in the proving, only the commitment to it. If love is a belief, then almost necessarily it has to be instant, a revelation, an epiphany, not a gradual logical process. Just like loving God, at some base level you either accept Him or you don't. You don't build to belief, the castle is already in the air, you just have to knock at the portcullis when you believe it is there. Oh dear, look at me, reading just like my maker.

There are times when you have to pay attention to every detail and other days you can settle into a pattern, switch to automatic, live between the daydream and the reverie while going about your life. The following days, almost a fortnight, were pretty much like that for all of us.

i spent the time adjusting to being the spurned one, carefully honing a cynicism and bitterness that is under-reasoned but over-justified by rejection. i contemplated nothing but myself and, in a way, i was happy doing that.

Barry and Peersnide spent the time languishing in a cell together as the search for Burnt stepped up and widened its net each day. Barry learnt Peersnide's first name and Peersnide Barry's last, and with those intimacies conquered they began a mutual appreciation on a deeper level than either could have imagined possible. Theirs were extraordinary circumstances, and it is accepted within the male collective psyche that they are allowed to act in extraordinary ways in such situations. So, each dark night was spent held in each other's arms, each day meeting each other's curiosity openly, without limits. They developed a platonic relationship; platonic in that it was pretty much the way that Plato and Socrates and most Ancient Greek men conducted theirs. Only perhaps a little less intelligently.

For Oswald Scrufstayn, being unexpectedly short-staffed and longing for promotion, the following weeks were spent manning the ladies' 'clini and sani' counters on the Second Floor. Or, to be more accurate, womanning the counters. After the first Monday's zero sales return, he had the wit to realize that his gender might be inhibiting the female customers, if not the courage to delegate the duties. In a comforting wig and twin set borrowed from Mrs Scrufstayn, Oswald single-handedly tripled the department's sales records and was even named employee of the week. Apart from having to be patted on the backside by the visiting MD, he found himself enjoying his new identity and insisted that all staff call him 'Miranda'.

A routine also developed for Mercy and Flirt which was divided between wandering the streets of Venice hunting for Miranda, sleeping and having sex. Flirt would veer wildly between the suicidal, staring into eddying waters at every bridge, and the ecstatic losing of himself in a paradise of sexual satisfaction, between the big death and the little one.

On the first day of their hut exile, Ferdinand stood in the gondola and Miranda lay at the door, her head on her hands. Their eyes were level and she swam deeply, dreamily, in his as he tried to explain their security procedures.

'When I'm out there, looking for the Bentley, you have to understand that they may find me and capture me.'

'No,' Miranda said crossly.

'No, it won't happen, but it may. And if it does, they will want you as well. They will make me take them to you, Miranda. Do you understand?'

Miranda nodded, his eyes were like emeralds. 'Why can't I come with you?'

'Look, Miranda, nothing would make me happier than you being with me all day, but it's simply too dangerous. I might just have a chance on my own. However unlikely, if they were to capture me, they will let me use the gondola to return here. They know I will have briefed you about approaches by helicopters, motor boats and so on.'

Miranda nodded again. 'Have you?'

Ferdinand shook his head. 'I will keep this carpet on the front of the gondola.' He picked up Guido's bright scarlet floor carpet and laid it across the prow of the boat. 'It takes half an hour from the horizon to here, and I will come back before sundown. If you see me coming without the carpet, there are petrol cans in the hut. There is a little row boat tied to the other side. You need to empty the petrol cans around the hut, get out and burn the place down. That way there will be no trace. Row for the island, Pellestrina, and hide. They will think you have gone up in a booby trap. Every spy sets booby traps.'

Miranda nodded. 'And what about you?'

'Miranda, when I know that you're safe, I'll tap the cap.'

'Tap the cap?'

'First upper molar on the right, see the white filling in the middle?'

Ferdinand opened his mouth and Miranda looked. 'Tooth is hollowed out, got enough cyanide to . . .'

'Kill you?'

'Miranda, I told you this was dangerous. They would do it anyway. I know too much. Either I'm on their side or I'm dead.'

'Then I'll stay in the hut. I'll go up in the flames.'

'Don't be stupid, Miranda.'

'I'm not, I would.' And the way she felt at that time she knew that she would. It was no idle boast. 'Ferdinand, I've made the choice, the choice is you, and it is absolute, in every way. Nothing, nothing would make life worth living without you.'

Ferdinand nodded, but to be so committed to a cause, even, especially, if the cause was love, still seemed a little far-fetched.

Ferdinand took the oar, loosed the rope and pushed off. He rowed off that morning, searched many of Venice's car parks, and he came back before sunset. His scarlet carpet blazed about the prow, but he hadn't found the car.

The next day he searched again and found nothing. Miranda read, and cooked, and sunbathed and, day by day, they too fell into a routine, a pattern, of loving and searching and sleeping and eating and loving. And he taught her how to catch fish and handle a Silverdart 45 calibre pistol. And she taught him how to sleep and how to drink. He taught her how to handle and control things, she showed him how to let go, lose control. His life in the service had been one of substituting alcohol, ordering shandies and claiming they were pints. Ordering water in Martini glasses. Never sleeping, never dreaming, never losing a moment's control, never releasing the primitive within.

And each day they were a little more in love. With each day it became harder for him to leave and he would return a little sooner. And at night they would drink a little more and the lagoon would be filled with their laughter and they would make love or fall deep asleep above the fishes.

One night, having eaten some eels Miranda had caught, a particularly stringy fish, Ferdinand found himself drunkenly trying to dislodge some eel flesh from his teeth and laughing too much to manage it. Miranda, a little more alcohol tolerant from long years of weeping into wine glasses, decided to take advantage of the situation to sort out something that was bothering her. In an inspired moment of helping him floss, she took some fishing line and placed it around his poisonous molar. Ferdinand was giggling too hard to even notice, he was still like a kid getting drunk for the first time. Miranda tied the line to the hut door and, after calling his attention to his fly, slammed it hard. The molar ripped out of his mouth and Ferdinand sobered up as fast as a tequila worm in an espresso. The nights that followed that, Ferdinand drank to tipsy rather than comatose. It's things like that that teach you. But Miranda was much much happier.

In a certain way they, we, were all happy and all fell into a routine of happy ignorance of the gathering storms. The time passed blissfully. Almost two weeks elapsed before it all went wrong.

CHAPTER XI.

WHO ARE THEY?

For, Heaven be thanked, we live in such an age,
When no man dies for love, but on the stage.
John Dryden (1631–1700), *Mithridates*, Epilogue

SO FAR THIS HAS BEEN A LESS THAN NATURAL HISTORY OF LOVE, an examination of its true character. If we accept that love may be unnatural then we can surmise that there is a purpose, a reason why this thing has been created. For, like all things, it does have a purpose, and like all things unnatural its purpose is dubious, far beyond the simple facilitating of positive feelings and, ergo, encouraging the procreation and survival of the species. A purpose which, I have been demonstrating, serves neither the lover nor the loved but, in fact, renders them both servants. It compels them to be as unchaste, ashamed hierodules fettered to the temples of love by that same imagination which, for centuries we have been told, was supposed to liberate us.

But then, who is it who applies these chains? Who cracks these whips and truly rules the world; who are these directors of our imaginations? Is it perhaps Hollywood spinning dreams? Or maybe it is the publishing industry concocting our stories or the media leading our hearts rather than reflecting them? No. They are merely the tools. Of who, or what?

The best description can be found in the minds of the paranoids and the conspiracy lovers. 'Them' — the nameless who exclude us are always 'them'. Those we view as not within but without. Those who do not include us but who we aspire to be included with. The other. The unknown. The dark.

Them.

But who are they?

I believe that we need look no further than those who wield the power today; for they have always done so. Consider who truly commands your fate; who really makes the decisions

55

about your life; who controls each path and every aspect of your life; and isn't your mother. Look to 'them' because they have always been there. Throughout history 'they' have never ceded power, their grip has never loosened, their anonymity has never been compromised. 'They' have always been silent so that we would never know from whom to wrest true power. But they are there.

In our pursuit of 'them' we need not look beyond our own pockets for, in the West, money and power have become synonymous. Thanks to Marx, the marketplace now provides the symbolism, the currency, of power in the world. Refer to 'a hot day for the market' nowadays and no one will think you were talking about the weather when you went to buy a bag of broccoli. No, look in your pocket and see who takes your money. Look with open eyes and you see a Janus beast, one with two faces, two heads: one skull financed in power and fear by our taxes, the other from preying on the residue. They are the nation and the multinational.

It is all too obvious how the multinational companies, the commercial interests, exploit love. I have already demonstrated how the carbonated drinks companies use love to promote their nectars and so, at a basic level for them, the perpetuation of the love myth is a beneficial selling tool. Of course, it goes much deeper than that, but it is the other head that this treatise is concerned with, the one which is far more insidious. The head of State.

Do not look to governments for 'them' though; those zoos are just the ever-changing colours of the State, the array of verbiage and clashing personalities and arguments put there merely to distract us, the public, the people, from the true machinations, tools and objectives of the State. Governments are like our clothes. We wear them until we are weary of them, and then we change them. They come in different styles depending on our mood. Sometimes we feel greedy, and at others caring. Sometimes we feel we should look after others and sometimes just ourselves. We select them as suits our humour. It is no coincidence that in Britain this clothes cupboard is called a cabinet. They have no real power, they come and go at the whim of the people, a political fashion statement for the time. And it is important that they appear to change so we shall be forever dazzled by their hypocrisy, their bickering, their pomp, their allusions to moral sanctity and their sanctimonious fervour for their job;

PART III

SOMETIMES I DESPISE YOU. YOU JUST BLOODY SIT THERE SILENTLY brooding, judging. That was funny, that wasn't, that's true, that's not. i told you it wasn't an easy story, i've gone and shown you all this, my complete failure to engage a real reader, i've told you it all and now i hate you. Letting me blather on and you, smugly saying nothing.

Right, you know what happened, what i went through, so you know what a dirty little tramp i am. Does that make you feel big? Like you've got the moral high ground? Don't shake your head, i can see it, you're looking at me and thinking: tart. i'm not what you thought i was, i'm just something that can be read and discarded with no commitment. Like a pamphlet, ephemeral, unwanted, direct-marketing literature. An Argos catalogue: Impress your friends with our exclusive Deep Thoughts and Tangential Asides – now only £2.99. What about an Historical Love Conspiracy, 'This Summer's Must Have Chat Subject' – at the unbeatable price of £3.99. You won't find this in the shops because no shop would be stupid enough to stock it. The Spy and the Shopgirl, a Saucy Romp and Love Liaison – just £1, batteries not included. i'm like something whose life is mapped out as a direct route from doormat to dustbin.

Well, who needs you? Books don't need readers any more. i'm going straight to celluloid. My story's too good just for you. They'll love all the spies and exotic locations and sex and violence in Hollywood. That's where i'm going with or without you. Who was i kidding with all that 'love of just one person' malarkey? Who needs it when you can have the adoration of the masses? Let them eat popcorn in the dark and be entranced. Now that's love.

But. Hang on. i'm missing something. i can't go to Hollywood like this. Where's the big action finale? Where's the army mobilizations, the hardware, the planes and helicopters, the mad millionaire scheming to take over the world, the huge and futile 'message' gestures?

What sort of story am i?

28

The Skeletons of Dreams

SO. LOOK, HERE'S HOW IT HAPPENED. REALLY. THIS IS TRUE BECAUSE it's how it happened, how i came to be with you in the first place. You can believe it or not but go with it, trust me, it's the easiest way. You see, i'll survive with or without you, i've done it before. That's why i'm here and, well, look around you, do you see Miranda? i'll survive because that's my type. i mean, maybe there are just two types in the world: those that separate the world into types, and those that don't. i do, but then typing is what made me.

Anyway, in the end there are only two types of stories about people falling in love: fairy stories and love stories.

The fairy story is usually about two people battling their own personal demons separately, solving their own conflicts, so that they can finally be together, happily ever after: Jane Look-In-The-Attic Eyre, Miss Elizabeth Wipe-That-Smug-Smile-Off-Your-Face Bennet, Snow Little-Men-Are-More-Manageable White and Sleeping Beware-Of-Pricks Beauty, to name just some of the archetypes. When the time to be together comes, a 'happily ever after' veil is drawn over their ensuing years, the ones in which the two lovers have to learn to cope with each other and all the problems that entails.

Love stories seem, however, a little different. The lovers often face conflicts jointly, get together in one way or another, whether in body or just mind, much sooner in the story, and try to overcome obstacles that threaten to tear them apart. Each one's problem is also the other's:

Juliet 'Tis-The-Moon Capulet, Anna Watch-Out-For-That-Train Karenina and Cathy Mad-On-The-Moors Earnshaw seem fairly good examples.

There is, of course, another basic difference between these two types of stories. Whereas fairy stories seem to end in laughter or marriage, love stories usually end in tears, if not death. Maybe that is because the alternative – the slow death that love more usually suffers, the bridling contempt born of familiarity, the anguish of realizing that all goals are compromised, the neutered ambitions, the habits once adored gradually abhorred, the limiting co-dependency, the repetitive arguing – is usually too repugnant or simply mundane to make a good story.

As far as my story so far has gone, it's been a fairy tale. The Prince and Princess have met, overcome their differences, come together and declared undying love. If you put me down now, never read another word, well, they will always remain like that.

i'm not saying that if you follow the story any further Miranda and Ferdinand are destined to walk the plank of love into the cruel sea of tragedy. But even i have to admit that there was something extraordinarily idealistic about the little utopia they set up at that time. Living surrounded by the gentle blue waters of the lagoon, its spring sunrises, its blazing sunsets, in their little fishing hut, back to basics, idyll.

Of course, if you do put me down and stop here you'll never know how you came to find me, and it may feel a little like a waste, buying a book and not finishing it, but then what price the possibility of sadness? As with any book where the hero and heroine sort out their feelings for each other before the end, you have to be aware that there is a certain risk that it might all go wrong. If you really want me to take you on with this story, and you can see that there is quite some to tell, you have to know that the likelihood that the fairy story will become a love story, a tragic one, is extremely high.

Maybe we should quit while we're ahead, just as Ferdinand was trying to do, while the dream is still possible, that two people can live happily ever after. Maybe you should find a comfortable shelf for me and then, whatever really happened, they will always be together. But then again, so would we, and i'd be there, a nagging thought in the back of your mind: 'How did it all turn out?'

Read on.

Nearly two weeks had passed and Mercy was beginning to despair of her friend. Their daily walks through Venice had become a trudge through all-too-familiar streets. They had been to the police, the British Consulate, the Reparto di Persone Perdute, receiving nothing but helpless and hostile looks. She had no proof that Miranda had ever come to Venice, no hotels had her registered, her passport was never logged anywhere, it was as if she had never been there.

Their visit to the Consulate set off alarm bells for the taskforce tracking down Burnt Umber, already assigned an operation name. For a few days after that, a couple of stock American tourists seemed to be everywhere Mercy and Flirt found themselves. When the gum-chewing, baseball cap-wearing agents realized that Mercy and Flirt were even more clueless than they were, they packed up their big shorts, 'Hard Rock Cafe Reykjavik' T-shirts, white socks, money-belts and inflatable buttocks, and returned to base with the only explanation: that the couple were probably enemy agents set up by Umber to throw them off the scent.

Nearly two weeks. Mercy knew that by now she wouldn't have a job to go back to so she was in no hurry to return. But every day Flirt whined a little more and his credit-limit loomed a little closer. She couldn't fight it much longer; they were going to have to return to England empty-handed.

It was a depressingly bright and unnervingly warm Sunday morning when Mercy woke up, angrily glared at the phone and booked their return flight to the cold London springtime. The church bells clanged melodiously from tower to tower, echoing about the trembling pink bricks of the city. Over bridges and quaysides, through piazzas and campos, Venetians dressed in their Sunday best and strutted, like the pigeons, to nest in churches. Happy, weather-cheerful faces nodded and greeted each other. Only Mercy and Flirt walked and hobbled silently, misery increasing gravity and pulling their faces towards the ground. They slowly followed their usual routine around the city, with the last vestiges of hope.

Mercy strolled, barely conscious of anything other than faces, just hoping one might be Miranda's. So many faces, and plenty she had checked and seen a dozen times, computed and discarded. And then there were the women who looked a little like Miranda, especially from behind, the same hair or the same walk, but every time she sped past them and turned, it was another face. Lastly, she looked for tall, dark and handsome men. Each one she saw she would wonder, is that Ferdinand? Once in a while she would be so convinced that she would shout 'Ferdinand' behind them to see if they turned round. They never did.

After their coffee, silently drunk in their own thoughts, they headed back to the hotel by way of the waterfront. A warm breeze greeted them as they turned onto the broad pavement of the lagoon front. As they climbed each bridge to reach the next stretch filled with flag-rippling souvenir carts, the wind tousled their hair and flapped about their clothes. It was a spring whisper sent by the Bora to warn of its coming, the hot ceaseless summer wind that tears off the Adriatic and drives men mad.

As they approached St Mark's Square, passing the dark front door of the Danieli hotel, Mercy noticed a man striding purposefully towards them. She was suddenly struck by his piercing blue eyes, his powerful frame, his well-cut clothes, his groomed black hair and she knew that it was Ferdinand. Just knew it. He passed within a breath of her and she stopped to watch him go.

'Ferdinand,' she called loudly. Within earshot there was just an old mask-seller reading a book and a muscular young gondolier easing his vessel into dock. The man turned. 'It's you. Isn't it?' She beamed.

'Non so,' smiled the man. 'Mi scusi, non parlo inglese.' He bowed slightly, turned and strode away again. Mercy was more crestfallen than a cock losing its head. She stared at his back in shock.

Ferdinand was reeling, stunned to hear his adopted name yelled so openly. Who was this woman and her crippled companion? He knew that MI5 officially had an equal opportunities recruitment quota, but he'd never seen a one-legged, one-armed agent. He thought it best to keep his distance. He secured his gondola with a rope, straightened his stripy shirt, and watched the argument that broke out between the couple.

'Will you stop doing that. It's hopeless,' said the man with one leg.

'I was sure it was him,' came back the buxom blonde.

'You're clutching at straws. Just give it up.'

'Not until I find out, I won't give up on her.'

'Look. We've got a few more hours here. Let's just enjoy them.'

'No, I'll look, and keep looking.'

'Maybe it's like your keys, if you lose them you can only find them when you stop looking for them. They just seem to app—'

'She's not a bloody set of keys.'

'I'm just saying that sometimes if you stop looking . . .'

'Just shut up. If you've got nothing worthwhile to say.'

'Nothing has come of this, Mercy. Nothing. Face it. We're going back with nothing.'

Mercy. Ferdinand stared at her. It fit. The looks, the attitude. It was her. Miranda's friend. But who was the man with the crutch? Was this a set-up? Ferdinand surveyed the Riva as the two argued. Nobody evident in any windows, the mask-seller was safe, he had seen her before. No one else about, but the area was too exposed. There could be a sniper miles away that he would never spot. Probably high up, what about the campanile on the island of San Giorgio Maggiore? Or in the belfries of a dozen churches with sightlines, St Mark's or San Zaccaria, the leaning tower of San Giorgio dei Greci or the roof of Santa Maria della Pietà? He checked each one, looking for any telltale lens flashes from sun-reflecting telescopic sights. Nothing.

So maybe this was just one of those moments of grace that life serves up and that should be grasped when recognized. Grace? The only thing that the various religions can agree on is that if the world is going to be saved it will be saved by grace. It seems odd that a little mantra before a meal can do such a mighty thing. But mysterious and wonderful are the workings of most of the deities. Or coincidental as the atheists would have it. Could it have been a coincidence? Venice is a small city. Even if they weren't a trap, should he approach them? What would Miranda say if he told her that he had seen Mercy but done nothing? All these bloody questions. Oh, for the certainty of a well-defined mission. At heart, the quandary was simple: Did he approach them, or not?

Still too early to wake up when there was so little to do with her day, Miranda stayed curled up in the indentation of Ferdinand's absent body, asleep and dreaming. A film of salt was dried stiffly about her twitching eyelids.

The fishing people of the southern Laguna Veneta believe that the sands of their beaches are made from dreams. The grains that you rub from your eyes each morning are the skeletons of dreams that you have worn in the night. When they are washed away they end up in the sea and thence on the beach, a massed graveyard of a billion years of dreaming. But, so they say, many dreams are not completely worn through, they linger in their husks and at night they wander out to find new eyelids to dance beneath, to complete their journey. This, they claim, is why they dream so much of things that they have never seen before, and why everybody dreams more on seaside holidays. It is accepted that when Pellestrinesi relate events they make no distinction between what they may have dreamed and what was real. It's true. Or maybe i dreamt it.

Miranda dreamt of solid land beneath her feet again, away from the constant ebb and flow of the moving water beneath the hut. She dreamt of cities scraping skies, shopping malls and big cars and chromium, flashing, bright, white big-toothed smiles. Have a nice day. More powerful than a locomotive, faster than a speeding building, able to leap bullets in a single bound, home of the free, land of the brave by the shore of Gitchee Gumee, by the shining Big-Sea-Water, big fridges, let's get outta here, Central Perk, I taught I thaw a puddytat, bang a corvette backfiring, huddled masses yearning to breathe free, bang a Smith and Wesson, Long Island iced tea, bang the Wall Street crash, bang to bill of rights.

Waking suddenly she looked out of the doorway. The breeze had picked up and had set the door banging against the wall. She shook her head. What would she do today? she wondered. Oh, I know, she thought. I can wait. For a change.

'Gondola? Good price.'

'No, fuck off. '

'Sì, I take you for good ride?'

'You called Guido?'

'No.'

'Well, fuck off then.'

'You look for Guido?'

'Yes.' Flirt nodded knowingly. 'I know: you know one. Or maybe one hundred.'

'No. I know just one. He is on holiday.'

'Well, could you just push off then, we're trying to have an argument in peace.'

'So be it. Sim Salabim.' Ferdinand turned to head back to the gondola. He had tried. He wasn't going to risk pushing them into it if they were plants.

'Hold on,' Mercy called suddenly, turning pale. Ferdinand looked back at her. 'What did you just say?'

'Sim Salabim?' said Ferdinand.

Mercy racked her brain to remember where she had heard or seen that before. That was it: the note on the flowers Miranda got inviting her to Victoria. She looked at the gondolier. He would be a lot taller if he wasn't so hunched. He would be handsome without that squint and from what hair peeked from under his straw boater she could see he was dark. 'You. You know, don't you?'

'What?' said Flirt incredulously.

Mercy continued, 'You know where she is, don't you.'

'You come for ride, sì?'

Mercy nodded. 'Sì.'

Flirt looked to the skies. 'Oh, God, no. Not another bloody gondola ride.'

Mercy threw a withering look at him. 'No. Not another one. THE gondola ride. The one we've been looking for.'

They walked over to Ferdinand's vessel, groaning against its post, pitching in the clashing wakes of the Bacino's motor-boat traffic.

Ferdinand silently rowed. Into and out of the wind, for a long while he kept tacking and changing direction, trying to keep an eye on each of the church towers they were leaving behind them. They say you'll never see the bullet that comes for you, so a process of elimination might keep them safe. Maybe picking up Mercy and her boyfriend was the craziest risk he had taken so far, apart, of course, from living on a diet of fish taken from the most polluted waters of the Mediterranean. He was advancing slowly southwards, away from the city, concentrating on every other vessel, every possible range point. His attention was completely absorbed with the anticipation of attack and he reserved none for his passengers. He wouldn't until they were, at least, out of range of modern small-arm ballistics. But somewhere in the back of his consciousness, Flirt seemed to be moaning about something and Mercy seemed to be chiding him.

'I've only got one leg left and now I'm going to get rheumatism in it, I know I am. It's been so damp all fortnight and now another bloody gondola trip and we're just getting cold and wet again. This is definitely the last.'

'Oh, shut up,' Mercy snapped. 'You don't understand, do you?' This was the moment she had been waiting two weeks for. The gondolier, she was sure, was Ferdinand. They were, she knew, going to find Miranda. Flirt was right about one thing though, it was fucking damp. She could almost feel the piles growing between her buttocks. She reached up for the carpet on the prow and shoved it under her aching bottom. Ferdinand kept his eyes peeled on every horizon.

Only when the city was a distant blot did he straighten his shoulders and speak with his normal accent.

'Sorry. Had to be sure. There are many people looking for me.'

Mercy nodded. 'You're Ferdinand, aren't you?'

Ferdinand nodded.

'I knew it. Where's Miranda? What have you done to her?'

Flirt looked at Ferdinand with a confused gawk.

'She's fine. I'm taking you to her. We're having to, um, hide out.'

'Why? What's happened?'

Ferdinand rowed on for a little, silent again, weighing up the risks. 'Can you keep a secret?' he asked Mercy with all due seriousness.

Mercy nodded. Flirt nodded. And as he rowed south, towards the hut, Ferdinand told them everything, spying, loving, killing, running, as best he could, and for the most part his listeners sat open-mouthed.

With so much to explain, it was a while before Ferdinand actually focused again on the waters in front of him and realized that a thick plume of black smoke was rising up from the direction of their hut. Panic rising, perhaps a first for him, he glanced down at the prow, black and carpetless, he took it all in, lifted his eyes back to the smoke and screamed uselessly, 'No. MIRANDA!' Mercy turned to watch what he was screaming at. She saw the smoke and suddenly a dizziness hit her, she knew that Miranda was there. Ferdinand jumped down and pulled the carpet from under Mercy and started waving it, but he knew it was too late. He thrust the carpet into Mercy's hands to keep waving and went back to his oar, pushing with every sinew in his body, trying to get some speed, harder and faster. Knowing all the time that he could never be fast enough. Keeping his eyes fixed on the flames at the bottom of the slanting black column. Hoping that he might see the row boat leaving the inferno. He pushed at his oar harder yet almost expected to see Miranda ascending the clouds of jet. Her words playing in his head, 'I'll stay in the hut, I'll go up with the flames.'

It was another twenty minutes before they were close enough to see the remains. The four damp, charred stakes which once held the hut above the water were still sticking up like smoking chimneys, creating a choking, blinding sea mist. They floated through the cloud and wreckage, the burnt wood, the few floating items which had fallen to the water before the flames consumed everything. Tears blurred their vision and protected their eyes in the now eerily silent haze. Ferdinand looked about calling her name, to hear nothing save the water rippling beneath the keel. Occasionally they would find some clothes or a book asleep on the grey water.

'There. There,' shouted Flirt suddenly, pointing. Mercy and Ferdinand looked and rowed towards the shape. Half floating, burnt and blackened, the hull of the row boat rocked and bobbed on the water, a frazzled thread still holding it to one stake. Ferdinand suddenly faltered, his hope finally broken. He sat down heavily and imagined himself already being transported by Charon. Miranda had gone, as good as her word. Dead. Dead. A matter of course in his work. Now it seemed new and strange and frightening. He had been responsible for any number of deaths yet it had never touched him and now, now it was as if he had never seen death before, as if it had passed him a hundred times and made no sign because he didn't care and there is no meaning to anything unless you care about it. Ferdinand cared, cared deeply and whispered to himself, 'No. No. No,' over and over as if words really could change things, as if the denial made often enough was all it took to reverse the reality. Miranda had watched for the red carpet, and he hadn't. Miranda had died to be with him on the other side. What had made him think he could just go over to civilian consciousness so easily? What arrogance put the poor innocent girl at risk and killed her.

Mercy looked at him. She needed to hear him say it.

'Was Miranda in there?' She pointed at the wreckage.

Ferdinand nodded, staring at it, their little ideal home.

'She's dead? Is that what you're saying?'

'Yes! Yes!' shouted Ferdinand, red-eyed. 'I fucking-well killed her. All right?'

Mercy still couldn't quite take it all in.

'Why? What happened? Why did she, I mean, in a fire.'

'A security measure. I promised to signal to show that I was all right, and I didn't.' He knew there was no point telling Mercy what the signal was.

'But, but she can swim. She could make it to the shore over there.' They had floated out of the thickest smoke and the island of Pellestrina could just be made out.

'She said she wouldn't. She said she would rather die. I, I didn't believe her.'

Mercy had held back her tears too long, now they flooded out. 'Dead? Miranda? Dead?'

Only Flirt retained his composure as the two sat in the boat, their heads in their hands. With his one arm, he began to paddle the boat away, towards the island.

so that we do not see the true cogs of the machine and those who really turn the levers. And so this is the real reason why democracy is promoted in the West with such zeal; it is democracy, better than any other form of government, which allows this play of shadow puppets and lets the true power-mongers remain secure in their anonymity. The powerful remain successful as long as they don't want fame as well.

So if parliaments and senates are the monkeys, who then are the organ grinders?

Who are always there, you must ask, when governments change and shift with the ebbing and flowing tide of public opinion? Let us ask which are the forces that stay as still and strong as stone, faceless edifices, the rocks of the nation whilst all else mutates as fashion changes?

To answer this, let me briefly bring it to the level of the personal sphere. Let us ask in a theatrical way: whodunnit?

And when we ask this question there is only one response: it is inevitably the butler. The butler did it.

Those who claim to serve are always dubious. It's a rotten job so if you actually want to do it you're pretty likely to harbour hidden agendas, and half the silverware too. I ask you, who would really serve if there were as little to gain as it appears? Who would be a servant, content to never be the master, unless there was more benefit than meets the eye?

The reasons to serve are, thus, always veiled, always based on a certain lie: that all men are not created equal. I, of course, am not suggesting that 'they' are an army of knowing Jeeveses, being archly sarcastic in a way that completely goes over the head of their masters yet seems to keep them amused despite the total lack of appreciation for the humour or their services, because it makes up for the humility of their station. Although this may be close to the case. No, it is when we look at who our servants are on a social scale that we discover the true 'them'. Our fingers must point at those we pay and who claim to serve us. Who boldly, duplicitously, cunningly call themselves 'the services'.

The military, the civil and the social. I must even suspect church services. These are the institutions which represent this shiftless power. These supposed machines of government merely pay lip 'service' to the prevailing fads of parliament or senate. But who elects the generals, the civil servants, the baby snatchers and the meals on wheels lady? Nobody but themselves. Nobody votes for them, they are self-succeeding entities which need pay no heed to the puppets of power. Ministers may come and ministers may go, but the services go on for ever. And the longer they are there, the richer and more powerful they grow. Why do you think the Knights Templar, the richest order of their time, were the ones who claimed to 'serve' the common pilgrim? Power-mongers, the lot of them. Freemasonry is built of people in 'the services' rather than people in government.

It is little surprise then that, over the aeons, 'they' have had the time and money to perfect some of the most subtle weapons of power and control ever known, and unknown, to man. We are aware of the less subtle ones such as censorship, inflation, taxes, war and dog licences. And suspect some of the less blatant like telephone taps, CCTV, means-based sanitation and ludicrously expensive and swiftly changing shoe fashions. The most vicious of all though, I beg you to open your eyes to see, is love.

Love? Could such a wild thing as being in love really be controlled from without? It certainly is not controlled from within ourselves so we must accept the possibility. And it would not be the first 'idea' to reside in the domain of the mind and the imagination which was, in fact, controlled in such a way. It wouldn't be the first madness of the crowd which was, in truth, manipulated from beyond its own parameters.

Witness the times in history when, for some spiritual reason, the individual souls of the masses seem to conspire in a shared imagination. Consider, if you will, as an example, when the imaginative forces of an era have appeared magically to collude: sixties hippydom; Victorian conservatism; the hundreds of years of religious wars; the political confrontations of the first half of the twentieth century; the ideological ambivalence of the second; practically every art movement which has been dignified and sanitized by an 'ism'. These are all called *Zeitgeist*. We brush these things off as a ghost, a mere immaterial spirit of the times. Times when our imaginations have been influenced by some unearthly power beyond us but within us. Sometimes we called it God, the Lord, but like the Catholic Church, it was nothing but a mass delusion.

Scratch these 'movements' and we see that they all work with, and around, the notion of power, legitimizing those who wield it. In the sixties the students believed that they could seize power through smoking dope and fearing baths.

29

Sycorax

I SUPPOSE THERE IS A LITTLE *SUNSET BOULEVARD*-STYLE LOGIC ERROR here; like telling the story when you're the dead man floating in the swimming pool. If i was in the hut and got burnt with Miranda, how can i be here with you now? Still, maybe Ferdinand had taken me to hide as a sort of protection measure, a bargaining chip if they got caught. Maybe. Whatever happened, i will tell you openly but forgive me for holding this answer back for a little longer. i have the Hollywood executives to think about now. The history of my love is over, i was out of the triangle, and the rest is just a story as far as you and i are concerned. A true one but, like any story, not much more than a tension between what is known and what is to be known.

Ferdinand dolefully helped Flirt paddle the gondola to the shore, all of them silent; minds occupied with the unanswerable questions death always asks, their faces stony masks, as if humans have not found an expression to come close to that shocking grief which is beyond tears.

Petulant seagulls, watching the smouldering remains of the fishing hut on the off chance of some smoked fish, lined the low stone wall that separated the lagoon from the overgrown and reed-filled land of Pellestrina. They warned the rowers off with vicious caws and threatening flapping of their wings. As the boat met the wall, they rose as a flock creating a dreadful noise and aiming some fantastically odorous excrement at the invading vessel. The seafarers stumbled onto the path and, unable as yet to even consider what they were doing, they sat, like the seagulls, on the wall by the long grass and listened to the birds fight.

The island of Pellestrina is long and thin, expanding to a wider part at each end. On a map it looks like a leg bone but on the ground it resembles a calm wetlands, a mellow marsh. It is barely more than an inhabited sandbank but it has served an historic purpose: for millennia, it has separated the occasionally ferocious Adriatic from the mostly serene lagoon. Where the three landed, just south of the village of San Pietro in Volta, it is barely two hundred yards across. A high concrete sea wall rises on the seaward edge of the island and a low bricked embankment lines the lagoon. Here the three sat, still in shock. Gradually, however, as the cinders settled about them, the need to avoid guilt and lay blame found voice.

'What happened?' Mercy turned on Ferdinand. He sat shaking his head, watching the smoke, breathing in the ashes as if some might have been Miranda's, as if there might be a way that they would always be part of each other.

'She burnt our hut,' he choked.

'Why? Why would she do that?'

'Because I told her to.'

'What?' Mercy could not believe what he was saying. 'You told her to? You told her to do that?' She pointed to the smoke.

'Yes. No. Not to burn herself. To set light to the place and take the boat and get out of there.'

'Why? Why should she do that?'

Flirt, now accustomed to Mercy's explosive nature, attempted a little optimistic appeasement. 'She could have swum ashore, couldn't she?'

Ferdinand ignored him. 'To prevent her from being caught if they caught me.'

'They?' Mercy spat. 'They? Your fucking secret squirrel spy-masters? Your pathetic games-players, dungeon-masters, M? Q? Is that the they?'

Ferdinand shrugged.

'What the fuck was she doing there?' Mercy shouted. 'Why her? Why didn't you send her back to London? Safe. How dare you take her into your sordid life! What right did you have to use her like that?' Mercy's nails flew at Ferdinand. Not feeling in the mood for gentle-manly courteousness, he struck her across the face with just enough force to stun her. Flirt tried to get up to defend her but then slumped back down again when he realized that a two limbed A&E Frequent Flyer wasn't going to be a great deal of help against an able-bodied trained military agent.

Ferdinand stood up and Mercy saw there were tears in his eyes. 'I never, never wanted this to happen. I warned her, I told her, she knew the risks.'

'So why didn't you make her go back?'

Ferdinand faltered, 'I loved her.'

'Loved her? What do you mean? Why did she set light to herself? What sort of delusion did you feed her with?'

'She said she would. If she thought I was captured. She said she would go up with the flames. Then when we were rowing to the hut, just now, she saw, she saw I wasn't returning alone, she saw . . .'

'Us. She saw all of us and thought that "they" had got you?'

Ferdinand nodded and turned to look at the smoke.

'Are you saying it was a mistake?'

Ferdinand looked back at her but said nothing.

'Shit,' swore Mercy, 'shit and bollocks. The moment we get to some sort of civilization I'm turning you in, mate. You are either fucking mad or the world's most wanted man. You're not turning it round like we killed her. I'm not buying that. You told her to torch the place. She's dead because of what you alone said and so are you, I swear it.'

'Do you think I give a monkey's arsehole about your threats?' Ferdinand, red-eyed, cool-lost, shouted back. 'Do you think anything matters to me now she's gone? Do you think that I wouldn't have done the same for her? Taken her place? You think you had the monopoly on her affections?' Then quietly into the wind and the smoke, 'And it's even worse than that. I've been so wrong all my life, thought that only the mad make ultimate sacrifices for love. All my life, and now I find that I'm the one who's mad. I'd have done exactly the same. If only . . .'

'You are a prick. You are a tosser. You are a killer, a murderer and an arsehole.'

'Excuse me?' said Flirt.

'Fuck off.' Mercy was rolling. 'I've cleaned a few baths in my time but I've never met scum like you. You will rot in whatever hell your conscience lurks in.'

'No, I really think that this might be important,' Flirt tried again.

'I appreciate you trying, but don't waste your breath,' Ferdinand muttered. 'Nothing will make me feel any more of a shit.'

'Take my invective like a man, you can't just grab all the hatred for yourself. I want you to have some of mine. All of mine, you worthless piece of shit.'

'Looks like rain.' Flirt pointed across the lagoon. Both Mercy and Ferdinand looked up. Rising in the north, from the direction of Venice, was what appeared to be a dense black cloud. As they watched, they noticed a distant buzzing noise growing as the cloud did, as if it was, in fact, a massive swarm of insects miles away, bearing down on them.

Ferdinand jumped into the boat and pulled a heavy dinner jacket out of the aft cubbyhole. As the swarm approached, individual insects could be made out, distinct from the horde, and the buzz became a mighty beating getting ever louder. Ferdinand donned the jacket and climbed to the shore, keeping his eyes on the black pestilent mass, screaming towards their fate like the promise of an apocalyptic horseman. Relieved to be facing some real action rather than the perilous depths of his own heart, Ferdinand watched the fearful cloud with a steady eye and muttered just one word under his breath: 'Sycorax.'

He knew that they would come, he had imagined it, dreamt it, calculated the timing, the speed, the direction. They had played on Ferdinand's mind like harbingers of doom and now they came to exact their revenge. Sycorax helicopters, the favoured transport of NATO Mediterranean forces carrying special operations troops. They hunted in packs and struck terror into all who saw them, flying low, fast, with terrible insect-like rocket-launching pincers at either side. Each one carried eight men, armed to the teeth and highly trained to get in anywhere, eliminate, and get out, before anyone, especially the media, could draw breath. Somehow, something had told them that he was there. Were Mercy and Flirt really agents after all? He looked at them and registered the frozen terror on their faces.

'Run!' he yelled.

'Can I hop?' said Flirt.

'Here,' Ferdinand helped Flirt up and, like over-eager parents entering the school sports day three-legged race, they began to speed-hobble in the direction of the village. All thoughts of turning Ferdinand in were wiped from Mercy's suddenly panicked mind. The terrifying things that were approaching, occasionally glinting as they grew larger, were definitely shoot first and ask later type machines. She turned to Ferdinand and Flirt and began to chase them.

They all raced along the bank as the dreadful black machines got ever louder and more deafening. They stumbled and hopped past the waterfront buildings, as the swarm above the lagoon split into three. One group swooped towards either side of the village and the last headed right for the centre. Ferdinand picked Flirt up and began to run as fast as he could, Mercy clawed her high-heels off and, barefoot, kept up with him.

The centre of San Pietro in Volta is usually a sleepy place. The last time it saw military action was the landing of Allied forces in 1944 in the course of liberating Northern Italy. The action in question consisted of one marine hopping out of a boat and asking, in laughably bad Italian, the way to Venice. At the village's centre is an L-shaped piazza; half of it fronts onto the lagoon, whilst the other two sides are made up of white houses, a small bank, and a café with the faded words 'Da Nana' painted above a green and white striped awning. On Tuesdays a fruit and veg boat docks beside the piazza, on Thursdays a fish-monger, and that just about sums up the activity of the place. Occasionally a new scooter is bought for one of the dwindling village's youths, and like all mainland Europeans, he removes the silencer and, driving up and down the three hundred yards of the village, supplies it with that unmistakable amplified lawn-mower sound effect. However, it being a Sunday and within three hours of lunch-time, the place was quite empty. The stand pipe fountain trickled water, ice-cream wrap-pers blew across the empty square, and a woman in dark glasses and a glistening black dress sipped lemon tea from a glass at one of the café's patio tables.

The noise of the Sycorax rotors was thudding now, shaking the whole village, as they came to a slow hovering halt a few hundred yards out above the lagoon, cutting the air with dull, regular menace. Almost limping from the strain, Ferdinand ran into the square look-ing for a place to hide. As he stood assessing the best location, a dozen gun sights aligned their crosshairs.

Mercy followed Ferdinand, they both looked at the café, at each other, then sprinted for the door. The woman in black tore her eyes away from the helicopters to register the newcomers running towards her with grim intent etched on their faces. Her glass of tea smashed to the floor. 'Mercy!' she screamed.

'Miranda?' as she tried to run and alter her focus from the café door to the woman in the sunglasses, Mercy tripped. She landed with her arse against the stone and whipped up a cloud of dust. Ferdinand helped her up again, dragging Flirt at the same time. The woman in black took off her sunglasses and for a moment there were no helicopters, time and motion took a break, physics succumbed to psychology. It was Miranda.

'Miranda?' Ferdinand echoed, amazed, impressed, happy, curious, fearful, disbelieving, i could carry on but i don't like to mix my thinks. Then a dread steeliness filled him: now he absolutely had to stay alive and protect her, he owed it to her. A furious command came loudly to his voice. 'Miranda,' he ordered, 'inside. Now.'

They piled through the café door as ropes dropped from either side of each helicopter. Ferdinand picked up a table and placed it in front of the doorway. He paced about the bar checking exits. The bartender was already taking all his precious whisky bottles down from the display behind the bar, as he had seen in all his favourite westerns.

A tannoyed announcement boomed from the central helicopter outside, a warning, in bad Italian again, to the residents not to leave their houses. They were pursuing a dangerous fugitive. The operation would soon be over. Then in English, the clear-cut voice of Remington-Wilkinson-Gillette: 'This is your first and only warning. You have exactly one minute to leave the building with your hands on your heads. Failure to comply will be considered an act of aggression and will result in immediate armed response from ground troops. Do you understand?' As the announcement echoed off the village walls, black lumps were flung from the helicopters which inflated into boats on the way down to the water. As Ferdinand pulled out his personal weaponry, one large black gun, the others watched from the window as men dressed in black, in balaclavas, weapons strapped to every part, piled out of the Sycoraxes and slid down the ropes to the waiting boats.

Mercy and Miranda turned to each other. 'My God,' said Mercy.

'How did you get here?' Miranda said in equally awed tones.

'You phoned me. You were in trouble. Miranda, I don't believe it, you're alive.' Mercy burst into tears caught in breaths of relief. 'You're alive,' she said, gripping bits of Miranda, her arms, her face, her legs, just to make sure.

Miranda looked at Flirt and nodded. 'Hi, you look,' Miranda tried to think of a good word to describe someone who was half the person they were when she last saw them, 'different' seemed the only inoffensive option. And then she turned to Ferdinand. He looked up and their eyes met. She smiled. 'So what happened? It wasn't my mistake, was it? I looked but it wasn't there.'

Ferdinand's brow roughed an imploring furrow. Mercy wondered.

'What? What wasn't there?'

'The red carpet,' said Miranda.

Mercy looked at Ferdinand and realized what had happened.

'Was that it? Was that the signal? The carpet?' She turned to Miranda. 'Shit. I took it, to sit on. Those wooden seats are really hard on your arse and . . .' Ferdinand looked uncomfortable.

Miranda crossed over to Ferdinand and gave him a long kiss. 'It's fine we're all here, we're all alive.' She paused and shook her smiling head.

'But we won't be in a few minutes,' Flirt interrupted, pointing out of the window.

The soldiers who had already landed were running into various positions, hiding behind strategic points and aiming their weapons at the café. Others paddled slowly to shore, hunched and huddled, casting about, expecting action at any moment.

'How did they know?' Ferdinand muttered, mainly to himself. 'Who, what, tipped them off?'

Mercy had no time in her head to order her questions so they all seemed to come out on top of each other. 'How did you get here? We thought you were in that hut.'

'I wanted to stay. I did. I spread the petrol and lit the place and the flames were coming up and then. It was so hot, Mercy. And I thought, fuck, I can't do it. By that time the row boat was on fire. I just jumped and swam.'

'Now all we need is a little more ordnance.' Ferdinand patted the pockets of his jacket. Miranda brought up a clear resealable plastic sandwich bag that had been at her feet. In it was the gun he had given her, a selection of essential make-up, her Switch card, the binoculars and, most importantly, me. She took out the gun and slammed it on the table.

Mercy's eyes widened. Miranda looked like Miranda, she sounded like Miranda, but her shy friend had certainly come out of a shell or two. For a start there was her familiarity with the penis-extension to end all penis-extensions, the gun. Then there was her dress. Miss don't-want-to-show-my-curves was sitting in a little black number to die for that wetly clung to her like she was a Doctor No dolly. She packed a widow-maker with the confidence of a professional. She had the cool to wait for the armed forces sipping tea at a café. And if this was the new Miranda, was there anything more she could teach her?

Ferdinand kissed Miranda again as he picked up the gun. She looked at him lovingly. Oh yes, lots to learn, thought Mercy. 'Only you could get into this sort of mess,' Mercy said, 'and we've got a lot of catching up to do.' But all of us fell silent. Words seemed futile now, only the feelings really mattered. Only the feelings.

The tannoy screeched on again. 'You have not corresponded with our request,' came the razor-sharp voice. 'You are surrounded. Come out now or we will remove you using the full force at our disposal.'

Mercy, Flirt and Miranda looked at Ferdinand. He had attached a laser sight to his handgun and was pointing it out of the window at one of the helicopters. As he squinted he said, 'Listen to me, this is the plan. In a moment, when we don't appear, he will begin to count down. I want you all to go through to the kitchen. When he reaches three, open the back door and place your hands on your head. There is an alley behind this place, one end leading to the lagoon, the other into the village. There will be two, possibly three, men in the alley and they will be aiming their weapons at you. You will hear a pause in the count-down and then a crash. The men will look away and, hopefully, move towards the noise. At that moment you must make a dash for it, they'll have gone right, you run left. Run through the alleys to the edge of the village. You'll see the sea wall, go through one of the openings and you'll find boulders and rocks to hide in. They won't follow you.'

'Why not?' asked Flirt.

Ferdinand looked at him, 'Because they'll think we were blown apart, no remains.' Ferdinand opened his jacket, explosives dripped from belts that lined it.

'You're not going to . . .' Miranda's voice petered out as she looked at the explosives. Ferdinand shook his head.

'Not if I can help it.'

'So promise me you'll follow us,' Miranda urged.

The voice started again.

'As you have failed to comply with our orders, we will give you ten seconds to leave the building. Ten.' It was standard procedure but Remington-Wilkinson-Gillette counted slowly, relishing the moment, knowing the panic that would be going on inside the café. Umber would be constructing some stupid plan, playing the hero, and giving the captain every excuse to waste him. He smiled, 'Nine.' Flirt and Mercy shuffled back to the kitchen.

'Promise?' Miranda pleaded.

'Just go. Go.'

'Eight.'

'Not until you promise.'

Ferdinand bit his lip, he would not lie to her, he'd sworn it.

'Seven.'

'Please, Ferdinand, you've got to come.'

'Go. Please.'

'Six.'

'I won't go without you.'

'Five.'

Miranda continued, 'I failed you once. I thought they'd got you but I couldn't bring myself to kill myself. Now I've got another chance.'

'Four.'

Ferdinand turned to her. 'I love you. Don't die, live. You only take one life into the shower – live and go, Miranda.'

'Three.'

Mercy and Flirt dutifully opened the back door and faced the masked gunmen with their hands on their heads. Miranda rushed to the back and placed her hands on her head too. Nervously looking about, one of the soldiers waved, sending a signal to another at the end of the alley by the lagoon. He, in turn, waved at the helicopters. One of the Sycorax peeled off to oversee the evacuation. As it turned to circumnavigate the building, it gave Ferdinand his one and only shot at reversing the situation. Its open cockpit was in his sight line, the pilot's shoulder caressing the cross hairs of his laser sight. Ferdinand pulled his trigger and the man's shoulder exploded. The helicopter suddenly veered out of control. It jumped one way, then another. Then, crashing into another Sycorax, they both plunged to the sea, letting out a mighty series of explosions.

The gunmen at the back door raced to the lagoon-front to see what was happening. Miranda began to run. Mercy helped Flirt hobble on his crutch. Miranda looked behind and saw her struggling. She ran back to help.

'Miranda, run,' Mercy shouted, 'run. They don't want us. It's you and him, we'll be OK.'

Miranda looked at her. She knew she was right. Mercy suddenly pulled Miranda to her with her free arm and kissed her, hard, passionately, lovingly on the mouth. 'Go,' she whispered.

Miranda started running down the alley.

Mercy and Flirt followed her, but the gunmen had turned back. A deafening round of gunfire echoed into the alley and Flirt fell.

'My leg, my leg, they've got my sodding leg,' Flirt cried. Mercy stopped and knelt by him, glaring at the eyes in the balaclavas. The gunmen edged forward, weapons at the ready and shouting, 'Get down! Get down! Lie on your front with your hands on your head.' Mercy complied and Flirt, as far as he could, did the same.

Miranda ran hard, she ran and ducked and hid until the beating sounds of the helicopters became faint. The houses suddenly stopped and the tall green reeds of open land beckoned. She paced along a sandy track towards the high sea wall, stumbling out onto a road that ran parallel to it. She vaulted up some steep concrete steps that led to an opening in the wall.

At the top the wind tugged at her hair and she caught sight of the rolling endless sea, windwhite breakers crashing to the shore. And to left and right a long string of massive white boulders and concrete blocks, dumped there to strengthen the island's sea defences. To her right they reached into a distance she could barely make out and to her left as far as a causeway that led out to a lighthouse. Before bounding down into the safety of the boulders she looked back towards the village. She could see the helicopters hovering above it and as she watched a massive cloud of smoke began to pile up from the village centre, closely followed by the sonic boom of a huge explosion.

'Ferdinand!' she screamed to the wind. Then achingly descended the steps to find a place to hide among the seaweed-strewn rocks.

While Miranda was making her run for freedom, and Mercy and Flirt were being dragged to the lagoon front to be whisked away on a motor launch, Ferdinand had been setting up his next move with the calm quietness of a somnambulist, albeit a deadly one. In the kitchen he found a roll of silver foil, then gracefully he went around turning the ovens and stoves on to full, stoking the pizza furnace until, unable to take the heat, he got out of the kitchen, leaving the explosives from his jacket on the work table in the middle.

In the restaurant area he leaned over the bar to where the owner was sitting, cowering and praying. 'Andiamo.' Ferdinand gestured to him to come.

Nervously, the man made his way to Ferdinand. Placing his hands on top of his head, Ferdinand ushered the man to the front door and pushed him out. He watched as the man ran over to the soldiers who, in turn, threw him to the floor and started to frisk him with their feet. Meanwhile Ferdinand had turned his attention to the glass-fronted dessert refrigerator near the door. He switched it to defrost and cold air began to blow from the vents. Then he began to pull out the shelves, the fruit-covered cakes and the tiramisus tumbling to the floor. Once it was empty, he wrapped himself in the silver foil, picked up a *coppa di tiramisu* and climbed into the fridge.

The muscles in Remington-Wilkinson-Gillette's grizzled jaw

pulsed with tension. The captain kept his guns trained on the café, his thumb rested lightly on the red rocket-launching button on his stick. He squinted through the bulletproof cockpit glass and glared at his thermal-emission mapping screen. A moment before he could see that there had been one other living person inside the café, and now he had disappeared. Remington-Wilkinson-Gillette would have liked to have gone in and got this smug bastard himself. Had he had the time he would have grabbed his favourite Uzi and gone in there raining bullets into the ponce from intelligence. Those university prats screamed so delightfully when torn apart. But now he couldn't risk Umber getting away, not after losing two Sycoraxes, which was going to be hard enough to justify on his ordnance roster chit.

'You can hide but you can't run from these,' he blew under his breath and pressed the button forcefully. The two heat-seeking rockets at either side of the helicopter flew out like streamers and streaked towards the café. They burst through the restaurant wall, smashing the fish tank and liberating a lobster, two puff fish and a crab. As Ferdinand watched them skirt around his fridge, weaving around each other, they headed straight for the hot kitchen and the scorching heat of the pizza oven. The next moment the kitchen exploded, filling with fire that burst out of the doors and licked at his fridge. Timbers started to descend as the first floor crashed down and into rubble. Dense smoke filled the air as Ferdinand calmly watched from his cool vantage point, eating his tiramisu and enjoying the pyrotechnics. At last, all that was standing in the ruins of the café were a few of the hardier pieces of kitchen furniture, the collection of whisky bottles that had been gathered beneath the bar and the dessert fridge.

While the smoke, fanned by the helicopter blades, was too dense for the soldiers to move in, Ferdinand scraped the bottom of his coppa, took a deep breath, stepped out of the fridge and ran. He ran through the smoke, into the same alleys that Miranda had navigated and out into the field. He ran to the road and up onto the sea wall. He dashed down the steps whispering loudly, 'Miranda? Miranda?'

So we three did meet again. Not in thunder, lightning or in rain, but a little cave formed by huge sea-wall boulders. And Ferdinand and Miranda laughed and kissed and were like excitable children. i watched stoically until at last they looked out to sea and began talking sense.

'Mercy and Flirt?'

'Alive. Caught. But they'll be fine; it's just me they want now. And probably you if they know that you mean anything to me.'

'What now?'

'They'll be after us soon.'

'So where do we go?'

'Well, the logical thing would be to go right and head for the southern end of the island. There's a boat to the mainland, we could just lose ourselves in Italy.'

'So let's go.'

'But,' said Ferdinand, not moving, 'they know that that would be the logical thing to do so they'll be guarding that end. So we go that way.' Ferdinand pointed left. 'Towards the Lido. Take the ferry over that end.' Ferdinand took Miranda's hand and led her down to the water. They took their shoes off and ran along the sand, the cold water crashing about their toes. They ran until they got to the causeway that led out to the lighthouse and climbed onto its smooth surface.

The causeway was barely half a mile long. It was a flat concrete path projecting out into the sea. On either side of it were more rocks. Seawater crashed under, in between and over the white rocks which stretched all the way to the faded red and white striped lighthouse at the end. The sea wall met the causeway at right angles and stopped. Beyond was a channel of water wide enough for small ships and on the other side the shore of the Lido.

Ferdinand turned away from the lighthouse and ran up to the sea wall with the binoculars in his hands. Peeping over it, he trained the glasses on the ferry-docking ramp jutting out into the channel, ending the wall's parallel road. Two Sycorax were parked on the road and a dozen soldiers were standing and kneeling in place, waiting for action.

'Fancy another swim?' asked Ferdinand cheerily. 'Because our ride has just been cancelled.'

Back on the causeway, they scanned the green trees and look-alike lighthouse on the Lido side. But before they could descend the rocks into the water, Ferdinand stopped Miranda and pointed. Balaclavaed soldiers were running along the Lido side stopping at, and establishing, shooting vantage points. The two turned quickly and scrabbled down the beach side of the causeway, crouching.

'Bugger,' said Ferdinand, 'they seem to have worked out that we're not still in the café.'

Miranda hissed at him, 'What do we do now?'

'Come on.' Ferdinand led her jumping from rock to rock along and out to the lighthouse. There, the concrete path splayed out in a circle around the lighthouse and high rocks surrounded them. This was the furthest point out to sea and so, from the landward side of the lighthouse, they could see everything going on on the two islands.

Tiny black troops had arrived at the now distant sea wall and were spreading out in both directions. Running on top of it and along it. Ferdinand watched them, he looked about, he assessed every angle, he searched for the loophole, the escape route. He hunted about the rocks as if he might suddenly find a jet ski they could take out into the waters. Finally, and quite suddenly, his body slumped. It was as if, in a moment, all the fight, all the hope, all the cool confidence, just left him. He went to sit next to Miranda leaning against the wall of the lighthouse. 'Now,' he muttered, 'I guess it's just a matter of time.'

'What?' Miranda could hardly believe what she was hearing. 'Is this it? Is this where it ends? It, it can't be. You always find a way out. Come on.'

'We could swim out to sea, but their boats and helicopters, they'll be around in a little while, we can't escape them like that. But miracles do happen.'

'What's that supposed to mean?'

'It's what we need. A miracle. Just meeting you. That was a little miracle. We've got together, we found what we were both looking for. We've survived long enough to say goodbye to each other. That's a miracle. You're a miracle. Miracles happen, Miranda. And sometimes they run out too.'

'Is that it? Is that your answer? Are you telling me to kneel down and pray?' Miranda looked around at the distant blue horizon, at the eternal waving sea, then peered behind them, around the lighthouse wall at the scurrying soldiers securing the island, getting closer. 'There's got to be a way, we've come too far.'

Ferdinand stood up to take in more of the sea and Miranda followed. 'Miranda. Look. Sometimes you've just got to recognize how far you've come. Whatever happens, it was all still worth it.'

They both peered behind the lighthouse. A troop of soldiers were advancing up towards it, checking every rock on either side as they went.

'This is it, Miranda,' said Ferdinand. 'I just want you to know that I do, will always, love you.'

Miranda burst into tears. They hugged and waited.

Through the wail of fear a buzzing sound began to grow. Ferdinand looked up. Suddenly a small sea-plane was circling above them. It buzzed around the lighthouse. It descended, took a sweep towards the island, turned and landed on the waves a few hundred yards away. They looked at the troops, who had stopped to see what was happening, and then turned back to the plane as it bobbed over the waves nearer and nearer to them. A figure stepped out of the plane and, standing on one of the floats that supported it, he started to wave at them. Ferdinand lifted his binoculars.

'I think he's waving at us. Nobody I know. Friend of yours?' He handed the glasses to Miranda, who peered through and focused on the smiling, waving man.

Miranda waved back. 'Yes,' she said, 'yes, it is. It's Tony Fromnextdoor.'

The Victorians believed that their form of conservative capitalism and the fear of poverty was the only way the world could work, wielding power on a global scale. Religious wars, we all recognize in these godless days, as excuses for grabbing power through creating a fear of wronging a god. Might was right and right to fear. Then, in the wake of the mightiest, the ultimate power of atomic death, came the turnaround to the ideological ambivalence of today. He who could seem least capable of power was trusted to lead. Fear of sincerity prevailed. Veteran actors, smiling PR men, idiots who looked good were the elected representatives as power was thrust onto the say-don't-do, sound-bitten world leaders. And art, like modernism, was always used to separate us and them. The masses couldn't afford art in the nineteenth century and couldn't understand it in the twentieth. Whereas those in power, or finances, could and did. Those without power have always feared art. Always will. That's the point of it.

Fear. Fear. Fear. These all played with fear which is, as I have already demonstrated, the direct conduit to the imagination, life's negative motivation. Do you really believe that these movements were a coincidence, a feeling of the time? Or, more likely, an orchestrated bid for power by one faceless force over another.

And when they've got power they want to keep it. In search of security, these powers have influenced societies to go to war for, or fashion their lives around, principles. Doctrines are invented to keep us in line, defining sets of ethics often considered barely important fifty years before, or after.

So the way we see, feel about, believe in, love, is it really impossible that it has been encouraged, influenced, administered, pushed, by 'the powers that be'? Them. Those we now anonymously call the services?

Certainly, since the twelfth century there have been times when love has had more encouragement, more influence, more air-time, than others. With Oliver Cromwell and the Parliamentarians there is a marked decline in love poetry. The Restoration period afterwards was noted for its rakes rather than its lovers. Then there is the so-called 'Romantic' period where it became central again. Who's to say that the political climates weren't an influence on, if not in direct control of, our attitudes towards love?

Love is the most insipid, subtle and insidious contrivance of these influences. I do not believe in conspiracy, it is as much an imaginative outlet for fear and paranoia as any other, yet looking at these histories with an impartial, open mind, I must accept the possibility that those services which wield power over our lives may be promoting lust, and indoctrinating us with a mythical explanation for it. Love.

30

Whites-of-Their-Eyes

I LOOK AT YOU NOW, SO ABSORBED, SO DEEP WITHIN ME, AND, WELL, I'M sorry, i've been a little irritable recently. It's probably because i, well, we both know that an end is coming, that it must come. i'm sorry though, for the things i said, i don't think i meant them, but now you seem so much more absorbed, certainly much more than Miranda ever was. Perhaps all i needed to do was tell the right story. Maybe all you ever wanted was the Hollywood version.

But we have come so far together and i feel so much a part of you. Maybe it's because you have the end in your sights, the ever-diminishing unknown in the pages in your right hand. And look how the past, in your left, has grown.

i guess i just want you to know, whatever happened and whatever happens, i will take you with me, your smell, the pages you creased, you. You will always be a part of my story as i might be a part of yours. O, and my story, my goodness, what has happened? This was such a temperately paced tale. But now, as i tell it, i realize that in the moment, i hardly had time to think about how fast we were descending from the gentle pace of a love story to some mad action-packed thriller. Suddenly it was all bristling with Gatling guns and stocked with grizzled, military, cigar-chomping characters. Verbs a-go-go. All doing and few feelings. i suppose it is inevitable that as you reach towards an end, a climax, the whirl spins faster. Of course, books are not like life, they always end prematurely.

i should be ashamed of myself or, more accurately, life should be ashamed of itself for creating such an adrenaline-pumped situation which was hardly good for anybody's nerves.

And then, of all things, a miracle, a saviour. Life can really stretch credulity sometimes and indeed is stranger than fiction. However, there was a reason for him appearing like that for, as we know, Tony the computer wizard was less a *deus ex machina* than a *nerdus in machina*.

'Dive.' Never slow to seize an opportunity, Ferdinand grasped Miranda's hand and raced with her to the rocks on the furthest edge of the lighthouse causeway. 'Dive,' he repeated.

They looked at the churning waters that eddied around and under the rocks, then at each other, and plunged together into the waves. In the suddenly cold, suddenly quiet, water, Miranda's dress fluttered gently against her body, quivering through the slow, floating other world of the sea. A moment of peace, encased in the tranquil, liquid movement of the tides.

Miranda's lungs abruptly tired. She broke the surface gasping and looking about. The soldiers, smaller now, were running up the causeway. Some had stopped and were kneeling, squinting into their gun sights. Occasionally there was the ominous whistle of water strafed by a bullet, but none too close. Ferdinand came up from the water a little further out. He looked back at her and beckoned. They swam on. They pushed through the water encouraging each other with smiles and kick-splashes until Ferdinand reached the plane. He pulled himself up onto the leg float. Then, with Tony one side and Ferdinand the other, she was pulled dripping from the sea.

'It looks like I got here just in time,' Tony beamed.

'Yes, thanks,' said Ferdinand busily and then pointing at the soldiers arriving at the lighthouse, 'though if we don't get this thing up in the air, we might still be too late.'

'This is?' Tony said to Miranda.

'His name's Ferdinand. Look. We're in a bit of a hurry. Can we just go? Please.'

'Of course,' Tony smiled, 'of course.'

Miranda climbed up to the cabin with a little bit of over-enthusiastic bottom pushing from Tony. He piled in after her, yapping orders at the pilot, and even as Ferdinand was climbing the ladder, the plane was already picking up speed, out to sea and away from the soldiers at the lighthouse.

'Please strap yourselves in. This may be a touch bumpy,' the pilot said with archetypal over-calming, cockpit understatement, even as they jolted and jerked violently over each wave that buffeted them. The plane was thrown from one side to the other with no regard to the delicate sense of balance the human inner ear needs to maintain in order to prevent upwardly mobile airline food. Ferdinand barely had time to pull himself in before the plane reached take-off velocity and began to skim the water, kicking through the higher waves until at last they were airborne. As it climbed steeply Tony looked at Miranda with glee.

'Holidaying? It looks a lovely place. Did you have fun?' he asked, as if absently flipping through their holiday snaps on a slow Sunday afternoon.

'Tony?' Miranda said.

'It really is good to see you, Miranda, in the flesh, it is always quite different.'

'Tony?'

'I thought they might have got you; it looks like you did a good job avoiding them. I knew they were on to me but I never thought I was putting you at such risk.'

'Tony, what are you doing here?'

'Well, I really just came to see you.'

'Tony, you live in a bedsit in Shepherd's Bush. Less than a fortnight ago were a penniless benefit artist, drawing the dole. What the fuck are you doing with a sea-plane, flying about Venetian islands and rescuing people from the army of Satan?'

Tony looked out of the window. 'Oh no, they look pretty human to me.'

'What I'm trying to say, Tony, let me put this in more familiar terminology.' Miranda gestured around her. 'This does not compute.'

'Well, of course it computes,' Tony replied, 'that's exactly what it does. That's how I found you, you logged on to the IBT network and you told me you were there.' He pointed out of the window towards the rapidly vanishing island. Ferdinand looked at Miranda quizzically.

'No, I didn't,' Miranda said, shaking her head.

'Switch card?'

'Well, yes, I did get some money out,' said Miranda.

Ferdinand's eyes widened. 'You used the teller machine in the village?'

'Well, I'd just swum out there, I didn't have any money. I fancied a drink and, well, yes. So?'

'That's how they knew,' said Ferdinand, 'that's how they knew you were there.'

Tony looked at Ferdinand. 'They?' he said. 'They were keeping a tab on her account too?'

'Of course. The moment you put the card in the machine, it dialled home and . . .' Ferdinand stopped and looked at Tony. 'What do you mean "too"?'

'I've had a basic alarm routine running on Miranda's account since she disappeared.'

'You can do that? Who are you? You're not Six? Seven?'

'I am not a number,' Tony told him triumphantly, 'I am a free man!'

'Sorry to bother you, sir,' the pilot murmured back with his silky calm voice, 'but the radar is showing three objects approaching from six o'clock, rate two hundred and twenty knots, closing.'

'Sycorax,' said Ferdinand, 'whoever you are, you're not their friend.'

At that moment, and yet again, Mercy found herself being talked to, or more accurately at, by a doctor. This time, however, it was a military surgeon at the Vicenza airbase, replete and ready for surgery, scrubs and mask on, gloves held up like a surrendering cowboy.

'Bullets never come in singles any more. It's all these automatic weapons they have nowadays, everything gets peppered with lead and really we're back to medieval solutions whenever limbs encounter that sort of action.'

'Amputation, you mean,' said Mercy, looking at him spitefully. She was not to be humoured with euphemism considering she was hand-cuffed and chained to a water pipe.

'Well, considering the state of his other limbs he might find that it even helps his balance, he is off centre and this might help his mobility.'

'How do you work out that having no legs will help his mobility?'

The doctor paused and Mercy watched the eyes above the mask search the air for a positive response. 'He'll be lighter on a wheelchair?'

'How far to home?' Tony leaned over the pilot's shoulder and looked at the radar's bleeping dots of light.

'Approximately fifteen minutes before we enter our airspace.'

'And how long before they catch up with us?'

'Sir, they're within missile-striking distance as we speak.'

'But they haven't fired.'

'No. Not yet anyway.' The pilot looked back at Ferdinand. 'You said Sycorax?'

'Yes.'

The pilot had immediately recognized something military about Ferdinand, just like him; another who had stepped onto the other side. 'Ordnance?'

'Usual side-arms, mounted machine guns. Combination of missiles. Pair of heat-seeking at sides and one guided, centre-mounted.'

'Any idea why they haven't fired yet?'

'Maybe they think they've got a friend on board.' Ferdinand looked meaningfully at Tony.

The pilot followed his eye-line. 'No. Not him. He's friendless.'

Miranda sulked in her seat and looked out of the window. It was all so masculine, talking in objects, guns, actions, time, space, movement. Where did the heart fit into all of that? What was the velocity of love, the position of tears, the fire power of feelings? But then, as she watched Ferdinand, so comfortable dealing with these right here, right now, problems of time and space, she smiled. Whenever he galumphed into her world of the emotional he lost that beautiful self-assurance that had struck her and made her desire him so much. He was like a virgin, touching and feeling emotions, trying them out, seeing what they did, how they fit, where they went. But here, in the world of guns and speed and things, he was so much more at ease. Maybe it was unfair of her to take him away from all this. And if they ever got away? Would he ever really be happy, doing something safe with his life, bringing up kids, letting her be the limits of his life, his goals, his ambitions? Maybe she would just be destroying the very things that she found so wonderful and reassuring about him.

Tony, having been frozen out of the conversation as the other men started speaking in acronyms and armoury, made his way back to Miranda. 'Exciting, isn't it?'

'I still don't understand how we ended up here.'

'Well, I don't quite know why you ended up so close to my gaff,' said Tony, 'but it's like I said. I was worried that they had got you so I came out looking for you.'

'They being?'

'You know. The ones following us, for a start. The ones who don't want me finishing Everything 1.1. The ones that know I have special feelings for you. I'm not sure who they are, a sort of international group of secret service agencies. I will find out. That bloke you're with probably knows a lot more than he's said.'

'Tony. They're not after you. They're after him, and me because I'm with him.'

'That's what he's told you, isn't it?'

Miranda thought for a moment. 'Yes,' she said, 'that's true.'

'So maybe,' continued Tony quickly, talking closely into her ear over the roar of the engines, 'maybe he's just told you things and set this whole thing up to get to me. Look, here he is, in my plane, being chased by some helicopters armed to the gunwales and they're not firing.' Tony nodded at her conspiratorially. 'It's a thought, isn't it?'

Miranda's credulity factor had been shot to bits some time before, so now she was willing to believe that anything was possible. But when any lie might be true, or any truth a lie, then you might as well be selective purely on the basis of your own desires. Tony could have been right, she supposed, but she didn't want him to be, so by that one and only token he wasn't. When reason abandons you, all you have to follow is your heart.

A new beating, throbbing sound quickly grew all about them. 'They're here,' shouted the pilot. Miranda looked out of the window. On either side of them a nasty black helicopter buzzed menacingly. The third, she supposed, was right behind them, or above.

Captain Remington-Wilkinson-Gillette wasn't born; he was moulded, formed from the very pink, durable, washable plastic that Action Man himself is fashioned from. For all we know, he may have had no genitals and the knobbly lettering 'Made in Taiwan' stamped into the small of his back. Pure-bred for swinging on ropes and bashing sharks, he was a man at the extremes of self-sufficiency. And in that, he was not a natural leader. It is difficult to tell others to do things when you can do it all better yourself. The trouble is that in a hierarchy like the army, you bash enough sharks, you then have to tell other people to do it. But Remington-Wilkinson-Gillette always wanted to fly that chopper, jump that gorge, fight that man, hand to hand, no weapons, just the muscles and brawn that Hasbro had blessed him with. He was what was known in the ranks as a WOE soldier, not because he was particularly sad or needed to be reined in, which he was and did, but because he would never want to engage the enemy until he saw the Whites-Of-their-Eyes. He hated to eliminate any opponent without seeing him first, especially one as slippery as Umber. That is why they had pursued the sea-plane south-east for ten minutes without launching missiles; he wasn't going to let Umber go down in a blaze of fire until he had seen the fear in his eyes. Confirmed the kill.

As the three Sycoraxes matched the speed of the sea-plane, drawing alongside it, Remington-Wilkinson-Gillette looked over to the cockpit and saw Umber for the first time. Typical military intelligence fast-tracker, good-looking, clean-shaven, probably spoke ten different languages, as if it mattered what the wops and wogs of this disposable world spoke. Why talk to them when you're only going to kill them or bomb them or at least impose toilet-paper sanctions and watch them shit themselves? He looked at Umber with all the hate that the passed-over repress through their lives. He waved to him, laughing past his cigar, 'You're dead himbo.' His helmet radio crackled.

'Sir, four and a half minutes to Serbian air space. We need to down him now, sir.'

Remington-Wilkinson-Gillette switched his radio handset to an open wavelength. 'Four Nine Sea Plane Delta Six, this is SYX Leader. You are in violation of international transport codes, harbouring a known terrorist, please change course to three point seven degrees north and proceed to Vicenza. Over.'

No answer. 'Four Nine Sea Plane Delta Six, this is SYX Leader. You have been warned. If you do not change course immediately we will have to engage our weapons to stop you.'

No answer.

'Three minutes and fifty seconds to Serbian air space. It is a no-fly zone, sir.'

'I know it's a no bloody fly zone, it's no flying for the bloody Serbs, not us.'

'Sir, I'm sure you know that if we enter the zone it may be considered as a violation of the current treaties and seen as an act of aggress—'

'Shut up, soldier.' He knew only too well, but now he was ready. He had booked the best seat to watch Umber's smug smile get wiped off his face and all over the Adriatic. 'And fire at will,' he snarled.

'Roger. Request for you to draw back, sir, the blast may have impact on your craft.'

'Oh, bloody hell.' Remington-Wilkinson-Gillette steered his Sycorax away from the sea-plane, drawing parallel again some five hundred yards away.

Ferdinand watched the Sycoraxes move away, at both sides and behind, and knew it was in readiness for the final blow. The pilot looked at Ferdinand.

'What do you reckon they'll fire first?'

'The heat-seekers are cheaper, but the guided one can be recovered if it misses and, let's face it, it's more fun to run.'

'Let's give them a run then.' The pilot suddenly pushed his stick forward and the plane nose-dived towards the water. The pursuing Sycorax went screaming after them. Miranda felt sicker than a month of binges, but with no toilet to crown herself and the g-force pushing her larynx into her ears, making even swallowing difficult, she kept it down, watching, transfixed, through the front window, the dizzying, shining waves getting closer.

A few yards above the big blue wall, the pilot swung the plane up again and violently pulled out of the dive. Miranda's head snapped back against the seat and smashed loudly against the cabin's back wall. They skimmed along the waves. The pilot watched as the following Sycorax descended and attempted to draw up behind him. The plane was so low it felt as if it was nearly surfing, the teeth-gritting speed was all too evident now they were so close to the surface.

'Hit a wave at this speed and we'll all be in the soup, the Donald Campbell's soup,' the pilot laughed, obviously enjoying the near-death experience more than most of his passengers. Miranda noticed that Tony had turned that unpleasant shade of pastel green that covers the walls of old hospitals and large institutions.

At this low altitude, the following Sycorax found itself in a little trouble. To retain the speed, it needed to be tipped forward at nearly forty-five degrees. Its propellers were close to clipping the water and the helicopter pilot realized that he needed to back off a little and gain some altitude again. The sea-plane had bought itself a little time. Tipped as it was, it was impossible for the Sycorax to establish a lock-on target for its guided missile and, so close to the water, the air-to-air weaponry had no space to right itself. Fired now, it would just hit the surface of the water, doing nothing more than damaging the fishing quota of the area for a few decades.

Ferdinand was saying something into the pilot's ear. The pilot nodded and pointed to where Miranda was sitting. Ferdinand approached Miranda and knelt down in front of her. He calmly parted her legs, smiling. Miranda supposed that if they only had seconds left to live anything was worth a try and smiled back welcomingly. Ferdinand reached down to the toolbox stored under her seat and found a small blowtorch used for emergency welding. He got up again, lit it and turned its dial until a pure blue flame pointed from the nozzle. He nodded to Miranda and shouted to her, 'I'm just popping out,' like he was Captain Oates. He opened the plane door and climbed out.

As the Sycorax rose to about fifty metres, the heat-seekers at either side were primed. Needing no direct visual lock-on, they would just sense out the sea-plane's engines and blow it neatly into the deep. The helicopter pilot flipped a few switches, arming the heat-seeker warheads.

Miranda undid her safety belt and rushed to the plane's door to look out. The cross-wind almost sucked her out of the cabin and she grabbed hold of the doorframe. Below her, she watched Ferdinand holding on for his life as he edged down the leg float to the back of the plane, his blowtorch still glowing.

Behind them Miranda could see the pursuing helicopter. It rushed close to their back and then slowed down to recover a decent missile-launching angle. She noticed that there was clear liquid jetting out of the chassis of the plane and smelt petrol. She shouted inside to the pilot, 'I think you might have a leak.'

'No,' the pilot yelled back again, his finger on a little switch above his head, 'I'm jettisoning fuel.'

Miranda looked out again. The Sycorax was far behind them but now it seemed as if its sides were detaching themselves. Her eyes widened as she realized that these were the missiles coming straight for them. They dropped down slowly to the sea-plane's altitude and sped towards them.

Ferdinand reached over towards the middle of the plane and dropped his blowtorch into the rushing water where the fuel was streaming out. The water beneath the plane instantly burst into flames which shot backwards as they flew forward. Suddenly the plane lifted sharply and Miranda slid down the floor. Ferdinand clung to a strut. Behind them, a blazing trail of fire spread out, flames licking the surface of the water as the inferno stretched like a vast, flashing, orange blade erupting from the sea.

The missiles hit the wall of flame first. Heat found, they exploded in two enormous flashes of pure burning white. The pursuing Sycorax, though it tried to pull up, never had a chance. It flew directly into the blinding force of the blast and was instantly ripped apart in a molten fountain of fiery clouds.

There was no noise to the explosion, just the billowing colours and shapes, the sparks that glided into the sky and then arced back to earth. There was only the roar of the plane as it climbed away from the fireball.

'Nearly on our patch,' shouted the pilot as he pointed down to one of the large warships that coursed the Adriatic, slowly patrolling the potential war zone edge of the Yugoslavian coast.

Remington-Wilkinson-Gillette watched the smoking wreckage of the Sycorax spinning down into the water with rage and disbelief. Umber had escaped the destroyed café and now he had blown up another bloody helicopter. The captain looked up at the sea-plane soaring away from the fire and there he was, Burnt bloody Umber, still clinging to the plane, unable to get back to the cabin under the sheer wind pressure of the climb, but still very much alive. As usual, the captain found himself thinking: if you want a job doing, you've got to do it yourself.

'Take us close in to that little bastard,' he barked at his co-pilot and stalked back to the fixed side guns. He tore the door open and, placing his hands on the twin machine-gun trigger-handles, he screamed at Ferdinand's little figure, 'You're dead, you little fuck!'

Even though he was out of range of both voice and bullets, he rattled off a few rounds just to relieve the frustration as they got closer. He was going to get to see the whites of Umber 's eyes after all.

At less than five hundred yards Remington-Wilkinson-Gillette let off a volley of bullets which strafed the side of the plane. That would scare them. He aimed carefully at Ferdinand as he got closer. He waited, waited for that delicious moment, his fingers twitched as the sights filled with Ferdinand's helpless clinging body.

There is much to be said for regular trips to the opticians, however good you think your eyes are. If this had all happened just a year before, Remington-Wilkinson-Gillette's slowly advancing near-sightedness would have been just those few yards better. But time and optometrists wait for no man. In the closing of the three yards between seeing the eyes and seeing their whites, between looking at and looking into Ferdinand's deep green irises, Remington-Wilkinson-Gillette's NATO Sycorax invaded more than just Ferdinand's personal space, but Serbian air space as well.

With a jolt, Remington-Wilkinson-Gillette was thrown backwards as the Sycorax banked sharply away from the plane.

'No,' he shouted at the gods, 'no.' He scrabbled back to the open doorway as the helicopter righted itself and watched the sea-plane fly off towards the Montenegrin coastline.

'Get me the Awacs,' the captain grunted into his helmet mike, 'they have to trace that cunt.'

*

Nobody spoke. They had done it, they had escaped, Ferdinand was still hanging on and the plane was now descending gracefully over the placid waters of a large bay, a long, lake-like sea inlet surrounded by mountains. It skimmed the mirror-like waters, churning up a shower of fine spray behind it, and steadily slowed to a drift. Ferdinand climbed back in as the plane gently motored towards a pier. 'We home, then?' he said. 'Tivatski Bay, isn't it?'

Tony nodded and Miranda looked out at the new scenery. Craggy mountains towered above the tranquil waters, their skirts covered in dense forest, their upper grey peaks tipped with Toblerone snowcaps. The shore line was fringed with tall trees arching over narrow beaches, in a state of unspoilt nature. Up on one mountainside, a large red-brick, half-timbered, Tudor-style house emerged above the trees. Smoke gently rose from some of the house's tall chimneys. 'Where are we?' she said.

'Welcome to Serbia and Montenegro,' said the pilot, 'home of the best warmongers this side of Attila.'

'And did Henry the Eighth live here and all then?' she said, pointing at the house.

'No,' smiled Tony, his colour returning, 'that's just a whim of mine. Home from home.'

'It's yours?'

'Practically everything you see is mine. I bought it last year.'

'Tony,' said Miranda, 'I know a giro can go a long way in a struggling economy, but this is insane.'

'Miranda, money is just a set of numbers like anything else.'

'Oh shit,' she interrupted him, 'we're not out of it yet, they've sent a landing party.' A group of heavily armed men in very tired, camouflage fatigues were pounding up the pier.

Tony looked and then smiled that smile which was getting rather annoying now. 'Don't worry, they're mine too.' He raised his eyebrows.

The plane drew alongside the pier next to a powerful-looking speed boat. The passengers climbed out onto the wooden-slatted jetty to be saluted by the armed guard. Tony began speaking to the apparent leader and Ferdinand whispered to Miranda, 'You've got powerful friends. Are there things that you haven't told me?'

'No,' Miranda shook her head. 'A couple of weeks ago he was the no-hoper living next to me, now he's Howard fucking Hughes.'

'Does he know who I am?'

'Don't ask me. He seems to know my inside leg measurements so it wouldn't surprise me.'

Tony turned back to them. 'Miranda and um . . .' He looked at Ferdinand.

'Ferdinand,' said Ferdinand.

'Ferdinand, of course, well, you are my guests. Come on; let's get up to the house, we'll just be in time for the six o'clock news and a lime juice and gin.'

'You betcha, man,' Ferdinand said, winking hospitably at him. The three walked towards the shore, with the soldiers marching behind them.

CHAPTER XII.

INSIDE THE MINISTRY OF LOVE

> Double think means the power of holding
> two contradictory beliefs in one's mind simul-
> taneously, and accepting both of them . . .
> . . . War is Peace, Freedom is Slavery,
> Ignorance is Strength . . .
> George Orwell (1903–1950), *1984*

. . . AND FEAR IS LOVE. IN THE COURSE OF THESE RESEARCHES I
have had to accept a number of startling conclusions about love.
Firstly, that being 'in love' is not a completely natural emotional state.

We don't, after all, actually need love. In the hierarchy of our
needs it rates far down the list, next to the luxuries, long after
air, water, food, warmth, shelter, security, genetic perpetuation,
self-esteem and so on.

However, what the emotion of being in love does do for us
is make us susceptible to victimization by anyone who may
have a more dispassionate controlling interest.

There is much to suggest that there are, and always have
been, controlling interests; that there is a systematic and well-
established form of emotional brainwashing – heartwashing
perhaps – in use today.

The true powers behind what we know as the State are, in
all probability, the ones who perpetuate this exploitative, mad,
sad and destructive emotional force that we call love to meet
their own ends: a stable populace, made up of insecure, unsta-
ble individuals, who have no interest in insurgence.

In his novel *1984*, George Orwell describes a civil service
department which orchestrates the mass brainwashing of the
public. Its headquarters harbour the infamous 'Room 101'
that contains one's greatest fear. Whoever is suspected of not
loving (Big Brother) is punished by being exposed to their
fear.

Does this sound familiar? Has my thesis, so far, pointed to the workings of such a State department? Orwell called it the 'Ministry of Love'.

If those in the services, the 'them' who co-ordinate and influence love, are some clandestine part of the State system, am I suggesting that we really do have a secret 'Ministry of Love'? Could there really be a covert powerful State unit orchestrating our emotions and encouraging our fixation on loving, not Big Brother, but our perceived 'beloved'?

To be honest, after I had gathered all the evidence that you have read so far, I did start to believe that perhaps this was true. All the facts that I had amassed to this point seemed to indicate that there really was a 'Ministry of Love'. Orwell was not writing fiction but fact simply dressed as fancy. We can only speculate that if he had written the facts as they really were, not only would we probably not have believed them, but possibly 'they', the true Ministry of Love, would have welcomed him into his own personal Room 101. However, as it was, Orwell that Ends Well.

A terrible pun and not much of a conclusion I know but, when I first completed this thesis, this really was as far as it went.

It seemed that in the course of my researches I had amassed a wealth of circumstantial evidence and yet not a drop of forensic proof. Thankfully, in this over-analysed world, one which has practically run out of true facts to expose, academia and historical hypothesis require much less rigour than a court of law. There, the overwhelming weight of circumstantial evidence may make a compelling case but not an established one. The lucky academic doesn't have to prove that anything is definite, just provide enough evidence to make the opposite case appear more sound than we had hitherto suspected. Love as the result of social brainwash appeared to me not just a possibility but a distinct probability.

Then, after an encounter in the heart of the very State mechanism I had been examining, I was furnished with all the forensic proof I could wish for.

There comes a time in many dons' lives, perhaps at high table, or, in my case, at the urinals of the St Giles Public Convenience, when they are approached with a message. The messenger will draw them aside and quietly tell them that they are required to see a 'Man In Victoria'.

31

Birnam Wood

'ZERO POINT ZERO ZERO ONE PER CENT ON THE STAMP DUTY OF EVERY share deal on the Hong Kong, Tokyo, London and New York stock exchanges,' said Tony, as he gestured around the echoing great hall of his mock-Tudor mansion. Miranda looked blankly at him. 'Every time anyone buys or sells shares,' Tony continued, blowing some mock-dust from a mock-grandfather clock, 'he pays a small levy for the privilege to the relevant stock exchange and that in turn pays a small levy to my funds through a chain of various international banks. All, of course, in a good cause. The wonderful thing is, it is quite undetectable because the system is so automatic, and even if anyone has noticed it, the drain hole is so small, it's not worth their time and money to fix it. But, altogether, it is a million or so every month. And that's what built this, bought them,' he pointed at a soldier stationed by the door. 'It's not stealing, Miranda. It's just prioritizing. It's making sure that Everything 1.1 runs to the end of its natural sequence. It really is for the good of the whole world.'

At that point Ferdinand called Tony a deluded, lying madman.

In fact, he just coughed. A little polite clearing of the throat, but it's amazing what you can do with ticklish tonsils. Ferdinand's cough was one of those subtle linguistic masterpieces that litter daily lives, where the sound itself speaks volumes but commits to nothing. He made it with the right force and timing to not only express a dubious cynicism but to declare that Tony had left the rails of sanity a long way before the last station. 'Everything 1.1?' he said, following up the cough with just enough conviction to throw its meaning into a little doubt.

But they all knew what he was saying. Tony looked at him as if he had just hawked up a yard of green bile and silently turned back to Miranda. 'It's an exact replica of Thomas More's house, the one he had in Chelsea, you know, man for all seasons. Utopia.'

Miranda didn't know. 'A replica, why?'

'I like it. But it's perfect here, the whole area looks like Europe did three hundred years ago. It's the only part of Serbia that's close to Europe and yet is a law unto itself. I'm hardly the only outlaw here.'

'Yes,' said Ferdinand, 'you and several hundred war criminals.' Tony finally recognized that Ferdinand was sentient.

'It's important for the world that my work is finished, so if it has to be here, somewhere where the West can't touch me, then it might as well be in the sort of environment I like. This country is the future. It's for the minds that think outside of the usual mind-set of the propaganda of the West. The minds who want freedom, a place where they can think freely without fear of persecution, without the heat and flies of the third world or the strictures of fundamentalism. They will gather here. Those who can think outside the box.'

'Out of their boxes,' Ferdinand said, 'loonies who can't hack the real world, and criminals. This is a country founded on genocide.'

'What country isn't?'

Ferdinand struggled and nodded.

'So, let me get this straight,' said Miranda. 'You were never as poor as you pretended. But you lived in a bedsit in Shepherd's Bush, what, just for the fun of it?'

'It was a good cover, some small-minded bureaucratic law-enforcement agencies would probably call what I'm doing fraud, and fraudsters are generally caught when people notice that they're suddenly rich. But it's not fraud. It's fraud when the money is an end in itself. I'm reappropriating, tapping funds which the West is too narrow-minded to offer me to continue my research.' Tony stopped and looked towards his shoes and almost whispered, 'And, and, and it was nice being close to you.'

Suddenly Ferdinand, a life-long betrayer of no emotion, mainly because for most of it he had no emotions to betray, quietly but visibly bristled. The oh so cool, neither shaken nor stirred, super secret agent was facing his first emotional crisis and didn't know what to do with it. Already he had been placed in a bedroom in the West Wing while

434

Tony and Miranda had rooms in the East Wing. Tony's interest in Miranda was obvious enough, geek or not; he dominated the space around her and, for the first time in Ferdinand's life, a little jealousy crept into his limited emotional repertoire. He was growing, he could tell, growing is always painful. Perhaps he should tell Tony, in no uncertain terms, that he and Miranda were together. But then, not only was he a guest, he really could not afford to anger his host, especially as Tony was the only thing between him and the combined wrath of the Nato forces. Then the killer thought struck him, one that had downed many a more emotionally aware person than he: perhaps Miranda would prefer this old neighbour of hers now he turned out to be a multi-millionaire. And the jealousy twisted a little more painfully inside him.

During the entire tour of the house Miranda found herself, annoyingly, thwarted of any opportunity to talk with Ferdinand. When, finally, Tony had to visit his own mock-Tudor 'little boy's room', Ferdinand, even more frustratingly, told her not to mention their relationship. She shouldn't let it burden her. So, when they all went off to their separate rooms, Miranda felt somewhat aggravated by the way these two men acted with each other. If she had realized that each, in his own way, was fighting over her, it might have made her feel happily smug. As it was, it was all whispers and half-truths and she felt that a tangled web might be being woven which she would, inevitably, blunder through at some point. Because that's what she did whenever she tried to lie.

As if they were refugees from a Noël Coward play, they all dressed for dinner that evening. Black tie was laid on for Ferdinand and Miranda found, on her bed, a dress that looked a million dollars, which meant it looked more conservative than it cost; with a galaxy of diamonds sown, like sequins, about it and a designer name-tag. After sneaking a look at herself in it, and realizing how cheap she looked in contrast to the couture smock about her, she laid it aside and donned the familiar, comfortable little black number she had been wearing since she burnt down the hut.

In the high-beamed, mock-tapestry-hung dining hall, in front of a massive crackling fireplace, sitting at a long, solid, dark oak table, soup was a quiet slurping of meaningful looks and indulgent smiles. At last, before the main course arrived, Tony at the head of the table put down his mock-tankard and turned to Ferdinand.

'So what do you do for a living, then?' he said, as if he were the sceptical father of a prospective bride.

'Actually, I quit recently but, until two weeks ago, I was a spy.'

Tony's cool broke. Let's face it, he was never very good at it anyway. 'Really?' he said with all the puppy's tongue-lolling admiration that only an anorak and fantasist can express. 'Wow!'

Ferdinand raised his glass to him.

'So, like, you were on to me?' asked Tony. 'You work for the State?'

'I did.'

'Is that how you could do all that stuff with the helicopters?'

'No. That was just bravado and stupidity.'

'So what do they know?'

'About you?'

Tony nodded and Ferdinand shrugged. 'Nothing as far as I know. Hacker working in the Balkans? That about the size of it?'

'I'm not a hacker, I'm an environmentalist, I'm redistributing wealth that was raped from this area over the last centuries.'

Ferdinand smiled; he had met a lot of Bloemfeldt wannabes, but this was quite pathetic.

Tony looked at Miranda, 'Do you believe him?'

Miranda nodded.

'So,' said Tony to Ferdinand, 'what were all those troops doing there?' As he spoke, a small, flat-chested, dark-haired Yugoslavian girl, swallowed by an ill-fitting mock-serving wench's outfit, entered bearing a Renaissance wholenut stuffed tofu vegetarian banquet.

Of course we, like Miranda, have been through all this before, but less omniscient characters, real people, i'm afraid, have to sit through the drudgery of catching up with each other and pooling their stories. The better class of book, which does not feel the need to reiterate or fill space, will politely look away at these points whilst the regurgitation takes place. So i think it is sufficient to say that Ferdinand told Tony the truth about love and about me. Being a dedicated conspiranoiac, Tony listened enraptured with the whole notion of the conspiracy behind emotions and behind conspiracies themselves.

'Can I see it?' he had pleaded. 'Please.' And when i was brought to him, 'Let me scan it, the whole book. I'll put the whole thing up on the internet, we've got to give this thing to the world,' appealing to a communal instinct that Ferdinand had not quite developed yet. Ferdinand shrugged.

'Ask Miranda, it's hers.'

Miranda suddenly looked up, realizing that she had almost dozed off. 'What?'

'Your book, can I scan it?'

'Do you mean you want to read it?'

'No. I mean make a computer copy so I can publish it on the internet so the whole world can see what the State has been keeping from them.'

'Er, sure,' said Miranda, 'I didn't write it or anything.'

But she had, in a way, hadn't she?

Over an indescribable mockery of a Tudor pudding, Tony told Ferdinand all about Everything 1.1 and how he had financed Balkan Telecom to get broadband telephone links to their shores to keep his connection with the program running in London.

'It's the future,' he looked dreamily up at the high mock-rafters describing his vision. 'The West is policing the internet more and more. Eventually it will be impossible for the free voice to speak out on it. And that's when the struggling countries of this world will come into their own. The authorities can only cut off the supply, not the distribution, so all the questionable "free" voices of truth will base themselves in places like this and will turn the economies of their host countries around. The third world will become the first.'

Snoring into her plate, Miranda suddenly woke. 'I'm sorry,' she said, pushing her chair back and standing a little unsteadily, 'I'm very tired and I must go to bed.' She departed wobbling.

'Long day,' said Ferdinand. 'Listen, Tony, can I use your e-mail?'

Tony looked at him suspiciously. 'To warn your bosses? Tell them where you are?'

'If I were, I'd use my cigarette lighter e-mailer gadget, wouldn't I?'

Tony thought about that. 'It doesn't really matter if you do. There's no way they'd get in here. This place is guarded by a small standing army, they'd have to send troops in, and considering the political sensitivity of the area that won't be happening soon.'

'I've still got to get out of here though,' said Ferdinand, omitting to include Miranda. 'I need to send an e-mail to the Americans. I have a date with the US.'

So the men left the table and descended to the bunker-like cellar of the Tudor mansion, an ultramodern air-conditioned computer room. Everything 1.1 was there, still running happily, picking up pictures from London.

Tony took me and subjected me to the most uncomfortable, clinical and degrading reading i have ever experienced. Each page creased open like some anatomical pornography and laid on a glass and eyed up and down by a photo-eye. The things one does for posterity. Only the photocopy machine, with its blinding, ink-fading light, holds more fear for the sensitive book.

Meanwhile, Ferdinand sent an encrypted e-mail to a friend @cia.gov.us.

Miranda woke up. She wasn't quite sure what woke her but she looked about her night-dark mock-chamber for mock-headless ghosts. Nothing moved. It had definitely been something. She knelt up on the bed, gripping one of its four posts. Then it came again, a muffled knocking. Miranda got up and crossed to the big old oak door. She opened it a little and peered out. Tony stood there with a candle. As soon as their eyes met he looked down and started talking to his feet.

'I was wondering, I was thinking, I was, well, I just thought, I might, like, ask again. I mean you might have changed your mind, now, now you've seen this, what I do.'

'Changed my mind?' Miranda was still a little sleep-bewildered.

'What I asked you, the last time I saw you, in Shepherd's Bush.' Tony caught her eye for a moment and looked back at his shoes.

'Oh, oh yes,' Miranda realized that memory best serves the things of relative importance. Tony could obviously remember their night in every detail. Miranda had wiped it.

'So, maybe you have?'

'Um, well, Tony.'

'Now that you've seen this place, now you've seen what I do, how I live.' Tony dared to meet her gaze. 'Miranda, you'd live like a princess, anything you wanted, it's all, all possible.'

Of course a princess was exactly what she wanted to be when she was a little girl, a fairy one preferably. And here was a prince, in his castle, offering her the world, and she realized that had it been a few weeks ago, before Ferdinand, she'd have probably taken it. I mean the prince might be a bit geeky but, well, men were built to be changed, weren't they? But, whatever she did, he'd never be Ferdinand. She looked at his pleading dog-eyes.

'Tony, I wish. Things have changed for me, my world, it's kind of broadened,' even as she was saying it she knew that the 'we're not suited' routine wouldn't work, Tony seemed to have the sort of money that could shift the world if she wanted it. She searched her repertoire of let-downs, she had been exposed to enough in her time, and she went for the very worst, the totally indisputable 'it's-not-you-it's-me' line. 'I just wouldn't be good for you, I'm too demanding.' Miranda hated herself as the words issued from her very own lips. 'You deserve someone good and sweet and who could really give you . . .'

To be honest i find myself loath to continue. What she said made her cringe and Tony cry. He sobbed, and turned and left. Miranda watched his candle disappearing down the hall and wondered for a moment why Ferdinand hadn't found his way to her room. God, she wished he was there.

Dawn broke over Tivatski Bay like a hymen, bleeding red sun into the still water and bathing the high, clear sheets of mountain snow in deep crimson. Something had disturbed the area, something had destroyed the virgin peace of that once unspoilt part of the world. Something large and long and hard and wet.

A grey battleship, flying the Union Jack and the Nato Globe, had stationed itself just out from the entrance to the bay. Huge, silent and menacing, it had anchored according to a very liberal interpretation of what marked the boundary of Montenegrin waters. Its guns pointed to the air like the morning glory of a military might.

'Red sky in the morning,' Ferdinand muttered as he watched the scene from his binoculars. 'What colour would you say that was? Rose Madder or Vermilion Lake?'

Ferdinand handed the binoculars to Tony. The two had been woken before dawn by Tony's Serbian sergeant-at-arms and had climbed up the side of the mountain to the lookout that had first spotted the ship. There, above the tree line, they could see far out over the Adriatic. Tony studied the ship through the binoculars. 'Do you think they mean business?'

'They might just be trying to scare us.'

'They wouldn't dare send in troops,' said Tony, 'not unless they wanted to risk sparking off the bloodiest Balkan crisis since Archduke Ferdinand took a Sunday drive in Sarajevo.'

Ferdinand was not so sure. He knew that they wouldn't go quietly. Something was cooking. He looked again to see if any other ships were in the area but it was just the menacing presence of that steel tub, filled with the men he was once proud to call his colleagues. 'Don't worry, they're not after you, they're only here for one thing.' Ferdinand looked seriously at Tony as he put down the binoculars. 'Me.'

Tony nodded and peered back through the glasses.

'And,' said Ferdinand, 'I'll be leaving in the next couple of days.'

'When do you think?'

'Depends on the answer to my e-mail.'

On the way back down through the woods the two men descended silently. As a prelude to talking and saying something that he was not exactly comfortable saying, Tony started shuffling his feet and stuttering.

'She's, she's, she's very nice, isn't she?'

'Who?' asked Ferdinand as if he didn't know.

'Miranda. She's, um, special.'

'Yes, she is very nice. Is that a wood pigeon, that sound?'

'I, I really like her.'

'It is. I haven't heard one of those for ages.'

'Ferdinand, I, I've always loved her.'

Ferdinand stopped Tony with a fraternal hand to the shoulder. 'Have you told her?'

'I, well, yes, last night I.'

'Last night? You saw her last night?' Deep in that darkling forest a monster was roused and its eyes were green.

'Yes, I, went to her door.'

'What happened?'

'Happened? Well, I asked her to, if she would like to, stay, here.'

'And she said?'

Tony looked up suddenly. 'You know, I think it is a wood pigeon.'

Ferdinand felt his deeper breath returning. 'Maybe now isn't the right time, eh?'

They trudged the rest of the way down pretending to be ornithologists.

Although, through the day, the lookout reported any and all movements on board the battle-cruiser, the ship maintained the appearance of being merely docked for routine exercises.

After lunch, Tony excused himself to go to his computer room and finally, at last, Ferdinand and Miranda were alone together. Seeking privacy and intimacy, they went up the spiralling staircase that led to the roof of the house. Up, high above the world, in their own private heaven, they sat next to each other on the steeply raked tiles of the chapel and looked out over the bay.

Still too low to see the warship over the mountainous promontory that protected the bay, Ferdinand silently wondered if he should tell her that it was there. She looked so happy. How could he tell her that they were not out of the woods by a long shot? That the enemy were not vanquished, merely gathering strength. The next time, whatever they did, they would come at them a hundred times harder than they did before. Not that he hadn't been in similar situations before, waiting for the enemy's move, watching Birnam Wood approaching; he had experienced that stomach-churning wait a hundred times but the calm before this particular storm was like no other. Now he had so much to lose. If the stakes had been this high at any time in his career, he would never have survived. The anticipation, the wait for the unknown response, boiled within him as if it was going to explode with the pressure.

'Gorgeous, isn't it,' he said, looking about and faking a deep relaxed breath.

Miranda nodded. 'I love you,' she said again, 'I do, I really do.' Her eyes were wide as they roamed frenetically about him, as if she could record him; keep all of him locked up in her head somehow.

Without warning, Miranda rolled on top of Ferdinand and pushed his head down on the tiles, kissing him, passionately, wilfully, only wanting to possess him.

She laid her head on Ferdinand's chest and listened to his heart, her heart, race. The beats melded and were comforting. And then they were confused with another sound. A sobbing sound.

Miranda looked round to the door of the stairwell tower. It was Tony. He was standing there, knock-kneed, cowering and trembling. He was crying like a child, red of face, tears streaking down his cheeks. There was a piece of paper in one hand, whilst the back of the other endlessly tried to wipe away the tears as if it could wipe away the crying as well.

'I came,' he managed to say, 'I came to tell you, you've got an e-mail.' Looking at Ferdinand. The piece of paper fluttered out of his hand. Tony turned and descended the stairs again, slamming the door behind him.

'We should have told him, we should have,' she berated Ferdinand. 'And broken his heart?'

'We did anyway, we were always going to, but this was the worst way,' Miranda snapped back as she reached the door. She opened it and followed the steps down, calling after Tony.

Ferdinand picked up the piece of paper, read it and smiled.

Miranda ran to Tony's room, but he was gone. She shouted his name about the house, running from room to room down empty corridors, but no answer came.

441

'Miranda.' A shout, Ferdinand's voice. 'Miranda.'

She ran outside, turned round and looked up. Ferdinand was standing up on the crenellations, pointing down the hillside.

'He's down there, going to the pier.'

Miranda started running down the dusty path between the trees, to the bay. When she got to the beginning of the pier Tony was shouting something at the pilot who had been sunbathing on the end. As she ran towards them she could see the pilot getting his shorts on and climbing into the sea-plane. Tony followed him. As he closed the door Miranda grabbed hold of the handle.

'I'm sorry,' she said, 'I really am.' She tried to catch her breath. 'I just never felt for you like that.'

Tony looked straight ahead. 'Come on, start the engines.'

'Tony, don't do this, don't go, I still want to be,' the weakness of her own plea stunned her for a moment, 'friends.'

The engines started. Ferdinand now came pounding down the pier.

'Tony, please let's talk about this.' Miranda gripped the handle tightly.

'Let go,' Tony said to her. 'Just let go.'

'No,' she said, 'not until we've talked.'

'Miranda, there's nothing to talk about, you've got what you wanted,' he pointed at Ferdinand as he arrived, 'now let go.'

Ferdinand butted in, 'Tony, you can't go, they'll think you're me escaping.'

'They, who's they?' Miranda looked at Ferdinand.

'It was never going to be just you leaving, was it?' Tony squinted at Ferdinand.

'I know,' said Ferdinand, 'and I'm sorry, I just thought it might hurt you.'

'Who's they?' Miranda persisted.

'Just let go, Miranda, it's over.'

'Who is they?'

'Navy warship, docked over there.' Tony waved his hand in a westerly direction.

'A what? There's a bloody warship out there and nobody thought to tell me?'

'Tony, they'll pluck you out of the sky before you even make your first turn.'

'Let's go,' Tony urged the pilot.

Miranda began to feel almost hysterical. 'No, Tony, don't, none of this is worth it.'

442

'Go,' ordered Tony.

The engine began to roar and the chassis shook in the water. It started to move and Ferdinand tore Miranda's hand from the door handle. As if released, the plane jumped away, gathering speed across the water and cutting a smooth straight path through the clear reflection of the mountains. And then, it was airborne. Silently the two watched from the end of the pier as it climbed into the sky, turning as it did eastward away from the ship. It rose high and completed its turn, straightening out to the east and then south. They needed to shield their eyes with their hands to keep sight of the plane in the bright sky. Then, without warning, the plane appeared to wobble, then it turned back west and north, flying straight towards the mouth of the bay.

In a futile desire for the laws of diminishing acoustics to alter drastically, Ferdinand shouted at the plane, 'No, not that way, turn round.' The plane continued. And then a burning light shot up, from behind the mountainous promontory, flying fast towards the plane. And they could only watch silently with growing horror as the light met its target and a fireball erupted in the clear air. For a moment the whole thing seemed to hang in the air, then streams of black smoke plummeted towards earth. Miranda watched, open-mouthed, speechless. The fragments of the plane dropped sizzling into the water of the bay, splashed and caused waves to explode from the stillness. The waves faded to ripples and the ripples evened out, until nothing, nothing was left.

'Look, look,' said Ferdinand, facing the other way. Far to the south east a single parachute fluttered down. Ferdinand pulled out his binoculars and focused. The pilot was steering the parachute towards dry land.

'Fuck,' said Ferdinand, 'fuck.'

my first death. Well, there were the Sycorax pilots, i suppose, but the first character death, someone i met and knew. It is rather shocking. Rather extreme. This all started so nicely as an urban melodrama but the stakes have risen so high, i suppose it was inevitable, just a matter of time. But such a nice boy as well.

The ship did not move all day. Occasionally a helicopter would fly in or out. Another British ship arrived and a third one, all of them anchored, blocking the way out. Waiting. Tony's army had been paid up to the end of the month so they were happy to report to Ferdinand until then. But now, with Tony and the plane gone, it looked like the chances of getting out of there alive were slimmer than the handbook of political intelligence.

Despite Ferdinand's best efforts, Miranda went into a kind of shock. She locked her door and spent a lot of time crying and then, when the tears ran out, staring. She ordered mountains of chocolates which all found themselves in the lavatory pan after a quick visit to her upper stomach. She ran questions through her head, and found a million different answers.

Ferdinand turned to brooding. He sat in Tony's computer room, watching the images that Everything 1.1 threw at him, looking like he was continuing Tony's work, but not really concentrating. The questions, which had started a few weeks before in such a liberating way, were now taking over, captivating his mind. He forgot about the warship and waiting for its attack, he just wondered at how far this love, this emotion, had brought him. He hadn't wanted to kill Miranda because she was an innocent, but now another innocent had died. He tried to justify it by telling himself Tony was a thief and a hacker, but it was no good, the bottom line was that Tony took a bullet that was meant for him. He didn't need to die. And for love? Did people really die for love? Would he have? Miranda said she couldn't, but then she said she would. Could he? Is that what it takes to truly love? What do people do who live long and die old together? Don't they love? Or maybe the slow death of love itself, borne on the contempt bred of familiarity, is worse. Maybe it is better to die before love does.

He read me, it was nice but i felt i was just a distraction, he'd read one of my clones a long time before, i was just a less than satisfying repeat. But all he could draw from me was that he loved, whatever it is called, whatever it is for, and would, until it either burnt up and died away or he did. In the meantime he knew that what defined him now, what informed his every thought, was love. Miranda.

The next morning, Ferdinand was back reading me when a message came from the lookouts. He closed me, picked up his binoculars, and we went up to Miranda's room. He knocked.

'Miranda,' he said softly through the door. There was a long silence.

'What?' eventually came back, a sleep-cracked, pillow-muffled reply.

'I have news, something you ought to see.'

'Can't it wait?'

'No. No, it's really quite important.'

Miranda opened the door. She looked at him. He hadn't grown

devil's horns; he didn't look like a co-murderer. His hands didn't drip with blood. His face was also not caked in tear-dried black mascara. His skin had no blotchy remains of despair. A little tired-looking but he had no bag-laden, pink, rabbit-twitching eyes.

'Come in.' She then saw me in his hand. 'But get rid of that bloody book.'

me, what had i done? i had been nothing but good to and for her. i was catalytic in turning her life around, i practically single-handedly found her the tall dark handsome stranger she had always dreamt of, i had quietly backed down and accepted her lack of feeling for me, and now she had the audacity to want me thrown out, after we had been through so much together. The ingratitude, what sort of fucking reader was she anyway? A stupid one.

Miranda tramped back to her bed. 'It's what caused all this trouble in the first place.' Ferdinand entered with me. 'If it wasn't for that book Tony would be alive, we wouldn't be on the run, the people of Pellestrina would still have a café, Mercy's boyfriend would probably have his limbs intact and, and, and . . .' She sat heavily on her bed.

'And we would never have met,' said Ferdinand.

'But we can't love if we know that it's going to hurt someone else, can we?'

'Who said that love wasn't selfish?'

Ferdinand surrounded her with his arms and he hugged her to his chest until she could feel the tears coming again.

'We both killed him. Sweet, harmless Tony.'

Ferdinand nodded. 'Nevertheless, we are sitting ducks in this place and we've just scored our ticket out of here.'

'What?'

Ferdinand showed her the e-mail Tony had brought, from his friend @cia.gov.us. 'The USS *Starbucks*® has arrived and is anchored out beyond the point. They're waiting for us. If we can make it out there, we're home free.'

'Free. Going to America?'

Ferdinand nodded.

'But?'

'But we'd have to get past the British ships to get there and, well, considering what they did to Tony, I don't suppose they're going to salute as we motor by. On the other hand there's another bit of news from the lookout. There's a launch from one of the British warships coming into the bay, they are probably formal negotiators coming to offer an ultimatum to surrender. There might be an opportunity to hold them as hostages or something.' Ferdinand passed Miranda his binoculars. She got up and focused out of the window. There indeed, crossing the bay towards their pier, was a boat. She could see the white suit of a naval officer steering the vessel. 'Looks pretty harmless,' she said. Then she locked onto one of the passengers, a woman. 'Christ,' she said, 'I don't believe it. It's Mercy.'

Ferdinand jumped to the window and she gave him the glasses. 'It is,' he said, 'and with her there's that Flirt, and Lake and Barry, and, my God, it's . . .' He put down the glasses to tell Miranda exactly who it was, but she was gone, running down the stairs in her dressing gown, flying to the front door.

This, on the whole, is a joyous occasion, signifying as it does a goodly rise in income and a certain enhanced popularity with some of the more intelligent and attractive members of the student body looking to a future career in the Secret Services. Becoming a talent scout for British Intelligence gives the financial and social status of even the fustiest of dons a considerable boost.

The 'Man In Victoria'? Of course, the intelligence building is in Victoria but the phrase, I'm afraid, is a crude donnish cryptic acronym. M.I.V translates as M.I.5, get it? *The Times* crossword culture has much to answer for.

To be honest, when the 'approach' was made, by a gentleman with a broom, blue boiler-suit and a string of Pee-Fume ring urinal fresheners, I was somewhat taken aback. Though not in the way that many of my cottage industry colleagues have been taken aback in that place. Even the next day on the 5.40 to Paddington I had still, somewhat naively, not made any connection between my studies' conclusions and the reality of the allegations I was making about the covert operations of the State.

At that point nobody, I thought, had even seen my work and though I was scheduled to lecture on my findings to the Zuleika Dobson Society I had been careful to reveal nothing of their content.

In retrospect, the books that I had been using in the Bodleian Library would have been catalogued and perhaps the 'Man In Victoria' drew his conclusions from that. However, when the bluff and balding Intelligence Officer who greeted me at the Millbank building passed to me photo-stats of the very chapters you have read so far, I was somewhat at a loss.

'Before anything is said,' he passed a pen to me, 'sign these.' He pointed to forms laid out on the table, a copy of the Official Secrets Act. My curiosity burning, I signed and handed the pen back to him.

'Before I start, Pennyfeather,' he began somewhat aggressively, 'you understand, now that you have signed this,' he pointed at the document, 'if, after you leave, you utter or write anything about what is spoken in this room, it is punishable as treason. We still have a death penalty for that in this country.'

I nodded.

'Now, the thing we would like to know is, exactly who gave you this information, names, addresses and so on.' He waved the photo-stats at me.

'It's just research,' I told him, trying to smile genially, 'conclusions drawn from books, studies. It's hypothesis.' My interrogator was somewhat hard-headed and persisted for an hour or so before it slowly dawned on him that I could possibly be telling the truth.

'And the fact that you've got me in here,' I tried, 'the fact that you want to know so much. Does that mean that it's all true, then? This really is the Ministry of Love? Metaphorically speaking, of course.'

Having turned a little pale, the officer left the room, only to return with a charming young man whom I recognized, a St John's graduate from about five years before. The young man warmly shook my hand and enthused about a lecture he had attended, offered me a drink and generally put the able into affable.

'Now, Professor,' he said at last, 'I'm sure it comes as no surprise to a man as intelligent as you that we have been monitoring you for quite a while. Basically, we believe that we, and your country, need you.'

'You're offering me a job?'

'Of course. We'd like you to join us, help us keep an eye on the next bright things coming up through the university.' The boy wrote some numbers on a piece of paper and pushed it towards me. 'You would be remunerated appropriately for such a delicate role.'

I looked at the figure, almost silicon-enhanced in its obscene size, and realized that I was being made an offer I could not realistically refuse. I, my thesis, was a threat and they weren't going to let me beat them, they would make me join them. They were buying my silence. How could I accept? Yet, if I didn't, I would live my life never knowing when they might strike, take me out, and, perhaps even worse, I would never know exactly how the whole love conspiracy worked, the mechanisms that I had spent so long trying to work out.

I joined, dear reader, not from fear but curiosity. I signed the enlisting papers and I held my hand up and swore on a good book and, well, in a matter of an hour I became a bona-fide, paid-up spy.

'Welcome,' the young man said at last, shaking my hand and beaming. 'Over the next few weeks we will set up the contact arrangements and so on.'

32

Love Did That

THE LAST CHAPTER, YOU CAN FEEL IT, CAN'T YOU. IT'S ALL GOING TO happen here. Everybody is gathering so all their stories can neatly wrap up. So much more satisfying than real life. But then maybe that's why books, stories, are still loved. They end and generally they come together so much more pleasantly than reality. But then, this was real and it is only my nature as a book that is willing this story to end clearly. We do have neat little rounds and closures to our lives, it does happen, but then you carry on living, you don't close your life like you can close me and say, right, that's all over. And though lives may well have gone on beyond this last bit, as a book, like an artist, i know when to stop. But the imagination goes on for ever. Now i'm getting all sentimental and i haven't even told you what happened. But there is so little left to go, i know in the back of your mind there is a knowledge that something will end and very soon.

Bursting through the ranks of the Serbian soldiers standing on the pier with their rifles aimed, Miranda ran to Mercy and hugged her.

'Thank God you're all right, thank God.'

She smiled at Flirt, hissed at Barry and Trotsky and helped the old man and his Zimmer frame onto the pier. Ferdinand carried out Flirt's electric wheelchair and then lifted Flirt into it. The naval officer saluted Ferdinand and Peersnide saluted back. He turned to Ferdinand. 'I've come to . . .'

'Later,' Ferdinand said. 'Why not come up to the house, freshen up, have a drink, and then you can tell me exactly what you've come to do.' Peersnide looked at the Serbian soldiers and their guns, and decided it could wait. The whole party went up to the house as the Serbian troops remained suspiciously eyeing the launch officer, until he had untied his boat and headed back across the bay towards the point.

As they traced the track up through the woods, pigeons peacefully cooing, Miranda walked ahead, showing the way, arm in arm with Mercy. Ferdinand pushed Flirt in his wheelchair and walked silently next to Peersnide. Barry helped the old man up the steep path while nodding to the sound of his Walkman, 'Minemis minemis minemis slimshaydee.'

As if she were the lady of the manor, welcoming her guests to a weekend in the country, Miranda stood in the entrance hall and designated rooms appropriate for all of them. 'Lunch,' she declared, 'is in an hour. We can all get together then and hear what Trotsky has to say.'

'Trotsky?' Peersnide bristled. 'I'm the bloody representative for the British Government and armed forces, you can't call me Trotsky.'

'You also tried to kill me and I can call you any fucking name I want,' Miranda said.

A murmur of agreement came from everybody in the great hall. Peersnide stormed off. 'I'll see you at lunch, then. Come on, Barry.' Barry bounded up the stairs after him. He stopped half way up and looked down at the rest of them.

'Don't be too hard on him,' he said. 'We've spent the last few days in helicopters and boats and he don't travel well.' Then he turned the corner and chased after Peersnide.

Miranda took Mercy to her room. Mercy giggled and jumped on the bed, bouncing up and hitting her head on the four-poster canopy.

'This is great.'

'Mercy?'

'Yes.'

'Tony's dead.'

'Tony? Tony Fromnextdoor? Is that who you mean?' Miranda nodded. 'No, he's not, saw him a couple of weeks ago, back in London.'

'This is his place.'

'Tony?'

Miranda nodded again.

'Are we talking about the same person? The no-hoper who lived next door to you?'

Miranda nodded again.

'This is his?'

'Was.'

'Did you know he had all this?'

'No. I didn't know any of it, but he got us off Pellestrina and yesterday he took off in his plane and the ships thought that he was Ferdinand and they shot him down and now he's dead.'

'Wow. Bummer. Another bloke hits the dust,' Mercy replied.

'And you?'

'Well, we've had a few square meals, they've hacked another limb off my boyfriend, and there have been loads and loads of sailors to drive wild. Nothing pisses them off more, with their oiled limbs and their honed pectorals, than to see me with a one-armed, no-legged man. The injustice of it drives them crazy. I wish I'd thought of it before, he's the ultimate man-slaying accessory. He's perfect. We're getting on really well. I can kind of understand having a partner if you get through the first week. It's great.'

Mercy sat down next to Miranda and hugged her friend.

And so they caught up with each other. Miranda found out how Flirt was pretty much Mercy's perfect man, male disempowerment on a literal level. Mercy heard about Miranda's plans to get to America with Ferdinand. They promised, whatever happened, they would get in touch, through life or even death. Friends for ever.

Lunch was a simple, three-course, local-speciality affair: cabbage in various disguises. Still, if that was what the Emperor Diocletian decided to leave Rome and set up the Empire in Yugoslavia to grow, then it would be surprising if, in nearly two thousand years, the locals had not managed to find a considerable number of ways to disguise the vegetable of choice for endless unpalatable school meals as digestible fare. Diocletian was obviously an emperor who realized the importance of force-feeding children, inventing, as he also did, monotheism and Roman Catholicism. The locals weren't happy back then about a foreigner coming in and setting up in the area and they still weren't now. The food was served with the usual disdain the Slavs have for their employers. At least they had the decency to spit on the food before it was brought in.

Peersnide laid a large navy walkie-talkie on the table as everyone sat down. He remained standing at the head of the table, glancing at everyone, catching their eyes, and when, at last, he had everybody's attention, he said, 'We have wasted enough time already. Burnt Umber, I think you know why I am here.' He was enjoying, finally, his moment of power, his Le Carré table gambit.

Everybody's head turned to look at Ferdinand at the other end, all except the old man, who was humming to his Walkman and nodding.

Ferdinand shrugged.

'I have been ordered to negotiate your surrender.' They all looked back at Peersnide as if it were a tennis match.

'Really?' said Ferdinand. 'Then why would they send you to do it?'

'Cabbage anyone?' Miranda offered a bowl.

'Because, unlike some, they respect my authority, they recognize my diplomacy. I know who you are, better than they do.' Peersnide gestured towards Mercy and Flirt. 'We have brought the Love Interest's friends as a good-will gesture, to show that they are unharmed, a peace offering.'

'A peace offering?' said Ferdinand. 'Since when did the British military make peace offerings?'

'Nevertheless, you can see that they are all right.'

Ferdinand pointed to Flirt. 'He's only got one limb left.'

'He's alive. With a nice electric wheelchair.'

'Coleslaw?'

'It's not them I'm surprised to see unharmed, Peersnide, it's you.'

Peersnide glowered over the top of his wire-frames. 'Don't call me Peersnide,' he hissed, 'I'm Vermilion Lake.'

'Just get on with the demands.'

'You have until half past t ... I mean fourteen-thirty hours. At that time a launch will come to pick us up. If you are on it you will not be destroyed with this place. If you aren't, well, may God have mercy ...'

'Yes?' said Mercy.

'No, I'm just saying I'm like the executioner, may God have mercy on—'

'On what?' said Mercy.

'Your soul,' fumed Peersnide.

'Thanks, and same to you,' Mercy said. Peersnide slumped down into his chair and Barry held his hand comfortingly.

Miranda passed a bowl towards Mercy. 'Chou rouge à l'orange?'

'So what's stopping us just walking out of here?'

'The whole perimeter of this area is now surrounded by Special

Forces Serbian police,' smiled Peersnide. 'We've got cruise missiles aimed right at this place. The only way out alive is to be on that launch.'

'Well, you're a pretty brave man, I give you that,' said Ferdinand, finishing a mouthful of sauerkraut.

Peersnide looked nervous. 'Why?'

'To come here when you know there's that sort of artillery aimed at us, at you.'

Peersnide glanced out to the bay and a little sweat appeared on his forehead. He wiped it off with a napkin.

'Caesar salad?'

'And,' Ferdinand said casually, saving the best for last, 'you've explained why this couple are here,' he pointed to Mercy and Flirt, 'but why exactly is he here?' He pointed to the old man, who was shakily practising some air guitar.

'He's the UN observer,' said Peersnide.

'He's geriatric!' Ferdinand exclaimed.

Mercy nodded at Miranda. 'Never trusted him when I saw him around Shepherd's Bush.'

'He's experienced, apparently,' replied Peersnide curtly.

'Oh, he is that,' said Ferdinand, 'but do you know who he is?'

'I said, he's the UN observer.'

'He bloody well isn't. He's Paul Pennyfeather.'

Of course it was just a name that Mercy and Flirt had heard from Ferdinand, but for the rest of us, it reverberated deeply. For me it was, perhaps, the most disturbing. i mean, to meet your maker. He didn't look how i remembered. This was a frail and mad old man, but even as Ferdinand said it i saw that he was right. It was him. For Miranda, who had decided to blame everything shitty on me, you know how the spurned can be, the name rang a terrible bell. It seemed incomprehensible that someone condemned to the periphery of her vision should suddenly become so central. 'The author, the writer, the . . .' She didn't really know what to say. 'The one who wrote the book. That's him?'

'Rubbish,' said Peersnide.

'Were you there when we started Operation Love Nuts?' asked Ferdinand.

'No, but. Well. He's not an academic, he's some sort of gibbering idiot. Anyway, I thought Pennyfeather was disposed of.'

'No, just lobotomized, with a message dependency, which comes through those.' He pointed at the headphones.

'Message dependency?' said Mercy, who was the only one who had seen Pennyfeather without them on.

'Lobotomies are pretty imprecise things. After the removal of such a critical part of the brain, the bit that holds your life's work, you're missing the bit which informs everything you do, you become quite incapable of surviving day to day. So, he has to have a twenty-four hour looped set of messages which remind him to do things like get dressed, put one foot in front of the other, eat, keep the headphones on. If he took them off for too long he would, after a while, just forget to breathe.'

They all looked at the oblivious Pennyfeather with sympathetic horror. He shook his head and sang.

'He seems to have worked out that it also operates as a personal stereo,' said Ferdinand.

'You knew about this?' said Miranda.

'It wasn't my decision.'

'It's inhuman.'

'I know that now. I've learnt a lot. Shall I kill him now, put him out of his misery?' Ferdinand pulled a large gun from his jacket.

'No,' Mercy and Miranda screamed.

'I meant him.' He pointed the gun at Peersnide.

Peersnide felt a wetting in his trousers.

'Oh, well,' Miranda shrugged.

'You've learnt a lot too, Miranda.' Ferdinand smiled, putting the gun on the table.

'What's Pennyfeather doing here?' said Peersnide.

'Good question.'

'Why don't you ask him?' Mercy said.

Peersnide approached Pennyfeather cautiously. Slowly, he lifted the headphones. Pennyfeather stopped rocking and looked at Peersnide, a little frightened; he looked around him as if he had no idea how he got there. He took some deep breaths and stared at each of them in turn.

'Now,' he said, staring at the headphones still poised in Peersnide's hands, 'my charms are all o'erthrown, and what strength I have's mine own.' He coughed. 'Which is most faint. Now 'tis true, I must be here confined by you.' He snatched the headphones and placed them back on his ears.

Mercy turned to Ferdinand. 'He was like that when I tried talking to him.'

Peersnide stormed out. 'This is ridiculous, I'll be down at two, fourteen hundred, for your answer. I want everybody back here then.' He grabbed his walkie-talkie and left before the cabbage mousse.

'Why,' said Flirt after the sort of silence in which a fart is about the only thing which can clear the air, 'do they call it something hundred when there's still only sixty minutes in each hour. I mean, do they say thirteen-fifty-seven, fifty-eight, fifty-nine, one hundred, isn't that like how to cheat at hide and seek?'

'Only sixty.' Barry was nonplussed and then he looked at his watch. 'The bloke who sold me this must have been having a laugh.'

It was after lunch, an hour to go before Peersnide's deadline, and the house was quiet. The soldiers were occupied at the perimeter fence in a stand-off with the police, Mercy was there negotiating a safe passage, as only she knew best, with a very handsome and foolish young police sergeant, Flirt had gone for a spin in his electric wheelchair down to the waterfront, Pennyfeather stood humming at the front door, looking out over the bay, as if he was actually enjoying the view, and Barry and Peersnide sat silently on the bed in Peersnide's room. Miranda and Ferdinand wandered the house, searching for answers, connecting, disconnecting, knowing that an end of some sort was coming. They entered the chapel and sat next to each other on the cool of a mock-pew. Miranda held Ferdinand tightly.

'You're not going to surrender, are you,' she said quietly. It wasn't a question, just a statement.

'If I did, we'd never see each other again, so no. But then, I don't know surrender is even on the cards any more.'

'What's going to happen?'

'I don't know.' He looked deep into her eyes. 'If we can work out why they're all here,' he nodded back in the house, 'then we'll know. Maybe they will blow up this place. Maybe they'll just let us go. Maybe we'll find a way out of here.'

Twenty minutes to go and Miranda and Ferdinand stood at the front door with Pennyfeather, watching him, trying to fathom the depths he must labour in. And despite the tragedy and their sympathy, they experienced a mutual there-but-for-the-grace-of-something-pretty-damn-powerful moment.

Pennyfeather took off his headphones, smiling at them. 'So glad of this as they I cannot be, who are surprised withal; but my rejoicing at nothing can be more. I'll to my book; for yet ere supper time must I perform much business appertaining.' He tapped his jacket as if absently looking for his glasses and turned to go inside.

Ferdinand looked at him. 'The book, his book, of course, that's it. What do we all have in common?'

Miranda looked confused.

'All of us here,' continued Ferdinand, a bright spark of realization lighting up his face, 'we're the only people, except for Madder himself, who know about the book and we're all here in the same place. He's got all his eggs in one basket and he's about to make an omelette. They're not going to wait for Peersnide to leave, they just want to make sure we're all together.' He ran into the house. 'Miranda, get your stuff, take Pennyfeather and get down to the pier. Now.'

'What? Why?' she shouted back at him.

'Because they're going to blow this place sky high.'

Ferdinand ran through the house telling the staff to get out, head for the perimeter. He ran up the stairs and burst into Peersnide's room. Barry and Peersnide jumped apart.

'Look,' said Ferdinand, already feeling he may have interrupted something, 'I wouldn't have done this a couple of weeks ago, but, well, now I feel everybody's got to have their chance. I just wanted to tell you, there's going to be no launch.'

'Of course there is.'

'We're getting out of here, you'd better too, they're going to strike the house when you signal them that we're all together.' Ferdinand nodded at the walkie-talkie lying on the bed.

'Ridiculous,' Peersnide scoffed. 'You're – we're – too valuable, they wouldn't do that to us.'

'It's nearly two now. The launch would already be on its way, wouldn't it? Go on, look out the window.'

Peersnide went to the window, took in the calm waters of the bay and saw it was empty. Turning again, he rushed back to the bed and picked up his walkie-talkie. 'Lake to Gold Leader, come in?' There was a high-pitched squeak that came from deep inside the transceiver.

'Gold Leader, over.'

Ferdinand recognized the little whining sound of an electronic homing beacon. 'Oh bloody hell, that's the signal.' He pointed at the walkie-talkie. 'You've just accurately triangulated your position for them.'

'Gold Leader, over?'

Somewhere out in international waters, Captain Remington-Wilkinson-Gillette grinned, a gleam appearing in the whites of his eyes. Machines bleeped and whirred, numbers appeared on his monitor. Latitude, longitude, altitude. Well within range. Even as he pressed the button, five miles away Ferdinand was leaping down the villa's stairs.

'Gold Leader, this is Lake, over?' Peersnide tried desperately. He looked back out of the window as he held the transceiver to his ear. Over the glistening water, a small dark shape, faster than a jet, turned the corner of the point and sped towards them.

'Fuck,' said Peersnide.

Barry leapt to Peersnide's side and saw the missile closing. Even as the cruise missile reached the shore and headed for the walkie-talkie homing transmitter, Peersnide talked desperately into it. 'Fucking Gold fucking Leader, over?'

Barry, ever a more instinctual creature, grabbed Peersnide and kissed him, hard, 'I, I love you,' he said.

And in that moment Peersnide let go and kissed him back, it was the most wonderful thing in his life.

The missile tore open the wall, and bricks, mock-Tudor beams, wattle, daub, mortar, Barry and Peersnide exploded into instant fire. Ferdinand ran out of the door just as the walls collapsed around him.

More missiles followed, scattering around the area, thudding into the woods and buildings. Ferdinand ran down the forest path as long-distance mortars rained down. Half way to the pier he met Miranda and Pennyfeather. Pennyfeather was sitting down on a trunk as trees burst into fire around them. She was pulling at him but he was refusing to go. His headphones were around his neck and he saw Ferdinand belting towards them.

Pennyfeather looked at Ferdinand pleadingly, as if he would understand. He beckoned him close and whispered in his ear, 'Let me not, since I have my dukedom got, and pardoned the deceiver, dwell in this bare island by your spell; but release me from my bands,' he touched the headphones, 'with the help of your good hands.' Pennyfeather grabbed Miranda's hand and Ferdinand's, clutching on to them tightly. A mortar fell near them and a tree split open, bursting into flame. 'Gentle breath of yours my sails must fill, or else my project fails, which was to please. Now I want spirits to enforce, art to enchant; and my ending is despair unless I be relieved by prayer, which pierces so that it assaults mercy itself, and frees all faults.' Pennyfeather shook their hands roughly.

'Please,' Miranda said to him, 'please come on,' trying to pull him, but he remained seated.

'As you,' said Pennyfeather, looking into their eyes, 'from crimes would pardoned be, let your indulgence . . .'

Ferdinand breathed the last three words in unison with Pennyfeather, 'set me free.' He nodded at the old man, he understood. 'Come on,' he said to Miranda, 'he wants to stay.'

'He'll die, we can't just leave him.' Ferdinand grabbed Miranda's shoulder.

'It's what he wants, let him go.'

The two ran together onto the pier. Ferdinand untied the speedboat and jumped in next to Miranda.

'If we go now and head for the American ship we'll draw their fire. Your friends, even Pennyfeather, might survive.'

'What are we waiting for then?' she said, and pushed the throttle forward. The engine burped and whirred but didn't roar and the boat didn't move.

'Damn,' said Ferdinand. He opened up the engine bay to have a look. As he examined the engine, and Miranda cowered with every explosion, Flirt rolled onto the pier. As he approached the back of the speedboat, he saw the weed that was wrapped around the propeller shaft. With an almighty heave of his one arm, Flirt pushed himself from his chair, landing heavily on the wooden decking of the pier. As the hills around them were alive with the sound of shell-bursts, he clawed his way to the edge of the jetty and leaned over. Putting his one arm in the water, deeper and deeper until he could feel the knot of weed, he began to pull and felt the weed tearing. Suddenly the engine roared and the boat shot forward.

The roaring of the released engine drowned the screams, as Flirt watched his last limb fly into the air in a shower of blood. Ferdinand, his head still in the engine bay, shrugged as he watched the propeller shaft spinning, then rushed to the wheel.

Flirt lay there and watched them go as more explosions rocked the whole mountainside, sending up black, foul-smelling columns of smoke.

The speedboat raced towards the point, towards the open sea, towards the British ships and the American dream. As the water exploded around them, it bobbed and weaved in and out, each burst of water getting closer to them.

As they rounded the point and sighted the open sea, the distant

American battlecruiser, and the British warships between them, the water became a frenzied curtain of erupting waves and fire. With Ferdinand at the helm and Miranda clutching him, the speedboat swerved and slewed through the detonating fountains until, in the smoke and fire and mist, one last huge explosion ripped from the centre, in a cloud, and shook the surrounding British warships. Then, when the smoke cleared, and the waves died down, there was no speedboat. They'd gone. Love did that.

'And that,' I said, pointing at the copy of my work, 'I have to say goodbye to all that?'

The young man furrowed his brow in a mock serious frown. 'Well, yes, I'm afraid that it wouldn't do for a member of the Secret Service to be publishing theories about the Service.'

'But they're not just theories,' I countered, 'are they?'

The young man looked at me for a good while. 'I see. Your enquiring mind won't go quietly.'

'Not after such a long time.'

'Well, for your satisfaction I suppose I could explain a few things.'

'I was right, there really is a Ministry of Love?'

'Well, yes and no. I mean in many ways there still is and, had it not been for certain events in the early nineteenth century, your conclusions might have been spot on. Tea?'

Coda

THAT'S IT, I SUPPOSE, IN A WAY. NOW, WHEN I LISTEN TO THAT symphony of human voices it is as if there is one familiar, joyful harmony missing, a single instrument gone from the orchestra, and the music will be for ever keyed with a subtle sadness. It will never touch me as it used to when i thought that i might hear her voice within it. But now there is you and you know and now, no matter what happens, we've got something, something that will last as long as we want it to, something that will defy age, time, substance and the world. Call it love, call it memory; it is eternal. Call it a story – but you will always have me, and i, i will always have you. What we are after this is not the mass, the material, it is the content, that is what really lives because it lives in the mind, beyond pages or flesh. That is love. Put me down, the paper, the cardboard, the ink, but you will never put me away.

In that way i don't suppose we have much more to say to each other except, well, except maybe you want to know how i got to where we met? Just to round things off. You remember where you found me? Well, picture it, a little time before, it could have been hours, or weeks. But there, a woman with amazing towering blonde hair, a massive heaving bosom, tottering on heels each sharp enough to be selling second-hand cars, pushes a wheelchair with a man under a blanket, only his head sticking out above it. They get to the place you found me, we both know where it was, and they look to either side. The man

463

hands the woman a book. She places me there gently, like no one would notice. And she pushes him off.

'Do you still love me, even like this?' he says as they leave.

'You're perfect. Especially like this. Of course I love you.'

THE END

A BRIEF HISTORY OF THE CONSPIRACY OF LOVE

I DO NOT CLAIM THAT THE FOLLOWING TRANSCRIPT IS ANYTHING but a rough approximation of what the young man related to me in his simple manner in that quiet office. But it will, hopefully, furnish you with the fundamentals, the salient points which define the workings of a system which I had, hitherto, merely speculated on.

All the while the young man smiled away, holding his bone china cup with the delicacy of a geisha, sipping so silently that the tea seemed to levitate to his lips.

'Of course, what you were writing about was an internationally developed system, not just something to do with the British, what do you call it?' He leafed through the manuscript. 'State. Such a harsh word; we in the business prefer to call it the Committee.

'Love may not have been British in origin but, like so many things in this world, it was we who made the essential contribution to make the whole structure of love what it is today, a world-beater.'

'Which was?' I ventured.

'Privatization.'

'We, er, the British, privatized love?'

The young man nodded and pursed his lips. 'Absolutely. You must understand that the love thing, promoting it anyway, became far too great a job for the Committee to support, what with the ever expanding demands of population growth, etcetera. It may print the money and fight the wars but mass indoctrination takes resources, writers, printers, distributors, martyrs, messiahs and so on, the media in short. The "State" just can't be as omnipotent as would be necessary.

'In the early nineteenth century love was sold off and, within a few years, most civilized countries who were still instilling it followed suit.'

By this time I must have been looking almost minused so nonplussed was I. The young man sighed with the sort of falsely indulgent impatience only youth can muster and tried to explain.

'You were right, about the emotional statecraft of love. Queens, then kings and princes created myths of love and saw what a spell of enchantment they wove on the human heart of their subjects. Britain owes its stability to romance. The empire was won on misguided interpretations of the ideals of knights. Knightliness forged in the era of courtly romance. Our army dressed in blazing red for centuries as if we were invulnerable because, by God, we were right. Completely based on the romantic fantasy that it was the rightest not the mightiest who would win at knightly joust. The English gentleman, cool, unflappable, respectful and distant, is based on the same delusion, completely invented characteristics of knightliness. Real medieval knights raped, pillaged and burnt if they were any good at it. But that gentleman knight created in the romance literature, like love, is still with us. We still like to think that we're like that. We let our imaginations lead us rather than recognize the world's harsh realities. And it was only because we were such a rich nation from our exploits raping the colonies that the populace could afford to be sheltered by such outrageous fantasies as knightliness and love. In spring a starving African's fancy never lightly turns to thoughts of love. He cannot afford fancy. Our romantic notion keeps hardship as far from us as possible. It's a drug, yes, an anaesthetic, an opiate. Love is our lotus leaf. Dine on it and we forget, forget the rest of the world.

'And still we keep this fantasy as an active and dominant part of our lives. This country reads more books per head than any other. We're a nation of escapists. Dreamers. Somewhere we all have the romantic dream, the dream cottage in the dream Cotswolds with the dream rose garden. And it's not just us. America was founded on and still regurgitates the "American Dream".

'But you know what? Dreamers aren't doers. The Committee never wanted doers because doers might just change the world.

'Right from the start the nobility commissioned poets, writers, painters and so forth to maintain the myth that infected the human imagination, the heaven-on-earth protocol. But "a man's grasp must exceed his reach or what's a heaven for?"

These artists, they were all on the crown committee. They spun and charmed the people. The human imagination, the dream, needs feeding and longs for narrative. The storytellers gave us an emotional ride from which we could never get off. Chaucer, he was one of the first best propagandists.'

'Chaucer was in on the, um, conspiracy?'

'A king's man in every respect, started out in Customs and Excise, became court poet. Knight's tale, reworking Boccaccio and so on. And Shakespeare too. I love it when all those academics speculate about who Shakespeare was. Why don't they just ask why we know so little about the world's greatest writer and the perfect ad-man for love? "Juliet is the sun and I the moon, thou art more lovely and more temperate, what brave new world that hath such people in't." It was because he was a King's man, through and through. Well King's Men actually.'

'Shakespeare?' I interjected, hardly countenancing what I was hearing.

The young man nodded. ' "Shakespeare", it just means, what's the modern word they use today? "Spear-carrier", you know, an anonymous extra in theatrical terms; someone who comes on stage and all he gets to do is shake his spear. Another term for anonymous. Anonymous because he never existed. If you want to know, and I suppose you do, we needed a canon, a body of work which would define love and its intrigues, keep people fascinated with it ever after. The plays, poems and so on were written by a whole group of "King's Men", civil servants the lot of them. And half of them wrote the King James Bible as well. Why do you think that the 46th word in the 46th sonnet is "Shake" and the 46th word from the end of the 46th sonnet is "spear"? A childish secret service joke. Twice twenty-three, remember Shakespeare's magic number. One score and three . . .

'Really, love went swimmingly as a divine piece of crowd-control, a complement to religious indoctrination. They were never in competition, as you put it, rather a marriage made in political heaven.

'Then there was Cromwell and the revolution and the Committee was disempowered. How were the poor souls of the parliamentarians to know that you control the people through lovesickness rather than dictates and morals. And Milton, he could have been the best, bigger than Shakespeare, the first mega-poet individual, had the Committee been operating in his time. As it was, forget love, it was all mourning and fire and brimstone and war and ethics and blindness. No romance, that was his trouble and the trouble with the whole parliamentary movement. Even today we look at the Royalists as wrong but romantic, the Roundheads as right but revolting.

'Then there was the Restoration and really things went a little downhill from there. Charles II, untrained as a king, never really rated the love work of the Committee. Maybe he was right. The Drydens and so forth tried, but the satirists and the rakes had the ascendancy. Rochester was the bad example we set for the public and even the church had to scrabble to claim him at the end of his life. What was that?' He smiled and started reciting, "And if I awake hot-headed and drunk, What a cry do I make for the loss of my punk, I rant and I shout and I fall in a rage, And missing my whore I bugger my page."

'It became clear that things would have to change by the end of the eighteenth century when the Committee faced the Hell-Fire Club. The ultimate rakish establishment where virgins were sacrificed on the phallic altars of society. The Prince of Wales, the Prime Minister and the Archbishop of Canterbury were all members and, in a way, it was their decadent, self-satisfied and totally debauched attitude that lost the American colonies. When it did, a sharp intake of breath could almost be heard in the Committee. The Americans had revolted, the French revolted, and neither country would have a clear understanding of love for centuries. Not really until the invention of mass entertainment, the phonograph and the celluloid film. Not since Cromwell had led the "great unwashed" had there been a better opportunity to force a republic on a weak and ineffectual government. The Committee feared losing control for ever and put into action a two-part plan. First it charged John Wilkes, once a member of the very same Hell-Fire Club, to lead a revolution that would never succeed and so recreate the proper respectful fear of authority in the people. Then, at the beginning of the nineteenth century, the Committee's love agenda initiated a clean-up operation. Love took a front stand again, a stand for a politically moral society. The Committee commissioned Romanticism. Wordsworth, Coleridge, Shelley, Keats, Byron, the best writers of the age, the best painters of the time, they were mobilized to reconstruct the primacy of love and romance. Even now we live with their legacy. Monogamy, passion, emotions, the purpose of life.

Love, life, life, love. It was all said there, everything was informed by the Romantic imagination. Order and stability were regained.

'Then in 1819, whilst everybody was looking at Peterloo and wondering if it marked Britain's next insurgence, another, quieter and far more important revolution began.

'You see, the cost of maintaining the Romantic ideology was becoming immense, impractical. India and other colonies had proved to be better run and organized by the private sector. And then somebody made a love you could eat. Well, something very like it. In Vevey, Switzerland, a chap called Cailler, François-Louis, he invented eating chocolate. Suddenly there was a mass-marketable portable love, a foodstuff which felt like love, a sweetmeat which released all the same chemicals in the brain, endorphins and so on. The Committee seized the chance to sell off the promotional side of love to the concerns that wanted to market this wondrous product.

'It was a commercial deal that changed the world. The company that first bought the rights to love and chocolate is now one of the world's great multinationals, probably the only food provider left when we enter the conglomerate age: Nestlé. The Committee sold the duty of the promotion of love into the care of the commercial sector whilst promising to maintain a defence against anything which might harm the system. Things like this.' The young man pointed at my manuscript. 'Perhaps the messiest part of the 1819 deal was the agreement to get rid of the people who had built up the product so nicely. Unfortunately the poets were idealists to the last, none of them agreed to come on board or go quietly. Within five years Shelley, Byron and Keats had been assassinated, Coleridge was hooked on drugs and Wordsworth was a social outcast in the Lake District due to a very misunderstood relationship with his sister. By 1824, the Romantics were effectively gone and the way was paved for the complete commercialization of love. Love which prevents revolution for us and sells chocolate for them, and virtually everything else in the world.

'So today, there is still a sub-committee that looks after the defence of the mystery of love and that, my friend, is who has sorted out this rather cosy deal for you.'

There was little else, I had understood only too well. It was only when I was about to leave that the young man grabbed my arm and said in menacingly quiet tones, 'If you are thinking of breathing a word of this just remember what happened to Barthes.'

Roland Barthes, the French academic. Perhaps he was suggesting that I would become a world-famous cultural critic and head of a prestigious college, but I doubted it. I pondered his last words as I left the Millbank building. What had happened to Barthes? He had been run over by a laundry van. Nothing strange about that. But then I recalled that it had happened after a lunch with François Mitterrand, a scion of the French State. And what was that book he had only managed to publish fragments of? *A Lover's Discourse.* Had he come to the same conclusions as I? Had he been brave enough to refuse the threat of his State? I realized that the young man had left me with a terrible threat and I crossed the road warily.

However, a weight had been lifted from my shoulders. I knew the truth. I had sworn myself to secrecy, but even as I signed the papers 'Prospero Duca di Milano' I knew I had to pass this knowledge on whatever the cost. It was too big for my little old frame of mind. If it wasn't Barthes, it would be me and if not me it would be somebody else, until the truth came out – the truth must out because telling it, in the end, is the only absolute duty a human in human society has.

So now you know. Just pray that they never know you know.

Of course, if you like, you may close this book and disbelieve every word in it but, before you do, ask yourself one question:

If love, as powerful and beautiful, as dangerous and useful, as tyrannical and deceptively liberating, as mesmeric and captivating, as controlling, respected and feared as it is, has never yet been harnessed by the State, why hasn't it?

ACKNOWLEDGEMENTS

I REALIZE THAT IN A WORK THAT WILL BE THE DEATH OF ME, anybody I mention here as an aide may attract the same fate. So I will not betray them, they know who they are. However there are others who have been, quite frankly, a nuisance and a hindrance, and were the Secret Services to contact and torture them, I would not turn a jot in my grave.

So thank you, Mr Matthew Harris, for not letting anything bounce off you unless it rebounded twice as witily. And thank you to my earliest readers and fiercest critics, Mrs Suzanne Brill, Mrs Agatha Sadler and Mrs Christine Kelly.

I'm deeply indebted *per l'Italiano del Veneto* and all matters Venetian to Professor Laura Bondi of the Universita di Ca' Foscari, Venezia: don't think that you are safe just because you are abroad.

I cannot let this death list go by without acknowledging the strenuous editorial collusion of Miss Jane Lawson and Miss Francesca Liversidge.

Other people to whom I still bear small grudges and could do with a knock from the Man In Victoria include the less than secret agent Mr Robert Kirby, Mr A.A. Gill, Mr Harry Burke, Mr Steve Leo, Mr Anthony Kosky, Mr John Henderson, Mr Leo deMyers, Mr Anthony Fulton of the Fulham Job Centre, Mr John Miller, M. Sebastien Berger and Miss Anna Pasternak. I thank you.

Lastly, for acts of extreme intolerance and a total lack of forbearance I feel the wrath of my gratitude is overwhelmingly due to Mr George McCrae, Miss Roxana Brill and the real Dr Claire Scudder.

They know who you are, they know where you live: it's only a matter of time.

SELECT BIBLIOGRAPHY

Andreae, S., *Anatomy of Desire*, 1998, London
Barthes, R., *Fragments d'un discours amoureux*, 1977, Paris
Brockman, J., and Matson, K., *How Things Are*, 1995, London
Carey, J., *The Intellectual and the Masses*, 1992, London
Csikszentmihaly, M., *Flow: The Psychology of Optimal Experience*, 1990, New York
Fisher, H., *Anatomy of Love*, 1992, London
Capellanus, A., ed. Parry, J.J., *The Art of Courtly Love*, 1971, Edinburgh
Jackson, S., 'Even Sociologists Fall in Love', *Sociology* Vol. 27, No. 2, 1993, London
Leader, D., *Promises Lovers Make When it Gets Late*, 1997, London
Lewis, C.S., *The Allegory of Love*, 1936, Oxford
Lewis, T., Amini, F., and Lannon, R., *A General Theory of Love*, 2000, London
Maslow, A.H., *Motivation and Personality*, 1970, New York
Paz, O., *La Llama Doble, Amor y Erotismo*, 1993, Madrid
De Rougemont, D., *L'Amour et l'occident*, 1940, Paris
Sullivan, S., *Falling in Love*, 1999, London
Zeuss, Dr., *Oh, the Thinks You Can Think!*, 1957, New York